CHASING
THE
WIND

C. C. HUMPHREYS

DOUBLEDAY CANADA

Doubleday Canada and colophon are registered trademarks of
Penguin Random House Canada Limited.

Library and Archives Canada Cataloguing in Publication

Humphreys, C. C. (Chris C.), author
Chasing the wind / C.C. Humphreys.

Issued in print and electronic formats.
ISBN 978-0-385-69048-5 (softcover). ISBN 978-0-385-69049-2 (EPUB)

I. Title.

PS8565.U5576C53 2018   C813'.6   C2017-906668-4
                                                C2017-906669-2

Cover and book design by Rachel Cooper
Cover images: (woman) Ilina Simeonova / Trevillion Images; (propeller)
Wisconsinart, (mist) CC0, (clouds) Positiveflash, all Dreamstime.com;
(blimp) Hindenburg, 1936 / Wikimedia Commons
Interior images: (part openers) *Graphic Ornaments*, The Pepin Press

Printed and bound in the USA

Published in Canada by Doubleday Canada,
a division of Penguin Random House Canada Limited

www.penguinrandomhouse.ca

10 9 8 7 6 5 4 3 2 1

Penguin
Random House
DOUBLEDAY CANADA

To my father, Flight Lieutenant Peter Humphreys,
Royal Air Force, Hurricane pilot. 1939–1945

Per ardua ad astra

Once having tasted flight you will walk this earth
with your eyes turned skyward. For there you have
been and there you long to return.

—*Leonardo da Vinci*

PART ONE

LOOP-DE-LOOP

ONE

CRASH

Curtiss Field Aerodrome, Long Island. November 2, 1929.

THE PILOTS TOOK SHELTER IN THE HANGAR AND KEPT THEIR earflaps down.

The storm had struck like a sudden military assault—the phosphorus flash of lightning, the cannon crump of thunder, hail hammering the tin roof like bullets from a Tommy gun. Having pounded the aerodrome, it gathered ferocity and headed west, to fall on New York City and wreak its havoc there.

Everyone moved to the wide doorway, straining to listen beyond the departing storm for the sound they all wanted and needed to hear.

"There!"

One pilot stepped out, and the rest followed, their leather jackets instantly glistening in the rain that was softening to mist. They squinted against it to the low grey ceiling of cloud. Now they all heard it—an engine's throaty cry.

"Travel Air?" called one of the pilots.

"That growl? Wright Whirlwind J-5." The first pilot smiled. "Without a manifold. It's a Vega—and it's who we've been waiting for." The grin widened. "Get to your birds."

They moved out to the planes lined up along the single runway's edge. Twenty-seven of them, wing tip to wing tip. Monoplanes, biplanes, open cockpit and closed. Some pilots leaned against the nose of their plane as they would against a horse's flank. Others reached up to gently hold the tip of a propeller as if it were a bridle. All looked to the wind sock, whipping like a silk dragon in the storm's coattails. Catholics crossed themselves, and the rest just shook their heads. Then all turned their attention to the heavens.

The plane came, stooping like a red hawk, falling steeply toward the ground. Everyone there knew the pilot had no choice; it was the only way to land in such a high wind. As the plane levelled for its glide, each flyer unconsciously mirrored the movements of their colleague in the sky—fingers opening the throttle a little so the engine would pick up fast if an overshoot was needed, toes shifting in their boots to adjust the rudder and keep the nose straight into the wind, hand gently but firmly pulling back on the stick.

The Vega levelled thirty feet from the ground—too high for the short runway. A hand raised inside the glass, a brief acknowledgement of the error even as the throttle was pushed hard forward, the plane gaining speed, rising, banking. It circled back smoothly despite the wind's buffets. Levelling again beyond the runway's end, the bird descended faster, lower. Few of the pilots there had flown a Vega—one of the swiftest, most exciting rides in the sky. But into a headwind on the short grass strip of Curtiss Field, the plane's strengths could make for a bumpy landing, and a crash in the long grass beyond.

Again they heard the throttle open a hair; again they mirrored the pilot's gentle caresses on stick and rudder, watched for the two-wheel touchdown, and held their breath against the third. If the rear wheel went down rough, the plane would bounce up; the whole sequence would have to be repeated.

The front wheels touched the grass as if leaning in for the softest kiss. Immediately, the throttle was closed off, the engine's roar diminishing to a purr. As the third wheel dropped, all the pilots released the breath they didn't realize they'd been holding. The Vega swung; the right wheel bumped through the old rabbit burrows on the perimeter, straightened, then taxied back down the runway. Finally, with a last burst of throttle and a panache several considered excessive, the pilot brought the Vega into the end of the line, sweeping the wing tip around until it was a hand's breadth from the plane next to it. As thunder rolled in the distance, the pilot cut the engine, slid back the canopy, climbed out, hovered for a moment on the narrow step, then dropped to the ground.

The crowd moved forward. The one who'd landed was, in some ways, their leader. It would have been harder to do what they needed to do today without the leader's endorsement.

"Damn tight," someone called.

"Damn Vega," called someone else.

The pilot stopped before them, pulled off gauntlets and goggles. A smile came as the other hand peeled off the helmet. "Fastest bird on this field," Amelia Earhart replied, running fingers through her flattened brown hair. "You should try it before you're a day older, Louise."

"What, and make that day my last? Not me, lady." As she spoke, Louise Thaden stepped forward, pulling her own helmet over her black curls and thrusting out her hand. "Better late than never, Amelia." She grinned. "A little like you in the Powder Puff Derby this summer, huh? Remind me. You were, what, third in your Vega? While I was— oh yeah, first, in my slow old Travel Air?"

Amelia joined in the laughter, gripping Louise's hand, then looking past her to the other pilots, every one of them a woman. "This it?"

"Yup. Twenty-seven including you."

Amelia searched over her friend's shoulder. "Roxy?"

"No-show." Louise shrugged. "You shouldn't count on her. I never do."

"Give the kid a break."

Louise grinned. "You might not be so charitable when you see her latest gag. She may not be here, but her plane is."

She swept her arm to the left. Amelia craned her neck and saw, at the far end of the row, the Breda BC. 33. She'd seen it the week before. Then, it had been painted grey. Now, it was red—the exact same shade as Amelia's Vega.

Amelia cursed, then laughed. "You could view it as tribute."

"Or you could view it as Roxy Loewen trying to steal your thunder. Again."

"Aw, hell." Amelia waved her hand, acknowledging the others as they set out for the hangar's back room, where refreshments were laid out and the meeting was to be held. Louise dropped into step beside her. "So, twenty-seven here. How many more pledged?"

"Seventy-two."

"Including Roxy?"

Louise shook her head. "She didn't pledge. I think her exact words were 'I'll be damned if I'll join any association that would have me as a member.'"

"She'd have joined," Amelia said quietly. "For me." She sighed. "Are we still going to name it after the number who did pledge?"

Louise nodded. "Looks like we're calling ourselves the Ninety-Nines."

"There you have it." Amelia smiled. "That's why Roxy stayed away. She knew it's a helluva better name than the Hundreds." The smile fell. "I just hope she isn't in too much trouble."

The storm pounding New York on November 2 was the second to batter the city in five days. It toppled telegraph poles, brought down street signs, smashed windows. But the first storm had been far more devastating. It had nearly destroyed the country. Hell, it had nearly destroyed the world.

October 29, 1929. The Wall Street Crash.

Roxy Loewen didn't care too much. But Roxy wasn't caring too much about anything as the winds raged outside, face down as she was on the bar of the 21 Club, New York's finest speakeasy.

The man beside her cared, though less for himself. Richard Loewen cared about the people who worked for him—or used to work for him, now that the shutters in his three factories were down. He cared for the people he'd borrowed money from to try and stop the collapse. When everything was liquidated—the New York brownstone, the house in Sag Harbor, the yacht, the cars, the horses—those people who'd trusted him would be lucky to see ten cents on the dollar.

Mostly, though, Richard Loewen cared about his daughter.

He reached out a hand, ran it through her tight blond curls. "Hey, Rabbit!" he murmured.

He supposed he'd spoiled her. Made up for her mother's early death by denying Roxy nothing. When she'd wanted to ride, he bought her ponies, then colts, then hunters. When she'd wanted to sail, he bought her a yacht. And when, that January, she'd wanted to fly? Even then he'd known he was tapped out, that every last cent he had should be thrown into the widening hole. But the hole was so wide and the plea in his daughter's green eyes so hard to refuse. Besides, planes were the coming thing. A plane might even hold its value—if she didn't destroy it first. Which she'd tried to do the first time she'd soloed, and on several occasions since.

"Roxy!" This time he called louder.

She sat up quite suddenly, eyes blurry. "I'm not asleep," she said. She pushed a curl off her forehead and grinned at him. "What were you saying, Pops?"

"I was saying . . ." What had he been saying? Something important. About inheritance. "Here it is," he said, reaching for the whisky bottle. "Enjoy it, Rabbit," he continued, pouring the last of the amber liquid into the two shot glasses before them. The whisky filled both to the brim, with no room left to take more and none to leave in the bottle. A perfect measure—though a helluva cruel way to treat so fine a Scotch. Still, it was one thing his creditors would not get.

"That the last of it?"

"The very last." He held the bottle upside down to prove the point, then up into the grey afternoon light that filtered through the filthy window set high above the door. The only window, as speakeasies didn't advertise their presence during Prohibition. "Macallan-Glenlivet 1904," he intoned, with reverence. "Paid one hundred bucks for it at auction."

"Worth every cent." Roxy took great care stretching for the glass, and as much care bringing it to her mouth. "What's the toast this time?"

"Wait." Richard lowered his glass to the wood, so his daughter did the same. "A few things to say first." He cleared his throat. Beyond the door he could hear the storm rising in savagery, cracks of thunder drawing nearer. The wind whining down Manhattan's stone canyons. Within the howl, there was the distant bell of a tram. "Roxy, my child, you are a credit to your old man."

"I thank you, sir." She tipped her head. "Drink now? Damn, but I'm still thirsty."

"In a moment." He frowned, focused. "Times are going to get hard. For everyone. You know what's happened. What I've done. Failed to do." He took a breath. "They'll come for it all. The houses and everything in 'em. Even that worthless cabin up near Newcomb. The yacht, your horses—"

"Nah! Blaze and Flame?"

"Gotta go." He licked his lips. "And they'll come for your plane."

"*Asteria*?" She let out a snort. "Let 'em try."

"But I have saved something for you, aside from the Scotch." From his jacket pocket he pulled out an envelope. "Ten bucks. And a train ticket to Montreal. Leaves from Penn Station at nine tomorrow morning."

"Canada? We're not going to Canada, are we? What the hell's there?"

"Canadians. And your mother's sister, Estelle. Oh, and *we're* not going. You are."

"Where will you be?"

"Here. Trying to put things right."

"I'm staying with you." She stared at him defiantly. "I'm not leaving without you."

"Sure you're not." He tucked the envelope into the pocket of the coat she hadn't taken off. It was cold in the 21 because it wasn't open; Max had opened it especially for him. Richard picked up his glass. "So a last toast, Rabbit. To the day. You know what today is?"

" 'Course I do. It's uh, uh—"

"November 2."

"November 2?" She slapped the bar. "Shoot! I'm meant to be with the girls at Curtiss Field. Forming an . . . an association."

"Max here was just telling me. Know what November 2 is in his native France?"

"Uh-uh."

"*Jour des morts*."

"Day of the Dead? Well, I have to say, father mine, that's one hell of a depressing last toast!"

"Nah, it's a celebration, kid. Memories of people we loved, who are still with us in memory." He looked at her over the brimming rim. "To your uncle Pete, killed in Flanders. To your ma." He peered at her. "Do you still wear it?"

She knew what he meant. "Always have it near." She reached under the neckline of her dress and pulled out the rabbit's foot, its grey fur capped in silver, attached to a chain. It had been her mother's, though how much luck it had brought Mabel Loewen, dead of influenza when Roxy was two, was hard to say. Still, it was all Roxy had left of her. And it had given Roxy a nickname.

Richard touched it. His eyes welled and Roxy shifted. "Come on, Dad. Too much talk."

He sniffed, then laughed. "You're damn right."

Both raised their glasses higher and spoke it together: "*Jour des morts.*"

They both shot. Roxy coughed, smiled, and lowered her head once again to the wood. "'Good night, sweet prince,'" she murmured. "Flights of angels, and all that."

He looked down at her for a long moment, then up at the bartender, a deeper shadow within the shadows of the speakeasy. "Take care of her, Max. Let her sleep it off in the back. I packed her a bag. Get her on that train."

"You can count on this, Monsieur Loewen."

Richard lifted his fedora from the bar and shrugged into his greatcoat. Outside, the wind gusted louder and the tram's bell sounded nearer. "Nighty-night, Rabbit," he whispered, as he bent and kissed her head through the thick curls.

She muttered something but didn't wake, and he didn't look at her. He stood with his back to the room as Max shot the bolts and opened the door, letting in a great cold swirl of air, a spattering of rain.

Richard stepped out. West Fifty-Second was jammed with people hurrying for shelter, clutching coats, heads bent, hats clamped down.

A woman shrieked as her umbrella skeletoned. She dropped it and ran on. That tram was getting closer and he thought of getting on, taking it anywhere. It would be the first time he'd dodged a fare since he'd come to New York in '05 with about as much change in his pocket as he had now.

Then he noticed them, the only people on the street not moving, not running from the storm. They were in the doorway opposite the bar, crowding it, three big men in dark coats, and hats with brims pulled low. Two he didn't know, though he could guess their profession by the one man he did.

"Hello, Sydney," he called, though probably not loud enough to be heard against the rain and the clanging bell.

The biggest man opposite didn't reply. Just raised an arm and pointed at Richard. The other two men nodded and stepped from the doorway.

Richard thought of running; he'd been fast in his day, had won races as a kid. But his legs were whisky weak, while these bailiffs were young and no doubt swift enough despite their bulk. He thought of talking. Talking was what had raised the near-illiterate boy born in Cicero, Illinois, from poverty into the top-ten league of America's wealthiest men. But yesterday Richard had talked himself hoarse to the man now pointing from the opposite doorway. Sydney Munroe had been a few ranks below him in the league when they'd met, and they'd become partners in multiple business ventures. Now it looked like the big guy was going to vault above. For all Richard's talking— pleading is what it had been—he had achieved nothing. Worse, he'd let slip the piece of information that not all his efforts in trying to dig himself out of debt were entirely legit. And he knew one thing: if he went to jail, Roxy would never go to Canada, never get on with her own life. She'd visit him every Sunday and work her fingers raw to free him. And he hadn't raised his kid to work like he'd had to.

As the men paused, waiting for the tram to pass, Richard Loewen looked up into the sky. A different world up there, blown wrappers and newsprint set against clouds that weren't so much grey as black. Even as he looked, lightning flashed. The thunder boomed not a second later. The storm was over him, right above, the tram's bell so loud. It was the second-to-last thing he heard. The very last was the screech of the tram's brakes as he stepped onto the tracks and the driver applied them too late, way too late.

◦◦◦

Roxy was dreaming, as usual, of flying. But whisky made it strange. She was doing a stunt, a barrel roll, but the plane had stalled halfway through and she couldn't get it going again. She was hanging upside down in the open cockpit and she hadn't buckled on her restraints.

"What?" she said, sitting up. There were so many sounds: thunder, crazy rain, screams, a woman weeping. "Pops?" she called. He'd been right there. When she put her hand on the seat next to her, it was still warm. She looked across the bar. Max was staring at the door. "Where's my dad? In the can?" she asked. "Max? Where'd he go?"

The bartender turned back to her. There was trouble in his eyes. "He just left."

She lurched up. "Open it."

"Miss Loewen, your father said—"

"Open the damn door!"

She swayed before it as he reached for the bolts, shrugging into her beaver fur coat and pushing the heel of her hands again and again into her eyes. It did nothing to clear them. She tried to focus on the tasseled ropes that gathered the plush velvet curtains to either side.

The door opened; the cold air hit her like a slap and the muffled sounds exploded. The weeping—it wasn't a woman but a man, a uniformed man in a grey jacket and a peaked cap. He crouched over a bundle of garbage on the ground, wedged under the front of a trolley car. Then she saw that in the garbage were Oxford brogues, looking just like the ones her dad ordered from Church's in London. Why would anyone throw them out, much less toss them into garbage in the middle of the street?

It was like the one key piece in a jigsaw puzzle: from separate images, she suddenly saw the whole. Saw the brogues, saw the feet they were attached to, saw everything. The tweed overcoat that would smell of his pipe tobacco if she could only get close enough. The narrow pinstripe of his Savile Row suit. The left hand with the pinky ring, and the bushy hair above each knuckle. She always teased him about that: "If I'm a rabbit," she'd say, "I've got a monkey for a dad."

Her father was lying on the street in front of a trolley car—which seemed crazy considering the weather, but perhaps not when you considered how much Scotch he'd drunk. But why was the driver crying? Babbling the same words over and over, tears and a thick Bronx accent muddying them: "I tell ya, the guy just stepped out! I couldn't do nothin'!" A crowd jostled near, fascination or horror on every face.

"Pops," she said, "you gotta get up. You're makin' a scene."

She stepped around to help him and saw his face. What was left of his face.

Somebody switched off the sound. One moment, nearby, the weeping of a man in uniform, the awed chatter of a crowd. Beyond, car horns, brakes, shouts. Above, thunder. Now, silence. Roxy looked at faces; people's mouths shaping words, nothing emerging. But she was wrong; there wasn't silence. There was a whine, high pitched, like a mosquito she'd wave away on the beach in the summer. Except, when she tried that now, her hand moved too slowly and the whine just got closer.

Somebody switched on a street lamp. The thunder clouds had turned the road as dark as night, lit only by sporadic lightning. Now it was bathed in a glow, yellow and sickly. It etched everything there— the silently talking people, the silently screaming man.

Somebody kicked her in the stomach, though she didn't see who, and the pain she felt was as bad as when Blaze had kicked her after she'd startled the colt. Her breath went and she cried out to the people around for help. Except, like them she made no sound.

Somebody. Some . . . body. Lying on the ground, her hand against a tweed shoulder. Nobody she knew lay down in the street.

There was a big man staring down at her, someone she did know: Sydney Munroe. He'd stayed at their house in Sag Harbor. He was a business partner of her father's. His eyes were fixed on her. She stared back as he spoke to the two younger men in front of him, without taking his gaze from her. Again she couldn't hear the words. But the fleshy lips moved in a way she could read: "Arrest her."

She saw him mouth the words—and they turned the sound back on, instantly so loud she had to block her ears with her hands. It did no good. The horns, the cries, the whining, the shouts slipped by them.

So did the younger man's reply. "But, Mr. Munroe, her dad just—"

"Died. He just died. So his estate—and the estate's debts—are now hers." He waved at Roxy. "Do your job."

Both men shrugged. Both took a step toward her, elbowing through the mob. Their movement whipped the yellow glow away as if it were a sheet. Roxy could see, she could hear, she could move . . .

"Move!"

It was a shouted command. Maybe she shouted it. She got up, turned and ran.

Her first steps were skittery. She went as much to the side as forward until she found her stride. Before she'd won races on horses and planes, she'd won them on her feet. Richard Loewen had left her more than ten bucks, a train ticket and some worthless land in the Adirondacks. He'd left her his green eyes. He'd left her his speed.

She weaved between people on the sidewalk and cars in the street, footfalls behind her, thumping heavy on the rain-slick pavement. They wouldn't catch her unless she fell. So she concentrated hard on not doing that.

When she hit the corner at Fifth, the lights were just turning green. Vehicles that had been gunning their engines lurched forward. If she stopped, she'd be trapped. If she made it across . . .

She didn't stop. She didn't look at the cars and cabs hurtling toward her. She barely heard them, their shrieking brakes and shrieking drivers. Only the very last vehicle caught her attention, because this one caught her dangling rear foot, even as her front one hit the eastern sidewalk. It spun her and sent her crashing into a mailbox.

The rider of a motorbike didn't fare so well. Yelping, he put it down on its side as both man and machine slid twenty yards up the street.

The bray of horns, the cries of shock, the shouts of fury, the rain falling in sheets. Dazed, Roxy pulled herself up and looked back. Her pursuers were picking their way through the stalled traffic. They were halfway across Fifth, but it was hard going for big men weaving through cars, some of which had locked fenders. She didn't have a lotta time, but she had a little.

She stood, cried out. Her ankle hurt. The running might be over.

She looked up the avenue. The motorcycle and its rider were both on their sides. He was moving; the bike was not. But she could see, with all the clarity of her drunken vision, the blue smoke that poured from its exhaust.

She lurched toward it, swinging her bad leg, pushing hard off her good one. She didn't look back, but the shouts told her the men weren't far behind. There was no time to do anything more than jerk the bike up, throw herself across it and hit the throttle.

She skidded. She felt rather than saw the hand that grabbed for her. Ducking that, she gunned the engine and took off up Fifth Avenue.

For the first few blocks she was occupied with not crashing and dying. The machine was an Ace, a stroke of fortune, because she'd ridden one on Long Island the previous summer. As she hit Sixtieth, she heard the first siren start up behind her. She needed somewhere to go and fast.

The road ahead was clearer, though rain still came down cold and hard, and wind slapped her around. Shrugging into the storm, Roxy kicked the Ace into fourth, opened the throttle, and headed for Queens. The Long Island Motor Parkway began in the borough. She didn't have any money for the toll. She'd just have to owe it.

∽∘∾

Amelia Earhart held a gavel of sorts—it was actually a monkey wrench—above the table in the hangar's back room. "So, before I declare the Ninety-Nines, the world's first all-women's flying association, officially formed, is there any final business?"

The other flyers looked around at each other. Officers had been proposed and seconded. The seventy-two absentees still had to send in their votes, but everyone knew the woman holding the wrench would be acclaimed as first president.

"No? Then it is my great pleasure to—"

"Amelia?" It was Louise Thaden who interrupted. She rose, gesturing outside. "What's that?"

That was an engine. The sound of a plane engine would immediately halt any business, in case the pilot was struggling to land and needed help.

The wrench hovered as they all listened. "Just a motorbike," said

Amelia, lifting her gavel, then pausing again. "Though I am curious," she continued, "as to why it is accompanied by so many sirens."

The pilots listened as engine growl and siren wail drew nearer. Amelia looked over the others' heads and locked eyes again with Louise. They both had the same thought. They both mouthed the same word.

"Roxy."

Amelia lowered the wrench.

✦

Between the soaking rain and the wind that had tried to rip her from her saddle, Roxy Loewen was halfway to sober when she tore past the hangar and over the grass of Curtiss Field Aerodrome. She was shaking, though, chilled to the bone. Her chenille silk dress suited the speakeasy, not the parkway, and she hadn't paused to button up her fur.

She pulled up beside her plane and dropped the Ace on its kickstand. Suddenly, she felt totally exhausted. What the hell was she going to do now?

"What the hell are you doing?"

Roxy turned. There she was, her friend, her mentor, at the head of a group of pilots. "Hey, Amelia."

"Don't you 'Hey, Amelia' me." Amelia tipped her head to the sirens growing ever louder. "They here for you?"

Roxy nodded, unable to speak. Amelia turned to the others. "Give us a moment?" As they backed off a ways, Amelia added, "Louise?"

"Uh-huh?"

"Those sirens? Distract them for a while, will ya?"

The younger pilot smiled. "Sure will try. Come on, ladies!"

As Louise and half the pilots ran to the road beyond the hangar, Amelia went to Roxy. "Kid, you're freezing. We've got to get you in—"

"No!" Roxy clutched Amelia's arms. "Help me. I've gotta get away."

"What trouble are you in this time?"

"The worst." She knew now, away from the sight, away from the sound and the soundlessness. And Amelia was the one person she could convey it to. "Pa's dead."

"What? How?"

"I think he . . ." Roxy couldn't bring herself to say it. She took a big breath. "They'll take everything, all he built, and—" She gripped Amelia harder. The sirens were so close now they had to be through the gates. "And now they've come to take *Asteria*. I can't let them," she said. "I can't."

Roxy turned to the plane and put a foot on the step, but it slipped off.

"Stop!" cried Amelia. "What do you think you're doing?"

"Getting the hell out of here."

"You crazy? You're drunk. I can smell it on you."

"No drunker than you were in Denver."

"That was—" Amelia broke off. "You can't. You'll kill yourself."

"I will if I stay here. May as well if they take my plane—" She looked into her friend's eyes. "Please! It's the last thing I've got of him."

Amelia gave a deep sigh. She ripped off her leather jacket, thrust it toward Roxy and called the other way, "Edna, a hand here?" The flyer ran over. "Lend me your flying helmet and goggles, will you?" The woman obliged. Some sirens had stopped, but others were still coming. Shouts came from the other side of the hangar, loud male voices. "Now, all of you—go help Louise hold them off."

The others rushed toward the hangar. Roxy hurled the fur up into the cockpit, slipped into the flying jacket and fumbled with the buttons. "Here," said Amelia, pulling her close. "I'll do those—you do this." She passed over the helmet. Roxy donned it and tightened the strap while Amelia buttoned her up. "Where are you going?"

"Canada. I've got an aunt in—"

"Wait, never mind! If I don't know, I can't tell. Now, move!" She boosted her friend onto the step and Roxy tumbled into the cockpit, spread the fur and sat. Amelia ran to the nose and put both hands on the top side of one propeller blade. "Contact," she yelled.

Roxy threw the switch. "Contact."

Using her weight, Amelia dropped hard and stepped back. Nothing. "Off!" she shouted.

"Off!"

As she grasped the blade again, a loud male voice bellowed, "Stop! That woman is under arrest."

But Amelia didn't stop. Instead she shouted, "Contact!"

"Contact!"

Amelia swung. The engine kicked and she dived to the side then back in behind the blades, to rip the blocks from the wheels. As the plane lurched forward, she hurled herself away and fell straight into the arms of the policeman who had run forward. "What was that you said, sweetheart?" she asked him, gazing up. "Didn't catch it."

The Breda was a racer, in the air or on the ground. Even as the cops forced their way through the crowd of pilots, *Asteria* had reached the edge of the runway.

Roxy squinted back. A handful of cops broke from the throng. In normal circumstances, she'd use the whole length of the strip to take off. The wind sock showed her the wind was blowing roughly straight down the field. In normal circumstances, she'd taxi gently into position and take off with it behind her. In normal circumstances, she'd never rush her cold engine.

These were not normal circumstances. If she took all that time, they'd get a car onto the track and block her. There was only one option left—she'd have to take off cross-field *and* crosswind.

Roxy opened the throttle halfway. The cool engine coughed in protest, but she sped forward. She had maybe a hundred yards before the fence marking the aerodrome's boundary. But *Asteria* was small, and light. She had good lift.

Pulling the stick gently back, Roxy brought the rear wheel up. Working the left rudder hard to counter the wind, she sighted on an elm at the edge of the far field. The narrow runway was smooth, its verge a lot less so. As she bounced over the first knoll, as she took a little air, Roxy thought, *Here's nothing.* Now opening the throttle all the way, she pulled the stick hard back.

Her right front wheel clipped a fencepost. It spun her, one wing tipping toward the earth. But she plied the rudder, threw her own weight back and the stick with it.

She missed the elm by a clear foot.

Banking, she swung back toward the aerodrome. She was only about a hundred feet up, so could see them all. The policemen—there had to be twenty—some standing with their hands on their hips, looking bemused; some pounding their fists in the air. Amelia, standing with her arm around Louise in the midst of all the girls, was smiling. Finally, she noticed a figure watching her, larger than the rest, a little apart. And he—Sydney Munroe—looked nothing less than apoplectically angry.

Roxy always liked a crowd, and suddenly remembered the stunt she'd failed to pull off in her dream. A barrel roll. Stunts were always done at least two thousand feet up. Hell with that, she thought. She snapped her safety belt on, pushed the rudder and stick left. Then, as *Asteria*'s wings angled, she kicked the rudder over and pulled the stick diagonally hard back.

Roaring, the plane barrel-rolled, one hundred feet over the spectators' heads. Even above the engine's roar she could hear the screams.

She reversed the movements of stick and rudder, stalled as she came out of the roll, drove the stick forward. The engine fired and, level, she started her climb.

It was cold, but her legs practically rested under the Breda's engine mount. Though only covered in wet silk, they began to warm. She drew the edges of beaver fur over them. The fleece lining and fur collar of Amelia's leather jacket also helped.

Roxy reached the low ceiling, burst through and kept climbing. The world went dark for a while. The buzz of good whisky had dwindled to a residue of pain. But it was all she had left of her father so she clung to it. All she had left of her mother was the rabbit's foot on the chain around her neck. Thinking of one, clutching the other, she cried now, because she could; because she was alone and not even God could see her in these clouds. Great shuddering sobs came, snot and teardrops freezing on her face. Up and up she went, with her sorrow, until it got hard to breathe and she thought she'd never make the summit. Then in a heartbeat, grey nothing turned to brilliant sunshine. Levelling, she rode the cloud tops north.

TWO

GUNS, RUM AND A COMMIE CALLED JOCCO

Seven years later. Somewhere over British Somaliland, Africa. May 1, 1936.

THERE'S NOTHING LIKE DYING TO MAKE A GIRL APPRECIATE living.

As she stared down into the pitiless black of the night, seeking, forever seeking, the one pinpoint of light that might yet save her—but it had better hurry up—Roxy Loewen thought about what was waiting for her.

A straw-roofed hut with a tin bath filled with tepid water on its third use that would feel like a clawfoot tub at the Plaza. Rum so raw it hurt your eyes but when mixed with tamarind juice would taste like a Negroni at the Ritz. Steak from a camel or an ass surpassing the finest filet mignon that Rex's 110th Street chop house could serve.

And at the end of all those, a German. Jochen Zomack—Jocco—with his big hands and his big laugh and the hank of brown hair that, when he let it fall over his face just so and in the right light, made him look like Cary Grant. Jocco, down there somewhere, scanning the black skies as she scanned the black ground, ready with his light.

If her message had gotten through. Communications had been sketchy since the Italians had begun what many were saying would be their final offensive. The gallant, heavily outgunned Ethiopians—guns, hell, a lot of them still fought with spears—would make their last stand against the invader near their capital, Addis Ababa.

The rumours had decided her. To fly her cargo of rifles west into that war zone was suicide. If the Italians didn't shoot her out of the sky, there probably wouldn't be an airfield left to land on. The one where she waited at Malco Dube would also be bombed again. Even if her Lockheed 227—*Asteria 6,* Roxy called her—wasn't hit on the ground, there wouldn't be enough time to fill in the craters on the runway that was already more gopher burrow than the racetrack it once had been. But if she could get her cargo to Jocco, he'd know what to do with it. He'd know where some of his comrades might still be fighting. He had run guns all over this continent. All over the world, truly. Hell, he might even get her paid. Though it wasn't so much the money she'd been thinking of as she'd taken off from the foothills of the mountains and headed toward a moon just peeking in the east. It was him. Lying with him. There was a time she might have blushed at that thought. But she didn't blush so much anymore.

Night fell fast this close to the equator, but the moon was a day off full and that had given her hope. Three hours' flight and a landing by moonlight? She'd done that before, half a dozen times.

What she hadn't reckoned on were the thick cumulus clouds rolling in from the Indian Ocean. She was under them now, halfway between the ceiling and the floor about two hundred feet below her. Flying star quadrants, covering ground above what she hoped was still the airfield at Dubaro. There were no lights. Italian pilots were so bored they would drop a bomb on a fella lighting a cheroot in his cupped hand. The terrain was featureless enough in daylight—arid, scrubby hills or thick jungle, especially this close to the coast. At night there was . . . nothing.

As she swung the bird again, dipping the wings each side and scanning the dark, the engine gave a cough, picked up, then coughed again. A small block in the intake valve, she prayed. That would, with luck, clear itself. The alternative? She truly had no clue how much gas was in the tanks. The gauge was busted, and though she'd woken from a snatched hour's sleep to be told they'd given her the last of what they had, she hadn't been able to confirm exactly how much that was before she made the decision to go.

It coughed yet again and she pushed the stick forward, dropped lower. If she ran out of juice, she would have to glide. Then it would be a choice between which piece of blackness looked most appealing. Trees would finish her. Scrub could break her undercarriage, flip her and hurl her through the windshield. She really wished she'd insisted they fixed her lap straps the last time a mechanic checked the bird over.

Waggling her wings, looking either side for even the flare of a match, she then glanced at the leather saddlebag at her feet. It didn't hold much. Compact and lipstick. A mickey of rum. Her Luger pistol. Three vials of morphine. One was for pain if she was hurt and had to wait for a rescue. Three were for when hope ran out. Between them and the Luger she was pretty much set.

The engine coughed anew—then kept coughing like a patient in a TB ward. Not long now.

She dipped her right wing . . . and saw them! Pulses of light.

Short. Long. Long. Long.

They came a second time. Short. Long. Long. Long. *J.*

J for Jocco.

She pressed hard on the rudder bar, swung the stick and the plane left. Too sharp! She slid outward on her seat, skidding, then corrected, but only just. If she had gas, she'd correct harder, shove the stick all the way forward, lighten up on the rudder, pass over and come in again. But since that cough was close to a death rattle now, she didn't have any choice. Her only prayer was that Jocco had more than a flashlight to guide her in.

He had better—he had fire. Hidden from flying eyes until now, exposed in sudden revelation. It was a view that got even clearer as the engine gave one last, great groan and cut out. It meant that she could hear the wind—and a knocking she realized could only be her heart.

She opened the cockpit window. She needed to hear that wind clearly. At night, with no moon, she couldn't use the horizon to judge her angle of descent. She could only use her ears. The hum from the bracing wires was high. Too high. Meant she was coming in too steep. She eased the stick back, brought the nose up a touch. The hum lowered and she held it on that note, like Caruso holding a high C at Carnegie Hall.

The fire, maybe a quarter mile ahead now, spread. Men were running different ways, holding torches. The last ones stopped. So soon? Flame demarcated the quadrangle of an airstrip, as short and narrow as any she'd seen. It had to be new, cut out of the scrub. That meant rough ground, divots and potholes, a horror of a landing by day, when you could see something. At night?

"Hail Mary," Roxy breathed, pressing the rudder to bring herself in line, pushing the stick forward. She wasn't thinking religion, though, but football. This was her last play. "Don't stretch the glide," she coached herself. "Don't flatten out too soon."

The first torches were coming close, fast. Caruso went off key as she put the bird into a sharper descent, pulling the stick back to level as she glimpsed an acacia tree, her front wheel clipping its top, its apex tickling the fuselage beneath her feet as she passed.

The first torches were to her left and right. The last was ahead, so near. She was coming in too fast. She'd take the wings off in the trees beyond the final flames. And one thing she knew—if she survived this, she'd need her wings.

It always surprised her how much time there was when there was no time at all.

Slow down! She kicked the rudder, now left, now right, fishtailing the Lockheed. Caruso sang higher. She pulled the stick to her a touch, levelled, and the note dropped again.

It was all or nothing now. Too slow and she'd flip. Too fast and she'd be picking leaves out of her teeth.

The bird slipped near sideways between the flames. Roxy couldn't see the ground over her engine. She could only sense it. Straightening up, she put the silent plane down onto earth that—Hail be to Mary!—was only a few inches beneath her wheels.

Her exhilaration lasted until the moment the left wheel hit a hole. The plane swerved sharply and thrust its nose into the hard, hard earth.

She'd been prepared to brace, since a rough landing wasn't entirely unexpected on a strip carved hastily from jungle. She took the jolt with one hand on the dash. But she still flew from her seat, the flight ended by her forehead hitting the windshield, her body folded by gravity into the frame. "Ouch," she said. She didn't black out, but she found it hard to move, near upside down as she was. Through the glass she saw a single flaring torch jiggling toward her. Every other one was already out. Not a moment too soon, she thought, trying to push herself upright. Because from somewhere not far off she could hear another plane engine. Though she was sure it was only her fancy that made its high-pitched whine Italian.

"Roxy?"

The voice, his, Jocco's, right next to her through the glass.

"Roxy? You okay?"

"Never better," she replied, and pushed herself out of the windshield. Jocco opened the canopy, plucked her out with one arm, set her on her feet, then thrust the torch into the ground, extinguishing it. In the sudden darkness she wobbled, and fell into him. "Well," she breathed, "that might be a slight exaggeration."

He picked her up again and she thought that was just fine. She liked his smell—Douwe Egberts tobacco, some hair tonic that always failed to control his mop. As he took a step away, though, she said, "Bag!" and, one-handed, he reached up and grabbed it.

It glugged. "Rum?" Jocco asked.

"Thought my baby might be thirsty. I'll trade you for a cigarette and a bath."

"I'll roll you one. The other?" He shrugged.

He strode to the clearing edge. She peered over his shoulder, and could still see the dark outline of her bird, its nose in the dirt. "You got someone here who can fix that? Wherever the hell 'here' is?"

"Yeah. Damn Eyeties destroyed the aerodrome. So all the boys are here. We carved this out today. Just in case you came."

"Kind of you."

They reached the tree line. Men were there, and Jocco spoke to them in rapid Swahili. She caught a little. Get the plane beneath the trees. Fix it. Then he looked down at her.

"You wanna walk?"

"How far?"

"Not far."

"Then I'm fine here." She nuzzled in as he set off. "And did you say something about a bath, and a cigarette, and a steak, and a drink?"

"You brought the drink. I've been saving a steak just for you, though it may be a day past its best. As for a bath . . ." He pushed through a stand of trees and she heard it before she saw it. "Will this do?"

He swivelled and she saw the beach. The moon poked through the clouds just enough to light the foam on the waves sweeping in. "Yeah," she said, as he set her down. "This'll do just fine."

∽○∾

She woke near dawn to the sound of waves and the taste of salt. Her sweat, his, the ocean they'd swum in—the only bath she was going to get.

He was sitting naked on the end of the camp bed, framed against the entrance of the tent. He'd thrown open the mosquito netting and was smoking one of his roll-up cigarettes, holding it in that way of his, his chin resting on his hand, his elbow on his knees, so the smoke would curl up into a trail and he could look at the world through narrowed, Meissen-blue eyes. She studied his back, her eyes going where her fingers had in the dark, tracing the raised lines of his scars, one map of his life. She'd wondered at it the first time they'd made love: how a twenty-six-year-old floppy-haired German had gotten himself into so much trouble. He'd laughed the scars off. "Skiing," he'd said. "I fell in a race." An angry cat. But something would flash through his eyes as he told the lies, something haunted, so she knew different; but she didn't probe. After all, were he to answer all her questions truthfully, she just might have to answer his.

"Roll me one."

He turned. "Good morning, Fräulein. Did you sleep well?" He was always formal first thing. He was "an inquiry after your health" kind of guy. A "hold your chair" guy. For all that he was a goddamn godless Commie, he'd gone to the best schools that big money could buy. "Breakfast first? There's mangosteen. I saved a custard apple."

"Tobacco," she growled. "Now."

He nipped the stub of the cigarette and put it in the tin with the dozen others—a last smoke if all else failed. He slipped in beside her on the narrow metal-frame bed, reached for his fixings and worked his effortless magic. Lit the result and held it between her lips so she didn't even have to move, just take a deep, life-sustaining drag. "Ah!" She breathed smoke out on her sigh. The day had begun and she was ready to think.

And remember. "How's my bird?"

She knew he'd left her after they'd made love. He was also one of *those* guys: get up straightaway and check that all was well. Primal, she'd teased him once. As if the moment right after lovemaking was when a man was at his most vulnerable, with beasts about, waiting for the opportunity to attack. In Africa, maybe not too far-fetched an idea.

"Prop is bent. The boys have been hammering it out for the last two hours—they just finished. I'm surprised they didn't wake you."

"I've barely slept in a week. I could sleep through a ground assault." She took the cigarette from his mouth, inhaled deeply. "Engine good? It cut out as I was flying in."

"I heard." He shook his head. "Engine works fine. But you have to remember to put gas in it." He looked down at her. "You only just made it, kid."

"Kid!" She snorted. He was just the one year older. He only called her "kid" because he was near a foot taller. "You got any?"

"In my bird. Half a tank. I'll give you half of that."

"Obliged. Where we going?"

"I'm going to Addis."

"What? We can still get in?" She sat up and put her bare back to the earth wall. "Then I'm coming too. Got three hundred rifles in the hold."

"Three hundred?" He whistled. "No wonder you looked so heavy. I thought it was just your flying." When she punched his arm, he laughed, and took the cigarette. "But it's too late for your guns. War's over."

"Hell it is!"

"Over." His eyes narrowed as he inhaled. "Fascism has triumphed. The Italians have won. Emperor Haile Selassie goes into exile tomorrow."

"And how do you know this?"

"Krueger. Came through yesterday, just before the Italians bombed the 'drome. Everyone left. Aside from you and me."

"Well, shit."

"I know—you won't get paid."

He said it as a statement, not a challenge. They'd had that fight too many times. When they first met, in that bar in Alexandria where mercenary flyers were gathering like kites over a new corpse called Abyssinia. Some, like Jocco, were going down for a cause. Most, like Roxy, were headed for the money. Big money, commensurate to the risk, flying guns to the overmatched Ethiopians.

"The first stand against the Fascists," he'd called it.

"Causes are for suckers," she'd mocked.

"Dollars are for exploiters," he'd replied.

The argument had continued whenever they met—Addis Ababa, Khartoum, Djibouti. She'd slapped him in Nairobi. He'd kissed the slapping hand. They'd slept together for the first time that night.

And was last night their last? she suddenly wondered. Wasn't it always meant to be just a fling? It was a law of the skies, nearly as important as gravity: You don't fall in love with flyers. You could only be in love with flight.

This war was over, he'd said. They would all be going their separate ways. Getting their birds to safety first. Figuring out where the next score or the next cause was after that.

Separate ways. In the past, she'd felt relief when such a thing ended. Yet was that what she'd feel—in Nairobi, in Alexandria—when the saloon door opened and Jocco Zomack didn't walk in?

"Hey, make a bit of room, will ya?"

He raised his arm to enfold her. There, pressed into his big chest, with the scent of tobacco, the ocean, the jungle and him all blended, she thought: I don't want this to end. Not yet. But how do I say that without sounding like a sap?

She peeled the cigarette from his lips, dodging her own thoughts in smoke and questions. "So why Addis if it's all over? Italians aren't going to treat any of us too well if they catch us. They won't make much distinction between Commies like you and mercenaries like me. Except me, they'll just shoot. You, they'll torture then shoot."

He shifted and she cut herself off. Damn, it was too early in the day and her tongue was loose. So she'd forgotten for a moment that this was his weakness; his sadness too. His best friend, a German flyer named Reinhardt, had been captured by the Italians and tortured to death. All because Jocco had refused to kill his wounded comrade when he'd had to flee or also be taken. It was a story he'd told her once when they were very drunk. It was the only time she'd seen him cry. He'd begged her that if it ever came to it, she wouldn't make the same mistake. "Put me out of my misery," he'd said, like he was some kind of mad dog.

Now he grunted. Perhaps he hadn't noticed. "I'll go to Addis, but I won't stay. Benedetti and MacBride are waiting at the one 'drome that still has a runway, according to Krueger. I'll collect them, then head for Egypt."

So there it was. He wasn't thinking about her. He was going to get his Red buddies. Cause had triumphed over . . . whatever it was he felt for her.

And then Jocco swung off the bed to kneel and take her hand. There was a look in his eyes. Jesus, she thought, he's not going to propose, is he?

"Roxy," he said gently.

She inhaled deep, and carefully stubbed out the cigarette in the tin. "Jocco?"

"Do you know what day it is?"

"Monday."

"The date."

"Uh, April . . . no, May. May 1."

"Exactly. May Day. International Workers' Day."

"Oh, come on!" She laughed, at least partly out of relief. He was prone to giving her lectures on various aspects of the world revolution. Kept making the mistake that she might learn to give a damn. Though usually there were at least a few rums as provocation.

"No, listen." He squeezed her hand. "The fight here is over. Mussolini has triumphed. The world looked away and waved him on. It will only make him and every other *fascista* bolder. They will already be seeking the next triumph elsewhere. Then the next. Until everywhere is painted black."

"I get it." She swallowed. She had seen the dead children stacked like firewood because Italian pilots needed some bombing practice; the old men and women with their skins peeling off because of the mustard-gas canisters dropped on their villages. "I know what they do. I just don't see what I can do about it. On May Day or any other day."

"There is something you can do. And get well paid for it too." He smiled. "Though I know you care more than you admit. That Italian general? He offered you double what you could make here to be his personal pilot."

"Since he made the offer with his hand on my ass, I chose to decline."

"And those three kids you flew out of Malco Dube?"

"They were badly burned. They needed a doctor fast."

"You had to dump three boxes of expensive ammo to make room for them."

"I figured I'd pick 'em up on the next trip."

"Did you?"

"No, but—"

"Roxy . . ."

"Ah, shuddup," she said, "and go back to what I could do. Especially the 'well-paid' part."

"Okay." Jocco reached for his tin, took out a paper, began slowly to roll another cigarette. "The next fight has already begun, even as this one ends. In Spain. The country is falling into revolution."

"Uh-huh. Sounds like a place to avoid. Unless—"

"Unless you can take something in to sell for a high price. Then take something out the next day that will pay you even more."

"I'm listening. What would I take in?"

"The three hundred rifles in your hold."

"What? Two thousand miles with that hold searched at every touchdown?"

"There are ways. You know there are ways. Night landings. The right officials bribed." He grinned, then ran his tongue along the paper's sticky edge. "Roxy, it's what you have been doing for the last two years."

"Good point. You got someone waiting to buy at the other end?"

"I do."

"Well, hell, I'll consider it." She eyed his handicraft hungrily. But this time he was fashioning a masterpiece. He was even ripping cardboard for a filter. She hated when he did that. "So now tell me about the 'even better paid' part."

"Right." He considered the end of the paper tube. "You know my father."

"You ever going to light that thing?"

"He's an art dealer. In Cologne."

"You told me. You hate him."

"I do not hate him. I hate his part in the system. His hoarding of money. He is a quiet man. What is it you say in English?" He frowned. "*Ungentle*? No. He does not show much affection. But I know he loves me, though I have caused him some pains."

"I bet."

"I got a letter from him. Krueger brought it from Addis. It was written last week."

"Really? That got here fast."

"German efficiency." He smiled briefly. "My father has found something in Madrid. Something very special. Lost for centuries." He slipped the cardboard in, crimped the other end. "Do you know art?"

"Some. My dad collected a little." It was an understatement. Before the Great Crash, Richard Loewen had had one of the finest private collections of post-impressionists in the United States.

"Do you know Bruegel?"

"Dutch guy?"

"Yes. Sixteenth century."

"You are going to light that now, right?"

He ignored her plea. "He painted the *Fall of Icarus.*"

"I saw it, in Brussels." She considered. "Legs disappear into the sea, while everyone looks the other way."

"That is it. Except, the one in Brussels is a copy. No, that is not quite right. But it is not the original." He reached for the matchbox, shook it as if accompanying a band. "Because Bruegel worked in the period when artists were changing from painting on wood panels with oils to painting on canvas with tempera. The first *Fall* was painted on wood. Then it was lost."

"Until your father found it. In Madrid."

"He thinks so, yes." Jocco slid the box open, pulled a match out. "In his letter he tells some of what I already knew: that Madrid and Spain are slipping toward chaos. He would like the panel flown out of the chaos. And the only one he trusts to do this is me."

"And what's in it for you?"

"He has promised me a share—a 10 percent share—in the sale. To put to whatever cause I want."

"Ten percent of—"

He shrugged. "Maybe one hundred thousand."

"Deutschmarks?"

"Dollars."

"Hosanna. And you are offering me?"

"Half. Half, if you get it to Berlin."

"Why Berlin?"

"He has a buyer already lined up."

"Five Gs, eh?" She whistled. That was the down payment on a new bird right there. There'd been talk of a second London-to-Melbourne race. Win that and she'd quadruple her five grand. But there was a catch here. "Why not fly it yourself and keep all the dough?"

"I am, uh, known to authorities in Spain. I was involved in the miners' strike in Asturias in '34. I would never get it out openly. But I will come, after you. I will help."

"To Madrid?"

"To Berlin."

She studied him. His chest. Those blue eyes in his tanned face. The white laugh lines. For a Commie bent on the serious business of world revolution he sure laughed a lot. She realized she hadn't looked forward to seeing the last of all that. Now she might not need to.

"I will write again to my father. Tell him to have a banker's draft to pay for *Icarus* waiting for you in Madrid," Jocco continued. "Also for an art expert to meet you there. Together you will go and see the bishop of Valladolid. He has the painting. The expert verifies . . . no, ah, *authenticates*—is this the word? You pay, fly the goods out. I meet you in Berlin, we collect our reward." He smiled. "Simple, yes?"

It was anything but. Yet she'd done things as tricky in the last few years. And the money was good. Really good.

Roxy looked down at his hands. "Put that down, will ya?"

"I thought you wanted to smoke it."

"Later," she replied, taking the cigarette, dropping it to the floor. "First you got to tell me a story."

"What story?"

"How did you get that scar?"

"Which one?"

"This one," she said, and ran her tongue along it.

∽o∽

She put a foot on the plane step and one hand on the door frame. She never liked goodbyes. They'd said everything—done everything—in the hut one hour before.

Or so she thought. "Roxy," Jocco said, putting one hand on top of hers, halting her ascent.

"Jocco?"

"A present."

He held out three cigarettes. She could see they were his fancy ones, filters and all. He must have rolled them when she went to the ocean for a rinse.

"It is the last of my tobacco."

"My, ain't you gallant."

She knew he'd be okay. There were all the ends in that tin, saved for such desperate times. And he'd be flying into Addis that night.

She tucked the cigarettes into the top pocket of her jacket, next to the three hundred dollars in mixed bills he'd given her for bribes and gas along the way. He'd be okay there too. For an avowed member of the proletariat, Jocco was never short of ready cash.

He gestured to the money as she buttoned up the pocket. "You sure it will be enough?"

"A gal could always use more. You have more?"

"Not till Addis."

"Kidding." She patted his cheek. "I'll be fine. I don't always pay for gas. I have favours to call in."

"Favours?"

"Yeah. First stop, Wajir. The RAF lieutenant there is a little in love with me. He'll fill the bird for free if I promise him a night of dancing in Nairobi on his next leave."

"Just dancing?"

Wow, she thought, that's not jealousy I see in those baby blues, is it? "Just dancing. He's one of those English guys. Stutters. Is 'ever so pr-proper.' "

She said it in her best faux-Brit accent. Jocco didn't smile; he looked away to the jungle. "And after Kenya? More favours?"

Wow, she thought again, he's got it bad. It pleased and frightened her in equal measure. Two flyers should not fall for each other. Not this hard.

"I'll be fine. Safe." She reached up, took his chin, turned him back. "And I'll preserve ma honour, sir."

The phrase, the Dixie accent she said it in, at last brought the smile back to his eyes.

"Good. And you remember? Captain Vásquez is your contact at the aerodrome in Madrid. He will pay you fifteen hundred for the guns—" He raised his voice to still her protest. "I know, it is not the best price. Call it a—" he smiled "—a good-cause tax. More important, he will get you into the city. When I know the name of the expert, I will wire you. Also, the bank for the draft."

"Baby, you told me this already. It's easy."

"Easy? Two thousand miles with a hold full of guns? Two dozen aerodromes with Brits, French, Italians, Spaniards to get past? In a world marching fast to hell?"

There was anger in his voice and his smile had gone—but she still had a hold of his chin. She pulled it down. "Easy," she breathed, and kissed him. He was a little stiff at first, until he wasn't, until he melted, until he sank into her and lifted her at the same time. Breathless, she finally pulled away. "Wow," she said, running her hand over her curls, "you sure know how to mess with a gal."

"And you with a guy."

His voice had gone husky and he bent again. She put a finger to his lips. "Berlin. Two months," she said. "Will this last you?"

He kissed her finger, then nodded. "I will wait for you in Berlin."

The way he said it, promised it, sent another wave through her, the same mix of joy and doubt. "See you above the clouds," she said.

He released her, and she moved through the hold, pausing only to check the straps around the gun cases, then up into the cockpit. She dropped her bag to the side, took her helmet from it and pulled it on. Her goggles she left up on her forehead. One of his boys had fixed her lap straps and she clicked them over her. The Lockheed 227 sat high, so she leaned out of the window to see Jocco, positioned now at the prop.

"Contact?" he yelled.

She turned the switch. "Contact."

He swung those big arms and the engine caught straightaway. It wasn't only the lap straps his boys had fixed. The engine gave off a contented, throaty purr.

"Clear," he yelled, stepping away.

She looked at him as she held the bird on its brakes, building her revs till the engine sang its warmest song. Had to look away to taxi along the short edge of the clearing. She gathered speed, and lost almost none of it on the turn. On the straight she pulled back easy on the stick. The 227 had a 420 HP engine with a twelve hundred feet-per-minute climb. Even weighted with all those guns, she lifted effortlessly over the acacia.

As she cleared them, she glanced back. Jocco stood in the middle of the runway, hand sheltering his eyes from the sun. She saluted, but he didn't wave, just stood there, and she lost him fast to flight.

She pulled her goggles down, looked ahead, seeking a landmark. First stop Kenya and then . . . all she had to do was fly a payload of guns all the way to Spain. Be a miracle if she made it.

"Hell," she said, aloud. "I've survived two years of war in Africa and made Jochen Zomack fall in love with me. One more miracle isn't too much to ask, is it?"

THREE

MAÑANA

Two months later. July 27, 1936.

AS SHE CUT THE ENGINE OUTSIDE HANGAR 7 OF GETAFE
military aerodrome in Madrid, Roxy slumped back and watched the
propeller feather down to stillness. She couldn't remember ever being
this tired. She couldn't really remember much of anything about this
last flight—apart from falling asleep twice and jerking awake as the
bird went into a stall and headed for the ground. She'd craved a few
hours of sleep in Lisbon. But when she'd finally reached Captain
Vásquez at Getafe, he'd urged her on. "The revolution changes things
every day," he'd shouted down the crackling phone line. "I do not
know if I will be here tomorrow."

Now she watched a man in uniform emerge from the hangar and
scurry toward her. It may have taken more miracles than a minor
messiah could manage, but she'd made it. And she also knew that
despite it being a city in revolution, Madrid would have everything
she craved. No matter how desperate the times, people with enough
money could always buy what they wanted; she'd seen it time and
again in war zones across the world. The uniformed man approaching

would give her all the money she needed—for a room in the best hotel in town, with a bath so deep she could drown; which, after drinking the finest whisky available and gorging on the finest steak, she might well do. She'd brought three hundred M1 Garand self-loading rifles with ammo to spare two thousand miles to a country at war. She'd done enough gun-running in Abyssinia, and spent enough time with Jocco, to know their value. Hell—she smiled—I might even take a suite.

She reached, pulled the cockpit window open. "Captain Vásquez?"

"*Comrade* Vásquez, please." He saluted, clenched hand rising to his temple. "You are Comrade Loewen?"

His English was good, if thick and lispy. "Just call me 'Roxy,'" she said, as she unstrapped, moved into the hold and sprang the door.

The captain—comrade offered a hand. She took it and jumped down. He was the same size as her—and she wasn't the tallest poplar in the grove. He had a thin moustache; his hair was pure black and glistened with pomade. He wiped a palm nervously over both sides, smoothing it. "You wish to rest before—" he swallowed and an over-large Adam's apple bobbed up and down "—business?"

"No, let's do the business. I've got a date."

"Who with?"

"Johnnie Walker."

She reached inside the Lockheed and pulled down the small steps set inside. Vásquez mounted, and she followed and opened a case for him. He lifted a rifle and gave an appreciative grunt. He checked another couple of cases at random, then nodded. "I will call my men to unload the plane."

He took a step to the door. She laid a hand on his arm. "Not so fast, Captain. Where's my money?"

"Business in my office," he said curtly. Frowning, she followed.

His office had a desk, two chairs, a wall-mounted telephone and a steel cabinet. As Vásquez went to that and took out a key, Roxy stepped to the grimy window and watched as a dozen men began unloading the oblong boxes from her plane. "Like wooden coffins," she murmured, yawning. For the first time she wondered how many coffins her delivery might help fill—and shivered.

"*¡Señorita!*"

She jumped, turned. Vásquez had taken his hat off and was pouring wine into two glasses. He lifted both, handed her one and raised his. "To the Republic!" he said.

"Mud in your eye," she replied.

He shot, and she sipped, grateful that she did—the wine could have pickled herring. Putting her glass down, she said, "And my money?"

He reached back into the open cabinet, pulled out an envelope. It was suspiciously thin.

Banker's draft, she thought. Shit. Cash—dollars—was the universal currency for guns.

"*Lo siento,*" he said.

And she knew enough Spanish to understand he was apologizing. Then saw something in his eyes and recognized that he wasn't apologizing for the draft. She snatched the envelope and ripped it open. A single sheet, poorly printed with some sort of ink-blotched seal stamped on it. Her Spanish wasn't good enough to translate.

"What the hell's this?" she asked.

"It is the gratitude of the Republican government."

"The *gratitude*?"

"For your contribution to the glorious cause."

"Yeah. And where's your contribution to my glorious cause?"

"*¿Qué?*"

She leaned down to rest her hands on the desk and eyeball him. "Where's my money, pal?"

He flinched at the steeliness in her tone. "This—" he waved at the paper "—is also a—what you call this?—IOU. So. You will be paid . . ."

"I know I will. Right now."

"*Lo siento,*" he said again. "But you will be paid when the Glorious Revolution is complete."

"Then that's when you'll get your guns." She took a step to the open door, put her fingers into her lips. The loudness of her whistle made the soldiers stop and twitch like bird dogs. "Put those back in the plane," she yelled, "pronto."

Vásquez grabbed her wrist, pulled her back inside, closed the door. "Let go of me, you son—" She jerked her hand free. "You are not screwing me here, buddy. You are screwing Jochen Zomack. These guns belong to him. You know him, right?"

He nodded.

"Then you also know that if your Glorious Revolution is to succeed, you are going to need him and his buddies to bring you a lot more than three hundred rifles. Which they won't if I don't get paid now." She glared at him. "And you won't get your cut, right?"

He flinched. "Many regrets. But we must all make sacrifices. It is only a week since the rebellion of the Fascist General Franco. The committee has said all deals made before then must be delayed. *¡Qué lástima!* What a pity, no? But if you will wait a little, arrangements will be made to your satisfaction."

"How little?"

He shrugged. "Perhaps a week?"

He might as well have said *mañana,* which they did all the time in Spain. Meaning "whenever." But anyway, she couldn't hang around, not even a week. Jocco had a telegram waiting for her in Lisbon. The German art guy was in play. He'd make contact, through Vásquez. She'd meet him, collect the banker's draft, verify the painting, pay the money then get the hell out of Dodge. This time tomorrow night she should be flying her booty out. To Jocco and the real payday.

Damn it. She glowered at Vásquez but knew she had no choice. She'd kiss the grand and a half goodbye; she had to. Because five grand waited for her in Berlin. Held by a certain German Commie who rolled a mighty fine cigarette.

"And there is something I help you with, yes?" Vásquez, seeing her hesitation, had let a smile back onto his face. "Get you into the city, through all the barricades, to your rendezvous?"

The flying game had taught her that what you couldn't fix you shouldn't sweat. She shrugged. "You got a bath in this joint, Captain? And something better than piss to drink? A steak?"

"Food, yes. Maybe some cognac?" He stepped close—too close. Inhaled so extravagantly his moustache twitched. "And why do you need a bath? When you smell like a woman to me. A real woman."

Aw, Christ defend me, she thought. Another one.

There'd been a Captain Vásquez at almost every stop she'd made. They all assumed that because she was a woman in a man's world, she must be an easy time. Lecherous and venal, at least they were never blessed with great intelligence, these captains. "That would be fun," she drawled, as his face came nearer, "if my new husband, Jocco, hadn't vowed to cut the balls off any man who got . . . even as close as you are now. *Fweet!*"

She made the cutting noise loudly, in his face. He winced, and stepped back.

His expression turned sullen. "Very well. I get you some food. You may sleep here."

"Thanks. I'll sleep in my bird. Which you will make sure is filled with gas, right? Tonight."

After a moment, he nodded. She caught him a last time at the door. "And the bath?"

He didn't even turn around. "There's a cold tap outside. No towel. *¡Qué lástima!*"

He left but returned after a minute to throw hard salami and even harder bread toward her. The vinegar wine softened the bread a little—and gave her stomach cramps. She went to the tap, used a silk neckerchief to wash the worst of the grime from her face and neck, then bummed a smoke from a sentry. She climbed into the Lockheed's now-empty hold, took out her pistol and put it within reach. Using her bag for a pillow, she lay down, lit up. Coughed. The cigarette was black tobacco, filterless. "You owe me a big night in Berlin, Zomack," she muttered. She smoked it to the nub, stubbed it out—and fell asleep surprisingly fast.

⋘⋙

Vásquez woke her at half past dawn with more rock bread and the kind of coffee she could stand a spoon in. He also handed her a business card.

"Professor Ernst Schlaben," she read. The name had a lot of letters after it, all done in gold copperplate. On the back of the card was a brief note dated July 21 that stated he would be outside the Banco Mundial, in the Puerta del Sol, every morning from ten till twelve.

Roxy used the edge of the card to dislodge a crumb from her teeth. July 21. One week ago. Considering she'd flown from the heart of Africa, she was pretty much on time. "Can you get me into the city this morning?" she asked.

Vásquez nodded. He was obviously not speaking to her. She couldn't care less.

Though four hours later, at the tenth checkpoint they'd had to negotiate, she considered giving him a kiss. She'd have struggled on her own. Each barricade was manned by a different fist-pumping militia with a fighting name—the Lynxes of the Republic, the Furies—all in the berets and workers' blue overalls that had become the

uniform of revolution. "*¡No pasarán!*" they'd chanted at every barrier, which was ironic, because each did let them pass after studying
their papers for an age—though most clearly couldn't read—and eye-
ing her lasciviously. Perhaps they didn't see her shade of blonde too
often in Madrid.

A church bell began to toll twelve, when Vásquez nudged his battered Hispano-Suiza into the Puerta del Sol, one of Madrid's biggest
plazas and crammed with more of the fervent revolutionaries they'd
met along the way. Roxy spotted the Banco Mundial straightaway,
a horde before it. Anxious—she really didn't want to have to spend
another night in Spain—she scanned the crowd for something different. And spotted it: grey in a sea of blue, a suit amid the overalls. It
had detached from the mob, and was moving away.

"Wait here," she commanded, and stepped out, sliding and shoving
her way through the crowd. She caught him just as he went around
a corner. "Professor Schlaben?"

The man turned. He was on the smaller side too, skinny, with the kind
of balding dome of a head that intellectuals often had. Pale-blue eyes
glimmered behind wire frame glasses. "Fräulein Loewen?" he inquired.

He pronounced her name with a vee. Lewven. Roxy still spoke
reasonable German—she'd learned more than how to drink schnapps
at her Geneva finishing school—and replied in his language. "That is
me. I am glad to meet you."

"And I you." He held out a hand and she shook it. "I was beginning
to despair. I did not want to spend much more time in this city." He
looked around as another revolutionary chant began in a single hoarse
female voice, then was rapidly taken up by scores of others. "It is
becoming dangerous."

He'd switched to English, so she did too. "Then let's get a move on."
She took an elbow and turned him toward the bank, though she
didn't squeeze very hard for fear of snapping him.

At the front door Vásquez joined them. Introductions were swiftly made. "You have the papers I gave you?" On Roxy's nod the captain continued, "Do not try to return to Getafe until the middle of the night. The militias will be sleepy then and perhaps drunk. Buy some brandy to pass to them to speed your way. You have money?"

Roxy shrugged. Her bribe fund was down to twenty bucks. But twenty bucks could probably buy a lot of the rotgut that passed for booze in Spain.

"Your plane will be ready," the captain said. "*Buena suerte*." He turned away, then turned back. "Oh, a warning. In their enthusiasm to liberate all the anarchists and other political prisoners from jail, the revolutionaries also freed every murderer, rapist and thief."

"Well, ain't that just dandy."

"Yes."

Vásquez gave a small bow, then pushed his way into the crowd. Roxy followed him with her eyes until she lost him. Was that a warning he'd just given her . . . or a threat?

She faced Schlaben, who was swallowing repeatedly. Well, if he was nervous, she couldn't be. "Shall we?" she said, taking his arm again, and leading him into the marble portico of the Banco Mundial.

FOUR

DEATH IN THE AFTERNOON

AT THE TOP OF THE STAIRCASE INSIDE THE CHURCH OF SAN Francisco el Grande in Madrid, Roxy's stomach let out another long growl. It was the loudest yet and this time the three men—Ernst Schlaben on her left, the bishop of Valladolid and his assistant on her right—couldn't ignore it.

"You would like, maybe, some food, Señorita Loewen?"

"Monsignor . . ." Roxy hesitated. Was that the correct form of address? Unlike her German, her Spanish didn't go much beyond the ordering of mescal in Guadalajara. Fortunately, the bishop of Valladolid understood some English. "What I'd really like is to see what I came for. Once my, uh, colleague here—" she gestured to Schlaben "—authenticates it, we can conclude our business. Let's eat after. Hell, after I'll buy *you* dinner."

She could, too. She had the funds. Because she'd collected *two* banker's drafts at the Banco Mundial. Heeding Vásquez's warning about the freed thieves, rapists and murderers—oh, wasn't she just loving Madrid!—she'd placed in her bra's left cup the one for five thousand dollars, which was to pay for the painting. The second draft, the surprise one, was for two hundred dollars. Bless Jocco, he'd probably guessed that there might be a hitch with the gun pay-off so she'd need some cash. She'd turned that one into the dollars and *pesetas* that filled her right cup. Uncertain how bribery worked here, what denominations she'd need to get her and the painting back to Getafe—Schlaben had a truck waiting outside, so that was transport paid for—she'd gotten a variety of notes. They weren't especially comfortable.

The bishop coloured. Was it her bra adjustments? Her mild profanity? Or was he stalling? She figured the last. Because from the moment he and his assistant—a younger priest as defrocked as his master, both wearing collarless pale-blue shirts, black trousers, braces—had let them through the side door of the church, something had felt wrong.

She was about to voice this, profanely, no doubt, when Schlaben spoke.

"We would like to eat. Thank you," he said.

She glared at him, raising an eyebrow. He continued softly to her in German, which they'd established the priests didn't speak, "They are obviously waiting for something, maybe for the item itself. And since we wait—" he paused to push his wire frame glasses back up his nose, his face as moist and slick as hers in the heat "—well, I am hungry. Are you not, Fräulein?"

"Jesus Christ," she muttered. "I may as well bloody well eat."

"After you, señorita."

She led them down the stairs. A door opened onto a cellar. It contained a table, four chairs and a tall mahogany cupboard with ornate rococo hinges and a doorknob of rolled iron. The room was furnace hot.

The bishop nodded to his assistant, who went to the cupboard, pulled some items out and placed them on the table: metal plates, more stale bread and three cans of sardines.

"What a feast," Roxy said, tearing a hunk off the bread, chewing it and watching hungrily as the priest opened each of the cans. She took one as soon as he set it down, as did the others, tipped the contents onto her plate and lifted a fork.

"Wait, señorita," the bishop said.

"Grace?"

"Chocolate sauce," he replied. He reached into his jacket and produced a bottle, poured a large dollop on his sardines, then passed the sauce to Schlaben, who followed suit.

"You guys pregnant?" she asked. Still, when the German offered her the bottle, she shrugged, accepted it and tipped.

It was strangely good. Or maybe she was just that hungry. The young priest put an unlabelled bottle on the table, and three glasses. The bishop poured, raised his glass. "*Madre España*," he intoned, and shot.

Roxy and the German sipped, and her eyes watered.

"Cognac," the bishop said, smiling, reaching again for the bottle.

"In your dreams," she replied, and coughed.

The eating took no time. They sat in silence then, listening to distant shouts, chants, the occasional gunshot. She'd seen a dozen bodies on the drive in. Old scores were being settled in a country slipping fast into civil war.

She sipped slowly. The liquor was starting to grow on her. But when a church bell sounded nearby and tolled two, she slapped the table. "Look, Your Bishop-ness—"

The man pointed to the stairs. "*Viene.*"

"He comes," translated Schlaben.

"That much I got." Roxy turned to the door. Whoever entered

through it would be carrying a wooden panel wrapped in cloth. He would lay it on the table; she'd let the expert do his thing. If he nodded, she'd reach into her bra for the draft. The younger priest might blush. But if she winked, then maybe he'd carry the Bruegel up to the street and load it into Schlaben's truck.

Roxy wasn't expecting anyone particular to walk through the cellar door. But the man who did was certainly not who she was expecting. Because she knew him instantly, and the sight of him made the cheap brandy rise like acid in her throat.

She didn't have a greeting for him. Maybe it was the taste of fishy chocolate in her mouth. Maybe it was the burn of the booze. Or maybe it was because the man who stood before her now, more than any other man in the world, was responsible for the death of her father.

He had a greeting for her, though: "Hello, Roxy," said Sydney Munroe.

She stood abruptly. She was aware of the others getting up too, which annoyed her, in case they had taken her rising as a signal that this was someone who should be shown respect, as opposed to a cockroach that should be squashed underfoot if you could find a big enough boot.

It was strange seeing him there, in the flesh. She'd seen him plenty in dreams, mostly on a New York street, with something that she would never look at crushed on tram tracks between them. Someone.

In her dreams he had always looked big. In real life he was enormous. Maybe six-six. Maybe four hundred pounds. When she drew herself up to her full five-five, her nose felt about even with his belt buckle.

"Señor Munroe. *Bienvenido.*" The bishop went around the table and held out a hand. Munroe took it; or rather, his hand swallowed the other man's. Even as he shook it, his eyes never left Roxy's.

"May I introduce—" began the bishop.

"Oh, it's all right, Your Eminence. Miss Loewen and I are old friends."

His voice hadn't changed. Still at variance with his bulk. She'd heard it before, at the family home; that day in front of the 21 Club. High-pitched, for a man of his bulk. "He's no friend of mine." Roxy sat, before the sudden weakness in her knees took her down anyway. "Why the hell's he here?"

She knew the answer; part of it, anyway. Because she didn't believe in coincidence. Luck, sure, every pilot did; you needed luck when the cloud ceiling was one hundred feet and you were an engine cough away from gliding to a strip lost somewhere below. She never flew anywhere without her mother's rabbit's foot. No. It wasn't coincidence that Sydney Munroe was standing there.

It was betrayal.

"Why am I here? A lucky break, you might say." He smiled. "Staying in the only decent hotel still open in Madrid while I did some business, I spent an evening drinking with Professor Schlaben. Under the influence of a few martinis, he let slip his purpose here. I was intrigued—but even more so when he told me who he was meeting." His grin widened. "So I approached His Eminence—" he nodded at the bishop "—and asked him to let me know when this rendezvous would take place." He stepped to the table and sat, the chair creaking loudly. "I am an art collector, Miss Loewen. I have a fine collection at home in Chicago. Indeed, many of my pieces you might recognize. A Braque. A Cézanne. A rather fine blue period Picasso. I picked them up cheaply at the bankruptcy proceedings against your father. Happily for me, he had rather more skill in choosing art than he did in running a business." He leaned forward, smiled. "You should visit me next time you're stateside, and get reacquainted."

Roxy swallowed, forcing the hot anger down her throat. "May I remind you, Eminence, that I am who you're dealing with here. Me

only. We have a deal." She glared at the bishop. "So can we get on
with this?"

But the churchman was still staring at Munroe, like a rat hypno-
tized by a snake. And though Roxy still didn't look at Munroe, there
was nothing she could do about that voice.

"Before we begin, I am curious about something else, Roxy. I always
hoped we'd catch up one day so I could ask you." Munroe pulled out a
handkerchief, blotted his huge, sweating face. "You see, I am the
chairman of the group your father bilked of their money." He paused,
as if expecting some objection. When she said nothing, he continued,
"We have twice-yearly meetings to decide if the time is yet right to
liquidate your father's few remaining assets. We got so little back in
'29 and '30, after the crash." He flapped the handkerchief, put it away.
"Every meeting it always seemed that one or two were absent. Then
the same were absent again—and a few more besides. Small debtees,
it is true. Craftsmen, in the main. Saddle makers. Jewellers. Plane
mechanics." He cleared his throat. "I made some inquiries. And do
you know what I discovered?" He looked around, as if throwing his
question open.

Roxy glanced at the young priest, at Schlaben. Both just stared at
Munroe, silent.

"I discovered that these small debtees had been repaid. Not a dime
on the dollar either. Their full debt. Sometimes with interest. So
here's what I want to know, Roxy." He faced her again. "Why them?
Why them and not me? Never even one red cent for me?"

She looked at him fully now, as the others turned to her. She
studied his face, the eyes near lost in all that flesh, the gleam and the
glisten and the sheer bulk of him. She considered all she could say, all
the things she'd said to him in her dreams. Because if he knew a little
about her, she knew a whole helluva lot about him. She had made it
her business to know. How he used his money for hurt. Siting mines

in countries where the majority were starving, and paying only enough to keep the workers alive. Building labs to develop the kind of weapons she'd seen used in Ethiopia to flay men, burn women and children. Opening museums next to Hoovervilles and swimming pools on the shores of lakes that his factories polluted.

Jocco could have given that speech. For her it was simpler than that. So she said it simply: "Because you drove my father to his death, Munroe." His eyes widened. He looked like he was going to speak some more. But she'd heard enough. Pivoting to the bishop, she continued, "Business, if you please."

The bishop came out of his trance. "Pedro." He gestured, and the young priest went back to the cupboard and began removing the few items remaining in it, then stacking them on the table—more sardine cans, some cutlery, some plates. Everyone concentrated on him as if he were a conjurer and they wanted to see how he would produce the rabbit.

Pedro tilted then lowered the cupboard onto its side. He took a screwdriver to the hinges, removed the doors, then worked down the back edges, the screws giving easily, as if they were used to the caress. Finally, he took a mallet and, with a few hard blows, separated the rear and side panels.

The cupboard lay in pieces on the floor. Roxy glanced first at Schlaben, then Munroe. Both men leaned forward, entirely focused, the light from the cellar's one naked bulb reflected in the sheen of their skin.

The priest lifted the long rear panel, stood it upright against the back wall. Using the back of the hammer, he began to pry out some small tacks that pinned a black cloth, thick like dry canvas, against the wood. As he worked down, alternating sides, the material fell away. Halfway down, dark mahogany yielded to a sudden explosion of blue and green.

"My, my," muttered Sydney Munroe, the coolness of the expression belying the heat in his eyes.

The cloth was gone in moments. The priest put down his hammer, then lifted and turned the panel onto its side.

My, my, indeed, thought Roxy.

The dullness of the surrounding wood brought out the colours more strongly—the emerald of the sea, the yellow of the billowing sail on the ship in mid-distance, the vivid red sleeves of the farmer in the foreground, his plowshare carving a terrace of lines in the green-brown earth; the fluffed whiteness of the sheep, the grey-blue of the shepherd's shirt. In the distance, the sun had sunk halfway below the horizon. In the lower right, a fisherman with a scarlet belt jigged a line in the water.

It would have been an everyday pastoral scene, country folk going about their business—were it not for what was occurring right in front of the oblivious angler: a pair of legs scissoring into the sea, as if a competitive diver had botched his attempt. That and the winged man flying in the top left corner, focus of the shepherd's stare.

Her mouth was dry. She got some moisture into it. "Herr Schlaben?"

The art expert jerked, stepped forward, knelt. Put on different spectacles. Bent close until his nose was nearly touching the panel; leaned back to get a wider perspective. He muttered in German, nothing Roxy could make out.

After a minute or so Munroe rapped the table with his knuckles. "Well, sir? What can you tell us?"

The professor leaned away. "The light is poor here. And there are certain tests I would make were I in my own department—"

"I realize the constraints," interrupted Munroe, taking out his handkerchief again, sweeping it across his face. "But will you hazard, is the thing?"

"It is almost identical to the one in Brussels. The one on canvas, thought to be the original. Except for these significant differences." Schlaben pushed his spectacles back to the bridge of his nose. "In that one, Icarus is the sole figure from the myth. His legs, anyway. Ignoring his inventor father's advice, he has flown too close to the sun with his wings held together by wax. The wax melts—*phisht!*" He made an odd sound accompanied by a downward motion of his hand. "He falls, he dies." He nodded. "The painting has always been interpreted as man proceeding with his life—plowing, fishing, looking after sheep—ignoring the arrogant who strive for glory and fail."

"You hear that, Munroe," Roxy whispered, loud enough to be heard.

Schlaben blinked at the interruption, continued, "But look here." He pointed to the figure in the upper left, wings raised behind him, gazing at the accident in the water. "Daedalus, witnessing his son's death. Look at the shepherd seeing him. Daedalus is not in the original painting. What we called the original." He rose, took a pace back. "This will make us reinterpret all we have thought to this date."

"So it is genuine?" Munroe stood, excitement clear in his voice, on his face.

"I would need to do some further tests to be sure—"

"Is this a lost Bruegel? Yes or no?"

Schlaben took off his spectacles, put them in the top pocket of his suit. "If you force me to speculate, *mein Herr*, I would say . . . *ja*, it is."

"Well, that's just dandy," said Roxy, rising fast. She pulled the banker's draft from her brassiere and held it out to the bishop. "Here's your money. Have your friend put this cupboard back together. We have a truck—"

Munroe's voice came, all silk. "Whatever she is paying you, I will double it."

The bishop had reached a hand to the draft. Now he paused an inch away. "She is to pay me five thousand American dollars."

"I have ten here." Munroe tapped the tan leather briefcase before him. "Cash."

"Wait a goddamn minute!" Roxy took a step toward the bishop, who took a step back, his hands rising as if she was about to strike him. She waved the paper. "We have a deal. You're a bishop, right? Surely you keep your word."

"The church has suffered terrible depredations in this revolution. Fifty churches looted and burned in Madrid this week alone. The same atrocities across the whole of Spain. Surely what the church needs most now is to restore its glory." Munroe's voice vibrated with a preacher's fervour. "Take double the money, Your Holiness. Rebuild God's house."

Roxy was listening to the greedy American—but she was watching the wavering Spaniard. Saw doubt replaced by certainty. Saw the fortune in the briefcase work its magic. "*Señorita, lo siento.* But the church is needing." He licked his lips. "I am sorry."

She was sorry too—but not surprised. Which was why, when Munroe first walked into the cellar, she'd opened the clasp on the holster inside her flying jacket, that she'd never removed despite the heat. Taking a step back now, she drew the Luger, flicked the safety off with a clearly audible *click.*

"*¡Madre de Dios!*" exclaimed the bishop, at whose belly the weapon pointed.

"All of you—move to that wall," Roxy said softly. "Not you, Pedro. You're going to do your magic act on the cupboard in reverse." She looked at the young priest, who was staring in horror at the gun. "*Ándale, amigo.*"

"I don't think so." Munroe's voice was still as soft, as sibilant, as high-pitched. The only thing that might have given it a little more iron was the iron in his hand—a Smith and Wesson .38. "Drop it."

"Well, why would I do that?" asked Roxy, the Luger's barrel now pointed at Munroe's belly, just as his gun was pointed at hers.

Munroe grunted. "Because I have shot someone before, Miss Loewen. Have you? It takes nerve. Do *you* have it?"

Did she? If ever there was a man worth finding that out for, it was Sydney Munroe. Her eyes narrowed—

And then an arm went around her body; a hand seized her wrist, jerked the Luger's barrel up to the ceiling. A moment later she felt cold metal thrust into the flesh beneath her jawbone.

"You will both give up your guns," ordered the German voice, as steely as Munroe's had been soft. Adding a shout of *"Raus!"*

Schlaben held her hard. She'd underestimated him. His professorial softness was belied by the strength of the fingers crushing her wrist as much as by the pressure of the barrel in her neck. She put the Luger on the table. But he did not let her go, just swung her more fully in front of him, pointing his own pistol at Munroe. "Put it down," he commanded.

After a moment's hesitation, the American obeyed. As soon as his gun was on the table, Schlaben threw Roxy forward. She braced herself on a chair, turned. The German took two steps back so he could more effectively cover the room. "Herr Munroe," he said, "move away from the door. All of you to that far wall. Now! Not you," he said, waving the barrel at the priest. "You do what the Fräulein said. Put back the cupboard."

What choice did she have? Like the others, she moved to the wall. Schlaben collected both guns, and dropped one each into the pockets of his suit jacket. Then, while keeping them covered, he opened the door, leaned out, put fingers to his lips and whistled.

Footsteps on the stairs. In a moment two men, one large, one smaller, both blond with close-cropped hair and narrow-set eyes, came into the room. "Help him." Schlaben gestured to the priest on the floor, who was shaking so much he was struggling to put together what he'd so easily dismantled earlier.

It was the bishop who finally spoke, outrage in his voice. "You are robbing us? Robbing the church?"

The faintest smile came to the German's thin lips. "Consider it a down payment, Your Holiness," he replied. "This country will soon be in a civil war. *Mein Führer*, Adolf Hitler, will wish to support those who seek a return to order, and an end to godless Bolshevism. He will send arms, men." He nodded. "I will make sure that the proper departments are notified and that your contribution to a great cause is noted."

"Cause?" The bishop's voice cracked in anguish.

"Yes." Schlaben's eyes glimmered behind his steel frames. "In a few days the sixteenth Olympic games start in Berlin. And alongside the sport, the most cultured city in the world will mount a *cultural* Olympiad. This . . . discovery—" he gestured down to the cupboard, near fully assembled now "—will be a wonderful surprise for mein Führer, who is, of course, a great artist himself. A revelation to launch it."

"A . . . *revelation*?" The bishop's reply came on a shout. Furiously he rushed forward.

The gun's crack, loud in the small space, set Roxy's ears ringing. She raised her hands to them. The stench of cordite filled the cellar, as the bishop collapsed to the floor.

"Foolish," said Schlaben.

"No!" the younger priest cried out, dropped to the floor, seized the bishop, pulled him onto his lap. The man's head lolled, his eyes open.

Roxy saw the light in them fading, fading . . . gone. Lightless eyes, like those of a man lying under a trolley car's wheels on a New York street. The echo of pistol shot changed, transforming from bass growl to whine. It took away all other sound. She saw the young priest cry, could not make out the words he wailed. Schlaben spoke to her, and she did not hear him as she slipped down the wall. Shapes moved before her—the German's two henchmen speedily completing their task, then lifting the mahogany cupboard. Schlaben swung the door open and they marched out.

Their leader turned back and surveyed those who remained, the living and the dead. She saw his lips shape a familiar phrase. "*Auf Wiedersehen*," he must have said, as he walked out of the room and closed the door behind him. Within the whine, the sound of the key clicking in the lock was so loud.

The man beside her crossed quickly to the door; pulled at it, to no avail. Then he turned. His lips moved around more words.

"You bitch."

The words, though she didn't hear them, let her in. It took her only another moment to recognize him. To realize that he'd been there that other time, the first time, when she'd witnessed Death come and take someone.

"Sydney Munroe." His name, spoken in her head, was an "open sesame." It brought her hearing back. The priest was rocking the bishop's body, speaking some prayer through his tears.

Munroe lurched toward her. "You stupid, stupid bitch," he shrieked.

She found her voice worked again. "Why is this my fault?"

"You brought him."

"I was given a name. I wasn't going to hang around for—"

She broke off. He'd stopped right in front of her, his vast face crimson, his hands clenching and unclenching. Now he bent down toward her. "I'm going to teach you a lesson."

She recognized the moment. She'd been there rather too often in the last seven years—the Last Chance Saloon. There wasn't much of a chance here. But she'd discovered that "not much of a chance" seemed to have become her middle name. Which was why, as the man bent, she'd already reached to her right ankle, into the fold of her thick wool sock. So now she drew out her grandfather's derringer and pulled the hammer back. The pistol gave a loud *click* as she raised it and stuck it in Munroe's face.

According to the family legend, Grandpa Loewen had plied the gambler's trade on the Mississippi riverboats and had once killed, with this gun, a man who'd cheated him at five card stud. Or who he'd cheated—the story was a little unclear. She'd believed it as a kid, though later she doubted, thought it could be just another of the tall tales her dad would tell her late into the night when she couldn't sleep. But like her mother's rabbit's foot, she carried it for luck. The antique weapon worked; she'd made sure of that. The drawback was that it only had one bullet. Still, she'd always believed there would be a time when one bullet was all a gal would need.

As now. "Back off," she said.

Munroe's eyes crossed as he tried to focus on the tiny weapon in her hand. "That . . . that is a toy," he blurted.

"Not really."

"It couldn't hurt a bird."

"You'd be surprised."

The priest on the floor was still clutching his boss, dead now. He was intoning something; Latin, she thought. For a few long seconds it was the only sound she heard—unless you counted the distinct clicking of Munroe's mind.

The big man smiled, though she could see the effort it took.

"Young lady," he said, spreading his hands in a peaceful gesture, taking a step back. "I have underestimated you once again." He gave a strangled chuckle. "You really are most formidable."

"Save it," she replied. "And back off."

"Indeed." He drew back the chair he'd formerly occupied, sat. "Is that better?" he inquired.

She didn't answer. Used the wall to lever herself off the ground. Keeping the gun on him, she moved around the men on the floor to the door and rattled the handle. The lock was rusted and old.

"Ah, yes! I can see the way your mind is working, Miss Loewen. You hold the immediate solution to our problems in your hands. A, uh, derringer, is it, has only one bullet, yes? You could use it to shoot out the lock." Munroe nodded. "Our German friend will be making straight for the airport. I have a car outside. We could catch him." He held out a hand. "An alliance? I will play straight with you from now on. Pay you." He tapped the briefcase still on the table. As she studied him, he continued, "Think how many of your father's debtees you could pay off with ten thousand dollars. Especially if, perhaps, I lessen your debt to me?" He smiled. "Come. Shall we shake on it?"

He held out a hand. She lowered hers, the one with the gun.

His miscalculation was to mention her dad. The hand he offered had once shaken Richard's. And her father had always put more faith in a man's handshake than in the smaller clauses of a contract. Munroe was right about one thing, though. The derringer had only one bullet. Which meant she had one choice.

She glanced at the lock again. A single bullet might spring her. This game wasn't over. Far from it. Because wasn't she being paid to get the painting to Berlin? Berlin—where Jocco waited.

She looked at Munroe again. Hadn't he been about to attack her? Mightn't he attack her yet?

Distant shouts came. Gunfire. People were being shot in Madrid every day. What was one more?

Roxy "not much of a chance" Loewen had a single bullet and a choice. Though when she thought about it, it was not really any choice at all.

"Roxy?" Munroe wasn't smiling anymore. "Don't do anything foolish now."

"Oh, I won't." She stepped forward. "On your knees."

"I—"

"On your knees!"

Munroe pushed back the chair, knelt. "Please don't do this!"

"Isn't that what my father said to you that day on Fifty-Second Street?"

Munroe's lips moved. No words came out. It was like she was deaf again. And yet she wasn't. Every faculty was clear as she stepped closer. Until the gun was six inches from her enemy's head.

"Please," he begged.

PART TWO

OLYMPIAD

FIVE

REUNION

SOMEHOW, THEIR FINAL CRIES HARMONIZED. HIS BASS, HER alto a near perfect fifth above.

Through the poverty-thin walls of the misnamed Hotel Superior, someone started to clap. A "Bravo!" came. "Take a bow," she whispered, and they both began to laugh, the beard he'd grown during their separation tickling her neck. She suddenly went all sensitive, her nerves tingling. She shoved him away. He flopped onto his back and they laughed some more.

Jocco rolled off the narrow bed, went to the window and pulled back the mesh curtains. "Hey!" she called. "We're not in Africa. No scary beasts here."

He turned. "You are wrong. The beasts in Berlin are scarier than anywhere else."

And he's back, she thought, sighing, pulling herself up so she could lean against the metal bed frame. She reached for the roll-up cigarette that had gone out as they'd made love, lit it and regarded him. She just had to accept that with him she was not going to get any after-sex canoodling. Even after fabulous reunion sex. The short moment of laughter had been unusual—Jocco would always be a "get up and go" kind of guy. Business done, next business.

He came back to the bed, took the cigarette, pulled in a deep drag, then breathed it out as he spoke. "So, Roxy?"

"So, Jocco?"

"You know what today is?"

She sighed again. How many of their conversations had begun with that question? "Let me guess. Karl Marx's birthday? No, wait! Of course. Silly me." She struck her forehead. "It's the anniversary of the storming of the *Potemkin*."

He shook his head, sat. "That was in June. Today is August 1. Today the Olympics begin here in Berlin."

"I knew that." She did. That rat Schlaben had told her as much in Madrid. He'd stolen the *Fall of Icarus* to launch some sort of arts Olympiad to go with the sporting one. Then, after Madrid, sitting at Orly in France, she'd had nothing to do, and no money to do it with anyway because of what she'd paid to replace the piston pins that had finally burned out. Only when they arrived from London and were fitted was she able to fly on. So she'd read old newspapers.

The press had been full of the story for what felt like years. She knew that they were controversial, these games. Many countries had wanted to boycott them, to protest Nazi Germany's behaviour to its own people, especially their harassment of Jews. In the end, the boycotts all fell away when her own country, the US, opted to attend. Quite right, she thought, taking the cigarette back. Politics and sport had to be separate. She was pretty sure Jocco wouldn't agree. Fortunately, he didn't launch into one of his diatribes on oppression.

"There will be a big spectacle now. The Nazis will put on a show for the world. So this gives us an opportunity," he said.

"For what?"

"To steal the painting back."

"Yeah?" In a snatched phone call with Jocco two days before, he'd cryptically indicated that it was the new game plan. Grabbing the cigarette, she took a last drag till her finger burned, and stubbed what remained of the butt into the ashtray. Even Jocco would struggle to get any more out of that one. "And have you used your time in Berlin to figure out just how we do that?"

"I have." He stood again, began collecting clothes from the floor where frenzy had hurled them. "Get dressed. You must meet our forger."

"Uh-uh." She glared at him. "I'm meeting no one smelling like a Cairo whore. Not until I get the bath you promised me."

He looked like he would argue, then shrugged. "The bathroom is left, down the hall. I am not sure there will still be hot water, but—"

"Oh, there had better be."

He continued dressing. "There is a café on the ground floor. Meet you there in twenty minutes."

"An hour." She glared at him. "You owe me that, Zomack."

∽o∾

She didn't get the hour. The water was lukewarm. Will I never get to soak in a tub again? she wondered, angrily scrubbing. But at least she didn't have to don her filthy flying suit afterwards. Jocco had brought her valise all the way from Africa. The day looked hot so she pulled on a light floral dress, and tied on a headscarf.

The air in the café was blue with smoke. Some of it shifted to a waving arm. She crossed to Jocco.

Two men stood. "Miss Loewen. Herr Ferency."

She held out a hand. Ferency took it, turned it, kissed it. "Please— 'Attila.' Charmed," he said.

"Attila as in Hun?"

"As in Hungarian, yes. Many in my land are named after him. Though if I may correct so beautiful a lady, the pronunciation is Áttila, not Attíla."

His accent was light, his voice velvety. He still gripped her hand. She took it back. "'Roxy.' Only one way to say it."

"I am also known as 'Chameleon.' Because I, uh, alter colours so often." He tipped his head. "You may call me that if you prefer."

"I'll stick with Áttila, thanks."

He looked disappointed. Then his face creased up and he sneezed. "Aychoo—ah!" He was one of those sneezers who made a meal of it: loud and on a clear sound.

"*Gesundheit.*"

"*Danke.*"

"Coffee, Roxy?"

"As a matter of urgency, Jocco. To accompany your finest tobacco. Ham and eggs to follow in swiftest order."

While Jocco conferred with the waiter, Roxy and Ferency studied each other. He wasn't quite what she'd been expecting. Jocco, in a passing sentence, had given the impression that the forger was weaselly, so Roxy had been imagining someone small, middle-aged, bespectacled. Someone ash-on-the-collar dishevelled like that Austrian actor always playing creeps in Hollywood, Peter Lorre. But the Hungarian was nearly as tall as her man, if half his width. He couldn't have been much older than her, and his clothes were stylish, if flamboyant—a loud check on the brown suit, a pale-lavender neckerchief. His face sloped down from eyebrows that were so thin they looked teased, above droopy-lidded hazel eyes. He had a cleft above his mouth that rivalled the one on his chin. Only his nose and his lips were a little larger, disproportionately fleshy. The whole look shouted "artist" at her. And the hand that had turned hers for the kiss had flecks of paint under the nails.

The coffee came, thick and bitter and glorious. She gulped it, alternating it with drags from one of Ferency's slim cigarettes—gold banded, offered from a leather-and-gold case. It had a filter, forcing her to suck hard. Hell, she thought, back to civilization.

While the waiter fussed and carried, they chatted of the games, of the weather, of half a dozen inconsequential things. It was only when the ham and eggs appeared and Roxy assaulted them that talk turned to business.

"Herr Ferency says he will be done in three days."

"Done?"

"With the copy, Roxy. The *Fall of Icarus*."

She chewed, swallowed. "Why do we need a copy?"

There hadn't been much time to talk since he'd collected her at Templehof Aerodrome that morning, what with the fucking and all. She knew the heist was on but knew little else.

"Because the painting is still concealed. It is being saved for the big art opening before Hitler next week. So we steal the original and substitute the fake one." Jocco turned to Ferency. "Are you sure the paint will be dry?"

"Paint is not the problem. It is making the panel look old that is the main difficulty." The Hungarian waved his cigarette about as if he were conducting an orchestra. "I had to destroy a very valuable antique table, distress it, and create special stains and varnishes that would duplicate the original panels used." He sniffed. "Sometimes I think I am more chemist than artist. The painting itself is—" he shrugged, entirely failing to look modest "—easy."

"Easy, huh? So you think you are as good as Bruegel?"

Something combative in Roxy's voice made Jocco intervene before Ferency could reply. "Our friend spent five years at the Brussels Art Institute, studying the masters, emulating them," he said.

"I have copied the original *Fall of Icarus* half a dozen times."

Ferency gestured as if bringing in the woodwind section. "I could do it in my sleep."

"The original?" Roxy halted the passing of the last piece of ham to her mouth. "The original is the one I saw in Madrid."

"And Bruegel reproduced that on canvas. He copied himself and I copied him." He nodded, adding airily, "It is what we artists do. We pattern ourselves on masters then we—"

Roxy dropped the fork with a clatter, interrupting, "But he didn't just copy it." The expert Schlaben's words from the cellar came back to her. "He changed it."

"What? An extra sheep? My dear young lady—"

"Icarus's father. Daede . . ."

"Daedalus?"

"Him. He's in the painting now. He witnesses his son's death." She thought back. "Top left."

"What?" Ferency's suavity deserted him. "You are certain?"

"I think I'd remember that. Oh, and the plowman, looking into an empty sky? He's not. He's looking at Daedalus."

"*Sheisse!*" Ferency slumped back and carried on swearing, switching from German to some language that sounded like stones caught in a gearbox.

Jocco leaned forward, anxiety on his face. "But this is all right, yes? Roxy describes this new figure, you recreate in the style—"

"No. If I do not see the exact figure, the experts will spot it straightaway. And your plan depended on at least a week before it is discovered to be a fake, no?"

"It did. The buyer can't be in Berlin until then." Jocco chewed his lip. "So, we hide it better."

"With every policeman in Berlin looking for it? You have only been here a week. You do not understand how ruthlessly this city is controlled. You would not hide it two days. Two hours!"

While they bickered, Roxy chewed the last of her ham. Then she reached for one of the Hungarian's cigarettes and one of the German's matches. After lighting up, she blew a stream of smoke between the two faces, which had gotten closer as the men had gotten angrier. "Hey, fellas," she said, as they both leaned back and looked at her. "Seems the only answer is to get our friend acquainted with the new old painting."

"Impossible. It is hidden away and well guarded."

"Impossible, eh?" She smiled. "Where is it so well guarded?"

"In the new Air Ministry, on the Leipziger Platz."

"Air Ministry? Why there?"

It was Ferency who replied. "Because the man who is springing this surprise on Hitler is *der Führer*'s chief deputy, Reichsmarschall Hermann Göring." He sniffed. "Göring considers himself an art connoisseur."

"Göring?" Roxy leaned back. "Heard of him. Flyer, ain't he?"

"A war hero. Shot down twenty planes. Among his many roles he is also commander of the Reich's air force, the Luftwaffe." Jocco shook his head. "He is a notorious seducer of women, and has an apartment at the ministry for this purpose. And, like every other capitalist exploiter, he feasts off the sweat of the workers to throw huge parties that always end as orgies, with him as the main hog rooting at the trough—"

"Jocco!" She snapped her fingers and he stopped. Sometimes she found his Commie rants quite sweet; he was so passionate. But there was a time and place. "Parties, eh? Is he throwing one for the Olympics?"

"The press is filled with little else," Ferency said. "All the Nazi leaders below the Führer are trying to outdo each other in splendour. Göring has been outfitting the Air Ministry for weeks. There are rumours of a whole Bavarian village. His party is tomorrow night—"

"The Air Ministry? Where the painting is?"

"Yes. Why?"

They stared at her, at the smile spreading across her face. "You know," she said, "I've heard of him. Being a flyer, there's a chance he's heard of me too." She leaned back, shaped an *O* and shot a smoky circle above their heads. "Stand back, fellas. Roxy's going to a party."

SIX

SHOPPING

THERE WERE TWO THINGS A GIRL NEEDED FOR THE BEST party in Berlin. An invitation and a dress.

"More?" Jocco looked pained. He'd already placed a sizable pile of dollars on her palm.

"Baby," she replied, "fashion costs, in New York or Berlin. Great fashion, that is. And I'm going to need the best. So, yes—" she closed then opened her hand, making the greenbacks crinkle "—more."

They left at ten, opposite ways, same mission. He knew someone, he said, who could get her close to Göring. She would have to do the rest, and get that invitation.

She had exactly three dresses—you didn't fly in bias-cut. All of them were a few years old and hopelessly out of style. The least glaring one of them she restored to a reasonable state with a few licks of the hotel's iron. She'd lost weight on her journeys and it hung off her like a potato sack. But the silk was still good and she wore her nicest Schiaparelli up-thrust brassiere. Tits and teeth, she thought, studying herself in a mirror as she applied lipstick. Often does the trick.

But not at the first two dressmakers she visited on the Kurfürstendamm, Berlin's liveliest, most fashionable street. Cafés sprawled over the sidewalks, each one of them packed with revellers. Champagne flowed, though it wasn't much past ten. Her charms failed to move the first two proprietors—one clearly homosexual, the next in too much of a hurry. "I am sorry, Fräulein," the man burbled, tearing his eyes from her chest to place his hands on the store's metal shutters. "Come back tomorrow and we shall see. Today we celebrate our Führer's gift to the nation. The Olympic Games!" Slamming the shutters as if he was shot-putting for Germany, he gave her a salute and a cry of *"Heil Hitler!"*

All the other shops were also either closing or closed. Starting to despair, she walked away from the central area and the more elegant cafés. The clothes of the clientele got a little more workmanlike. Though each building still sported the Nazi symbol of the swastika— she thought it had to be a regulation, because every single business had one—the ones farther from the centre were less prominently displayed, a little smaller. She looked down a side street—more shops there, more flags, more shutters. Still, she'd often found what she was looking for off the beaten path. It was almost her life rule. So she walked ten paces down it . . . and saw it immediately. A word that wasn't there.

Jude.

Even if she hadn't spoken German, she'd have known that word.

Jew.

It wasn't there because someone had obviously tried to scrape off the paint from the window. But either the paint was too tough, or the person doing the scraping had given up. *Jude* still stood out on the unshuttered window. As she stepped closer, she saw above it an equally spectral Star of David.

Above that was the name of the shop: Bochner für Mode— Bochner for Fashion.

Roxy turned the door handle. The door was unlocked. She went in.

A bell tinkled. A man, leaning with his head on his hands behind a counter, reading, looked up sharply. Even at half a dozen paces, Roxy could see fear flash in his eyes. Replaced by sullenness as he saw her.

"Closed," he said in German.

"Do you speak English?"

He took a moment before he replied. "I speak." She shut the door behind her. "And I say to you in English the same. We are closed."

"You haven't got your shutters up."

"I wait for someone." He flinched, like he wished he hadn't said anything. Stepped around the counter, waved his hand. "You go, please."

Everything about the guy was big—a cannonball head, a broad chest, a prominent stomach. Everything except the hand he waved. It was disproportionately small. Delicate.

"You opening later?"

"No. Yes. Maybe. We see." He made the shooing gesture again.

She didn't move. Looked around. The room was quite empty—a low table, some well-thumbed fashion magazines on it, German and American; a leather couch with its back to the window. One wall had cupboards, sets of drawers. The opposite wall was lined with clothes racks. They held nothing but wooden hangers—and one fabulous green dress.

"Wouldn't that one fit me?"

He appraised her. "No. It is a ten. You are an eight."

"I used to be a ten. Hard times." She smiled. He still had his hand out. She ignored it, crossed to the dress and ran a finger down it. She'd been right. "Chenille."

"Yes."

"Hard to work with, right?"

He shrugged, said nothing. But he lowered his hand. So she went up to him, took it. She'd been right about that too. It *was* delicate. When she shook it vigorously, he winced.

"Roxy Loewen. Pleased to meet you. Herr—?"

He hesitated, then returned a limp shake before withdrawing his hand as if bruised. "Bochner," he said.

"The proprietor?" She gestured outside. "As in Bochner für Mode?"

She mangled the German, more than it deserved. A hint of a smile came.

"You do not speak our language, Fräulein Loewen?"

"Call me 'Roxy,' please. And I do speak it, a little. But I speak fashion more. You make the dress?" He shrugged, said nothing. "Awaiting collection?"

There was a slight hesitation before he replied. "No. She . . . the lady . . . she has gone away." There was something in the way he said it. The smile went, the eyes hooded. "Now, please."

The hand rose again. She ignored it again. "So it's going spare? And one size out? So you could adapt it, am I right?"

He ran a hand through thinning hair. "Fräulein—"

"'Roxy.'"

"Fräulein, I am not truly open for business. I may not be open again for a time."

"Thing is, I'm kind of desperate, Herr Bochner." She stepped closer to him again. She had the feeling that tits and teeth weren't going to cut it here. But studying the store had told her something might. "And I can pay."

A faint gleam came to the eyes. "How? I cannot . . . I take no American cheques."

"I can pay cash."

"When?"

"Now. Because I need the dress now. Today."

He exhaled loudly. "Impossible."

"Herr Bochner, 'impossible' is not a word I speak. In any language."

He studied her for a moment before he spoke. "You are very—how you say this—forceful, Fräulein. Do you always get what you want?"

"Always."

He put on some glasses, took a few steps around her, studying. "This cash you pay—"

"We haven't agreed on a price."

"I will make you a fair price. The dress is already made so . . ." He sucked at his lower lip. "You have Deutschmarks?"

"Dollars. Is that a problem?"

"No. I need dollars, I—" He broke off. "You will please take off your dress."

"Gee, you're fast. Guy usually buys me dinner first."

This actually got a laugh. It was clear laughing wasn't something he did very often. Or maybe he'd forgotten how. Anyway it took him by surprise and he covered it up fast.

"This dress you wear. You buy it off the rack or it was made for you?"

"Made. In New York."

"All is clear. Well made, but a little rushed. The fault of American designers. Of Americans." He peered at her over his glasses. "But it will tell me a little of how clothes hang on you. Is today absolutely necessary?"

"Absolutely. Early afternoon. One o'clock."

"One?" He looked ceilingward. "Good god! You want a dress or a potato sack?"

"A dress. A very, very nice dress. There's someone I need to impress."

"I think you could do this without a dress. Oh!" He blinked. "I do not mean. That is not to say . . ."

"Why, you sweet thing, you're blushing." She laughed. "Take the dress off here?"

"No, no. In the back, there is a curtain. Behind you find—*ach, was heissen Sie*—a sleep?"

"Slip? For under the dress?"

"Zo. A slip. You put on, I look at your dress, then we measure."

Roxy went back, took off her dress, handed it through the curtains, put on a filmy wrap she found there. When she emerged, Bochner was bent over his cutting table, her dress spread before him. "You come here." He raised a measuring tape. "You permit?"

"Sure. But touch me in a certain way and you'll have to marry me."

He laughed again, finding it easier this time. "I am already married, Fräulein. Forty years. And you are younger even than my daughters."

The laughter died on the last word. "Do they live with you, your daughters?"

"No." He knelt, placed a tape end at her hip, ran it to the floor.

"With your wife?"

"No."

"She's not . . ."

"No!" This came out more forcefully. He rose, moved around her, leaned back to write a number down, then turned back to her. "I sent my daughters away when . . . when their mother went missing."

"Missing?"

He put a hand to his forehead. "I am sorry. Please let us just do business, yes?"

"Um, sure, if you like."

"I am sorry. I am rude." He looked straight at her. "It is simple as this. My country is not a good place for . . . for people like me."

"For Jews?" He stiffened. She gestured to the front window. "I saw the word there, Herr Bochner. And the Star of David. Someone tried to erase them."

"I tried. Was ordered to by the Schupas—the Berlin Police. It was hard. The paint they used was strong." He shrugged.

"But why was it in your window anyway?"

"Why?" Another laugh came, but this one had no humour in it. "Because I am a Jew. Germany's new leaders, many of its peoples— they hate us. They persecute us. Stop our businesses. This woman whose dress I change for you?" He pointed. "Twenty years a loyal customer. She had no money—I make her dress on credit. Then she comes for fitting, sees the window. 'I had no idea, Herr Bochner. I must go elsewhere.' Like this!" He snapped his fingers. "Now with these Olympics they pretend. They wipe away the signs. The papers don't write their lies. Jews are even allowed to play some sport again—for the Reich. But when the games are done, the paint goes back up. The persecution starts again."

"Why don't you leave?"

"Where would I go?" He took a breath. "Your country will not take Jews. Most countries will not. I send my daughters to a cousin in Belgium. But I must wait—and try to find some money. For my wife—" He broke off.

"Missing you say? Any idea where?"

"I have an idea. It is not a good idea." He shook his head. "My Marthe is bold, like you. She speaks her mind. She spoke about what is happening to our people and I think they took her . . . to a camp. Sachsenhausen."

"What kind of camp?"

"A work camp. Though some people call it a concentration camp. A terrible place."

"You know she's there?"

"I do. I have a contact who says so, says he may be able to get her out. But he wants money."

She laid a hand on his arm. "I have some of that."

He stepped back. "Fräulein, I do not sing you this sad song to get more money from you! I make you a price. A fair price."

"Good. But remember: I pay a bonus for speed."

"Ah, you Americans. Always in a hurry." The ghost of a smile returned. He went and lifted the dress from the hanger. "You do not mind that it is green?"

"Why would I mind?"

"Some think a green dress is unlucky."

"Well, you obviously didn't notice my eyes." She stepped and looked up at him, batting her lids.

"These are the first thing I notice. They are—" he gazed upward, as if seeking the word in the heavens "—lustrous."

She gave a delighted giggle. "Why, you old flirt, Herr—what's your first name?"

"Reuben."

"Well, Reuben. Shall we get this done?"

While he took the rest of her measurements, they negotiated a price. Rather, he asked for twenty dollars and she insisted on thirty. Spared him embarrassment by saying it was for his speed as well as his skill. He wouldn't call her just "Roxy," though. "Fräulein Roxy." Or "*Gnädige Fräulein*." But he moved fast around her, taking measurements, writing them down. Then he sat at his table and began unpicking thread, while she leafed through the magazines on the table. She tried to ask him more questions, but his replies were grunts. He obviously liked to focus on his work, so she shut up.

An hour later, he was too deep in thought to hear the footsteps on the cobbles outside. There'd only been the sound of a few people before, hurrying past. These new footsteps came and stopped. Then the door opened, the bell tinkled and a man thrust his head in. "Reuben?" he called.

Bochner rose. "Josef," he said, beckoning.

The man rushed into the room, slamming the door behind him, talking fast, some language she didn't recognize, not German. The tailor held up a hand to stop him, then pointed behind the man, at her.

She'd been lying in the deep sofa. She sat up and the man jumped. He was of an age with Herr Bochner, slighter, even less grey hair. "Sheisse!" he yelped, and actually staggered back into the tailor, who held him and muttered something that must have reassured in that same language. The man straightened, swallowed, stepped forward. As Roxy stood up, he put out his hand.

"Fräulein Loewen. Herr Blumenthal."

The man took her hand in both of his and gave a sharp bow. He then turned back to the tailor and there was a further fast exchange. Her father had done business with many Jewish artisans in New York and now she recognized the language: Yiddish.

Whatever they were saying, it concerned her. The new guy had kept hold of her hand and kept moving it side to side as if it blocked his view of her. Bochner was nodding at his words. Finally, he said, "My friend speaks no English—I am sorry."

"Little, little," Blumenthal muttered, smiling and still shaking her hand.

"But what he does speak," Bochner continued, "is—how do you say this?—yes, the language of high fashion." He smiled. "In fact, Heime Blumenthal is one of the finest craftsmen in Europe."

"Blumenthal?" Roxy sucked in her lower lip. "Sounds familiar."

"It should." Bochner was beaming now. "For he makes the shoes for every queen and movie star in the world."

"Shoes, shoes," the smaller man agreed.

"And what he says to me now is: if I am making this fantastic dress, and my other friend Eli is going to bring a fantastic hat—did I not tell you this, *ach*, no, it is only now decided—then how can we let you go to your party in these terrible shoes?"

"Terrible, terrible," chimed in Blumenthal, his grin as wide as his face.

SEVEN

THE MASTER RACES

WHEN ROXY HAD WALKED DOWN THE KURFÜRSTENDAMM IN search of a tailor that morning, she hadn't turned many heads. Now as she strolled, seeking the café where Jocco had said they should meet, almost everyone looked up and kept looking. Waiters gawked; women in furs glared. Men paused, beers at their lips. From her Blumenthaler stilettoes, to her Stieffen cloche via sheer silk stockings beneath her emerald bias-cut Bochner dress, she looked like a million bucks. Only she would ever know that the whole ensemble had cost just shy of fifty.

A bell nearby had just struck one. Hope Jocco's on time, she thought, running her tongue over lips now glossed with Blumenthal's daughter's cherry-red lipstick. Baby needs a drink.

He was. She spotted him when he rose from a table outside a crowded Café Münster and beckoned. She had to cross the street to reach him, and she stopped the traffic—literally—when a policeman in black uniform, shiny peaked cap and large white gauntlets, with a smile and a bow, halted a line of limos, whose drivers all hit their horns. Someone gave a wolf whistle. It might have been the cop.

Jocco was staring, his mouth wide open. "Easy, sailor!" She reached a hand to his jaw, pushed up. "You'll catch flies."

"Roxy, you look amazing."

"Yeah, I clean up okay. You just never see me out of flying dugs. Well—" she smiled "—that ain't quite true."

"Roxy," he said again, though this time there was warning in his tone. She realized why when he stepped aside, and she saw that he was not alone at the table. A young lady sat there, about her own age, with the sort of white-blond, shoulder-length waves that came from birth, not bottle. She was probably pretty when she didn't frown so hard. Which she was doing now.

Jocco turned. "May I introduce? Fräulein Roxy Loewen. Fräulein Helga Schlurre."

The blonde held out a hand. Roxy shook it, sat. Jocco did too and beckoned a waiter. "We are drinking Riesling. You would like the same?"

"Scotch. Water on the side."

The waiter nodded, left. "Scotch? So early in the day?" Helga's frown changed slightly, warring with a smile. Her English was clear, only very lightly accented. "You live up to your reputation, Fräulein Loewen."

"I have a reputation? How thrilling." She pointed. "May I steal one of those?"

She'd pointed to a pack of du Maurier on the table. They were girlie cigarettes, but she'd have to wait before she asked Jocco to roll her one of his specials. Something in his second "Roxy" had told her that she should tread lightly here.

"Of course."

She extracted a cigarette, and Jocco flicked his brass Dunhill lighter. His hand was shaking slightly. She put her fingers to his to steady him, looked up as she bent and lit. The warning was still in his eyes. Snapping the lid back down, Jocco continued, "I was telling Helga how we met."

"Barnstorming?" It was a story they'd concocted before. Stunting at air shows was how a lot of flyers made their living—and provoked fewer questions than gun-running. "Yeah. He told me that before we even met, he'd loved me for my barrel rolling."

"Loved?"

One teased eyebrow rose. It was shaded in light brown, which was necessary since Fräulein Schlurre was as pale as a primrose. "Sure. Went on that my falling leaf was exquisite. My loop-de-loop unsurpassed." Roxy shook her head. "But since he said this while drunk and in German, Franco thought loop-de-loop was from the Kama Sutra and cold-cocked him."

"Franco?"

"My husband. Franco's not a flyer, so he doesn't get the camaraderie. Plus he's Sicilian, so he's always jealous."

"Your husband . . . he is not here?"

There was still a touch of suspicion in her tone, though the eyebrow had lowered.

"Stateside. Earning dough. Someone has to pay for my bird's upkeep." She patted her belly. "And kids are expensive I hear."

She made sure she didn't catch Jocco's eye, though she heard a slight intake of breath. For her gilding of their lie? Or for fear it might be true?

"You are with child? Congratulations." All jealousy had cleared from Helga's face. Relief had replaced it. It was clear she had designs. Or maybe she sought to renew an acquaintance. Roxy had never questioned Jocco too much on his past. But a shiver went through her now—probably the same kind that had gone through the German girl. My, my, she thought, last time I felt real jealousy was when Amelia soloed the Atlantic in '32.

She blew a stream of smoke out above them. The waiter returned with the Scotch. She slopped in some water and raised her glass, and they raised theirs. "*Prost*," they all said, and clinked.

"So, uh, how well do you two know each other?"

Roxy had kept the edge out of her voice. But she saw it cut anyway as Helga coloured. Hard for her not to do, pale as she was. Lovers once, thought Roxy, feeling that jab inside. My turn for that, she thought. And her turn to lie to me.

"We met at Hornberg, Baden-Württemberg. At gliding school."

"Gliding?" Something stirred in Roxy's memory. "Schlurre? Didn't you set a high-altitude record?"

Helga looked pleased. "Yes. Held it for three days. Until our instructor, Hanna Reitsch, took it back."

"Still gliding?"

"Not often. I am flying the new Focke-Wulf 44. Working for a film company."

"Film, huh? What, like *The Eagle and the Hawk*?" She sighed. "Don't you just love Cary Grant? Glamorous work, I bet."

Helga shrugged. "Not really. The company I work for is making— how do you say—film about facts?"

"Documentaries?"

"So. We call them similar. *Dokumentarfilm*. It may not be glamorous. No Cary Grants." She glanced at Jocco when she said that. "But it is very inspiring. Because we make films about our country. Its rebirth."

"Rebirth? When did Germany die?"

"At the end of the war. Your country helped kill it." She shook her head. "I am sorry—that is rude of me. But the war ended very badly for us and the peace was worse. You made us pay, too much. We were beaten, powerless. We became weak, decadent, exploited now also by enemies within." She smiled. "Until a man came. A man of destiny."

"Adolf Hitler?"

"Der Führer. Ja."

They'd all had to talk a little louder, because the music that had been playing in the distance had gotten closer. They looked to the street. A column of boys, all about thirteen or fourteen, were approaching, following a large red banner, a huge black swastika at its centre. The boys were dressed identically—black shoes, brown knee-length socks, black shorts, brown shirts. On their right arm each sported another black-on-red swastika. Most of the boys were blond, their short hair groomed. They marched in perfect order, to the beat of the drums and brass that followed them. Many people stood at the tables and cheered. Several, including Helga, who'd risen, also saluted, their right arm straight out from their shoulder, palm flat and down.

Jocco and Roxy took the chance of the distraction to look at each other properly. She tipped her head at their cheering companion, raised her eyebrows. He shrugged.

The boys and band passed. Helga sat, her face flushed. "This is the youth corps of the National Socialist Party, the Hitler Youth. They are so inspired by our leader. Are they not magnificent?"

"They're certainly something," Roxy said under her breath. Then asked louder, "Where are they going?"

"To the stadium. For the opening ceremony of the Olympics. Where we should be going also." Helga stood again.

"We?"

"Not me." Jocco picked up his glass, settled back. "Helga has only one spare ticket."

"He is gallant, our friend. I wanted him to accompany me. But he offers it to you." She laid her hand on Jocco's cheek. Roxy had to resist the urge to rip her eyes out. "He says it is because your life desire is to meet Reichsmarschall Göring, ja?"

"Life desire . . . is right!" Roxy glanced at Jocco, who kept a straight face. Really, they needed to work on their lying, not spring stuff on each other. "*Life* magazine did a spread on him when I was fourteen. His flying career, his great planes. I had it up on my wall till the pages turned yellow."

"Well, we may get the chance. We are not in the—how do you say this—the special enclosure where the leaders and dignitaries sit? But we are close. So perhaps it works." She stooped, gathering her ciga-rettes and lighter, dropping them into a small leather purse. "He likes me. He likes flyers. And—" she looked Roxy up and down "—he may like this brazen dress." Before Roxy needed to disguise her outrage, Helga turned to Jocco. "Auf Wiedersehen," she trilled, leaned in. They did the triple-kiss thing.

"Auf Wiedersehen," he echoed, leaning in to Roxy.

She forestalled him with a thrust-out hand, which he took, shook. "See ya," she said, thinking he controlled himself well, considering how sharp the nail was she dug into his palm.

"Come, we go," said Helga, moving away.

"Taxi?" queried Roxy.

"Impossible today. We take a train part of the way. Then we must walk." She glanced down. "Even in these shoes." She smiled. "The atmosphere will be good, yes? You will be able to see just how happy der Führer has made the people by bringing us these games."

∾∾

Happiness outside the stadium. Ecstasy within.

Roxy rubbed her left foot—new shoes, blisters already—and looked around again. She hadn't been in a sporting crowd since she'd last watched the Dodgers with her dad in '29. And Ebbets Field, Brooklyn, would have tucked cozily into one corner of the grandiose, marble-columned Olympic stadium, Berlin. Hell, she thought, there are as many people playing in the marching bands here as watched the Bums that day.

One hundred twenty thousand were crammed in, Helga had told her. And millions were outside the stadium on the streets, viewing on giant screens as the event was broadcast on television, the first time the newfangled system had been deployed for such an occasion. Roxy had seen newsreel footage of the opening ceremonies at the last Olympics, held in Los Angeles. There had been some ceremony. It was nothing like this.

A couple of light showers had swept through, but they had done nothing to dampen the crowd's enthusiasm. Or her clothes—a young German to her left had kindly shared the shelter of his overcoat. Now with the sun once again streaking the stadium, the band, which had been playing nonstop since they'd taken their seats an hour before, changed its tune from Wagner to something even more bombastic. Brass took charge, a fanfare was blown, drums struck up. A tune began, one she recognized, the crowd joining in with the huge choir of boys and girls whose clear voices first rang out into the air:

"'*Deutschland, Deutschland, über alles.*'"

Then, as the nation's anthem crescendoed, Adolf Hitler walked into the stadium.

Helga squeezed her arm. "He comes," she cried. She looked as if she were about to swoon.

He was preceded by an honour guard in shiny black, bearing a huge swastika. Following him were other men Roxy recognized from newsreels: Rudolf Hess, Joseph Goebbels, Heinrich Himmler. All, like their Führer, wore battlefield grey. All save one. He would have stood out anyway as easily the largest man among them even without the uniform that was a dazzling sky blue.

"Reichsmarschall Göring." Helga took a break from singing to breathe, then jumped back to join in as a different song began. This had a jauntier swing to it, and the people and the bands embraced it with enthusiasm.

Since Helga was in full flight—off key—Roxy turned to her neighbour and protector, who wasn't singing. "What's this?" she asked, in German.

"Das 'Horst Wessel Lied,'" he replied, looking less than happy about it. "It is an anthem, written about an SA man the Communists killed."

"SA?"

"Sturmabteilung. Hitler's storm troopers. They—" He stopped as Helga, still singing, leaned forward and glared at him. He blanched, then immediately and halfheartedly joined in the chorus.

When the song ended, the crowd, who still largely had their arms forward in their salute, cried "*Sieg Heil! Sieg Heil!*" again and again as Hitler and his party climbed to the dignitaries' enclosure. Reaching it, Hitler turned, took the adulation for a moment, then with a short wave commanded silence. One last cry echoed around the stadium, and he was obeyed.

Remarkable, Roxy thought. She and Helga were less than fifty yards from the leaders and she could see Hitler quite clearly—smaller than she imagined, his moustache bushy and narrow. His skin was waxy, but his protuberant eyes gleamed, and glancing about, Roxy saw it was a flame caught and held by the majority around her. Helga's were afire.

To another fanfare of trumpets, the athletes came.

If she didn't recognize the first flag, the guy walking beside it gave it away, with his kilt-like dress, embroidered jacket, white shirt with puffed sleeves and his red beret.

"The Greeks lead the parade, as is their right," Helga shouted above the blare. "But you may guess who will conclude it." Helga had fully taken on the role of guide and interpreter. "And see! See! The Greeks adopt our salute too! I hope all nations are as courteous."

As she shouted this, Helga also thrust her arm out in the same gesture she'd used during the songs, which Roxy had seen people using everywhere. Though it predated him, apparently everyone now called it the Hitler Salute.

While people cheered the Greeks and their courtesy, the man who'd sheltered her leaned down and said, "The Fräulein is mistaken. This is not the Hitler salute. See, the angle of the arm is lower? This is the Olympic salute."

Helga overheard and an argument began in German so rapid Roxy only caught some of it. She focused instead on the teams. Some gave the salute; some didn't. Some angled it skyward; some paralleled the ground. The crowd responded loudest to those who looked most Germanic—or to those from whom the gesture was least expected. Though they were recent enemies, the French team's angles were impeccably Nazi and got a huge cheer. While those other adversaries, the British, kept their arms to the side and so were greeted with notably less enthusiasm. The Italians not only saluted but also goose-stepped, drawing the biggest acclaim yet. Roxy only just restrained herself from spitting. Several of the Italians were in uniform—no doubt recently returned from their rape of Abyssinia.

Fuckers, Roxy thought. She hoped her own nation would not disgrace itself.

When at last the USA team appeared, they didn't—the only salute they made was for the men to reach up and sweep their quaint straw boaters from their heads.

Not all the heads were white. "You have African athletes in your team?"

"Not African. American." Roxy turned to Helga. "Don't you?"

The German snorted. "There are very few Negroes in Germany. And if there were, none could get into the team. They could never beat our native athletes."

Roxy couldn't help it. "Same with the Jews?"

Helga opened her mouth to reply—but her words were lost in the roar that greeted the arrival of the final team: Germany.

There were soldiers preceding them—but the athletes also marched like warriors. In step; arms raised in that salute; eyes fixed on their leader, who stood, as he had for the entire parade, right arm straight out, acknowledging the acclaim, receiving the adoration.

The noise, the cries of "Sieg Heil," the trumpets' blast, the thunder roll of drums. It was pretty overwhelming. She had to give Hitler and his managers that—they knew how to put on a show. Which continued, for even as the last athlete of the German contingent swept into his place behind their flag in the centre of the field, a great gasp came.

"Oh, wonderful," sighed the man beside her.

She looked at him. He was looking up. So she did too—and watched as a giant airship nosed into the air above the arena. It moved over, towing behind it a banner with the five Olympic rings. Though for Roxy what stood out even more clearly were the vast swastikas on its fin.

"The *Hindenburg*!" Helga cried. "Is it not fantastic? Would you not like to pilot that, Fräulein Loewen?"

"Wouldn't if you paid me."

"Oh, but why?"

"How much control does the pilot have? Can he loop-de-loop? Do a falling leaf?"

"It is much safer than a plane. Hardly any accidents."

Roxy shuddered. "I wouldn't even go as a passenger."

Helga was about to reply, when another fanfare sounded. Previously it had brought crowds. Now only a solitary runner came.

He was dressed in white, a singlet and shorts. A fair-haired young man, early twenties, with the lean torso and muscular legs of a distance runner. He ran in from the far end of the stadium, turned left onto the track, swept around it in long, graceful strides. He carried the Olympic flame.

Everyone was cheering, applauding. Helga resumed her role as guide. "Runners have brought it all the way from Olympia, in Greece, the cradle of the games."

"Is that usual?"

"No. It was our Führer's idea."

Roxy's snort was lost to more roaring as the athlete reached the bottom of the great staircase at one end of the stadium and ran up them. There was a part of her that wanted him to trip. It was all so . . . flawless. It didn't seem human, this relentless display—the parades, the music, the cheering crowd. All wore the same look that Helga did: part ecstasy, part worship. That's what this is, she thought. A religious ceremony.

And the god stood fifty yards away, arm still out, still saluting. It was as if he was connected to the runner who had successfully run up the stairs and now stood beside the cauldron, torch held to the side. He stared at the leader for a long moment. The leader stared back. In the pause lay the power and it brought an awed silence— like elevating the Host in a cathedral at Mass, she thought. A second passed, then two and three. And then the runner reached and laid the torch in the cauldron. Flames shot up, white smoke stark against the grey sky.

I was wrong before, Roxy thought, as cheers erupted again. Sport and politics are not separate, not at all. This display is all about power.

The crowd quieted for a white-haired dignitary who made a short speech of welcome mainly in German, some French and a little English. Yet he was just a warm-up act. For when he finished, another yearning silence came, as the man next to him stepped up to the microphone.

Adolf Hitler spoke slowly, clearly, simply: "I proclaim the games of Berlin, celebrating the eleventh Olympiad of the modern era, to be open."

That was it—though she'd have thought from the roar that greeted the words that it was an extract from the Sermon on the Mount. Immediately the full orchestra began to play the Olympic anthem, to accompany the rising of the flags behind the flames, swastika banners on either side of the five rings.

"Look!" cried the ecstatic Helga, seizing Roxy's arm.

Roxy obeyed. A huge flock of pigeons, had to be five thousand strong, rose in one great mass, wheeling in instant avian harmony over the athletes and the crowd. Perfectly timed to react to the next moment of the carefully structured program: the firing of a single cannon.

At which sudden noise, five thousand pigeons did what pigeons do when startled.

They crapped.

"Scheisse!"

It was a near universal cry, description and cuss both. The pattering that came was like the raindrops earlier, though this had a more immediate, visible effect. People flinched as if under gunfire, with time to do nothing else. It was Shit's Lottery, though, and not everyone was hit. Roxy felt her hair, checked her dress. All clear. Helga had not been so lucky. A large white-and-yellow dollop sat on her forehead, like someone had cracked an egg there. Choking back her laughter—and they say God doesn't have a sense of humour, Roxy thought—she got out her handkerchief, licked an end, began dabbing. As she did, she glanced at the special enclosure. No one in there seemed to be engaged in cleanup—perhaps even pigeons feared the wrath of the Führer and had aimed elsewhere.

But wrathful he was, berating some functionary who cringed

before him. A space had cleared around the pair, others avoiding the fallout of fury. And Roxy noticed that the man in blue, the man she most wanted to meet, had moved down to the edge of the enclosure to talk with one of the young guards there who, like, Göring, sported the winged insignia of the Luftwaffe.

He was about thirty feet away. "The Reichsmarschall," Roxy said, grabbing Helga's arm. "Now's our chance."

"Oh." Helga dabbed at herself with her own handkerchief. "But I am covered in this—"

"All gone," replied Roxy. In truth there was still an arrowhead of white shot through one eyebrow. But she didn't want to waste this moment.

They moved—and they were not the only ones. Like a movie star, Göring drew a crowd of admirers and they were stalled by backs about a dozen paces away. "Herr Reichsmarschall! Herr Reichsmarschall!" Helga called, but she was one of several. The man couldn't hear her.

So, Roxy curled a thumb and forefinger into her mouth and blew.

Her dad had taught her how when she was a kid. She'd once stopped a departing train in Colombia. It had as arresting a result here. People directly before her cried out and clutched their ears. Others turned—and a small passage opened through the crowd. "Go," commanded Roxy, giving a startled Helga a shove.

She moved, and repeated her cry. "Herr Reichsmarschall!"

He'd looked up on Roxy's whistle. She'd kept her eyes on his—and now saw them narrow in recognition. "Fräulein Schlurre!" he called. Then added, "Let her through."

The crowd parted. The two women advanced, till they were pressed against the barrier that divided the special enclosure from the rest. "Fräulein Schlurre. Helga," Göring said. "How nice to see you again."

His words were for her. His eyes were for Roxy. Especially one part of her anatomy, artfully enhanced by Herr Bochner and friends. Helga swallowed, and made the introduction. "Herr Reichsmarschall, may I present Fräulein Roxy Loewen."

She'd said it in English and he replied in the same. His accent was thick, while the timbre was soft for such a large man—he had to weigh three hundred pounds and stand six feet.

"Charmed to make the acquaintance, Fräulein."

He stretched out a huge hand, took hers. His fingers were like white sausages, several sporting elaborate gold rings. He managed to lift his eyes to her face—and she saw that they were lightly lined, subtly shaded.

She wasn't sure whether to kiss his hand or shake it; his gesture seemed bishop-like. She opted for the latter, and received a limp return—though his grip tightened when she tried to withdraw her hand.

"English?" he asked.

"American, sir."

"Ah yes. The stuffy British would never name a child Roxy." His pale eyes narrowed. "But Loewen? Jewish?"

"Hell no, sir. Lutheran born and raised." She smiled. "But the only church I attend these days is the annual meeting of the Ninety-Nines."

"The female flyers' association?" He squeezed her hand. "You are a member? You know Amelia Earhart?"

"Sure do. It was Amelia taught me how to do a dead-stick landing in a crosswind."

"A fellow flyer, eh?"

One eyebrow—also, she noted, shaded—rose, even as his eyes returned to her cleavage.

"Helga, you must bring your delightful friend to my party. Do say you will come, Fräulein Loewen. It would give me great pleasure."

"As it would me, sir."

"Herr Reichsmarschall." An officer had come up behind Göring. Now he simply added the words "Der Führer."

All looked. Hitler was glaring down at them. "Duty calls, my dear," Göring said, giving her hand, which he'd not given up, a final little squeeze. "But we will reacquaint tomorrow, yes? We will then discuss . . . your flying career, yes?"

He ran his gaze over her body again before he released her, muttering a few words into his adjutant's ear, then moving off to where Hitler waited. The officer reached into a satchel, pulled out a creamy envelope, handed it to her. When he turned and left, she opened it, took out the stiff board card within. Rimmed in gold, it had that thick Germanic lettering she always found so hard to decipher. Two words stood out: *Einladung* and *Luftfahrtministerium*.

Helga translated, though it was pretty clear. "So now you have your invitation to the Air Ministry. And, I think, the appreciation of the Reichsmarschall."

She sounded less than happy about the last part. But Roxy could not care less. Tapping one gold corner against her teeth, she smiled.

☙❧

When she got back to the Hotel Superior at six that day, Jocco and Ferency were sitting at a table in the dining room, a full ashtray and a deck of cards before them.

Jocco stood. "Well?" he asked.

She tossed the invitation onto the table. "So, Master Forger," she said, addressing Ferency, "show us how good you really are."

EIGHT

THE PARTY

FERENCY SNEEZED WITH HIS USUAL STYLE.

"Gesundheit," she said automatically. "Bad cold you got there."

"Is not cold. I am allergic to—" he waved to the trees "—these. How you call them?"

Roxy looked up. "Horse chestnuts?" They were in full bloom all over Berlin. More words were mumbled. "What did you say?" Ferency's voice was muffled not only because of his allergies. His wolf mask helped.

"What do we try now, Fräulein Loewen?"

"I have no idea."

She chewed at her lower lip. She'd assumed that the Air Ministry would be one building, filled with offices and maybe one hall for a party. Göring's headquarters was built more along palace lines, with vast grounds—now occupied by a combination of Bavarian village and fun fair. The theme of the extravaganza was taken from German fairy tales, mainly the work of the Brothers Grimm. So all the staff were in costume, as were a majority of the guests. Snow Whites served foaming tankards of beer to stags and foxes. From a castle turret, seven singing Rapunzels let down their hair, a blond backdrop to the firepits, where whole boars were being roasted. Hansels and Gretels offered gingerbread and other dainties from tables piled high with food.

Many people were dressed like fashionable peasants. Well-tailored lederhosen for ham-thighed guys, while beautifully cut frilly blouses accentuated the deep cleavages of their sturdy German Frauen. At the main entrance spare costumes and props had been laid out for those who wished to borrow them. Ferency had opted for the wolf. She had opted for a simple domino that covered only her upper face but had gone back to grab a Red Riding Hood cloak because within twenty yards of the front gate at least three drunken Herren had propositioned her. She'd save her charms for the Reichsmarschall.

That was their plan, beyond getting through the gate—get Göring to give her a private tour with her new Hungarian pal, and flirt with him aside while Ferency made his study of the artwork. What they hadn't reckoned on was the size of the turnout. If the host was present, they hadn't seen him. At least a thousand people were there. Between their inebriated yelling, the shrieks of riders on the six fun-fair rides and the continuous playing of the oompah band, it was hard to think.

"One more time?" she said.

Their revised plan was somehow to sneak into the only place they figured the painting could be. So now they circled the main building again. But the rear still had no unlocked doors; the windows were still closed and bolted. Back at its front entrance, the same eight black-clad guards were standing at attention.

"SS," Ferency murmured. "Hitler's elite. No way past them."

"There's gotta be a way."

They stood, watched. A Cinderella and her prince swayed up the stairs, laughing—to be hustled swiftly down them again and firmly ejected back into the whirligig of people.

"Shit." Roxy took Ferency's arm to steer him away. "Let's try and bluff our way in *there* again."

She pointed. Right in front of the Air Ministry was the most luxurious of the beer gardens. A further invitation was needed to get into it—as they'd found out when they'd tried to gain admittance and been refused. Most of the people in there weren't speaking German; it was the enclosure for the foreign press. She felt sure that the central table, a microphone before it, was where Göring would eventually show up. What was all this but an opportunity to show the smiling face of the Third Reich to the world? Find him, charm him, maybe get that private tour. But all tickets were still being scrupulously vetted.

They stood before the gate, uncertain, until they were shoved aside by four soldiers in field-grey overcoats. "Hey! Watch it!" she called, but they paid her no attention, passing fast through the gate; past the ticket checkers, who could not delay them. It was strange, overcoats on a hot summer night. None of the other guards wore them. Then she saw that they didn't carry weapons but a rolled-up six-foot cylinder of cloth. They ran with it up to the small stage, threw off their coats—they wore simple civilian clothes underneath. They unfurled the cloth. It was a banner and on it, painted in red, were words in English:

"Let the world know: Hitler murders all who oppose him. Help us."

The oompah sagged like a punctured bladder. People shouted in fury. The men began to chant, again in English: "Hitler . . . Killer. Göring . . . Killer. Goebbels . . . Killer."

They got out three renditions before men rushed them. Men in black uniforms. She swivelled—they'd come from the ministry. The entrance was unguarded. "Come on!" She grabbed Ferency's arm and ran.

They took the stairs fast, pushed open the heavy oak doors, halted in the entrance hall. Outside, the chants had changed to screams. She had no doubt who was winning that fight.

Ferency was looking at the board listing the Air Ministry's departments and their floors. "Where would he keep this painting?" He sniffed. "In the cellar?"

The words on the board were typically German—compounds of endless, near-unintelligible syllables. Only one stood out because it was a single word. And because it was borrowed from English. "No," she replied. "Didn't Jocco say he had an apartment in the ministry set aside for his seductions? What better line than 'Come up and see my Bruegel'?" She grinned. "The painting will be in the penthouse."

"You are right."

Ferency took a step toward the stairs—but Roxy stopped him. "In these shoes?" She lifted her foot, displaying the four-inch spike. "I don't think so." Moving across to the elevator, she pushed the call button. It was only one floor up. It had a door, not a grille, and when he pulled it open, they saw it was one of the newer fangled ones that didn't require an operator. They stepped in, the Hungarian pulled the door shut, and she hit *P*.

He sneezed. "What if there are other guards up here?"

"Bless you." She'd thought the same thing. Now she could only shrug. "Too late. Get ready to act drunk."

The elevator rose rapidly, and glided to a smooth stop with a soft but distinct *bing*. They waited, listening. No one approached. "Tallyho," she said.

The door opened directly onto a room, not a corridor. It was dark in there, the light spill from the elevator and flashes from the party through tall windows revealing little more than larger shadows that could be furniture. No sounds came from inside the room, only the world beyond. The oompah music had recommenced. Voices rose again in laughter. No doubt the little unpleasantness had been dealt with discreetly. Painfully.

"We're okay," said Roxy, running her hand up the wall beside the elevator. She found a switch.

"What are you doing?" Ferency snapped. "If anyone looks up . . ."

"Just getting my bearings." She flicked it off. She'd seen enough to verify that the room was just an office, though a large and pretty ornate one. A huge desk dominated one end before a vast hearth, closed doors either side of it. Above the fireplace was a tall painting of Göring in full military flying gear, an elk hound at his feet. Smaller desks were positioned under the three windows. To the right were twin entranceways, their doors closed—though from under the right one came a faint gleam.

"Let's try there," she said softly.

They were halfway along the wall when the searchlights came on.

They froze. The room was suddenly filled with bright light and deep shadows. The brightness wasn't inside the room, though, but beyond it. She crossed to the windows, then glanced outside and along a beam.

On the roof above them someone was playing with searchlights. Six powerful beams were directed onto the people below, some of whom screamed in shock, while others yelled in delight. The band struck up the "Horst Wessel Song"; people immediately joined in. Then, as one, the beams rose to the clouds above, like six columns holding up the heavens.

"Göring playing God, that's all," Roxy said, moving back to the door.

It opened easily to her touch, onto a bedroom. She flicked a switch and the ceiling light came on. To her left, a tall lamp stood behind a leather wing-backed chair, a small table beside it. She crossed to it, saw papers, reading glasses, a crystal decanter with snifters and a book. It was open, and she glimpsed some naked flesh in photos. Next to the book was a small leather whip.

She shuddered. Across the room, there was a desk, with thick velvet curtains behind it, folded back before two windows that looked onto the unlit rear of the Air Ministry. Between her and those was a large sleigh bed, headboard and bottom curved and carved from dark wood. Three animal skins were spread near it—a brown bear on one side, a polar bear on the other, a huge tiger skin at the base.

A closet stood beside the door, Göring tall, twice Göring wide. There was another door to the right of the bed, open; light spilled onto the black-and-white tiled floor of a bathroom.

"So Jocco was right about the seduction room." She swivelled, then pointed. "And I guess I'm right about one of its lures." There was only one other object in the room. It was under the windows, behind the desk. It was out of place in all that polished smoothness—a rough-hewn trestle. Someone had thrown a blanket over it. It stuck out at four corners. "There," Roxy said.

Ferency carefully peeled back the blanket. He hadn't gotten a third of the way down before he started sniffling—and cursing. The words were Hungarian, unknowable. His emotions were clear. When the blanket was all the way down, curses gave way to English. "Good God! I didn't believe . . . I couldn't . . . I am amazed . . ."

"Yeah, it's spiffy."

"Spiffy?" He shook his head. "I have been studying Pieter van Bruegel all my life. He is one of art's true geniuses. And here is one of the first examples of that genius." He slowly stretched a quivering finger out and laid it on the edge of the board. "It is like I am reaching down the centuries to touch him."

"Yeah, well, do you think you can reach down these next few minutes and copy him?" Roxy tipped her head to the distant party sounds. "Don't want to rush your rapture, or anything . . ."

Ferency straightened; wiped his nose. "Of course. I will get time to study. I will get time to . . . commune. When I recreate." He reached into his coat, took out a small camera. "Bring that lamp over here, please."

It was easier said than done. It was heavy, all brass, and the nearest outlet was a little far away. She managed to tip it to shed some light on the subject. Grunting, muttering, sniffing, shooting, the Hungarian moved up and down the painting. After ten minutes, he took out a penknife and five tiny plastic bags, then scraped small amounts of paint off different parts.

At last he just stared down again, totally still except for his eyes ceaselessly moving—and one wet drop forming on the end of his nose.

"Hey. We better move."

"Ja, ja," he muttered, and stooped for the blanket. But as he did, a clear sound came, a distant single bell—followed immediately by the sound of a motor.

"The elevator!"

Ferency quickly covered the painting and stepped back. "Where do we go?"

His voice was panicky. Roxy tried to get calm into hers. "There have got to be stairs. Come on."

They went into the main room. After glancing at the floor indicator—the elevator had just reached the ground—Roxy led the way across to the door on the left of the hearth. It was locked. So was its twin on the right. "Windows. Maybe there's a ledge."

She moved. He didn't. "I cannot," he said. "I have vertigo."

She crossed to the windows anyway, tried each one. All locked.

Sounds rose from the elevator shaft. A door opened, closed. Gears engaged. The arrow moved. "They may not be coming up here," Roxy breathed.

The arrow pointed to 1. Kept going.

"They'll stop."

The arrow reached 2. Passed it.

"We should hide." Ferency grabbed her arm. "Behind the chairs!"

"Are you crazy? Göring's probably sent someone for papers."

The arrow hit 3. Sailed by.

"Then the bedroom?" He pulled at her. "They come for papers, they go, we—"

She jerked her arm free. "Wait!"

The arrow moved to 4 . . . and stopped. "Ha!" she exhaled on a long breath.

They listened, waiting for the door to open on the floor below. Instead they heard a single word: "Scheisse." Then the sound of the elevator, rising again.

"Bedroom," she said. They ran in; she closed the door behind her, continued to the bathroom. But it had only a bath, no shower, no curtain. She left it, knelt—the bed base was too close to the floor. They heard the elevator glide into place. She looked about. "Closet," she said, hitting the ceiling light switch before moving to it.

He followed, too slowly. "But I have also claustrophobia," he whimpered.

"Of course you do," she sighed. Voices came from the main room. "But we have no choice."

Seizing his arm, she shoved him in, and followed. As the bedroom door opened, she pulled the closet one almost closed, leaving only a crack.

NINE

THE CLOSET

IT WAS TIGHT IN THERE.

Though the closet was large, it was crammed with clothes. Heavy wool pressed them. Perfume combined horribly with the chemical stink of mothballs.

"I cannot breathe," Ferency whimpered.

"Shh!" she said, pinching his arm.

The bedroom door opened. Laughter came, followed by light. Three voices, she thought, the first of which she recognized when he spoke. In English.

"Gentlemen," Hermann Göring said, "welcome to the pleasure room. Where high art and low appetites combine."

More laughter. Through the crack she saw the Reichsmarschall move into the middle of the room. He was wearing some outlandish blend of hunting garb and court dress, leather trousers and strapping around a costume uniform that glittered with medals. She couldn't see the other men—though when one of them spoke, she recognized his voice instantly. She'd heard it in a cellar in Madrid one week before, and it made her stomach spin.

"The Reichsmarschall," said Ernst Schlaben, "has one of the finest private collections of art in Germany. Perhaps in Europe. I know, because I have been acquiring it for him many years."

If this voice was a surprise, the next was a shock. Because she'd also last heard it in that same cellar—though then words had come on a high-pitched whine, as the speaker begged her not to shoot him. She hadn't. It wasn't her style. But she had certainly enjoyed the sight of Sydney Munroe curled into a sobbing ball under the table before she shot the lock out and ran up the stairs.

His voice was calm now. "And I may claim to have one of the finest collections in the United States," Munroe purred. "We are a match, sir."

"But is your collection not primarily degenerate art?"

As he spoke, Göring crossed before her and she heard the pop of a stopper, the tinkling of liquid into glass. He crossed back with two brandy snifters and handed one to Munroe, still out of her sight, before continuing. "Jews, Communists, the insane, with their distorted view of the world? Cube-faced whores and green skies, *nein?*"

"Some of it is. But I collect such works only for trade, since the current tastes run so that way, at least stateside." Munroe shifted into view, but Roxy could only see his vast back. "Yet I suspect, Herr Reichsmarschall, that I despise the degenerates as much as you do. As I despise the Jews, with whom I must so often deal for the art. It is one of the reasons I so enjoy coming to Germany. What a bright new world you are creating here! The clean streets, the shining people. You seem to have found a way of—how shall I say—handling your degenerates, have you not?"

"We have gone some way in that direction, certainly. There are many further steps to be taken. You may be sure we will take them, in good time. But come—" glasses were clinked "—this is not a night for politics but for pleasure. For the appreciation of the good things in life. This Armagnac, for example. I have the finest Havanas, if you would care to smoke. No? Well, how about other pleasures? It is what you came here for, is it not, Herr Munroe?" She saw Göring turn to the side, heard him switch to German. "Schlaben, show our American friend the painting." Then he grunted and added, "Hmm! Strange. I do not remember moving the lamp to that position."

Roxy stiffened. Beside her, Ferency gave a little grunt as he suppressed a sneeze. But the sound was covered by that of the blanket being pulled back over the wood. With Göring distracted by the revelation of beauty, judging by his sigh.

"Magnificent, is it not? I know you saw it before, Herr Munroe. And I do regret the actions of my subordinate in needing to secure the art for me. Take your time and study it now. I assure you, no gun will be pulled on you here." He gave a coarse laugh. "At least not immediately."

Roxy saw Munroe cross, a vast bulk swathed in red.

"Yes, yes," he said. "As you say, truly magnificent. But the first glimpse I had of it enraptured me. I do not need to study it for long . . . now." He stepped back. "How much can I pay you to let me take it back to America with me and study it forever?"

Beside her, Ferency gave out a tortured wheeze. Even in the little light that reached into the closet, Roxy could see his face had turned a strange colour. She loosened his tie—it was all she could think of doing—then shifted as far away as she could before turning her attention outward once more.

Göring laughed, then spoke again. "My dear Mr. Munroe, this painting is not for sale. First it will be presented to the Führer at the exhibition opening next week. Then experts from around the world will be allowed to come and examine it. After a suitable period, the painting will be removed—for further study, shall we say—to my forest home, Carinhall." The sound came of large lips smacked together. "It is named for my first wife, my beloved Carin. I am creating a shrine of beauty for her there. It was she who taught me about such things. You'd never believe, but I was—how is the term?— a philostrate before we met."

"Philistine, Your Excellency," Schlaben said.

"Zo. Philistine." A laugh came. "My beloved Carin loved this style of art. It will be my gift to her."

"One hundred fifty thousand dollars." There was a gasp, but Munroe continued. "Now, sir, I like to get straight to the point."

"You 'cut to the chase'—is that not what you Americans say? I am a hunter, so I appreciate the chase." Göring chuckled. "But this paint- ing is not for sale. At any price."

"I so enjoy it when someone says that to me, Herr Reichsmarschall. And then I buy what I want anyway. There is always a price. For anything—a woman's body—" Roxy saw Munroe cross back "—a family business. A painting." The bulk stopped. "How about a hun- dred fifty and a fine Edvard Munch? You like him?"

"He sometimes leans to the degenerate—but at least he is a good Aryan, a Norwegian." A grunt came. "But this is an undiscov- ered Bruegel, Herr Munroe."

"You see, sir?" There was no mistaking the satisfaction in the American's voice. "We are negotiating."

Ferency's wheezing had gotten louder. His face was mottled, flushed. She put a hand over his mouth.

Göring's rough laugh came again. "I am enjoying your, how you say it? Your Yankee directness, mein Herr. We will have further dis- cussions. But I am neglecting my other foreign guests. Let us return to the party." A glugging sound came, another smack of lips. "It appears you are right. Everything, even the finest Armagnac, has a price. Let us go!"

Twin bulks moved past the crack in the door. Under her hand, the Hungarian was shaking. She pressed harder. She watched Schlaben pull the blanket over the art work, turn off the lamp and follow. In the distance she could hear the elevator door being opened. The overhead light went off. The door closed.

"Aaaaaatchoo!"

She kept her hand there, despite the stickiness. "Let me out," moaned Ferency.

"Just a—"

The door opened. The light went on. Schlaben said, ". . . heard something."

Göring said, "There is no one here."

There was a moment's silence. Then Ferency sneezed again. Louder.

Roxy had no choice. There was the disaster, then there was the greater disaster. So she stepped out of the closet. "What? None of you gentlemen going to say gesundheit?" she said.

The three gentlemen stared at her, mouths open. No one spoke. Until everyone did.

"Fräulein Loewen!"

"*Gott im Himmel!*"

"Roxy!" It was Munroe who blurted the last. Then his piggy eyes narrowed in memory. "She has a gun."

Roxy raised her hands. "In this dress? You gotta be kidding me!"

A gun did appear—Schlaben drew his Luger, came and lifted her small purse over her head. Stepped back and tipped the contents out onto the bed. Not much. Compact. Cigarette case. Lighter. Rabbit's foot. Derringer.

Göring stooped for it. "Interesting," he said, turning it over in his hands. "An antique. I would like this for my collection."

"My grandfather's. Not for sale." She looked at Munroe. "At any price."

"What are you doing here, Fräulein?" Göring raised the pistol, aimed it at Roxy's face.

She pulled a curl off her forehead, put on her best coquette. "Didn't I have a standing invitation?"

"She's here for the painting," Munroe snapped. "Tell him, Schlaben."

The art expert lowered his gun but didn't put it away. "I told you a little of this, Herr Reichsmarschall. A rival bidder for the Bruegel. How I had to extricate it."

Göring was staring at the gun again, turning it over and over in his hand. With luck it'll go off and he'll shoot someone, Roxy thought. The derringer wasn't the most stable element in the periodic table.

"So that was you, Fräulein Loewen?" He whistled. "You are a collector as well as a pilot?"

"She is a thief. Working with the dealer Wilhelm Zomack," Munroe rasped. "Or rather with his son, Jochen."

"Jochen Zomack?" Göring's heavy brow creased. "I have seen this name on a list. He is a Communist, is he not? An agitator?" He looked at Roxy. "Tell me you are not a Communist, Fräulein Loewen."

"Not at all." Roxy smiled and thought she'd play a card. "Just trying to make some bucks so I can buy one of your Focke-Wulf racers and enter it for the London-to-Melbourne race."

If she hoped the camaraderie of the flyer might make Göring sympathetic, she was wrong. His expression didn't change.

"She is lying," Schlaben snapped. "Herr Munroe is right. She is here to steal the painting."

"I don't think so. At least not on her own."

Göring smiled and tossed the derringer in the air, caught it. Roxy held her breath. Still no bang.

"She is resourceful, yes—but is she strong enough to carry this heavy board out of this building? Look at her. She is . . . *dünn*." He said it in German, the word *skinny* escaping him. "So, it follows, she must have accomplices. Would you care to tell me about them?"

Accomplices were on her mind, what with the faint sound of snuffling coming from the closet. She took a big sniff. "Sure. What say we
go downstairs, you buy a girl a beer and we talk about it?" As she said
this, she took a step toward the door.

Two barrels came up and pointed at her. "I don't think so," said
Göring. He went behind his desk, opened a drawer and placed the
derringer inside. "I believe we need to continue this discussion
somewhere less public. And I have just the place." He turned, shouted.
"*Kommen!*"

Boot steps, and two black uniformed officers appeared in the
doorway. Göring rapped some orders at them in rapid German, not
all of which she caught. What she did catch wasn't good. The word
keller was involved. Cellar. But she was pretty sure it wasn't going to
be a *Bierkeller.*

The two soldiers grabbed an arm each. "Hey, easy. I'm not going
anywhere."

They dragged her through the door into the main room. Everyone
followed, which gave her a flash of relief—with luck Ferency would
find his way out of there. The feeling lasted only till she heard Munroe
speak again.

"May I come? I would like to witness this interrogation. Perhaps
I might be allowed to ask her a few questions myself. Perhaps I
might help."

The voice was silky, excited. Göring frowned. "Herr Munroe, I
can see how you dislike the charming Fräulein. But this is Germany,
the land of Goethe, of Schiller and Wittgenstein. The most civilized
country in the world. We do not abuse our guests, if this is what you
are seeking. And Fräulein Loewen is far too lovely and fragile to
damage." He gave Roxy's cheek a pat. "Besides, there are better . . .
methods. Swifter ones too." He tapped one of his officers on his
epaulette and spoke a phrase that Roxy understood totally—and that

chilled her in a way not even her destination had: *"Bringen Sie meinen Arzt,"* he said.

"Jawohl, Herr Reichsmarschall," the officer replied, then clicked his heels, unlocked one of the far doors and disappeared through it. Off to obey his leader's command . . .

. . . and bring his doctor.

TEN

A TINY PRICK

SCHLABEN WAS ORDERED TO WAIT FOR THE ELEVATOR TO BE sent back up and then to go and tell the master of ceremonies that the Reichsmarschall would be a little while. It was crowded enough in the elevator without him, what with Roxy, the one guard and especially Munroe and Göring. The American man was dressed much like the German, in some bizarre approximation of a fairy-tale hunter. They faced each other, their bulging stomachs almost touching. Tweedledum and Tweedledee, Roxy thought but didn't say. She was in enough trouble. What she did say—quite jauntily, she thought, given her terror—was "I suppose there's no point in me screaming."

"With all the noise from the party? No one would hear. Besides, Fräulein—" Göring smiled "—no one pays attention to screams in Berlin anymore. How would you ever sleep?" He chuckled as the elevator shuddered to a halt. "Ah, here."

Unlike the marbled entrance hall and the oak-pannelled offices above, the corridor they stepped into was purely functional—bare light bulbs above a row of steel filing cabinets, these punctured every ten paces by metal doors. On Göring's grunt, the officer pushed her down to the last entrance. Shoved open the door, shoved her in and flicked on a light.

It was a doctor's office. Opposite the door, on the wall behind a wooden desk, was a gilded diploma from the University of Heidelberg. On the left wall was a framed photograph of Hitler and an eye chart, a metal chair beneath them; opposite that a single hospital bed. This had a curtain rail above it, the cloth curtains tucked back. There were foot stirrups at one end, different from those she'd seen before— these had straps and buckles. Higher up were other restraints, leather and metal again. The sheets, both top and bottom, were wrinkled. Both also had red stains. At the bed head was a stand, a metal tray on top of it, filled with various medical implements that, like the sheets, could have used a clean.

"Here we are." The Reichsmarschall ushered in Munroe and continued, "Welcome to a very special place."

He nodded at the officer, who still held one of Roxy's arms—which he wrenched, before pulling her around and shoving her hard down on the bed. Göring went to the desk, perched on it, pulled out a gold cigarette case, flicked the catch. It opened and he offered it to Munroe, who shook his head. After extracting a slim, black cigarillo, he held the hand of the officer, who lit it for him; he inhaled, then blew out a plume of smoke.

Roxy tensed like a bloodhound. "Give me one of those and I'll tell you everything you want to know."

Göring laughed, nodded. The officer took out a cigarette, handed it to Roxy, lit it, stepped back. She sucked deep, and exhaled on a sigh. "Fine, is it not? Specially made for me by a tobacconist on the Haymarket, in London. Cuban and Turkish blended. They always make me feel so good. You know, I suspect they may even sprinkle in a little hashish. Can you tell? They make you want to converse, do they not? Get intimate. Share secrets." He drew shallowly, let smoke run up his nostrils. "Would you like to share some secrets with us, Roxy Loewen?"

"Sure. What do you want to know?" She had to keep him talking. Partly because she really wanted to smoke this cigarette down to the tiny gold rings around its filter. Mainly because she didn't want to think about what would happen in that room, on that bloodstained bed, when the talking stopped.

"You can begin by telling me why you were in my closet."

"Isn't it obvious?" She veiled her half-open eyes in smoke. "I'd snuck into your room hoping you'd come up and join me. Alone. But when I heard voices, I panicked and—"

"Horseshit. The little bitch is lying." Munroe took a pace toward the bed. "She was there for the painting. Why not let me—"

He raised a hand—and Göring his voice.

"Herr Munroe! You will restrain yourself. You are here as a guest, not a participant." His voice then changed from steel to silk as he came off the desk and leaned down to Roxy, putting his face a few inches from hers. "Besides," he said, breathing smoke and garlic onto her, "it is not an—unplausible, is this the word?—answer. Women offer themselves to me every day. Also—" he raised a chubby finger and ran it along Roxy's jawline "—it would be a pity to let you spoil this beauty. I doubt you are experienced in these things. Whereas I—"

The blow came sudden and sharp. Not hard enough to do much damage. Hard enough for her to use it as the excuse she'd needed ever since she first entered the room. Following the slap's trajectory, she threw herself sideways and crashed against the implement cart. Most of the metal bowls and tools cascaded onto the stone floor, ringing loud. Not all of them, though. Not the scalpel she snatched up, slid up her sleeve and pinned under her watchstrap before she turned to glare at Göring and yell, "What the hell do you think you are doing?"

The officer stepped forward, arms out to fend her off. The Reichsmarschall stepped back, grinning. "Oh, I am sorry, Fräulein. This is not a game you like to play?" He shrugged. "Yet there are others, aren't there? Different ways to communicate, no? Ah!" He turned to the corridor, to the *bing* of the elevator. "And here comes my expert in one of those ways."

A man appeared in the doorway. "Heil Hitler!" he cried, clicking his heels together, his right arm shooting up.

"Heil Hitler!" echoed Göring, though his salute was more casual, a hand thrown back on a limp wrist.

The newcomer was small, narrow faced, with a hank of hair plastered over his head in a poor attempt to conceal baldness. He looked at each of them, blinking through bottle-lens glasses. He was wearing a frilly white shirt, and lederhosen considerably too big for him, which made his pink legs look like uncooked turkey drumsticks. His prominent Adam's apple slid up and down a suitably avian throat. "Herr Reichsmarschall. A thousand apologies," he said in German. "But I thought our appointment for your, uh, treatment, was in the morning?"

"It is. Though since you are here, perhaps we shall—" Göring swallowed. "Yet this is not why I summoned you." He switched to English. "This is an American friend, Herr Munroe." The two men nodded at each other. "While here—" Göring turned as he spoke "—is the reason I have called you away from charming Frau Glück, and the little Glücks. This is Fräulein Loewen."

The man looked at her—and the tics, the blinking, the twitching all stopped. Roxy got the distinct sense that she wasn't the first girl that Glück had examined for Göring. The thought made her shiver, as the man licked his lips.

"And you wish, Herr Reichsmarschall . . ."

Göring grunted, "Nein, nein, nothing of that sort. No, the Fräulein here has information we require. She may be reluctant to give it—"

"No, no!" Roxy interrupted. Pulling her gaze from the unnerving stare of the doctor, she blurted, "Not reluctant at all. Happy to give it. In fact, can't wait."

"Or," continued Göring, as if she had not spoken, "she may lie."

"And you wish these results swiftly?"

"I wish to rejoin my party as soon as possible."

"Then may I suggest . . ." Glück lapsed into German, rattling off terms that Roxy couldn't follow.

Göring held up a hand to halt the flow. "Yes, Doctor, exactly so. Proceed."

Glück clicked his heels again, then moved around his desk. He opened a drawer, then began to pull out objects—a white towel, which he spread out to receive a small bottle; a bandage roll; and lastly a syringe, which he filled from the bottle.

Roxy bit her lip. "Look, sir, I will tell you anything—"

"Like the whereabouts of the Communist Jochen Zomack?"

"Absolutely. Last saw him in Africa, uh, two months ago."

"But did you?" Göring shook his head. "You may have. But I will not be able to be certain about that, or about why exactly you were in my room tonight. Not with just your answers. Yet my doctor here—" He turned back and snapped, in German, "Me first, you fool. My vitamin shot, and quickly." Glück flinched, and immediately reached into the drawer again to pull out another syringe, which he used to draw a colourless liquid from a second bottle, produced from a locked drawer. Göring's smile returned. He sat on the chair under the eye chart and began to undo the laces on his right boot. "You see," he continued, "the good doctor here can guarantee that what you say will be the truth. Please, Dr. Glück, be so kind as to explain as you prepare. I am sure Herr Munroe would find it fascinating. Perhaps Fräulein Loewen even more so. Since she is, after all—" he grinned wider "—the patient."

Glück came around the table. "Of course, Herr Reichsmarschall." He took a deep breath. "It is work I have been engaged in for some time. And I have benefited from the experiments of a countryman of yours. He is from Texas, where the cowboys come from, is it not, Herr Munroe? His name is Robert House and he was the first to develop this." He held up a bottle. "I have improved upon it."

She didn't want to ask. She had to. "What's in the bottle?"

Glück's eyes gleamed behind the lenses. "In Germany we call this *Wahrheitsserum*. It was your good Dr. House who named it. It means 'truth serum.'"

Roxy's stomach did a flip—her nausea increasing when Göring slid his boot off, followed by his sock, and wriggled toes like pink sausages in a pan. He reached over and picked up one syringe. He looked up at the six people focused on him. "About your business," he snarled in German.

Everyone looked away, to the doctor now coming from behind his desk. All except Roxy, who watched the Reichsmarschall fiddle among his toes, seeking, finding, pressing the needle in, pushing. He sighed, his eyes rolling back in pleasure. Then Glück moved before her, blocking the sight, holding up the second syringe. "You will raise your sleeve, please."

"And why would I do that?"

"I need to access your vein."

"Access this, you prick." She raised her middle finger in his face.

Glück blinked at them, looked around. Behind him Göring rose. His eyes were eerily bright, his smile sloppy. "It is easy, Fräulein Loewen. Do what the doctor says or I will have my men hold you down while he does so. They are rough men. You may bruise. It would be such a pity to mark such delicate skin." He laughed, the pitch high.

"I'll hold her down." Munroe stepped closer to speak. If his eyes weren't as shiny as the Reichsmarschall's, they weren't far off.

Roxy looked around, at odds too great. She looked at Glück again, then at his needle. Talking seemed good just then. "What's in that?"

The doctor ran his tongue over his lips. "A compound of my own devising. A relaxant, which will send you to sleep very quickly for a little time and is based on chloroform. There is also a euphoric, which you will enjoy. Together, these will make the experience quite pain-less, Fräulein. But the strongest ingredient is derived from henbane. It is called scopolamine." He smiled. "Now, please."

She still didn't see that she had a choice—and anyway, people always underestimated her because of her size. She'd drink Göring and his guards under the table, that was for damn sure. She'd weather this storm, and she'd keep lying, until something better came up. Something always did. Well, she thought, nearly always.

Glück pointed again at her right arm. But she had her one ace in the hole up there. So she unbuttoned a silk sleeve, rolled it up and held out her left.

The needle pricked. She looked over his shoulder at the eye chart. She could read every row, though the letters were those German monstrosities. She read the lowest: "*Z. B. J. Ü. M. T*," she breathed to herself. Then repeated them.

Göring had sat again to replace his boot. "How long till she is receptive, Glück?" he asked.

"Fifteen minutes. Though for a time she will still be a little dazed from the relaxant."

"So if I was to rejoin the party and return in, perhaps, half an hour?"

"It would be perfect, Herr Reichsmarschall."

"Good." Göring stood again. He laughed, stretched. "Thank you, Doctor. I feel revived. Come, Herr Munroe. We can discuss art on the way."

"You will let me return here, though, won't you?" Munroe gazed at her hungrily. "If Roxy is in a talkative mood, there are a few questions I'd like to ask her too."

"Of course. Of course!" The big German slapped the big American on the back.

"Tweedledum and Tweedledee," Roxy muttered.

Göring paused in the doorway. "What did she say?" he asked.

Glück bent to the bed. Roxy felt an eyelid being lifted, which was strange because she didn't know she'd shut them. "*Z. B. J. Ü. M. T,*" she informed him.

"She is going under," the doctor said, from far away.

"Heil Hitler!" Göring began it, and the usual chorus followed.

"In your dreams, you asshole," Roxy replied, as she slipped into hers.

ELEVEN

VISIONS

IT WAS WHEN SHE PUT THE FOCKE-WULF INTO ITS SEVENTH
loop of the loop-de-loop-de-loop, yelling "Focke! Focke!" that she
heard the scratching. It was monstrously loud and right by her ear.
With some difficulty, she turned her head.

A rat was emerging from the wall, shovelling aside bits of plaster.
It saw her seeing it and stopped its digging to grin, before whispering
something in German, which she didn't catch. Then it turned tail . . .
turned its tail . . . and vanished back into the wall. Which sealed up
behind it, leaving not a trace of passage.

Though the scratching went on. From behind her now. It was another
mighty effort to turn back, but she managed it. And there was her pal,
the eminent Herr Doktor Glück, pride of Heidelberg, at his desk. He
sat in the circle of light shed from his lamp, writing. The pen's nib on
the paper accounted for the scratching—though it failed to explain
why the letters were forming in blood, not ink. She thought she'd ask
him that. It seemed a reasonable question, under the circumstances.

She tried. Words wouldn't come. Words weren't the problem.
She had words. Icarus. Johnnie Walker. Scopolamine. Wahrheitsserum. Many others. She could form a sentence—if only her mouth

would work. It was sand dry, desert dry, dryer than the driest martini.

Which was what she needed—a martini. She'd settle for water. "Wah-ter," she crackled.

The scratching stopped. A chair screeched. Footsteps, as if someone was walking across a drum. *Boom*, they went. *Boom boom*.

"Fräulein Loewen?"

She'd been looking at the wall again. She had something to confide to the rat. The voice came from right above her and she jerked back, cried out—at least inside, because her throat made zero noise.

Glück was all eyes. There were his own; then there were the ones in one half of the glasses he wore; then there were the ones in the other half. Bifocals, she thought, couldn't say. Then he lifted a third eye, which was on a rubber cord around his neck. Blew on that eye, then placed it on her chest, under her left breast, and listened.

"Yes, yes," he said. "It does accelerate the heart, does it not? And that can make one anxious. Also, the mouth? So dry, yes? One moment."

He went, came back with a glass. Helped her sit up and held it to her lips. She drank greedily, finished fast. "More," she managed to say.

He went, returned again. This time, though, he only let her sip. "Not too much. It will make you sick. You can never get enough and this—you call it side effect, nein? I'm afraid this will last for a day or even two. Just a little to keep the mouth moist, yes?"

She wanted to bite his hand off. She thought that at least she could grab the water from him. Drink as much as she wanted. What was she, some sick child? But when she tried to raise a hand, she couldn't. Either one. She looked down.

Both her hands were tied to the bed by leather straps.

He followed her gaze. "A precaution only, Fräulein . . . may I call you Roxy?" He went on without waiting for an answer. "Some people wake up frightened and thrash around. I had one subject, broke every knuckle hitting a wall."

"I won't. Let me hold the glass."

She was pleased to have spoken in complete sentences.

"Perhaps. If you are good."

"I will be."

"I hope. The Reichsmarschall will return in a few minutes. He is a very busy man. He will not wish to waste any time. So let us see if you are in a—how is it—a receiving state? Answer and I shall release a hand, let you sip yourself, ja?"

"Absolutely ja."

"Very good." He let her have another sip. "Answer the question again you answered before. This, uh, Jochen Zomack. You said you last saw him in Africa two months ago. Was this true?"

"No."

"When did you see him last?"

"He fucked me senseless at eight o'clock this morning."

All six of Glück's eyes shot wide. He looked like a deer in a forest that suddenly sees a wolf. It was the funniest thing she'd ever seen and she fell back onto the bed, laughing loud.

The doctor grunted. "Where was this?" he snapped.

"Once on a bed. Twice on a table. Last on a chair."

The eyes popped again and Roxy laughed even more. This guy was killing her! Then that thought suddenly sobered her up. Perhaps he *was* killing her. Didn't he jab her? "I'm sorry," she said primly. "But you did inquire."

"Sometimes subjects find things funny," he said sourly. "I would ask you to try to resist this. Especially before the Reichsmarschall."

"Well, luckily for you I never liked clowns." She jerked her head at her hand. "But I answered you. Do I get my deal?"

He grunted then undid her right strap. She reached for the glass—but he held it away. "Sips only," he said.

She nodded, took the glass and sipped, resisted the urge to gulp.

Her head started to swim, and she thought if she lay back again, she might throw up. "May I sit?" she asked.

Glück nodded. "But we only undo this strap, not the other. I do not want you moving around, perhaps falling over. The hallucinations will continue to get stronger for a time. Your balance will be off for a while."

She sat up, swung her legs around to dangle off the bed, swayed. "No kidding," she said.

"Tell me this, Roxy." Glück leaned forward at his desk. "Why were you hiding in the Reichsmarschall's closet?"

She wanted to stick to her story—infatuation. But she'd just called Göring a clown. Besides, there was nothing wrong with telling the truth. Everyone was going to know about it anyway, soon enough.

"I was planning on stealing his painting," she said.

He did the eye thing again. She wanted to, but this time she didn't laugh. Instead she looked away, to the eye chart. Read that bottom line, though the letters twisted like snakes and tried to throw her off. "Z," she began, grinding her teeth, rubbing her right hand along the bed. "Z. B. J. Ü. M. T."

"What are you saying?"

"What's that?" she cried out.

"What? Where?"

"That. Those!"

He came, looked where she did. "On the chart?"

"Ja. Yeah. Those two dots? They're . . . eyes. Staring at me."

"Above the *U*?" He peered at it. "This is an umlaut."

"And this is a scalpel." She put the blade to his throat with her right hand, gripping a scrawny wrist in her left, which she'd freed when he'd turned to the chart. "I will kill you with it if you move even a hair."

His six eyes bugged. But he obeyed her, because she would have and he knew it.

∽०∾

Fortunately, it wasn't until she finished the last knot that her fingers stopped working. One moment she was executing hitches and slips that would have had that old sailor, Pa Loewen, whooping approval; the next she was staring at ten pink oblongs that each had four spectre-pink oblongs behind them. She waved them, and it was like watching an anemone bed off Jamaica through her diving mask. "Whoa!" she giggled, and kept waving. "That's great!"

Glück said something, which she didn't understand because of all the medical gauze she'd shoved in his mouth and taped over. But what had he said before? That the hallucinations would only get stronger? That couldn't be good. She had to get out of this room, the cellar, the building, the whole damn country. Before Tweedledum and Tweedledee got back and asked her questions she'd have to answer.

Which was when? What had Glück said? She'd been asleep for about fifteen. Had Göring said he'd return in thirty? And she'd been awake now for a couple? Roxy looked at the clock. Hitler looked back and said, "Games." She gave a little scream. All she wanted to do was lie on the bed, talk to that rat and watch the anemones sway in Montego Bay.

Somehow, she'd lain down when she thought it. She sat up again. Clutching her scalpel in one hand, she bent to check Glück's knots with the other. "All secure, Cap'n," she muttered, then lurched to the door.

In the corridor, bare-bulb light shimmered on steel cage and cabinet. The only way out that she knew was the elevator. Besides, her legs weren't working too good. She didn't think she could handle stairs even if she found them.

The elevator came to the call of her finger. Pulling the door open was harder work. Somehow she must have managed it but when it closed softly behind her the box she found herself in was so tight, so close, so crammed she thought she might be in her coffin. She moaned, bit her lip to stop moan turning to scream. Buttons were before her and she stretched her tendrils to the one above the bottom. She missed, raised to stab again . . . and stopped. She'd aimed for the entrance hall. Guards would be in it. Appear there and they'd grab her. She had to go higher. She lifted her hand again . . . and remembered something else.

Göring had stolen Grandpa Loewen's derringer.

Roxy hit the penthouse button.

She heard young men's voices in the hall as the elevator cruised past. They didn't sound concerned. They were probably used to late-night trips from the cellar to the penthouse. The memory came, of Göring's pink toes, and she shuddered.

The elevator glided into position and the bell went *bing*. She leaned all her weight on the door and it finally opened a crack. She listened. Had Göring and his group come back up there? But she heard only the party beyond the room, nothing in the room itself. Taking a deep breath, she stepped into the dark.

It took her a while to get her bearings, even though it was bright enough in there—those columns of light were still rising from the searchlights outside. In the gardens, the laughter had only gotten more raucous, the oompah band more strenuously jolly. Her heart thumped in rhythm as she staggered into the bedroom. "Ferency?" she called. But the cupboard was bare. The Hungarian had sneezed and bolted. Only the polar-bear skin answered her. "*Wilkommen,*" it said, lifting its head.

She ignored it. Her purse was still open on the bed, its contents spilled. She dropped the scalpel, shovelled them all in, then weaved to the desk, pulled open a drawer. There, in the centre of a jumble of letter openers and penknives, lay the derringer. It felt good in her hand.

A bang! She cried out, wondered if she'd pulled the trigger, felt desolate at the thought. But no smoke rose from the barrel. Another bang came, then another, then a series, the noise coming loud from the office beyond.

"Move!" she said to herself, turning away sharply, and crashing straight into the edge of the painting, still covered on its trestle. The cover slipped. Crying out, she bent to rub her knee and stared as the painting came alive, became a movie. She'd seen one the year before in Cairo, called *Becky Sharp*. It was made in Technicolor, which almost none were, the colour garish. The *Fall of Icarus* was twice as lurid. The son's legs scissored in the water, though he didn't sink below the surface. The plowman plowed, the fisherman caught a cod, wind billowed the boat's red sail. The father, Daedalus, his face a mask of anguish, turned to her and pleaded, "Help him! Help him!"

She fled the room; looked out the office windows and saw trails of light soar up into the sky. She staggered across. The fireworks display had begun. To cries of wonder and joy from the gardens, rockets screamed and rose, starbursts lit the sky, rainbows cascaded. It was beautiful enough anyway. On this drug, it was breathtaking. She stood transfixed.

The *bing* wasn't nearly as loud as the fireworks, but it startled her even more. It was the elevator. The sound of it descending, the turning of its gears, was monstrous.

She turned and watched the arrow dial descend. Floor 3, 2, 1, ground. It stopped. She held her breath but jumped when it started again. Down. Down to the cellar.

The monster twins, Göring and Munroe, were back to question her. They would find Glück. They would sound the alarm. They would hunt her down.

She looked around, at a room lit by rockets. It made no sense. Five floors up? There had to be stairs. Wait! Yes! Göring's officer had gone a different way to bring the doctor.

She ran up to the doors that stood on either side of the hearth and the Reichsmarschall's monstrous portrait, his eyes following her. Both doors were still locked.

The elevator *binged* and began to rise again. They were coming for her. She'd be trapped; they'd take her back to the cellar, where she'd truthfully answer any question they asked her because she'd have no choice. She'd betray Jocco; she'd betray herself. And then? They weren't just going to let her go. People disappeared all the time in Berlin, that tailor had said to her. His wife was one of them. They'd throw her in a camp. Or they'd kill her. And maybe not quickly.

She looked again at the gun in her hand, as the elevator dial rose to ground level and kept coming. A single bullet. But sometimes a single bullet is all a gal needs, she thought. And thinking that, she raised the gun—and shot in the lock in front of her.

The dial was at 3 when she walked through gun smoke into the office beyond. She'd been right, there were stairs—one set down the interior of the building, another outside the rear windows. Those were the ones she chose, seeing as men appeared to be rushing up the others now. The door to the fire escape was locked, but a window beside it was open, held by a bolt above. The gap was less than a foot wide. So was she. As the shouts sounded on the landing below, as the elevator *binged* its arrival, Roxy slipped through the gap and out onto the metal platform.

She didn't stop as lights came on above her. Kicking off her stilettoes—Farewell, my lovelies! she thought—she began a fast stumble down.

It was hard work. For a fixed staircase, the thing swayed a lot, like a building in an earthquake. Or maybe a battle, the stench of one as she descended through sulphur-and-cordite clouds, as firework bombs still exploded above her and flares split the night sky. Her gait was half lurch, half tumble. She caught herself on cold rails to stop a trip, used them to push off and continue the trajectory. It was dangerous but speedy, and it was not till her feet hit cold pavement that she heard the smashing of glass and the first boot thump onto the metal platform five flights above.

A treed darkness was ahead of her—the back of the building, leading some place unknown. It was tempting to dive into it, to play hide-and-seek among the spectral silver birch. But she didn't fancy her chances against the goons making all that noise on the stairs. So instead of plunging forward, she tottered to the right. As she cleared the edge of the ministry, the brightness of the fairground beyond near blinded her. Raising a hand, taking a deep breath, she dived into the light.

No one paid her much nevermind, gazing to the heavens as they were, sighing out on oohs and aahs. As she thrust herself into the crowd, she knew that her gait was a stagger. A guard glanced at her as she weaved forward. She kept going, passed him heading . . . where? She had a feeling that the main gate was up ahead. But fifty paces away she saw him—one of Göring's SS guards sprinting in, conferring with two of his fellows there, all three turning to look sharply along the avenue. Roxy stepped between two fairground booths. Like everyone else there, the proprietors were gazing upward, and she slipped by, unnoticed.

She could see the high wall of the ministry dead ahead. It was too high for her to climb unaided, and she suspected by the time she got something up against it, guards would have been dispatched along its length. She didn't know what to do, so she turned back into the main fairground. Two soldiers came toward her, sharp gazes sweeping about. Swivelling, she grabbed a stout man in lederhosen and spun him around to the oompah beat. He laughed, reaching for her, but she slipped his grasp as the soldiers passed by.

What was she going to do? What the hell was she going to do? She could hear Glück's words, almost as if he was whispering them in her ear. The effects were only going to get stronger. She didn't see how that was possible. Already the noise of band and rockets and crowd had blended into one steady roar. Already faces around her were distorting, noses elongating, mouths spreading in cavernous red smiles. Her gait was full-on lurch now, only the drunkenness of so many blending her in. Men were seeking, grey-and-black steadiness amid the mayhem. She had a surge of desire to just run up to them and end it; felt a jab of longing for the doctor's bloodstained couch. She'd answer their questions and they'd give her water to sip—her mouth was still a scorched desert.

She snatched a beer stein from a table, drank hard, dropped it and kept going. Stop and she'd freeze. Move and she had a small, small chance. As small, perhaps, as the derringer in her pocket. She always kept a second bullet about her; had one tucked in the top of her right stocking. She thought of stopping, trying to load it. Instead she sped up.

Because she'd noticed something . . . someone. Following her. A man's eyes were on her; she could hear his feet treading the ground. When she moved quicker, so did the footsteps. When she slowed, so did they. Which meant he wasn't a guard. Perhaps it was the gentleman in lederhosen, who was seeking another spin. Perhaps it was the devil. She'd been expecting him.

She reached the corner of the ministry main building again. A glance to its entrance showed her Göring, shouting, gesticulating wildly, guards running off in every direction at each spittle-flecked wave. Munroe was beside him, and as she looked, he began to turn in her direction.

She slipped around the corner, broke into a lurching sprint, rounded the next corner and threw her back against the wall. Those footsteps were still behind her.

A man came, fast. She stuck out a leg. He fell, and she was above him in a moment, derringer pointed at his head. "I'll blow your head off, you—"

"Roxy?"

It was the moment she knew that she'd tipped over the edge. The drug now had her in its full grasp. The hallucinations were complete. Because the man who lay at her barrel's end was Jochen Zomack. Or a version of him. The one who no longer had a beard and now, instead of a flying suit, wore a waiter's black-and-white uniform.

"Fuck," she said.

Jocco was up in a moment. Gently, he pushed the gun aside. "Roxy! What has happened? Why are you—"

She'd talked to hallucinations earlier that night. Polar bears and paintings. At least this was someone she knew, even if he wasn't real. "Drug. Something to make me talk. Escaped. After me."

She thought she did pretty good, considering that her tongue was a piece of leather and her brain was closing down. Her legs too. They jellied and she started to fall. He caught her, which was kind.

"Come," he said. "We get out. This way."

"Can't walk. Need to lie down."

"Not yet."

He bent, lifted her, put her across his shoulders.

Her head spun; she retched, but nothing came. "How'd you find me?"

He began to move fast along the wall. "I was looking for you. I was desperate after Ferency told me—"

"Ferency made it out?"

"Yes. He waits outside with a car." Jocco paused, peered around the ministry's end. "I was going to try to get into the building. Then I heard them say you'd escaped. I was standing right next to you when you danced with the burgomaster."

"You should watch that guy. He has some fancy moves." He started again. "Listen! They have guards everywhere."

"I know. But there is a way in for servants. We try."

The world was even crazier upside down. Jocco took her to a side entrance, where there were piles of wooden crates, dirty glasses, plates, steins in boxes. He leaned her against a wall and she slipped down it, as servants bustled in and out. She put her head back, closed her eyes—then opened them fast. Worse things went on behind her eyelids. Way worse.

He was shaking her. "Roxy?"

"Mmm?"

"I am going to hide you in a box. It will be dark for a while but—"

"No!" She gripped his arm. "No box! No coffin!"

"Just a little while. I will get you out the gate. It is our one chance."

"Not much of a chance." She released him. "'Not much of a chance' Loewen."

She watched him through half-slit eyes. There was a trolley, and he loaded tall boxes of glasses onto it. One, she saw, was empty. He put that down, then came to her, bent, lifted. "Be calm, love. Make no noise," he said, kissed her head and placed her into the box.

She curled up tight. Kept her moans to herself, even when he pulled her Red Riding Hood cloak over her and began to cover that with beer mugs. Another crate banged on top of hers, another on that. Then, through the gap he'd ripped in the side of the box, enough for her to breathe, to see a little, she watched the world go past—legs, uniformed and costumed; bushes strung with firefly lights. The cart tinkled as it halted. Men questioned Jocco. She saw the trouser crease on a black-clad thigh. Hands shook the trolley. Then they were off again. She heard him whisper, "Close. Close."

Babel faded. A car went past, another. A horn sounded. They halted. Crates came off, glasses. Her tomb was opened. Hands reached, lifted.

She still couldn't stand. She leaned against him like a cartoon drunk outside a speakeasy, as a car pulled up. Jocco opened the back door and slid her in. "You're safe now, Roxy."

"Ain't that the truth," she said, and passed out.

PART THREE

HEIST

TWELVE

PLANS

THE TALKING RAT FINALLY TOOK HIS LEAVE AFTER TWELVE hours. Chirped a last Auf Wiedersehen and sealed the hole behind him. Roxy was going to miss him. He was way more polite than the porcine Nazis who brandished syringes and demanded answers. Since they and their monster friends only appeared when she closed her eyes, she'd contrived to keep them open despite Jocco's urgings that she sleep. She was drowsy as hell. But sleep was a long, cold nightmare.

Other symptoms of the drug lingered longer. Her mouth absorbed water like waves on sand. She couldn't drink enough to curb it, and the hotel water was over-sulphured, tasted foul. She'd insisted that it was flavoured with whisky—the only drug that she'd accept, though he kept offering different ones—aspirin for the headache, sleeping pills. When she'd realized that she was bloating too much and peeing too little, she settled for boiled candies. Lemon drops were the best, needed less spit to get 'em going. What concerned her most was that she didn't want tobacco. Helluva way to kick the habit, she thought.

What mostly settled her down was watching Ferency paint.

Jocco had insisted she not be left alone. But he had to be out, organizing the heist. So the Hungarian had grumpily agreed to babysit her in the cellar they'd rented for him. There was no chance they could have stayed on at the Hotel Superior. Her description would have been circulated fast. Jocco had gone back to snatch some of their things and just made it out the back door as the Gestapo came in the front.

Ferency had insisted she didn't talk while he worked. But talking was what she needed to do to keep things moving, sanity-wise. She'd discovered, however, that his prohibition didn't extend to questions that spoke to his genius. She learned quickly how underappreciated he'd been as an artist in his own right. Which made his career in forgery almost a crusade.

"The establishment," he'd sniffed, "thinks only they can decide what is worthy art. I have been ignored, debased, shunned. I take my revenge . . . so!" He'd jabbed a paintbrush hard onto the wood. "Fooling them. Exposing their pretensions."

Roxy popped another lemon drop into her mouth, took a sip of Scotch-and-water. If she closed her eyes, the mix almost made her imagine she was drinking a Whisky Sour at the 21 Club back in Manhattan. Yet if she closed her eyes as she imagined it, she'd remember who she'd seen crushed under a streetcar outside the speakeasy. Opening them wide now, she said, "So how's it going?"

"You ask this every twenty minutes."

"I do?" She frowned. "So how's it going?"

He grunted and she thought that might be that. But he straightened, stretched. The two panels leaned against a wall, resting on a table shoved against it; they'd not found easels strong enough to hold such heavy wood, and the angle was a little low for his back. He peered at his work. "It goes well."

"It certainly goes fast." She'd been amazed at how swiftly the pictures had emerged. "How come you're so quick? I thought you'd need to be methodical."

"I am. But one must be methodical with speed. Bruegel's brush-strokes were swift. All artists have a rhythm. An expert could tell instantly if I painted more slowly."

"Yes, but—why are you painting it twice?"

He looked pained. "Again with this question, Miss Roxy?"

"Really? Bad memory. Indulge me."

He sighed, spoke in the manner of a schoolmaster teaching an especially dull student. "I practise on the one panel. When I am certain I have it, I reproduce on the other."

The room was small; she wasn't far away. But her eyesight was still blurry, so she got up and, using the copper knob of the bedpost to support herself, stepped closer, bent, peered. "They both look exactly the same to me."

"Zo. I am good, yes?"

"You are." She hadn't spent a long time studying the original, not in the cellar in Madrid, nor in Göring's office. But both these copies looked pretty damn accurate. Though . . . "Isn't the paint a little, I don't know, fresh?"

He sighed again. "This is why I do not like someone watching me. Always impatient with the questions." He shrugged. "The painting is almost the easiest part. When you have studied the master as long as I have. When you have painted and repainted him in emulation so that you feel like you are almost—what do you say—with his spirits? Possessing you?"

"Channelling?"

"Channelling. Pieter Bruegel the Elder is here with me. Smiling. But the years since he painted, not. We must make the painting look old."

She thought back to some of the older portraits in her dad's collection. "Yeah, when you look close at a painting, you can see these lines . . ."

"That is called craquelure. Older canvases have them because they stretch with age and the paint cracks. But wood does not crack. Here we have different problems."

He picked up a stubby length of bent wire and pushed it into the wood, twisting and turning it slightly each time. "You see these marks in the photographs?" He pointed to the large blow-ups of the shots he'd taken in the office, mounted on the wall. "I could see the original had not been always well taken care of. I suspect it had been left in a cellar in an old house, and sometime worms had eaten away little parts. That's what these holes are."

He tapped the photo, and she could see little pits, like acne scars on a face.

"Wood worm. I make new ones. Not many. Where they are most clear."

"That looks like hard work. Why not use a drill?"

Ferency smirked. "Some forgers do—and are detected immediately. Do you think worms bore straight?" He bent, punched an irregular pattern in the plain red sail of the ship.

"None for Daedalus?" Roxy pointed to the flying figure, top left. His face was a mask of anguish as he watched his son plummet to his death in the sea.

"No." Ferency smiled, showing his irregular teeth. "Remember, this figure is not on the canvas one in Brussels. This is the figure that will get the most attention. Him, I will perfect. Not worm eaten, no?" He raised a hand to halt her next question. "But like the rest, he will be dirtier, yes? The dirt of years. He will have been in a room lit by oil lamp for centuries. Where men sat by a wood fire and smoked and looked at him with pleasure. So, once I have put a special varnish on, while it is still wet, we will smoke, yes?"

He raised his Meerschaum pipe. There were figures cut in the large yellow bowl. An elk raised its antlered head; a hunter stalked. Roxy looked away. "Maybe later. Can you manage without me?"

"Of course. The tobacco is a small part." He gestured to an old-fashioned oil lamp beside him. "This will burn all night. The oil is bad quality. And I have prepared a special kind of soot to blow over it with this." He lifted a straw. "By tomorrow morning you will not be able to tell which are the fakes, which the real."

"I might not. But wouldn't an expert like that guy Schlaben? He talked in Madrid about the further tests he could do in his laboratory."

"Which he will already have done. He will not study it again."

It was a new voice, and both she and Ferency jumped. For a big guy, Jochen Zomack moved pretty quietly. He stood in the cellar's doorway, making it look kind of cramped.

"You are up," he cried, moving across to her, putting the briefcase he held down.

She sank into him. "Jesus, you startled me. Yeah, yeah, feeling a little better."

"Good." Jocco looked at the paintings. "Two?"

"I have explained. I practise, then I—"

"Never mind. You are the forger, not me." He bent to stare. "I heard you say you will age them overnight. Does that mean they will be ready Wednesday?"

"Tomorrow?" The Hungarian sucked at a lip. "I thought you said I had till Thursday?"

"I did. But things have changed." Jocco gently released Roxy, went to the whisky, poured himself a tot, shot it. "In my journeys today I discovered that they have brought the art opening forward to Thursday. Hitler's schedule requires this." He poured himself another. "So we must have the painting in the gallery tomorrow—Wednesday night."

Roxy sank onto the bed. Moving quickly seemed a hard thing. "Why can't we wait till after the opening? Let Hitler see the real painting, hit the gallery when the ruckus has died down, substitute the fake?"

"Because I also found out that Göring plans to move the painting that same night back to the Air Ministry." He raised an eyebrow. "And we do not want to go back there."

She shuddered. "I sure as hell don't."

"Also, you say you think you told Glück that you were going to steal the painting?"

"I may have. I—"

"No matter. This only means we need a bigger distraction. And I do not think there is a bigger one than the arrival anywhere of Adolf Hitler."

"I am glad you are so confident." Ferency chewed his lip again. "I would have liked the extra day. More smoke. More aging."

"Smoke harder. Roxy will help—she's good at that." Jocco smiled briefly and waved at the paintings. "However it is, now will have to be enough. No one who values his life is going to shout 'It's a fake' before Göring and Hitler."

As Jocco filled his glass again, Roxy said, "Better pour me one too. And roll me a cigarette. If Bruegel and I are going to be ready for tomorrow—"

"No, Roxy. You are not recovered. Also, they know your face too well now. I have made the plans to do this without you. You will only be waiting to fly the painting out . . ."

"You know me. Once I make up my mind . . ." She crossed to him as he shrugged and poured three shots. She raised hers, and she was pleased to see that her hand was steady. Well, steadier. "To the plan." They all three shot, and she continued, "Whatever the hell it is. So tell me."

For a moment, he looked like he was going to argue further. Then he sighed and reached into his briefcase, pulled out a map. He glanced about. Every surface was crammed with the materials of forgery. "Bed?" he said.

"Gladly," said Roxy, sinking down.

Jocco unfolded the map onto the coverlet. It was a city plan: Berlin Central. Within it, a red-crayoned circle marked out an oval, bounded in blue. "This is Museumsinsel. The Museum Island. It is the heart of art in the Reich." He tapped. "Five buildings, each one dedicated to a different form. This is the famous Pergamon Museum. It is for antiquities— the reconstructed Pergamon Altar. The Market Gate of Miletus." He moved his finger. "This is the Bode, mainly for sculptures and Byzantine art. And this—" he pressed down "—is the Alte Nationalgalerie. Where our painting will be unveiled at the ceremony—"

Ferency interrupted. "But the Alte Nationalgalerie is for nineteenth-century art. The *Full of Icarus* is sixteenth century."

"Yes. But this is also Herr Hitler's favourite building. It is neo-classical, similar to the Acropolis in Athens—which, did you hear, Hitler and his archaeologists now say was built by an Aryan tribe? The arrogance!" He laid a fingertip on the middle of the building. "Here there is a cupola, a dome with light streaming in from all sides. Some of Hitler's favourite painters are on display here: Schinkel, Friedrich, Von Menzel. Here in the very middle, on Thursday at noon, *Icarus* will be unveiled."

"What's the river called?"

"Der Spree."

"An island, eh?" Roxy peered down. "So these lines are bridges, right?" Jocco nodded. "Kind of tricky to get things across them, especially with the security you say will be in place. Especially something as big as this painting. Got a plan for that?"

"I do." Jocco smiled. "We do not cross the bridges. We arrive and leave—" he ran his finger around the island "—by water."

"Explain."

"You are right. The bridges, every entrance to the museum, all are already heavily guarded—Berlin police, SA, even SS. They will be even more so on the day itself. But here—" he laid his finger down "—at the back of the museum is a wall that circles the riverside. There used to be a gate, but it was torn down and the gap blocked when they remodelled in 1926. They didn't demolish the water staircase that leads up to the gate. The steps are old and crumbly, but still there. And the highest one is just six feet beneath the top of the wall."

"How tall are you again?"

"One hundred ninety centimetres. Or six-foot-three."

"So you will dock, climb over the wall, the fake gets passed up to you . . ."

"Exactly."

"Okay." Roxy squinted down. "So two problems I see here. Who steers the boat? And how the hell d'you get into the museum?"

"Only two?" Jocco grinned. "You still haven't asked about security on the river."

"I was getting to it."

"There is a police patrol boat. It circles the island once an hour. The rest of the time it rests here, on the east bank."

"Right opposite your watery staircase?"

"Correct. But when it goes on patrol, it goes around the island and does not appear for two minutes fifteen seconds."

"Precise."

"Give or take a few seconds."

"You can do it in that time?"

"Yes. I have found a good boat . . . person."

There was something in the way he said it. "Person? You mean, a boatman?"

"In this case I mean a boat woman."

"Oh yeah? And who is she?"

Maybe it was her tone. But he coloured when she asked it. So Roxy knew something was different here. "She is . . . her name is Fromer,

Betsy Fromer. She is the widow of Karl Fromer. The three of us were members of the Young Communist League. Karl was killed in a street fight with SA storm troopers in '32."

His colour had gotten deeper. For such a solid guy, Jocco was a bit of a blusher. And even though she didn't want it to bother her, it did. "So you, uh, comforted the widow?"

"Roxy!" He threw up his hands. "Why do you ask this? Why does it matter?"

"If it doesn't matter, then tell me."

He ran his hands through his thick blond hair. "Yes, Betsy was very sad. We were . . . briefly involved."

"How briefly?"

"I had to flee Germany in 1934, so—"

"So two years?"

"Eighteen months."

"Still." Roxy ran her tongue over her lips. "And why does this old flame have a boat?"

"Karl was a boat mechanic. They lived on a boat. She still does."

"Had a nice reunion on the water when you went recruiting, did ya?"

"Roxy!" Jocco blurted her name, then took a deep breath. "It was over many years ago."

"Not so many. Really you came from her bed to mine. With a few stops in between, no doubt."

"Oh. And you were so—"

"Quiet!"

It was Ferency who spoke, and it made her jump—for a few moments of fury she'd forgotten he was there.

"None of that is important. Only this is." He gestured at his work. "And this. This woman with the boat. Can she keep the boat close and pass you up this painting? No, I answer. Unless she is a shot putter in the Olympics, she cannot. The panel is too heavy."

Jocco was relieved to turn away from Roxy's glare. "You are right. I am in the process of recruiting another old comrade. I looked for the man, but he is hard to find. I hope tomorrow—"

"Another? So now there are us three, plus whoever waits in the museum—who you still have to tell us about. Plus this boat woman?" He shook his head vigorously. "Already this is too many people. No." He drew himself up. "I will be in the boat."

"You?" Jocco frowned. "But you were very clear that you wanted only to do the forging."

"But I will not get paid all I am owed for that until the painting is gone. So I will help see it go. And protect myself also from too many mouths."

"I—"

"No, it is settled. And now you tell me of this other mouth, who is inside the Alte Nationalgalerie?"

Roxy was a little stunned. She'd never seen the weaselly Ferency so firm. Maybe Jocco was too. But he recovered first. "His name is Johann Müller. He is the gallery director of acquisitions. He is—" Jocco thrust out his lips "—a lecher with a wife, five children and a mistress in an expensive apartment on Kleiststrasse. So he supplements his salary by selling art by Van Gogh, Braque and Picasso. 'Degenerate art' or the 'product of diseased minds,' as it is called by Hitler and his minions. Such art is abundant in Berlin since it has been banned. He is offering to sell my father a small work by Georges Braque. I go to see it, bringing the money through the back door on Wednesday night. But what actually I bring is a cosh." He nodded. "I knock him out, tie him up. Wait till Hitler arrives and all eyes are out front for him. I exchange the paintings. Betsy collects me . . ."

He trailed off, the mention of the name making him look from Ferency to Roxy—who smiled.

"Baby," she said sweetly, "why use a cosh when you can use a stiletto? And I am not talking about the knife. Here's what we'll do."

She cleared her throat and briefly laid out her plan. Jocco objected, mainly at her being exposed to the danger. Finally, though, he had to admit, her plan was a lot less dangerous than his. "The banker's draft from Madrid," he said, reaching into his briefcase and pulling out a wedge of greenbacks. "I have cashed it. I will give you some."

"More," Roxy said when he stopped too soon, flexing her hand. He frowned and she continued. "Listen, for my plan to work, I'll have to sell myself straightaway as the real deal. So I am going to need a fancy new American dress."

"You have a new dress."

"That one? Pretty beat up during the escape. No time to fix it. Besides, it's not the right style." She shook her head. "Nope, I am going to need a new one and I am going to need it fast. Just so happens I know a guy who can make it."

THIRTEEN

DISGUISES

THE TAILOR WASN'T THERE. THE STORE WAS SHUTTERED, dark, and after hammering and calling for a while, Roxy closed her eyes and rested her forehead against the door.

She'd managed a few hours' sleep, relatively fantasy-free. Then, at 6:00 p.m., to convince Jocco that she was ready to do what she'd promised, she'd strode from the smoky cellar all cocksure and waved to him before turning the corner. Out of sight, she'd sunk onto the curb and retched. The drug's hold may have receded, but the serum still seeped through her system; her vision was still kind of blurry, her mouth sandpaper, her balance off. But she'd made it to the Kurfürstendamm, through the early-evening revellers upon it, all the way to the shop. What she really needed now was a chair and a drink.

Which I am not going to get here, she thought, though she didn't feel like moving, the metal of the shutters cool against her forehead. What if he's gone? Find another tailor? Who can make a great dress in a night? She'd have to return, tell Jocco, "Baby, it's back to the cosh."

A few people passed. One lady asked if she was okay. Roxy had managed a smile and a murmur, though she hadn't opened her eyes. Now she heard footsteps again. They stopped near. Roxy readied her smile.

"Fräulein Loewen?"

"Herr Bochner. For mercy's sake, can you let me in?"

"No. I cannot. You must—"

"Please. Just for a moment. I am having a little difficulty staying upright, as you can see."

She staggered as she stepped away. He grumbled but raised the shutter, unlocked the door, opened it, beckoned her inside. Pulled the shutter back down, locked the door again. It was dark in there, for which she was grateful. He went and turned on a small light while she sank onto the sofa.

He returned to stand above her.

"You are ill?"

"It's not contagious. Something I . . . ate."

"You cannot stay, Fräulein. I am expecting someone. He—" He broke off, gestured her up. "You cannot stay."

"But I have brought you business. I need another dress."

"I am out of business. Finished." He ran his hand through his thinning hair. "You will go, please."

"Another dress, Herr Bochner. I can pay. Cash. US dollars."

He was shifting from foot to foot, while his eyes kept moving to the door. "There will not be time. I am hoping that the man who comes—" He broke off again. "I told you of my wife. This man, I must persuade him to take less money now. To wait for the rest. To free her." Tears sprang, and ran down his cheeks. "Go!" he shouted. "Why will you not hear me?"

Roxy put her hand on the sofa's arm, prepared to lever herself up. It was no good; the man was too upset. She'd tried. It looked like Jocco's risky plan was the only game left to play.

The knock was loud, a hand hammered on metal. The shutter vibrated. "Bochner!" A man's guttural voice.

"It is him!" The tailor looked about wildly. "He cannot see anyone else here. He will—"

"Is there a back door?" Roxy said, pushing herself to her feet.

"No."

"Bochner? You better be there, Jew. I am not waiting."

He took her arm, dragged her fast past the counter. Then he almost threw her into the change cubicle. "Shh!" he ordered, finger to lips, before jerking the curtain across. "I come, I come," he called, moving away quickly.

There was a stool and Roxy sat on it. She heard the door open, the shutter go up, then the reverse as the man came into the room. The tailor had left a gap between curtain and frame. Leaning carefully forward, she could see into the store.

The man was as tall as Bochner, heavier built—and the tailor wasn't small. The man's large head thrust out from the collar of his uniform jacket like a white cabbage perched on a grey box—a match for the grinning skull insignia on his right collar patch. His hair, revealed when he took off his peaked military cap, was thick, short, bristling like a blond brush. He was sweating heavily. "Scheisse, it is fucking hot," he said, taking out a filthy handkerchief and wiping himself. "Have you anything to drink? Beer?"

"I am sorry, no. I have water. Some schnapps."

"That," the man commanded, throwing himself down onto the sofa, lifting his feet to drop them onto the small table, polished boots thumping onto the material and magazines there.

Bochner went to the counter, pulled a bottle and two glasses from beneath it, returned.

The man peered at the label. "Christ! Küpfels? You treat yourself well, don't you, you people?" As Bochner uncorked it, bent, the man used the toe of his boot to knock over one of the glasses. "Not for you. I do not drink with Jews. Leave the bottle."

Bochner did as he was told, straightened. "Of course, Herr Webel."

"That's *Obersoldat* Webel. I am a soldier of the Reich, Bochner, not some fucking tradesman."

"I am sorry. I do not mean to offend."

"I cannot be offended by a slug. Though a slug's smell?" He gave a loud sniff. "Do you Jews never bathe?" He laughed, a sound without mirth. "At least your wife has an excuse for smelling so bad. She gets one shower a month in Sachsenhausen. What's yours?"

"My wife. I—"

Roxy leaned back on the stool. She didn't need to look at Webel anymore. He was adding to her never-quite-departed feelings of nausea. The drug still had a small grip on her. But it had a benefit, she realized. She'd struggled with German on occasion if people spoke really fast. A few glasses of Scotch would always improve her comprehension, though, and so, it seemed, did the last effects of the injection. She was understanding almost everything the Nazi said.

She heard the glass being put down, the cork popped, sloshing.

"So," Webel continued, "the money? Have you got it?"

"Not all. I have over two hundred marks." Bochner overrode the cry of "Fuck" that came. "It is nearly half what we agreed. If the price has not changed again."

"You Jews! Always haggling! The price changed because I had to bribe more people. The night guard—who is on tonight, remember?— she needs paying for her silence. The gate guard too. Also, I decided I set the price too low before. So, this little extra."

"I will get the rest for you, Obersoldat. This now, the rest after—"

"After? There is no after! There is only before," Webel shouted. "After, you and your wife will vanish into one of your Jew rat holes. Or you will flee the country, perhaps. Good riddance. But first you will pay. And if you do not—"

Roxy heard him slam the glass down, rise.

"Well, at least I have half a bottle of Küpfels schnapps to accompany me back to Sachsenhausen. I am sure your wife will be so happy when I get word to her of your 'afters.'"

"Wait!"

"Wait? For what? For you to give me five hundred *Reichsmarks* this instant? For you to give me five hundred more when I return with your Jew bitch of a wife tomorrow night?" Silence. "No. I thought not."

Roxy had never been great at math. But it appeared to have improved along with her German. One thousand *Reichsmarks* was about two hundred fifty dollars. And she had one hundred in her purse.

She could see in the first moment that like a lot of braggarts Webel was a coward at heart by the way he flinched and shrank when she jerked the curtain back. "Who the hell—" he blurted as she marched forward.

"Roxy Loewen," she said, adding, "journalist with the *New York Times*. Here covering the games. But I'm looking to write other articles too—about work camps, and corrupt guards and such like. Care to give me a quote, Obersoldat Webel?"

Webel obviously had some English, enough to get her gist. He blinked at her and sweat started again on his pasty forehead.

"What is this, Bochner? Have you tricked me?"

He said it in German, so she switched too. "Herr Bochner is an old friend of mine. He's asked me to help. And I will." She reached into Webel's coat pocket, extracted the bottle of schnapps he'd stashed there, poured herself a tot. "Oh, don't worry, Obersoldat. You'll get your money. If American dollars are acceptable?"

He swallowed, nodded.

"Good. You get fifty bucks now, which is two hundred marks. With Herr Bochner's two hundred you got four. And there'll be one hundred twenty-five more dollars when you bring Frau Bochner here tomorrow. Five hundred marks more." She smiled as his eyes nearly crossed with the calculations. "Nine hundred marks total. The hundred less pays for the schnapps. And my silence. Deal?" She shoved a glass into his hand. "Deal?"

Once more he simply nodded, wordless.

"Good. Then prost!" She finished hers in a gulp. He sipped his, put it down. He was in a hurry to go now, and did, as soon as she counted the greenbacks and marks into his hand. After he'd closed the door behind the guard, Bochner sank onto the sofa with a moan. "What have you done? He will not return."

"He will. Didn't you see the greed in his eyes?" She sat beside him. "Believe me, I know that look. What's he earn as a camp guard? Ten bucks a month? He'll come back for a year's salary, trust me."

The tailor smiled. "Fräulein Loewen, you are a force."

"That's 'Roxy,' remember?"

The smile went. "I will pay you back, Frau—Roxy! If we can get out of Germany, I will work day and night to pay you back."

"Well, you can start this day, this night." She reached into her purse, pulled out the page she'd ripped from *Vogue*. "Because you are going to make me this."

She handed the page to him. He unfolded it and his eyes widened. "In one night? Imposs—"

She halted his words with a finger to his lips. "Not a word I use, remember." She took her finger away. "And there's something else you can do for me."

"Anything."

"Tell me where you and Mrs. Bochner are going to be the day after tomorrow."

⌘

The next day, just as Roxy put one elegantly shod foot on the Freidrichsbrücke, a bell inside Berlin Cathedral began to sound the hour. She glanced left to its dome, burnished in evening light. The River Spree was not wide here, the bridge not long, the toll of the bell stately, and she reached Museum Island at nine's last stroke. Its deep note lingered in the warm air through which house martins swooped and tumbled, better at aerobatics than she'd ever be. She envied them their carefree moments in the sky. Yet if all went to plan, she'd be up there again soon. She may not have been able to loop-de-loop in *Asteria 6*—the Lockheed 227 transport was not shaped for sport. But she'd waggle the wings as a salute to those watching her go. And if her hold was filled with the cargo awaiting her in one of the buildings ahead, with her share of its sale she'd be able to buy a new racer, name it *Asteria 7* and do the falling leaf from many a summer sky. If they did run the London–Melbourne again, she'd enter. Then she'd show these birds a thing or two.

If all went to plan . . .

Her knees started to give. She made it off the bridge, more stagger than walk, and leaned her head against the first stone column she came to.

Bravado had gotten her there. She'd always been good at bravado; it had taken her far: off the ground, into the skies. Persuading others, never letting them see her doubts, sweeping everyone along with her certainty. Which, half the time, was about as deep as her blusher. Bravado had brought her this far: to a museum in the most policed state in the world, preparing to steal a priceless painting from under the nose of that state's dictator.

And it wasn't just the odds. The drug may have been out of her system, but the memories weren't. She'd been lucky at the Air Ministry; as lucky as she'd ever been in a plane, low on gas and no landing strip in sight. For if Göring and his crew had caught her again, she'd have blabbed, no question. Told it all. Betrayed everyone. And then what? Would she be in Sachsenhausen now with Mrs. Bochner? Would they even have bothered to take her that far? More likely she'd be just another body floating in the Spree. A tragic American suicide.

Mr. Bochner's face came to her, tear stained and terrified. And though the circumstances were vastly different, a memory of another decent man popped into her head.

"Dad," she murmured. It hit her sometimes, had never gone away in the seven years since his death. She missed him, utterly. She bent over the jab to her stomach the memory brought.

"Dad," she said again. Differently. He was tough, Richard Loewen, and she was his daughter. She took a shuddery, deeper breath. "C'mon, girl," she urged herself in a whisper. "Move."

There was no turning back, not now. If she did, Jocco would understand. He'd tuck her up in bed with a few of his fancy rolled cigarettes, then go off to execute his riskier plan. She couldn't let him do that. Not when he might not come back. And not if she had even an ounce of her bravado left.

It had brought her to this threshold. Surely its echo could take her one step further.

"Jocco," she murmured, using his name like a last gasp of fuel for a coughing engine. Standing straight, she discovered her legs worked again. Enough, anyway, to propel her along the colonnade, an avenue of columns that swept away each side of her to turn and continue on—a square *U* with her destination, the Alte Nationalgalerie, the umlaut at its end.

There were still quite a few people around. During the Olympics, with all the city's visitors, museums stayed open into the evening. The one ahead closed at nine. She was meant to be there at half past eight. Fashionably late again, she thought, and took a deeper breath. Ain't that the double truth, she thought, and looked down.

Bochner, for all his grumbling at the haste, had done a magnificent job. He'd found a bolt of teal gabardine in his storeroom, perfect weight for the summer heat, far lighter than the wool crepe of Ginger Rogers's Metropolitan dress in the *Vogue* clipping she'd brought. Other than that he'd reproduced it perfectly, except where he'd improved upon it. The way the peplum jacket fell over her hips just so, final adjustments only being made when she stood in the shoes his friends found her—green also but a lighter shade, with gold leather trim that separated all into scallops of silk, their instep straps buckled also in gold. Sheer silk stockings, a thin black line down each back, rose to vanish into the skirt, cut perfectly just below the knee. Three other craftsmen had finished her off: her cloche was not camel felt but straw to fit the season, its strands darker, shades of forest. Her wrist-length gloves were calf leather, emerald. The little purse she carried gave the only accent—a vivid slash of scarlet, buckled and chained in silver. It contained just five things: a slim leather cigarette case, a lighter, a compact, her cherry-stain lipstick and a vial of colourless liquid. Her derringer was tucked into her stocking top, at her right thigh. Herr Bochner would have complained about the slight bulge, this spoiling of line. But she was happy to sacrifice style for a bullet's worth of security.

She pulled out her compact, and stepped into the light spill that came from the brightly lit building ahead. Touched up her powder, then ran the cherry stain over her lips. Made a moue, tucked all away and glanced down at herself one last time.

The dress had probably cost twice as much as Ginger would pay for an outfit to attend a premiere in Hollywood. And yet? Maybe not. Because with the two hundred fifty bucks she'd paid for this also came a human life. Frau Bochner.

With the hope on her tailor's face in her mind's eye, and the Alte Nationalgalerie in her gaze, Roxy set out across the grass.

As Jocco had said, the museum looked like a rebuilt Acropolis. Corinthian columns supported a pediment in which some classical goddess welcomed everyone with widespread arms. Before it, a man in cloak and part armour rode a stallion. The sponsoring *Kaiser,* no doubt. "Wish me luck," she breathed.

She passed up the steps beside him and tried to enter by the main door. But she was going against the flow of those exiting, and when she'd pushed through, a uniformed guide raised a hand against her and told her, "*Wir haben geschlossen.*"

She'd decided it was better to keep her German to herself. "Sorry, don't understand. Do you speak English?"

He shook his head, yet still answered "Closed," as he waved her out.

"I have an appointment. I—"

"*Wir haben geschlossen,*" he said again, taking her arm.

"Frau Winter?"

The voice came from behind the attendant, who turned, revealing a man approaching down the central stair. For half a second, Roxy forgot the name she'd assumed. Then she beamed and said, "That's me."

The guard still had a hold of her arm. "You know this woman, *Herr Direktor*?" he asked in German.

"Yes," he replied. "We have an appointment. Is that not so, kind lady?"

"Uh, sorry, don't really speak—"

He tipped his head. The English that now came was perfect, very lightly accented. "We have an appointment, do we not? But you are late."

"Sorry," she said. "Stocking accident. Had to go back for a new pair."

She raised the hem of her skirt to the knee and turned her leg as she said it. Watched the other man colour. Lecher, Jocco had said. Confirmed.

The guard's hand also tightened a little on her arm as he looked. "Hey," she said, "may I have that back?"

He may not have spoken English, but he released her quickly. The director, Herr Müller, stepped aside and beckoned her to precede him. The staircase was wide, like something from an opera house, that feeling heightened by more columns all around and classical statues on pedestals and in niches.

There was a hall straight ahead, but Müller directed her up the next flight of stairs to the right. "Before business, there is something very special I wish to show you," he said softly, leaning too close.

On the next floor, they took another short wide flight into a vestibule, a small room with paintings crammed onto its walls. He didn't let her linger, waving her on to a larger space beyond, which was again crowded with paintings, most of these romantic nineteenth-century landscapes. However, the next room, the biggest room yet, was where he halted, and she immediately noted three things: the monumental canvases on every wall; the four soldiers clad in field grey, one in each corner, with rifles at slope; and the easel draped in cloth in the middle of the hall.

"This," Müller whispered, "is what you must see."

He beckoned and two of the soldiers leaned their rifles against the wall and came forward. At a further nod, each bent to a corner of the easel and slowly, carefully, pulled the cloth up and over.

She'd been studying Ferency's forgeries. Looking now, she realized how good they were, even the one he said he used for practice. Yet in that first glance she also realized now how completely false they were. There was something about the real art—and she was sure it was not because she knew one was true and the others fake—an air it gave off, as if the artist's breath, Bruegel's actual breath, was caught and held in the paint and varnish. In the anguish on Daedalus's face. In the wind that bellied the sail of the ship. In the ox's swishing tail.

She hadn't noticed it at the Air Ministry—she was too scared they were going to get caught. She saw it here.

Her gasp was also not fake. The moment took her breath. Only partly, she realized, for the art. Mainly because she realized something else.

There'd been a small voice inside her arguing that even if she'd done some questionable things, she'd never been a thief and that the heist was wrong. That voice was gone. Taken by the real painting and the knowledge that it was about to be displayed for Göring's glory and Hitler's pleasure—the men responsible for all the Frau Bochners in Germany. Responsible for what had happened in that cellar in Madrid and the man who'd died there. She heard the snarl in the camp guard's voice as he cursed the tailor and his race and gloated over his cruelty. Felt the whisper of the drug in her veins.

This wasn't theft. This was liberation. And the only crime would be if they didn't succeed.

She realized that Müller had been talking to her for a while. She looked at him, shook her head and began to act. "I am sorry, Herr Direktor, but . . . what am I looking at?"

"Frau Winter, you are looking at Bruegel's *Fall of Icarus.*"

"That is not possible. Because I was looking at his *Fall of Icarus* only last month. In Brussels."

"Ah, but that is not the original painting. This is. The long lost one, painted on wood. This—"

He began his lecture, which she only half listened to. She knew the facts already, though she kept herself looking as interested as the guards, standing to attention on either side of the easel, looked bored. The only time she listened harder was when the story differed or left out elements of the truth. Ernst Schlaben was hailed as a great art detective, working for his supremely cultured master, Hermann Göring. He had discovered the painting in Madrid and rescued it from under the noses of the godless Communists, who would doubtless have used it for kindling. The provenance had been proved with painstaking chemical analysis and scrupulous paper research, which he, Herr Direktor Müller, for long hours, deep into many nights, had selflessly undertaken. She only listened harder when the story came onto the subject of tomorrow's great reveal.

"Ah, what a moment that shall be!" Müller's eyes glistened and he flapped his hand at the hall. "Here will be standing all the great men of the fatherland and the age. Of any country, any age. Watched by the great leaders who forged our nation." He gestured to the walls, on which hung many portraits of grim-faced men in uniform. "And the greatest of them all, Frau Winter, will be standing exactly where you are standing now. A sublime artist himself, he is perhaps the only one who will fully appreciate this glorious piece of art." His voice rose and he cried, "Heil Hitler!"

Four pairs of heels crashed together, as the four guards echoed him. "Heil Hitler!"

"Yes, kind lady," Müller continued, his voice softening. He withdrew a handkerchief to dab at overflowing eyes. "That will be a moment when all my dreams will be fulfilled."

Oh, you'll be dreaming all right, she thought.

He nodded at the guards, who bent straightaway, seized the cloth and drew it once again over the painting. "Well," he said, after a moment, "perhaps not all of them. Shall we?"

It was swift, the change. One moment, nothing but patriotism and hero-worship. The next, all venality and lust. "Let's," she answered, and let him take her hand. As she glanced back, she saw the guards return to their positions in the corners of the room and snatch up their rifles. Four rifles in the room. Jocco hadn't mentioned them. Had they been added because of what she'd let slip to Glück? It was possible.

Müller led her out the back door of the gallery, and to a door set flush within the next room's back wall. It gave onto one musty corridor ending in stairs, which he led her down to another. He turned along it—but there was a door at the bottom of the first stairs. She stopped before it. "Herr Direktor, where does this go?"

"To a terrace over the river," he replied. "The guards go there to smoke. This is forbidden in the building."

"Wise." She crinkled her eyes. "Look, Herr Müller, I do smoke. Would you mind?"

He frowned, then shrugged. "Of course." Then he reached into the shadows by the door, withdrew a key from some hook she'd never have seen. Phew, she thought, but said, "Thank you," as he let her out.

While she smoked, he chatted about art, the prices it could fetch these days. She knew what he was doing—talking up his product. She let him, gave him hope, while she studied the river, noted the newer area in the surrounding wall where the gate had been blocked. She lit up a second, to his mild protests, just as the police boat crossed from the far bank and then disappeared around the island's upper tip. She was just stubbing that cigarette out, when the boat reappeared at the lower end. The way she smoked, that made the trip pretty much two minutes even.

Müller ushered her in, locked the door, replaced the key, then gestured her along the narrow corridor. He held a last door open, then let her squeeze past him.

His office was cramped, a desk cluttered with papers occupying most of it, though she noticed a small cot bed under the window at the back. He noticed her noticing and smiled. "Yes, gnädige Frau. Sometimes my work forces me to sleep here. And it is good also for . . . naps, yes?" He grinned. "Naps . . . *und Schnapps!*" he declared, pulling a bottle and two glasses from a desk drawer. "To beauty," he toasted, raising the glass to her.

What the hell, she thought. I could use a steadier. But when he tried to refill her glass, she put her fingers over it. "Maybe later, Herr Müller," she said. "To toast other beauty, perhaps?"

"Ah, you are, as you say, 'getting down to business,' yes? I like dealing with Americans! Always so direct." He poured himself another tot, only sipped it, studying her quite shamelessly over the rim. "I was pleased when your—how do we say—quite forceful colleague was unable to come, and sent you in his place. Very pleased." He took a second sip of his drink, then put the glass down and swivelled to a cabinet behind him, pulled out a key, inserted and turned it. "But beauty? Well, it depends upon your taste." He sniffed. "I agree with der Führer. So much modern art *is* degenerate. Do you not think so?"

"Mostly I do. Happily, my clients are not as picky as I am."

From the cabinet, he removed an object wrapped in oilcloth, and laid it on the table. "Then," he said, folding back the covering, "I am sure your clients will like this."

She peered down at the painting. Braque had been one of her dad's favourite artists. Ferency had filled in a few gaps in her memory about the style and the art, though Jocco had said having such knowledge wouldn't matter much—she just needed to keep the guy occupied till everyone else, guards aside, had left the building. Her lateness had probably taken care of most of them. And the bed indicated that Müller was probably known for putting in late shifts. Or doing some late entertaining. Either way, it was unlikely he'd be missed.

"Can I get some more light, please?"

He flicked on a desk lamp.

"Hmm," she said, bending, scanning. "A later work, huh? A coastline. Normandy, right?" She got a grunt in return. "Even a human in it, not a blob. He's gotten back into people lately, hasn't Monsieur Braque?" Another grunt and she shrugged. "Though I was hoping it was going to be one from his cubist phase. That's the stuff that's really selling stateside these days."

"I told your colleague it was not a masterpiece," Müller replied, a touch huffily. "But as the beginning of our relationship? Besides, trust me, there will be more like this. Cubist. More degeneracy. Better . . . degeneracy."

"This is, what, ten years old?"

"From 1924."

"Oh yeah. There's the date, and his signature. If it's genuine."

He looked deeply offended. "Frau Winter, I am curator of the Alte Nationalgalerie of Berlin. I do not deal in fakes."

You'll be singing a different song tomorrow, buddy, she thought, as he continued, "Besides, if you buy this and it is proven fake, you will not return and that—" he smiled "—would break my heart."

"And mine, Herr Müller. And mine." She picked the painting up, held it at arm's length. "Still, it's pretty. I'll take it. Now, as to price . . ."

They haggled for a while. She had the feeling that she paid more than she should have. Which was fine, considering she wasn't going to pay anything at all.

They shook on it. She discovered that his palm was damp when he held hers too long. She extracted her hand, opened her purse, pulled out her cigarette case.

"I am sorry, dear lady, but—"

"Oh, right, no smoking." She dropped the case onto the desk. "How about that second drink then? Though put this away," she added, pointing to the Braque. "Wouldn't want to spill on it."

Herr Müller wrapped the painting back up in its cloth. As he turned to place it back in the cabinet, she opened the vial, which she'd palmed when she took out her cigarettes, flipped its lid, tipped the colourless liquid into his half-full glass, then dropped the bottle and cap back into her purse. When he turned back, she waved her empty glass at him, and delightedly he filled it, before topping up his own. "To Transatlantic trade," she declared, and shot.

"Prost," he said, and joined her. Smacking his lips, he continued, "And now, kind lady, can I interest you in anything else?"

It was easy enough to flirt with him for the five minutes Jocco said the drug would take. And her man was pretty much on the money. One moment the Herr Direktor was reaching across the desk to take her hand, claiming he had the gift of reading palms; the next a slightly startled look came into his eyes; and the one after, he laid his head down with a faint moan. "Herr Müller?" she called. "Herr Müller?"

She snapped her fingers. His only reply was a faint snore. She considered the sleeping man and decided to move him. She got behind him, bent, and raised him from the chair; laid his torso on the cot and afterwards lifted his legs. He muttered something she didn't catch.

She sat back down, looked at the clock. Ten p.m. Four hours till showtime. Müller would be out for close to twelve. As would a horse, according to Jocco's veterinarian friend.

Gotta stay awake, she thought. So she pulled out a cigarette. Against the rules, of course. My, but what a brazen criminal I have become, she thought as she lit up.

FOURTEEN

SEDUCTION

IT WAS THE BELL THAT WOKE HER, ITS DEEP TOLL SOUNDING two from the nearby cathedral. She jerked her head up from the desk, uncertain where she was and what she was meant to be doing. Müller's soft snores calmed her a little. She checked him, pulling back an eyelid. Gone. He was drooling heavily but otherwise well.

She reached for the schnapps, then thought better of it and poured a glass of water from a carafe on the desk instead. The liquor had made her drowsy and she needed to be wide awake.

She opened the office door, listened to silence. No doubt the soldiers, or their replacements, were in position around the painting. After closing the door behind her, she went along the corridor, found the key and opened the back door to warm night air and the muted sounds of a sleeping city. A car moved over the bridge ahead. Somewhere on the opposite bank, a woman gave a little cry, pain or pleasure she couldn't tell.

The opposite bank. Jocco had said that he would make his move anytime from 2:15 on. There was a clock she could just see, on a building beyond the bridge. She watched its minute hand creep along. At ten past she reached into her purse and cursed. She'd left her cigarettes on Müller's desk! She thought of going back for them, but the time was too tight. Instead she chewed one nail down to a stub.

At exactly 2:15, the police boat set out for its quarter-hourly run. She pressed herself back into the shadows of the museum wall and watched it pass. As soon as it passed the tip of the island, she ran to the filled-in section of wall, struck her lighter and raised the flame in the air. Immediately, another engine started up and a boat cut straight across. It wasn't much smaller than the police vessel; it had an open cabin forward and was covered in behind. But it was fast and was there in thirty seconds, a tire fender bumping into stone.

She peered down. You couldn't tell it was a woman driving, what with the seamen's pea coat and the flat cap. Only when she glanced up did Roxy see her for a flash, and then there was only an impression of curls around a wide face. Betsy Fromer.

She dropped the engine to an idling purr. Jocco stepped over the bow onto the hidden stairs, the water coming up to his shins. Ferency was behind, and with an audible grunt, he lifted a cloth-shrouded object and passed it over. Jocco took it, stepped fully off the boat, and Ferency followed.

"Roxy?" Jocco whispered up. "Is all good?"

"Better than good," she replied. "Müller's—"

"*Was machen Sie hier?*"

The new voice was sudden, loud and made her cry out. Below, Betsy cut the engine, and Roxy heard Ferency gasp as she turned.

A soldier was standing there, a silhouette in the doorway. Backlit, she couldn't see his face.

"*Was machen Sie hier?*" he said again, stepping forward.

Her German deserted her entirely. "I . . . I came out here to . . ."

"*Engländerin?*"

"Uh, no. American. *Amerikaner.*"

"Ah." He came forward and Roxy managed to move her feet so she met him a few feet from the wall. Enough light spilled from the open doorway and he was able to see her. Turning a little, he came into the light, and she could see him too—young, maybe twenty. His peaked cap was tipped back, so that a few strands of blond hair poked out.

"Ah," he said again. "I speak *Amerikanisch*."

"You do? That's great. Ever been?"

"No. But I have—how you say *Vettern*?" He shrugged. "Aunt sons?"

"Cousins?"

"So. Cousins in Milwaukee."

"Oh great!"

For some reason she gave a little laugh, and he frowned.

"What make you here?" he said.

She turned and looked at the clock. The minute hand was on twenty-two. She looked back. "I am a guest of the director."

"A guest of Herr Müller?"

She could see he knew exactly what that meant in the little smirk that came.

"So where is he?"

"Office. Resting. He, uh—" she looked around "—he doesn't smoke."

"Ah!" Smirk changed to smile. "So you are—"

"Yes. But, stupid me, I forgot my cigarettes. I'll . . . I'll go get them."

"I have cigarettes." He dug into his jacket pocket. "Amerikanisch cigarettes," he added proudly, pulling out a packet of Lucky Strike.

"Oh." She couldn't think of anything else to say. Or do, when he offered her one. Except take it. "*Danke*," she said.

"*Bitte*," he replied, lighting her, then himself.

Out on the water, an engine coughed into life. Not close to the wall, not far off. He frowned, took a step. "Hey," she called, catching his sleeve, holding it. "What are these fantastic patches on your uniform?"

It was the right question, and when Roxy suggested he explain them where she could see them, he happily accompanied her over to the lit doorway and talked her through the double SS on his collar and the eagle-and-swastika combo on his sleeve. She learned that young Klaus belonged to the Leibstandarte—Hitler's bodyguard. It was a sign of how important the beloved leader considered tomorrow's opening, she was informed, that he'd assigned his own elite troops. As she'd suspected, they'd only been deployed yesterday. Improved security after some vague threat.

Roxy glanced to the water. The patrol boat reappeared and returned to its dock on the opposite bank—without shining a light along the wall and spotting two men holding up a heavy wooden panel. Betsy must have made herself scarce. The clock's hand tipped to twenty-five past two when the soldier stubbed out his cigarette in an ashtray inside the back door.

"Duty," he said. "My break is over. May I escort you back to Herr Müller?"

She noticed that he didn't smirk when he said it this time, that there was almost a sadness. "I'm in no hurry to get back to him," she said. "Can I steal another Lucky Strike?" She took one. "Join me?"

She hoped he'd answer as he did: "I cannot. But I get another break in two hours. Maybe then?"

"I think I'll be gone. Don't your, uh, fellow guards smoke?"

"No. The Führer doesn't like it. I try to stop but—" He lit her, then clicked his heels together. "*Gute nacht, Fräulein.*"

She waited for the door in the corridor to close before she dropped the cigarette and ran back to the wall. The two men were still there, ankle deep in water, their faces strained.

"Is he gone?" Jocco hissed.

"Yes."

"Quickly! The weight is killing us."

Ferency let go. Jocco gave a huge groan as the Hungarian scrambled over the wall, turned and bent back down. Jocco pushed the painting up; the forger took it and managed to lever it over the wall before collapsing with a moan. A few seconds later Jocco pulled himself over, to fall also. "Shit!" he said. "I thought we were finished. One more minute and the Bruegel was in the Spree."

For some reason the sentence struck her as funny, and she laughed. Ferency glared at her, which made her laugh more. "Come on," she said, "let's get this in." Roxy put out a hand and hauled Jocco up. "When's the boat coming back?"

"Betsy will have to wait till the police circle again, before she picks Ferency up."

"Ferency and you."

"No. Change of plan. I stay now." He raised a hand to still her protest. "Betsy was in a riverman's bar. For the ceremony tomorrow they are doubling the boats circling the island. To get back and forth once will be difficult. Twice, impossible. So I will stay and she will come for us once."

He bent over, lifted the painting, grunted and carried it across and through the doorway. Ferency hung back by the wall. The exercise hadn't done him any favours, judging by his colour—red and a queasy yellow. She remembered his nickname—"Chameleon"—and wondered if he was in mid-transformation. "You okay?" she asked.

"No. This is madness," he moaned, then looked down and clutched his trouser cuffs. "And my suit is ruined."

"With your cut you can buy yourself a dozen suits. Don't miss your ride." She nodded toward the water, then joined Jocco in the doorway.

They went in; she relocked the door, then led him along the corridor to Müller's office. With a relieved groan he set the painting down just inside the door. From the cot came some muttering. Jocco's eyes narrowed. Roxy went and checked. More drool, no light in the eye when she peeled one lid back. "Out for the count. Poor bastard's probably chasing cube-headed girls through sunflower fields."

"Good." Jocco spotted the schnapps, and poured himself a tot, shot it back. "That," he said, holding up a shaking hand, "was too close."

"It's only going to get closer," she said, crossing to him, pouring two more tots and then handing him one. "There are four guards upstairs, not two."

"Scheisse!"

"Yeah and they are Leibstandarte—Hitler's own bodyguard."

"What?"

"I know. Scheisse." She raised her glass. "Here's some in your eye." They both drank and she continued, "But you suspected there might be some guards. You never told me your plan to get rid of them."

He put down his glass, then started undoing the buttons of the greatcoat he was wearing. It was unfamiliar, battle grey and winter heavy. Crazy on a summer's night. It partly explained the sweat, the thick wool adding to all the exercise and the panic. She smiled when she saw what was underneath. "Well hello, soldier boy!"

Jocco took the greatcoat off, dropped it over the chair. "Heil Hitler!" he said, making the salute. "Obersturmführer Proltz, at your service, Fräulein."

She'd never seen him in uniform. It suited him. His tall frame filled out the field grey. He'd had his hair cut short and he'd shaved, something he was usually careless about. The grey brought out the intense cerulean blue of his eyes. From the peaked cap he pulled from a satchel and put on, to the tip of his knee-high leather boots, via the polished gun holster at his hip, he could have been on one of the posters she'd seen around Berlin, the epitome of Aryan military might. She looked him up and down three times and asked, "Where the hell did you get it?"

"It belonged to my cousin Helmut. He died last year—influenza, nothing heroic. My widowed aunt asked me to return this to his unit. I thought it might come in useful, so I kept it. And I was right."

He turned, peacocking a little. She touched one side of the collar. She'd seen enough of the insignia to know. "SS, huh? Hitler's elite."

"That's right." He took her hand, placed it on the other collar patch—three pips and a stripe. "An Obersturmführer would be a first lieutenant in your army."

"Officer, eh? I'm liking you better and better."

"Roxy, this soldier you met upstairs? Did you see his comrades also?"

"Yeah. Müller showed me the Bruegel before he brought me here. That's when I saw the four guards."

"Were any of them officers?"

"I wouldn't be able to tell. But I doubt it. They were all standing to attention in corners. Would an officer do that?"

"It is unlikely. Good." He nodded.

Roxy ran her hand from the collar down his arm. "So, you are going to be their officer?"

"Correct. When Hitler arrives, there will be much commotion." He smiled. "German soldiers are trained to obey on the instant. I will march in there and command them to line the stairs outside the gallery. Then you and I will bring the painting in, switch them. Easy."

"Oh, a breeze."

Jocco took off his hat, placed it on the desk by her cigarettes. He extracted one. "Hey, buddy, didn't you read the sign? '*Rauchen Verboten!*'"

He paused, cigarette on lip. "Oh, and do you forbid me to smoke?"

"Why take the chance? I smoked one earlier. But that was before I met the soldier. He's the only smoker among 'em. He'll already be feeling it and smoke travels to a nicotine fiend. Trust me, I know. He sniffs it, comes to tell the Fräulein to obey the rules—"

"Damn. But you are right." He put the lighter down, slipped the cigarette back into the packet. "And I could really use one now."

"Nervous?"

"We are going to steal one of the most expensive works of art ever, in the most heavily policed country in the world, from under the nose of Adolf Hitler." He shook his head. "Why would I be nervous?"

"So we can't smoke, and we shouldn't drink." Roxy pulled her lower lip between her teeth. "Hmm. What could we do?"

His eyes went wide. "Roxy."

"Jocco?"

"We can't."

"We can."

"The guards?"

"You'll just have to be quiet."

"*I'll* have to be?" He looked behind the desk. "And Müller?"

"Sound asleep. May as well not be there."

"Roxy . . ." he said again. Though this time he sounded less certain.

"Obersturmführer Proltz?"

His eyes widened. "Are you asking me to—"

"Oh no." She put a finger between her teeth. "Who am I to ask anything from such a brave soldier?" She ran her gaze up his uniform, from boot tip to face. "You're the officer. You're in command." She put her finger to his lips. "Command me."

His eyes narrowed. "Young woman. You will take off this expensive dress."

As he spoke, he lifted the holster strap over his head. She was glad he hadn't just started to pull her dress off—it was too expensive to muss and she was going to need it. "Help me?" she said, turning her back to him, lifting her hair. He pulled the zipper down. "Danke," she murmured, not turning around, hoping for what came—his breath, then his lips on her neck.

She stepped out of the dress, laid it carefully across the chair. She took her derringer from the stocking, put it down, then turned to him. She crossed her arms over her chest, opened her eyes wide. "And now, sir? The rest? Start with the shoes?"

"No. I like the shoes, Fräulein. I like . . . the spike." It was his turn for his gaze to climb her. As it rose, she lifted her slip with it, over her knees, up to the clasp that held the stockings. His voice, when it came now, had thickened. "Leave the shoes. Leave everything."

He reached up to his neck, the buttons there.

"Please, sir, if I may be allowed just one request?"

"State it."

"Leave the uniform."

He growled, seized her shoulders, spun her fast to face the desk. While he fumbled at buttons, she pushed everything aside—cigarettes, lighter, art books. Clearing space.

His hands were at her ankles. He ran them up each leg, following the seam of her stockings. When he got to the straps of her garter belt, he slipped his fingers behind them, pulled, snapped them. She gave a little cry. "Silence," he hissed, his breath hot behind her ear, and he wrapped a hand around her mouth. She took his thumb into her mouth, bit it.

His cry now. A stifled oath. He pushed her down onto the desk. There was some movement as he dealt with the cloth between them. And then . . .

Field-grey serge chafed her skin as he pressed deep.

It didn't take long. Explosions shuddered through her, and, soon after, through him. He was in control—until he wasn't.

Eventually pain, and not the good kind, displaced the pleasure of just lying there linked. "Baby," she said, and he raised himself, stepped back.

She turned and looked him slowly up and down. "Thank you, Obersturmführer," she said.

The voice startled them both, and she jumped off the desk. Both of them looked—at Herr Müller, rolling over on his cot.

"Degenerates," he muttered.

Roxy turned away, burying her mouth and her laughter in her hand. Jocco eyed her, and shook his head.

"What?" she said, grinning. "He's got a point."

FIFTEEN

FÜHRER SURPRISE

JOCCO HAD BROUGHT SOME BREAD AND CHEESE IN HIS satchel, some water and, blessedly, a mickey of Scotch. She slept some, curled up in her slip in the chair, while Jocco sat by the window and stared out into the night. She was awake by seven, her neck stiff, her mouth a desert. They didn't talk much, though Müller's muttering increased by the hour. Yet it was only when the minute hand on the desk clock hit quarter to eleven that Roxy really started to feel nervous. She felt that she would actually kill someone for a cigarette, but she couldn't risk meeting the smoking soldier again on the terrace or lighting up inside.

It didn't help that Jocco was pacing up and down, checking and rechecking his wristwatch, pausing to look out the window at the Spree below and curse the two patrol vessels that buzzed around the island like flies. Under the growl of their engines, sounds had been building from the front of the museum—vehicles drawing up, men in shod boots marching in formation across the Friedrichs Bridge, the swelling noise of a crowd. Adolf Hitler was visiting the museum, and wherever he went, mobs formed to adore him.

"For crissake, Jocco, will you just sit already?"

He stopped. "I can't. If I sit, I think too much. If I think too much—"
He broke off.

"You wonder just what the hell we're doing?"

"Precisely." He peered down at her, rubbed the morning shadow on his chin, a sound like sandpaper, eerily loud. For a pale northern European he sure grew a fast beard.

She crossed to him, took his hands. "Don't think of the risk. Think of the result. All that money. Think what we can do with it. You can buy guns to free the workers from their oppressive overlords, while I . . . I can't decide between Lockheed or Boeing. Monoplane or biplane? Which do you think will get me to Australia faster?"

He finally cracked a smile. And as the minute hand crept toward the hour and the crowd noise swelled, they talked world revolution and stalling speeds.

It was at five to eleven that Müller woke up.

His muttering hadn't increased. There was no sign. One moment he was out, and the next he bolted upright and was staring at them. "Who are you?" he demanded in German. "What are you doing here?"

Roxy took a step toward him. "Remember me, Herr Direktor? Frau Winter? We had a helluva—"

It was as far as she got before Jocco moved past her. He didn't talk. He just dipped his huge frame and uncoiled it, putting everything he had into the punch. His fist connected with Müller's jaw and the man's head snapped back. His body followed, rearing back from the cot to smash into the wall under the window.

"Jocco! What the hell?" Roxy was around the desk fast and bent over the crumpled German. His head lolled and blood ran between his shattered lips. That bubbled, so at least he was breathing. She took his body, lowered him to the ground, turning him on his side. "What have you done?" she shouted. "You might have killed him. It wasn't necessary."

"It was." Jocco joined her and grabbed her arm, jerking her to her feet. "Look. Look!"

She looked where Jocco pointed—to the Friedrichs Bridge. Saw the soldiers, double ranked on each side of it, holding back the ecstatic mobs behind them, who screamed in joy just the one refrain, their arms shot out in one salute. "Heil Hitler!" they cried, again and again at the man dressed simply in battlefield grey, sitting in the open-topped Mercedes. Though perhaps some of the acclamation was for the man who sat beside him, who made him look small and perhaps a little dull—Reichsmarschall Göring, in his sky-blue uniform, sun-light refracting off the starburst of medals with which his chest was studded. Trumpets started blowing a fanfare of welcome.

"Quickly," Jocco said, bending to lift the fake Bruegel.

She opened the door and led the way down the corridor. They were halfway along, when the voice came.

"Herr Direktor Müller?"

They froze—but Roxy only for a moment. Because she recognized the voice. Waving Jocco to a stop, she continued, turned the bend and saw her smoking companion of the night before, descending the stairs from the gallery. "Hey, just the guy I wanted to see," she said, moving fast up to him. "Got a light?"

The soldier frowned at her. "What are you yet doing here, Fräulein?" he asked, doubt clear in his eyes. "Der Führer arrives. Der Direktor is requested. I must bring him."

He went to step around her. She blocked him. Her heart was thumping so hard she thought he must hear it. She knew her face was wet with sweat, and her hand shaking like she had a palsy. "He's, uh, he's just getting ready. Asked me to stay. To meet der Führer."

Something else came into the young man's eyes. Contempt replaced doubt. He glanced down. "In this dress?" he said. "It is not . . . respectful."

He was right. Herr Bochner had made a dress for a classy seduction, not a demure reception. "True. I'll go back and get my coat, I promise. That, uh, light? I'm gasping for a smoke."

His stare was as cold as his words. "There is no time. Der Führer is here. You and the director will come immediately."

He went back up but stopped on the landing to yell "Rauchen Verboten" at her before he opened the gallery door and stepped through. Göring's distinctive voice came, echoing through the galleries, amplified and a little distorted, some speech of welcome from the front steps of the museum. The door closed again, muffling the voice. She leaned over the stairs. "Quick now," she said. Jocco came up and passed her, grunting. She followed.

Göring concluded his oration just as she opened the door set in the gallery wall. The excited buzz of people reached her, then quadrupled in volume as the front door opened. Hitler was entering the building. They had two minutes, if that.

She closed the door quietly, turned back. Jocco had put the painting down. "You're up," she said.

"I know. I . . ."

His voice sounded fragile. She peered at him in the corridor gloom. His face looked fragile too. He was running his tongue over his lips as if he was trying to lick them off. "It is the moment. I must—"

In all their time together, through some pretty hairy episodes, she'd never seen him hesitate. She didn't want to see it now. "Baby," she said, "let me do that."

She took his face in her hands and kissed him hard. He held back for a moment—then gave, sinking into her. She pulled away a couple of inches, dropped her hands to his collar and did up the top button there, between the skull and the silver pips. "Off you go, Lieutenant," she said. "Do your duty."

He stretched to his full height, adjusted his cap, shot his cuffs. "I go," he said, and marched out the door. Ten seconds later his voice came clear, cutting through the noise of the approaching party. The German was fast, barked-out militaristic commands she didn't understand. She got the gist, though.

"The Führer approaches. You will line the balcony and greet him with salutes."

"Jawohl, Obersturmführer."

Four voices chorused their obedience; four pairs of heels clicked. She heard men marching away on the wooden floor. And one coming toward her fast. Jocco.

"Hurry!" he said.

He came through the door and set down his burden. She caught the briefest of glimpses—the anguish on Daedalus's face as he watched his son die. Hoisting the fake again, Jocco made for the gallery. She followed.

A swelling noise came from the stairs. Jocco stumbled, nearly falling, but Roxy stepped up, took some of the weight. Together they ran the painting to the empty easel and heaved it up. As another chorus of "Heil Hitler" rose from behind them, they stepped back, preparing to flee—and gasped.

They'd hung the painting upside down.

Roxy had her hands on it one second before Jocco. They lifted, swivelled, placed. It wasn't perfectly centred, but it would have to do. Flinging the shroud over the painting, they turned and ran.

As they left the gallery by one entrance, others came into it by another. And Roxy had the strangest sensation: that though all eyes were on the hero entering the space, the hero's own eyes, Adolf Hitler's, were on her, centred on her teal dress. Yet no cry came, no pack was unleashed to pursue them. They went through the doorway, closed it softly. Both sagged, leaning their butts against the wall. From the gallery behind them, his voice unamplified this time, they heard Göring speechifying again.

"Come," Jocco said, bending, heaving.

Roxy lifted the back of the Bruegel and somehow they negotiated the stairs down. She unlocked and opened the terrace door, as Jocco hoisted the painting alone and ran it to the perimeter wall. He set it down as they crouched, peering over the parapet.

One patrol vessel was almost directly before her. One glimpse before she ducked showed her the faces of the crew—the helmsman staring ahead; two soldiers at the bow poised around a mounted heavy-calibre machine gun; an officer, judging by his braid and sleeve stripes, his hand sheltering his eyes, scanning the far bank. She peeped until its stern disappeared around the tip of the island to her left and then she looked right—where the bow of the other vessel appeared almost immediately. It had the same four-man crew, same set-up, but was moving a little faster, she thought.

As it passed them, approached the island's tip, Jocco looked at his wristwatch and said, "Tell me when it vanishes."

She watched. "Now," she said.

She reckoned it was about a minute and a half before the first boat reappeared. It was less. "Eighty-three seconds," he said.

They waited, until the second boat came and went again. "Now," she said. He stood up and waved frantically. There was an immediate roar of an engine and in a moment the Fromer boat was powering toward them. There in less than thirty. Fifty left, Roxy thought, as Ferency jumped onto the steps, took the painting. Jocco leaped down and reached up for her. She used his hands but still landed heavily, her left stiletto heel snapping cleanly off. She kicked the other shoe into the river and climbed over the gunwale after the two men.

"Grab hold!" came a woman's shouted command.

Which Roxy failed to obey, and thus tumbled into Ferency as the boat reversed fast away from the steps, bringing them both down. He cursed her in Hungarian, either for the pain of her landing on top of him or the further spoiling of his beautiful suit, stained now with diesel-rich water.

"Under, all of you!" the woman yelled.

Ferency grabbed Roxy and pulled her none too gently to a wooden hatching, a cover to some hold below. Jocco grabbed a large tarpaulin, flung himself down beside them and pulled the heavy, greasy material over them.

"What the hell," Roxy began.

"Shsst!" Jocco hissed. "It is planned. Shsst!"

That's when the engine cut out.

SIXTEEN

MIXED CARGO

"WHAT—"

This time he didn't cut her off with a hiss but by laying his hand over her mouth. "What are you doing?" she whispered. There was no reply. Roxy just listened—to water lapping against the vessel, to her two companions' strained breathing.

To the engine. Not theirs. A far more powerful one, getting nearer fast. Then voices came, muddled by thick cloth and shouting. One male voice, strident and demanding. A softer female one, cajoling. They spoke in thickly accented German—that and the speed of their talk, together with fear enhanced by her lack of air, rendered the conversation all but incomprehensible to her.

The strident voice got less so. She heard something lifted, thrown back; a hatch, perhaps. Then there came a banging, metal on metal. Some female cursing, as crude as any man's. Some male laughter at it. The hatch went down—and the engine fired up.

"*Dankeschön, dankeschön!*" Frau Fromer cried.

The engine went up a notch in power and Roxy felt the boat shifting. She made a tent of the tarp in the hope of more air, but Jocco pulled her hand away.

"Not yet," he whispered.

They lay there for several more breathless minutes that felt like an age. Finally, she heard Betsy call the all-clear. Ferency and Jocco threw the tarp back and they emerged, gasping like newborn chicks. "What was that?" Roxy asked.

"She claimed we were broken down. There was no way to flee without this bluff." As he spoke, Jocco got up and moved toward the wheelhouse, letting forth a burst of enthusiastic German. As she followed, Ferency bent over the painting, lifted it and carried it to the boat's stern.

When Roxy reached the wheelhouse, Jocco hastily stepped back, releasing a woman from his clasp. Betsy Fromer was dressed in shabby worker's overalls, had a dirty red bandana around her neck and a seaman's cap wedged onto a mass of curly hair. Her face— makeupless, an almost perfect oval, with unruly eyebrows and a ski-jump nose—was smudged with diesel. She looked like a movie star acting the role of a tramp. And she didn't look too displeased at Jocco's thank-you. Gave Roxy one swift, appraising glance before turning her eyes ahead to the business of steering the boat under the Friedrichs Bridge.

Jocco at least had the courtesy to look a little abashed. "Roxy, this is Betsy. I was just congratulating her on her brilliance."

"Is that what you were doing?" Roxy replied. "Charmed," she added, holding out a hand.

Which Betsy ignored, only grunting while she turned the wheel. They moved from light into dark as they passed beneath a bridge arch.

"Betsy speaks no English, I am afraid," Jocco continued, as Roxy lowered her hand.

"Well, I'm sure we'll get along fine." Roxy turned to him. "Where's my gear?"

"In the back there. Under those tarps."

"Thanks." She stepped out of the wheelhouse, adding, "You two kids be good now."

As she moved to the stern of the boat, she heard them start up again, her querying voice, his soft answers.

She found her gear, such as it was—her satchel and her valise which held her few clothes; flying trousers, boots, shirts, spare dresses. She looked around, at the banks of the Spree, the city passing by. The boat moved fast; they were already nearly under a second bridge, the vast bulk of the cathedral on her right. She needed to change but didn't really want to go back and ask the captain where she could. Shrugging, she lifted the dress to her hips—then noticed Ferency sitting with his back to the bulk of the painting. He was watching her keenly.

"Hey," she said, "care to give a girl a little privacy?" He shrugged, made a pretense of looking away. She sighed, and stepped into her trousers, then hoisted them up and over her stockings, before pulling the dress over her head and laying it on top of her case. She put on the cleaner of her two shirts, though it was a narrow choice, then pulled on her flying jacket. She'd be warm for a while, but she'd be grateful for warmth soon enough, up in the air. If all went to plan. After rolling her dress, she shoved it into the suitcase. She'd press it when she got to somewhere civilized. Herr Bochner would be annoyed, but nothing to be done.

"Hey, Mr. Chameleon," she called. "Know where we are?"

"Berlin."

"Funny. Do you know the city?"

"I live here three years. From 1929 to—"

"So?" She gestured to the bank passing fast to their right. "Where are we?"

He squinted. "This area we approach is called Treptow. There is a big park—"

"Treptow. Heard of it. Beyond that there's another park, uh, Plant-something."

"Plänterwald. Isn't it a little late for sightseeing?"

"How will I know when we reach Plänterwald?"

He looked ahead. "The river widens. A—how you say?—narrow land comes in from the left."

"A promontory?"

"Perhaps. Opposite its tip is Berlin Island. You will see a church on that, a square tower. Just beyond is Plänterwald."

"How long?"

"I am no sailor—"

"Guess?"

He shrugged. "Fifteen minutes?"

"Good." She looked at the draped painting he rested against. "Why did you bring that back here?"

"Spray at the front. Excuse me."

He rose, gave a curt bow, then moved back toward the wheel-house. Roxy sat on the least dirty bollard she could find and pulled on her boots. There was a breeze off the water that cooled her a little, but she was still hot. She leaned out over the side, peered ahead, scanning for landmarks. Fifteen minutes, the forger had said, but she couldn't relax. Not yet.

It was nearer twenty before she noted the yacht coming out of another body of water to her left; saw the sunlight reflecting off a spire to her right, on an island. It was time to act.

She walked to the wheelhouse, stuck her head into the doorway. Jocco was perched on a shelf, his long legs dangling. He'd changed back into civvies too. Betsy glanced at her, grunted something, then put her gaze forward again.

"We gotta make a stop," Roxy said.

"No. There is a toilet below here." He gestured to a small doorway behind him, some stairs.

"Not that kind of stop." Roxy stepped into Betsy's eye line, spoke in her clear German. "We have to pull in to the Plänterwald dock."

"What?" The blue eyes swivelled to her. "No," she replied, "we make no stops."

"Roxy?" Jocco came off his shelf, took her arm. "What is this nonsense?"

"You'll see. Just pull over to the dock."

She said it without any edge. But Jocco took his hand away as if he'd been burned. "No. You know the plan. We go straight to Templehof. If things go wrong and they somehow discover the fake—"

"Plans change," she said in English. "And if we don't stop, you'll have to change them again, because you're going to have to fly the plane out. I won't do it."

"You must. I cannot leave now." Jocco's eyes narrowed in anger, his strong jaw set.

She leaned into him, lowered her voice. "This is part of my deal. Take it or leave it."

He noted the look in her eye, one he recognized. "But why this stop?"

She smiled. "You'll just have to wait and see."

They held each other's gaze, neither blinking—until he did. "We pull into Plänterwald." Betsy started to speak. "We pull in," he said, and pushed past Roxy to leave the cabin.

Roxy grinned. "He's got such a temper, don't you find?"

"No English," Betsy said, sourly. But Roxy thought Frau Fromer understood well enough.

Two minutes later, Betsy was spinning the wheel, heading for a dock. A small ferry was just pulling away from it, filled with families out for a day's fun. Roxy moved to the bow, scanning the crowd on the dock. She spotted Herr Bochner straightaway, because, unlike the gay, summer-clad crowds around them, he was dressed drably in a heavy coat and wore a hat. Frau Bochner had to be one of the women near him. Relief flooded her. So many things could have gone wrong. But they'd made it.

She stood tall, started waving. It took him a while to spot her, but when he did, Herr Bochner gave her one short wave back.

Jocco came to stand beside her. "What is this? Who is that man?"

"His name is Bochner. He made the dresses."

"What?"

She turned to him. "I helped get his wife released from Sachsen-hausen concentration camp. I promised I'd fly them out."

"You did what? Fuck, Roxy! You take this risk?"

"A small one, considering what we've just done." She tried for a joke. "C'mon, Jocco, you know the score. Always go for a mixed cargo. Guns. Rum. Bruegel. Refugees."

He did not smile. "But no one is released from such places."

"She was. I used your dollars well." She smiled, squeezed his arm, held on to brace herself as the boat bumped into the car tires set into the dock wall. Betsy shouted something. Shaking his head, Jocco grabbed a rope, leaped off and wound it around a thwart.

The boat steadied and Roxy jumped off. Bochner was moving to her and they met at the dock's edge. "You made it," she said, then peered past him. "Where's your wife? Washroom? Let's get her. We gotta go."

She went to step around him. He raised the arm that held the small case he carried, blocking her. "She is not coming," he said.

"What?" Roxy went cold. "That sonofabitch cheated you? Then we need to—"

"No, Fräulein." He swallowed and lifted eyes she now noticed were swollen and red. "My Marthe is dead."

There was no corpse before her. Yet the sensations that came were almost the same as when she saw one. The world's noises almost all gone, a high-pitched whine in their place. A pain in the stomach as if something had kicked her, taking her air away. She looked up and saw that Bochner was still speaking, but she couldn't make out the words. Though from somewhere distant she heard her name being called insistently. She managed a breath, tried to focus on what the tailor was saying.

"What?" she said. "Stop. What?"

Herr Bochner closed his eyes. "She died in the camp."

Roxy staggered, clutched the man's arm to stay upright. Because it hit her now, what she'd done. She'd sought to save a life. But by trying to strong-arm the guard, she'd killed Frau Bochner, almost as directly as if she'd held the gun.

The world fully returned on the thought, the terrible thought. Jocco hissing her name from the boat. Tears squeezing between the tailor's reddened eyes. "I killed her. Oh God, this is my fault."

She still held his arm, the only thing keeping her up. Now he reversed the grip, took hers. "No, no. Marthe died last week. I got the official letter. Influenza."

She shook her head, trying to clear it. "So that scumbag—"

"He was trying to get money. He knew I would not know yet."

Anger focused her. "That bastard. What can we—"

"Nothing. We can do nothing." He shook his head. "I thought to stay, to punish him when he came for more money. Maybe . . ." He shrugged, a helpless gesture. "But I am not them. I am not a murderer. And I thought of my daughters in Belgium, orphans if I did. So I came alone."

"Roxy!" Jocco's voice, his hand on her other arm. "We have to go now. Police are coming."

She looked. Two policemen were indeed walking down the wharf toward them. So she let him help her aboard. Bochner followed and a moment later Jocco cast off. Betsy pulled away fast and they were soon in midstream.

Roxy found she was still unsteady, lowered herself to sit on a hatch cover. Bochner joined her. They sat for a long moment, unmoving, until the tailor took her hand.

Quite soon after the Plänterwald, a waterway opened from the river to their right. A canal, Roxy knew, though the name had slipped her mind. Bochner supplied it. "Der Britzer Zweigkanal," he said. "Where are we—" His brow unfurrowed. "Of course! It leads near to Templehof, the airfield, ja?"

"That's right." It was Roxy's turn to frown. "Though, a canal has locks, right? How long will this take?"

"Locks?" When she'd explained the word, he said, "No. This canal has no locks."

"Good." Roxy found she didn't want to move just yet. Or speak. She realized with a sudden, intense clarity that all she wanted, all she needed to do now, was to fly.

The canal was narrow. There were times when they scraped sides with boats that came the other way, or the slower cargo barges they had to pass. The crews on those, and the strollers on the towpaths, glanced at them as they went by. An occasional greeting was called, to which Betsy always grunted a reply.

The canal entered a wider basin. Lots of boats were there, mainly barges, lined up on the dockside. Workers unloaded vessels. Jocco went to the prow, and beckoned to Roxy. "Templehof is over there," he said. "Do you see the cranes?" She nodded. "Hitler has ordered a massive expansion of the airfield. It is one large construction site. It is how we planned to get the painting in. But now?" He looked past her to the refugee, hesitated. "What happened here?"

She told him fast. Her hope. Her failure.

"Roxy, what were you thinking?"

She swallowed. "I wasn't. I was . . . I thought I could help and I just . . . just screwed things up."

She looked away. After a moment, she felt him touch her shoulder. She turned into his arms.

"You care, Roxy. You pretend you don't, but you do." He put a hand on her hair, stroked. "And you have had this success. We will get him out."

He kissed the top of her head, then moved away. She watched him go, watched as he picked up a rope. Jesus, she thought, startled by the sudden force of it. I love this guy.

Jocco jumped onto the dock and swiftly secured hemp to metal. "Quickly now," he called, reaching down as Roxy helped Herr Bochner up and over the gunwales. Ferency appeared from the rear, struggling with the painting in its grey shroud. She helped him too. Jocco took the painting and set it down on the dock, then hauled her out by one hand, her other clutching her life's possessions, all in one small bag.

"What now?" she said.

"This way."

He bent over, lifted the painting and moved off. She and Bochner followed. "Hungarian not coming?"

Jocco didn't stop. "He waits with Betsy. They both wait for me. I return here after you take off."

She stopped, looked back. "Good luck, Mr. Chameleon," she called.

Ferency didn't reply for a moment, simply stared at her. Then he said, "Have a safe flight, Miss Loewen," before turning and moving away.

Betsy was not in sight. Aw, Roxy thought, no fond goodbyes? Still, if she'd lost Jocco to another woman, she'd probably be less than gracious too.

She caught up with the two men at the gate out of the small dock. Beyond was a line of trucks, freight from the barges being loaded onto them. Jocco, having set down his burden for a moment, hoisted it again and strode to a truck at the far end. It was smaller than the others, an outsized van, open backed, with a lot of house painter's junk in it—cans, brushes, stepladders, paint-spattered sheets. He carefully lowered the painting into it all, stood back and stretched.

"Herr Bochner, we will have to cover you back here. You will keep very quiet, yes?"

"Yes."

"Roxy, you will ride in the cab with me. You have your papers?"

"I do."

"Then let us help your friend in."

There was nowhere in the back that could be comfortable, but Roxy folded some of the tarps for padding and placed them in one corner. Herr Bochner slid in. Roxy covered him with a couple of sheets and helped Jocco build a ramshackle nest of paint tins, buckets and stepladders around him. "Not for long," she whispered, then jumped down.

"What?" she said, to Jocco's amused look, as she climbed into the cab.

He shook his head. "Roxy Loewen. Always for the little people."

"Well, you guys with your revolutions and your wars always forget who you are fighting for." She jerked her thumb over her shoulder. "It's for him." She slapped the dashboard. "Now, drive. I've been on the ground way too long."

Jocco pulled his truck into a line of them, all heading slowly away from the wharf on a narrow road that soon joined a bigger one. They followed, heading toward the cranes. They passed a shiny new sign, which sported a swastika and a picture of happy Teutonic workers labouring on the ground while planes flew off in all directions overhead. "Templehof Field: Gateway to the New Reich."

There were two gates ahead admitting traffic. One had a smaller line. Jocco pulled into the longer one. She raised a querying eyebrow. "Watch," he said in reply.

She watched. The other line may have been smaller, but it moved more slowly. Three guards came out and poked around the bed of every vehicle. While at the head of theirs she could see a man in uniform, waving papers wildly at the driver of a cement truck, who just kept shrugging.

"And watch this," Jocco said, hitting the horn.

He started a fanfare, an orchestra of discord, high and low, staccato and stately, a crescendo of sound that first froze the gate guard ahead, who turned and stared, slack jawed, and then started shaking his fist with one hand while shoving the papers back at the cement driver with the other. The man climbed into his cab, accelerated away; the next pulled up and was even more cursorily dismissed. With Jocco and some of the others still plying their horns—the orchestra had switched to a more free-form jazz style—a swifter appraisal of papers and goods continued. Their line moved. It was only when they were one back that someone at the other gate noticed and Roxy saw an officer—her lessons in collars and cuffs back at the museum telling her his rank was lieutenant—emerge from the hut and start toward them. As he did, the truck ahead pulled away and Jocco was on.

"Well, friend," he said, "what crime did you commit to land the worst job in Germany?"

The guard had to be in his late fifties, his pudgy features slick with sweat. Thick white hair, revealed when he took off his cap and wiped his brow on his sleeve, lay dank on his head. "It's the truth, friend. Five hours I've been standing here. No cigarette break. Everyone angry. It's the shits."

"It is good and necessary that the state banned trade unions, of course," Jocco said. "But it's a pity that some of our protections went with them, no?"

The man's eyes, shifting between the approaching and now-shouting officer and the tooting line of trucks, focused on Jocco's for a long few seconds. "A pity indeed." He glanced once at the papers Jocco held, once more at the bed of the truck, then looked again at the officer, in range now and making his displeasure known in a stream of foul language. Slapping the roof of the cab, he said, "Proceed, comrade."

As the officer strode up, swearing, Jocco pulled away. "Comrade?" Roxy asked.

Jocco gave a swift grin. "When Hitler took power, there were nearly as many Communists in Germany as Nazis. We'd killed one another for years—now they'd triumphed. But they couldn't kill all of us, or throw everyone in camps. Who would work in their factories, build their coliseums? The leaders, yes. The workers?" He shrugged. "They adapted. They took jobs if they wanted to survive."

"You knew the guard?"

"No. But friends did."

On the other side of the fence, several roads diverged and progress was faster. The whole area looked like some kid had spilled his toy building set. Trucks were parked higgledy-piggledy everywhere; piles of stacked wood and twisted mountains of metal wire lay scattered about. They drove toward what Roxy recognized as a control tower, standing proud of the chaos. "That's not what I remember it looking like," she said.

"It's not the one you saw," he replied, swinging the wheel left at a junction. "That one is."

She peered ahead. A smaller tower was there. Jocco's words confirmed her memory. "Separate runways. One for freight and one—" he turned again onto a slip road, making for a big hangar "—for passengers."

They pulled in at its side. Roxy looked anxiously all around, didn't spot *Asteria* where she'd left her. "There," Jocco said, leaning across her, pointing. "I called ahead, told them to prepare her. You go speak to the mechanic. I will deal with the papers."

She gave a happy little cry and stepped out of the cab, then remembered. "Are you all right?" she asked, leaning over the truck-bed wall.

Herr Bochner's reply came, muffled. "I am all right."

"Not long now."

She moved away, trying to stop herself running. "Hey, baby," she said, laying her fingers on the Lockheed's propeller blade, "how you been?"

A young mechanic in overalls as dirty as his blond hair and face appeared from under one wing. He had sullen eyes, a tic in the corner of the left one. He was chewing gum. "Yours?" he asked in German.

"Mine," she replied, in the same tongue.

He had a clipboard under one arm, which he now flourished. "Instructions were to perform only a top overhaul. I have done so." He re-ticked each item on the checklist, telling how he had inspected every valve, screen and rod, replaced all the spark plugs and two piston rings. He was mechanical, precise—and yet there was a tension to him Roxy couldn't quite understand. But then she decided that she must just be giving him her butterflies. They'd returned to her stomach and, like her, all they wanted to do was fly.

The mechanic coughed abruptly, and thrust the clipboard at her. "I am sorry, uh, what is your name?"

"Jürgen," he replied, as if doing her a favour.

"Thanks for all you've done. Will you help me start her?"

He looked away, to the control tower. "Okay."

She climbed up through the cabin hatch, hung her jacket and slid into her seat.

The ignition switch was on Off. She set the gasoline switch to On.

"On," she called. As Jürgen turned the propeller slowly, she pumped the primer three times, then shut the primer valve and opened the throttle a touch.

She could see the mechanic's hands on the propeller.

"Contact?" he called.

Roxy flipped the magneto switch to Both, then repeated, "Contact!"

She saw the propeller swing fast through, heard Jürgen cry "Clear!" She turned the magneto booster fast.

Asteria breathed into life. She could hear immediately that Jürgen, although he was taciturn, had done good work. The engine moved smoothly, no knocks. She took the revs up to 550 per minute. Within half a minute, the oil pressure gauge began to register. All was well, and she advanced the throttle, took the rpm up to 1,000. The engine would need to run like that for ten minutes.

She flipped open her hatch window. "Thanks, Jürgen," she shouted.

He stared at her for a long moment, then pivoted and walked away.

She sat back, felt the hum passing through her like an electric current, charging her up. Closed her eyes and smiled.

"Hey!"

The shout brought her from her reverie. She looked back down the cabin. Jocco had his head thrust through the hatchway.

"All good?" he called.

"All perfect," she replied. "Mechanic was a bit of a pill but . . ." She rose, went back. As she went, she noticed a foot-square steel box that hadn't been there before, against the plane's right side. Saw that someone had scrawled *Ersatzteile* across it in black pen. "Spare parts." A good mechanic would include a box of what a pilot might need for running repairs. Jürgen, for all his grouchiness, was clearly one of the best.

Jocco had pulled the truck up close to the plane, its rear facing the stairs. He got out and looked around, then pulled down the truck's back flap. She grabbed her valise and threw it in the hold. Then came the painting. Jocco rested it on the edge of the hatch, Roxy held it there until he could climb up. He brought it up near the cockpit, strapped it tight into the side wall to the pilot's right, just in front of the spare-parts box. "Quickly now," he said, and jumped down. Roxy followed.

Bochner blinked into the bright sunlight. He was stiff and Roxy helped him up the steep, narrow stairs. The Lockheed had been fully adapted for cargo, but there was a row of four webbing seats down the left side. She lowered one and strapped the tailor in. When she turned, she saw that Jocco sat in the co-pilot's seat.

She flopped into hers. "Joining me?"

"You know I hate it when you drive. You take too many risks."

"Ha!" She grabbed his arm. "Damn! We have to go back to the gallery. Now!"

"What? Why?"

"The Braque painting. I left it there. It's worth five grand."

"Heh," he said, shaking his head. "What do you take me for? A thief?"

They laughed. Then both fell silent for a time. "Did we do it?" she asked finally.

"Nearly. You remember all I have told you."

"Yeah, yeah. Your father meets me at Liège Airport. He's bribed the airport personnel—"

"Shh!" Jocco glanced back at Bochner, though there was no chance of him hearing above the engine's purr.

"I'm sorry, Jocco. I just had to."

"Always for the little guys, Roxy."

"Not always," she said, reaching for him. "Sometimes I like the big guys too."

The kiss was long, fervent. It sent a different shudder through her, along the same currents the engine had opened up. Both made her glow. She broke away. "I mean it—why not come with me?"

He pulled back. "I cannot. I have things to do."

She raised an eyebrow. "Things to do like Betsy?"

He shook his head. "No. Betsy and I are long finished. Besides—" he grinned, shaking his head "—I think you would actually kill me."

She ran her fingers along his chin. Then she lifted them away and slapped him lightly. "Better believe it," she said. "Hey, didn't I need to show a passport or something?"

"The manifest says it is me who is flying. And only for a sightseeing tour over Berlin. With so many tourists here for the Olympics, it is most common. It is why we are at the end of the passenger terminal. They are overworked, so they do not check so much. Put on your helmet, lower your voice—they will not be able to tell."

"Well then." There were so many things she wanted to say and no way to say them all. So she put her fingers on his face again and pushed. "Get outta here already. I gotta fly."

He levered himself out of the seat, paused to stare down. "I see you in Brussels in three weeks."

"Don't be late." She reached back to her satchel, pulled out her flying goggles and helmet, and slipped them on. Her flying jacket was on the hook beside her seat where she'd hung it. She shrugged into it, began buttoning. Looked up. "You still here?"

He nodded. She knew he knew that she hated goodbyes.

"Be careful, Roxy." He glanced back at the painting. "Don't fly too close to the sun."

"Me?" she replied, then shooed him away. She followed him to the back hatch, pulled it shut, locked it and returned to her seat. Opening the throttle to full, she murmured, "Let's go, baby," and leaned out the window. "Chocks away?" she called loud.

"Chocks away!" he shouted.

When she saw him step clear, she pushed the throttle a little way forward, and the plane began to taxi. There was only one plane ahead of her, an older Boeing 80-A. It had twenty seats, each one was taken by tourists, no doubt. Just as she pulled in behind, it must have received clearance, because it lumbered forward and swung onto the runway. She pulled a little farther forward, and watched the departing bird for clues as it took off into the wind. Satisfied, she reached for the radio and switched it on. Someone—Jürgen, no doubt—had already tuned it to the correct frequency.

Guttural German came from her headset, clear enough to understand: "Lockheed 227. Mark 3A DDD, you are cleared for takeoff."

She growled a "Received. Out." And replaced the radio.

The plane before hers had made it look easy. She glanced at the windsock. It showed a light wind blowing nearly straight on. She taxied to the runway, then turned into it, advancing the throttle steadily, increasing her revs. The engine dropped into a throaty roar.

As she built speed, she pushed the stick forward to lift the tail wheel, then eased it back. The Lockheed had a light load—a Bochner and a Bruegel. So she hit the right speed fast and smoothly pulled the stick. At two hundred feet she glanced at her compass. Liège, her destination, was only two points off due west and about 360 miles away. With this load, a full tank and this purring engine, she could fly her top speed all the way and be there in just over two hours. This time, with Jocco's advance in her pocket, she was going to check into the best hotel. She'd have a steak brought to her while she bathed. They wouldn't even have to cook it.

Her heading took her back over the airfield. She was probably three hundred feet up as she passed, low enough to see the dock, with Betsy's barge still there and what looked like Jocco's truck pulling up. Then she thought she saw a body of uniformed men moving toward it—but the low cloud she entered took away her sight.

She shivered. It was probably nothing, just her nerves. Besides, Jocco was a big boy, and he'd take care of himself. Her part of the deal was taking care of *Icarus*. All their futures depended on that. She glanced at the compass again and headed west.

About an hour and a half in, the clouds had gone and she could look down on the big industrial sprawl of Cologne. Beyond it, a river widened; she'd found the Meuse. Follow that and it would lead her straight to her destination. She could almost taste the Scotch.

She heard a faint popping sound. A scream reached her a second before the smoke.

Whipping around, she saw flames. They were just behind her, on the right side of the plane. Herr Bochner had unstrapped himself and was beating at them with his coat. His efforts only seemed to spread them. That, and the accelerant she could smell—gas, stingingly sharp. "Leave it!" she yelled. "Strap yourself in!"

Roxy pushed the stick forward. She knew only one thing. Flames on a plane meant she had to get to ground—quick.

She glanced back. Bochner was strapped in again. But before him, the flames were spreading from their source—that box of spares, all consumed now. They reached and dissolved the shroud over the painting. She had a sudden sense of Icarus plunging to his death; of Daedalus, his father, screaming his anguish.

She touched the parachute under her seat but knew she could never use it. It would mean death for Bochner.

She'd closed her throttle, about all she could do to sustain her glide, which was still way too fast. She tried all she could to slow it.

The ground had to be close. She turned and screamed "Brace yourself!" even as the first wheel struck. But for a brief, terrible second she didn't turn back. She could only stare at the painting, fully revealed now, dissolving in fire. She saw Daedalus; saw that instead of a father's anguished scream, this Daedalus's face revealed only a wild and triumphant glee. And seeing it, she knew in a moment what Ferency the forger had done; knew what Jürgen the mechanic had done. Knew what betrayal was.

The second wheel struck. Opening her throttle wide and pulling hard back on the stick, she tried to jump over the barn that was suddenly, certainly, there.

PART FOUR

ZEPPELIN

SEVENTEEN

LETTERS

Eight months later. April 16, 1937. Hazelhurst Manor,
Northamptonshire, England.

HEY, KIDDO! WHAT TROUBLE YOU IN TODAY?

Roxy closed her eyes. She didn't actually need to read her friend's letter again. She'd gone over it so many times since its arrival one month before she thought she had it by heart.

"And where are you now, Amelia?" she murmured.

She opened her eyes. Clutching the letter, she stood, wobbled a little, then crossed to the wall opposite her bed, and the map of the world that was on it.

She'd borrowed woollen threads in two colours from Nurse Watkins. A short red one ran from Oakland, California, to Honolulu, Hawaii. A pin thrust into the island had a tiny scrap of paper wrapped around it to form a banner, neatly printed: *March 17: begin first leg. March 20: crash.*

She moved her eyes and her mind to better words and a brighter colour. Blue   this thread crossing America from Oakland to Miami. Because her friend wasn't going to let a bump in Honolulu stop her plans. She'd fixed her plane and changed her mind.

Amelia Earhart was still going to fly around the world, but now she was going to do it eastward.

Roxy looked down at the letter. Not because she needed to remind herself of the route and the timings, but because, in her friend's tight black letters, she could feel Amelia in the ink, her excitement transferred from heart to hand:

If my mechanics and me get the Electra all tickety-boo, we'll be in Miami the third week in May. Puerto Rico, Venezuela, Surinam in short order. I want to be in Brazil by June 5. Then it's the short hop to Senegal.

Typical Amelia. Two thousand miles of Atlantic, fourteen hours in the air, another continent . . . a hop?

Roxy studied the map again. She was glad she'd picked blue thread for the journey. The wild blue yonder. That was what Amelia was chasing. What they were all chasing. Though the straightness of the threads was misleading. You didn't fly straight across jungles—you zigzagged; found the best strips, where the best mechanics were. It all took time. But her new bird, the Lockheed Electra, was a twin-engine beauty, the most modern in the air. Her navigator was Fred Noonan, and there was none better—if he could keep off the sauce. He'd zig and zag her down those blue, blue lines.

Roxy ran her fingers along the map, along the threads, intoning the names: "Chad. Gulf of Aden. Karachi. Calcutta, Bangkok. Java. Darwin. New Guinea . . ."

She trailed off. The last blue line went across the vast Pacific to join up where it all began—Oakland, California. But a pin split it near the middle, thrust into an expanse so empty she'd had to draw a circle and mark the name that her friend had given her.

"Howland Island," she said loudly, as if saying it loudly made it more real. It was maybe two miles long. And even if two Coast Guard vessels would be cruising around it, signalling like crazy, Roxy knew that finding that speck was not the breeze Amelia made it out to be.

Roxy looked down to the writing again. To the part that always blurred her eyes a little. The part where even Amelia Earhart had her doubts:

> *But you know, even if it's tough, there'd be no point doing it if it wasn't. So I put my faith in God, in the Coast Guard, in the Lockheed Corporation, in Fred, in my husband and in every blessed mechanic and airstrip maker along the way. And in myself, as one of the founding members of the Ninety-Nines. Because a woman's going to do this first, kiddo, not a man: fly around the equator. Around the whole damn world. When I'm done, that's what they'll remember me for. Though, knowing you, you'll find some way to eclipse me yet, eh?*

Roxy could hear Amelia's laugh as she wrote that.

> *So you get better fast, ya hear? And meet me in Oakland. I'm going to start a flying school when I get back—and I'll need you around to demonstrate to the students what not to do! Do you think you could ever handle an actual job?*
>
> *Yours, aye, and ever affectionately,*
> *Amelia*

Roxy's eyes blurred again. She pressed a hand to the wall, took deep breaths and waited for the nausea to pass. When it had, she looked at the map again.

If Amelia Earhart can make this amazing journey, Roxy Loewen can make one too, she thought. It was much shorter, it was nearby and she wouldn't even need a plane.

She was going to walk across a roof.

Ten minutes later, Roxy stood on the roof of the house, wondering if she'd ever been more scared.

She could think of a few occasions that came close. That time when her yacht had capsized off Montauk, she'd been thrown into the frigid ocean and, as usual, had failed to put on a life vest. Or when the Italians bombed the airfield in Malco Dube and she'd lain in a hole six inches deep and eaten dirt for an hour. Or eight months before when she'd tried to land a plane that had turned into a flying, flaming spear.

Nope, she thought. This is worse. Because those other times had happened *to* her, so she could only react. This time she was doing it to herself.

Go back inside, she told herself. You're not ready. She reached to her neck, where her rabbit's foot should hang. That too had been burned in Belgium, destroyed. Perhaps I need to get another one before I try something like this, she thought.

She was leaning against the windowsill anyway. All she had to do was slide back in. She raised her hands to each side of the frame.

And yet, it had taken all her willpower to get herself to this point. If she went back in, she wasn't sure she'd ever make it out. And if she never made it out, she'd never beat this. Fail to beat it and she'd never fly again.

She heard it, faintly, high up. She raised her eyes, swayed and gripped the sill. Distance was still a problem—more than a problem. But through the motes that danced in her vision, she could see the plane, flashing silver in the clearest of April skies. It wouldn't hold still long enough for her to identify it. The engine's sound told her it was small, possibly a fighter. Hurricane, she thought. There was a base not far away. Dr. MacPhilips had suggested they motor over one day, he could introduce her to some of the pilots. She'd always put him off. It was hard enough thinking that she might never fly again, without meeting flyers who knew they would never stop.

Sunlight on metal made her suddenly nauseous. She retched, looking down, and closed her eyes. She opened them slowly. Focus, she commanded herself.

It stretched out ahead, her pathway. A line of bricks, crown and apex of the tiled roof that sloped steeply away either side. She knew that to her left was the gravel courtyard, the main entrance to Hazelhurst Manor. To her right, the garden where she'd been spending more time now that the season had changed. She looked at neither. Looking down from a height was even worse than looking up. But looking straight ahead?

She'd learned a brick's dimensions. An English brick was eight and a half inches long, Dr. MacPhilips had told her, puzzled by the question. Yet since he considered her psychologically as well as physically damaged, he'd answered it.

She focused again on the bricks. They were horizontal to her. So she had a pathway eight and a half inches wide. The bench she'd been practising on, which she'd nearly mastered—only slipping off once in the last week, and that because someone had burst into the rehab room—was not quite six inches. So here she had more than two and a half extra inches to work with. Though the bench, of course, was only two feet from the ground, not fifty.

Time to go, Roxy thought, and released the ledge behind her.

She felt her feet solid beneath her. Breathing slowly, she stared at just one brick, the one a pace ahead of her. Inhaling deeply, she raised her right leg and covered the brick with her foot. There was another brick the next pace ahead. She stared at it for a long moment, then placed her left foot on that.

She supposed that if she began to sway, she could turn and hurl herself at the open window. She thought she might make it, and the sudden temptation to try was strong. Instead she thought she'd look longer at the brick, three away from the one her left foot was on. This one looked newer, was more yellow to the others' red, the mortar around it less weathered. Hoping that a more modern bricklayer had done as solid a job as his eighteenth-century forebear, Roxy stepped.

Nothing shifted. She stood carefully, breathed easier. There was something about being beyond sanctuary that eased the mind rather than the other way around. It was kind of like when she'd first tried stunting. Once you committed yourself to a barrel roll or, worse, the falling leaf, you had no choice but to stick to theory. Listen to the engine. Move the rudder bars and stick correctly, use the throttle judiciously, and hope that it would work out. It always had. In the end, it was a matter of will. Here, there was that faint sea surge of blood in her ears; her legs were her controls and her will was the same, urging her to the next brick, the next step, the next after that . . .

She was holding the frame of the other window. She grinned into the glass, saw her lopsided expression—the plastic surgeon had done a wonderful job, but he hadn't quite been able to centre Roxy's smile. Then, through the window, she noticed Nurse Watkins, the thread donor. She was fashioning perfect hospital corners on a bed. Glancing up, she saw Roxy and screamed.

Not long now, she thought, so she turned around and, instead of focusing on bricks, focused on the window opposite and walked straight across to it.

The shout came on her fourth traverse, halfway back to her point of departure.

"What the bloody hell do you think you're doing?"

Since she'd been expecting him, she paused, swayed only a little, then moved forward again. "My exercises, Dr. MacPhilips," she said, "just as you ordered."

She smiled as she neared the wall. She could hear the curious rumblings and grunts that usually preceded one of the good doctor's eruptions. As if he was building enough phlegm, which would overflow like lava.

Spit and sound came as she reached the window and turned: "For Christ's sake, girl," he bellowed, "are you trying to kill yourself?"

She had thought of doing so the day the doctors first told her that her flying days were over. Vestibular disorders, they'd declared. Severe. The medical people might one day get her back onto her feet without nausea. It would be the limit of their ambitions and nigh on a miracle if it happened, given the extent of her injuries. Flying? Impossible.

Once she got past the weeping and gradually got them to reduce the morphine dose they had her on to near zero, she thought about how she'd always hated that word, *impossible*. And proving them wrong might be a better choice than killing herself. Anyway, she'd reasoned, she could at least try the first option. The second would always be there.

"Hello, Doctor." She smiled across at the red-faced physician. "Care to join me for a stroll?"

Her cockiness, as usual, was nearly her undoing. Halfway across and maybe moving a shade fast, she put her left foot on a brick edge and it slipped off. Nurse Watkins's yelp and the doctor's curse came loud as she windmilled her arms. But balance returned, her foot found solidity, she sank down and gripped brick. Only for a moment.

She rose and carried on. When she reached the window, the doctor grabbed her. "You are crazy, girl," he grunted, relief warring with fury on his face.

"It has been noted," she replied, and smiled as, with a strength unguessed at in a small and wiry Scotsman, he pulled her off the roof and into the room.

∾∽

MacPhilips tried to ground her. But since she was at the hospital as a voluntary patient, that was difficult. He threatened to call in a psychiatrist and have her sectioned. Roxy just sweet-talked him, as she always did. The doctor had three daughters about her own age. He was a sucker for female persuasion.

"Besides, Doc," she said, sitting on the edge of his desk and swinging her legs, "didn't I just prove that I am cured? You're a genius."

"I am not. And neither are you." He took off his glasses, placed them on the desk and stared at her. "Disorders such as yours are never fully cured. Your skull—" he waved over his shoulder at her X-rays on the light box "—was fractured in two places. The vestibular system was compromised. The best one can hope for is a retraining of your body and mind to overcome the symptoms related to your loss of balance, using the exercises we have devised here at Hazelhurst and others gleaned from specialists around the world. Work on eyesight, on the somatosensory system, on—"

"Somato tomato, Doc!" Roxy loved Dr. MacPhilips, but once he started, he could talk for hours on subjects that made her dizzier than her disorders. "Didn't I take a big jump forward today?"

"A jump that could have ended in a life-ending fall, Miss Loewen."

" 'Roxy'! I keep telling you."

"Roxy." The doctor leaned forward, his stern manner slipping away. "You are my patient. I don't wish to see you rush at this and perhaps set yourself back. This is a steady progression we are exploring here."

"Steady? I've been here five months."

"And remember the state you were in when you arrived. You couldn't stand, you could barely speak. Our psychiatrist diagnosed you as severely traumatized. Not to mention the burns—"

He broke off, and Roxy sighed. She knew what she'd looked like. The flaming plane had caused second-degree burns on 60 percent of her body and third-degree on part of the left side of her face. Fortunately, the hospital in Belgium where she was treated after a week in intensive care was a centre for plastic surgery. Many soldiers from the trenches had been treated there, and the doctors applied the same techniques to her. Straight on, she didn't look that different, unless someone really remembered her smile. If she turned sideways, though, the scar tissue was more obvious because of its smooth shininess.

But it was the hair that stood out most. Once it finally grew back, it came in entirely white. It's also a terrible cut, she thought, running her hand over the thick white hedge of it. First thing I fix when they let me out of here, if I can raise the dough.

It was this consideration that had pushed her into accelerating her treatment. Hazelhurst was expensive and the money Jocco had given her hadn't lasted long. Dr. MacPhilips and the staff had ignored her account for quite a while now, but they wouldn't be able to for much longer. An administrator was poking around, querying things. She'd overheard a blazing row between the man and MacPhilips on the subject. She needed money. To earn money, she needed to fly. It was the only thing she knew how to do. To fly she needed her balance. It was that simple.

She turned and looked again at the doctor. As usual, when she switched sight from middle to close distance, it took a little time to bring him into focus. When she had, she saw the concern still there. And it was as if he'd read her mind.

"I would feel I had failed you if I had not restored more of your functions. That will yet take some time. So do not be concerned about money. I will talk to the powers that be. Arrange something."

"Doc Mac, you are the tops." She slid off the desk. "But you and I both know my time here is up."

"Damn pencil pushers," MacPhilips muttered. "Well, I will delay them at least till the end of the week. Say I am trying out new techniques on you. Now, young lady, you will go to your room and practise your vision exercises for the next half hour. And you are to go nowhere near that roof again. Is that clear?"

"As glass, Doc Mac."

She wanted to get to her room without touching the walls. She managed it with just one slump and lean. The roof walk was already paying dividends.

There were various alphabet letters stuck around her room at different heights. She stood in the room's centre and focused on one *A*. She kept it in focus as she moved her head from side to side, up and down. When she felt tired, she glanced down to rest her eyes on the plain grey coverlet of her bed. Which was when she noticed the envelopes.

There were two. One was marked with an American stamp and bore the return address of Herr Bochner, in Brooklyn. The second . . .

She refocused. Noticed the lines first, the crossings-out. The letter had followed her through the various hospitals from Belgium to Hazelhurst. She bent closer, and her name came into focus. And she recognized the handwriting.

"Jocco," she breathed. She sat on the bed, laid her hand on the envelope and closed her eyes.

The hope that he'd write had left her in stages. First there was the terror of that last glimpse from her bird over Templehof: his truck by the dock, black-uniformed men moving toward it. Had Jocco been arrested? If he had, he'd be tortured. He was a well-known Communist, after all. After that, they'd probably kill him. The thought had tormented her days and nights. Once she could write again—it took three months—she'd written to his father. There had been no reply. She'd tried twice more. Nothing.

As she recovered her strength, her spirit came with it. Her fears receded and she thought: What if he escaped? He was always good at escaping, had more lives than a cat. In which case, he was in hiding. He had friends all over Germany.

Lately, she'd settled again into her uncertainty. She would never know until she regained as much of her balance as was possible; got a bird and took to the air. She'd meet him, up there somewhere. As a ghost or a gunrunner. Because one thing was for sure: if Jocco Zomack was alive, he'd be flying. He loved it with a passion that matched hers.

She looked down. The first postmark on the letter was from Germany and was dated March 16—one month before. But the sending of the letter could have happened months after the writing of it.

There was only one way to find out. She slipped her thumb under the flap and drew out a single sheet; when she unfolded it, a newspaper clipping fell out. But Jocco's distinctive copperplate was scratched across the page:

My Love,

I hope this finds you, and finds you well.

I learned about the crash. I only now learned that you survived, and the hospital where they took you. That is why it has taken me so long to write. Now I must be quick. Today my friends are getting me out of Germany. I have been in hiding since the theft.

Ferency betrayed us. You will suspect this. He switched the second fake for the real painting and that's what you flew with. He was working for Munroe, and Munroe was working with Göring—a devilish alliance. Munroe got the painting; Göring the fake and 200,000 Reichsmarks. But our enemy wanted more than that, so he must have paid someone to plant the bomb on your plane.

She'd reached the end of the page. That mechanic, she thought as she turned it. Jürgen.

By the time you read this I will be on my way to Spain, continuing the fight against Fascism. If you are recovered and have discovered an appetite for this fight, you could find me there. Yet I know for you, battles are always personal. So I have enclosed something that may be of interest. I think it is offering you a choice.

Roxy glanced down at the folded piece of newsprint. She looked back at the page in her hand, waited for her eyes to refocus.

My advice, though, is to forget Munroe. In the world now, the capitalist oppressors hold the power. But it is the system itself that must be fought. Individuals will be dealt with when the revolution is complete.
Go well, my comrade. I will see you again at two thousand feet.

Jocco

Unlike the rest of the letter, written in his exemplary handwriting, his signature was a little ragged. Maybe, unlike the cool phrasing, when he actually came to sign, he was overcome with emotion?

She closed her eyes again, and dropped the letter. It had begun with "My Love" and ended with "my comrade." But what had she expected? A passionate declaration? Not Jocco's style. The only time he wasn't playing the revolutionary was when he was playing the lover. Perhaps she'd hoped that if she got him alone again, she could persuade him to give up one of those identities. It was crazy, she knew, even as she thought it. Africa, and all they'd been for each other there, was a long way away now. They'd needed a dangerous backdrop for their love, flying in, seizing moments, taking off again. Till the next snatched moment, lit by tracer fire.

And yet . . . Spain? She'd read the newspapers, about the vicious ongoing civil war there. The rebels under Franco were heavily supported by his Fascist buddies, Hitler and Mussolini. The Republican forces, increasingly Commie, were backed by Joe Stalin in Moscow. Munitions were supplied to both sides by gunrunners and governments.

And both sides were getting airplanes. It was common knowledge that German flyers flew for the rebels. The Condor Legion, they were called. The Republicans had guys like Jocco from nations all over the globe. Guys . . . and gals?

She read the letter again. Behind the call to arms, did he want her to go? Did he understand their natures as well as she did? He'd find her a plane, something she'd not be able to afford on her own. He'd find them a bedroom. He'd roll her one of his special cigarettes.

She picked up the news clipping.

Someone—Jocco, perhaps, though it wasn't similar to his letter style—had written across the top: "*American Gazette*. Berlin, March 10, 1937." Just above a photograph of a man on some steps.

The man was Sydney Munroe.

AMERICAN LEARNS HIS GERMAN LESSONS

As she read the headline, Roxy flushed hot.

After nine months in Germany, the American businessman and millionaire Sydney Munroe is going home.

"It has been a real eye-opener spending time here," says Munroe, 59, from Albany, New York. "I have been so impressed with the energy and enthusiasm of the people, and the acumen of their leaders, in both the business and the political worlds. Germany is thriving because of sensible political policies and the encouragement of industry to do what it does best: make money. I am hoping to take many of the ideas of National Socialism—that last word I used to abhor, by the way—and persuade my own government to adopt them.

The US could certainly use some help to get it out of its current mess."

When asked if he himself intended to run for office, however, Mr. Munroe was coy. "People always ask—and I don't entirely rule it out. For now, though, I intend only to run my businesses. This includes some exciting new adventures in art. In my time here I have managed to purchase several incredible works from Germany's finest contemporary realist artists as well as some choice historical ones."

The *Gazette* inquired if he was taking the leisurely way home, by boat.

"Certainly not! I am too excited to get home fast and begin work. So I will be travelling in that other great German gift to the world, the good Zeppelin *Hindenburg*."

The *Hindenburg* departs from Frankfurt for Lakehurst, New Jersey, on May 3. Of course we shall be sorry to see such a good friend leave us. But Germany's loss will, perhaps, be America's gain.

Roxy read the clipping twice more, calmer each time. It wasn't the absurdity of a self-aggrandizing, gaseous windbag like Munroe running for office that struck her most, or the pro-Nazi posturing. It was the talk about art. Because she was certain about one thing: if he was only now returning to the USA, he would not be leaving his prize behind. Munroe might be going first class on the *Hindenburg*—but Bruegel would be travelling storage.

She sighed. What did Jocco mean that he offered her a choice? Spain? Or did he mean America? Pursue Munroe back there. How the hell was she meant to do that? Also, she hadn't been home since she'd left so precipitously in 1929. Eight years of exile.

She shook her head—never a smart thing to do, as she'd get dizzy, as if her brain was a little loose in her skull. She looked down, focused on the coverlet again, waited for the whirring to pass. And then she saw that the envelope wasn't empty.

She reached in and pulled out a folded piece of card.

It took her a while to understand what she held. It wasn't that her German was all that rusty. Besides, when she looked closer, she could see that most of the writing was also in English, French, Spanish and Portuguese. It was the word that stuck out, its first letter a capital *Z* in blue. A word she'd just read in the newspaper article.

Zeppelin.

It was only when she glanced down that she realized what she held.

Billete. Bilhete. Contrat de passage. Ticket.

Beneath that was a passenger's name: Madeleine Lille. Beneath that, the name of the ship.

Hindenburg.

She was holding a ticket for the Zeppelin. And the date of departure was the same date as Munroe's.

She laughed. "Jocco, you old—"

That's what he'd meant by a choice. But was it also some kind of test? Follow him to Spain and rekindle their love? Follow Munroe aboard the *Hindenburg* and . . .

She was thinking too far ahead. Either choice was insane for a girl who could barely walk and was totally broke.

She moved to the chest of drawers and opened the lowest one. Her satchel was still there, blackened with smoke and singed from the flaming crash. Herr Bochner had pulled it out when he'd pulled her out.

It contained all she had left. She'd smoked the cigarettes, injected the morphine when the Belgians hadn't given her enough. What remained was her Luger, her derringer and her IDs. Two weapons. Two passports.

She took the bag back to the bed, sat and pulled out her US passport. It had just over a year to run. The photo in it was of the younger her, during her "bottle blonde" phase. The second passport was French, had three years left, and this photo showed her in full Gallic pout. Madeleine Lille was the name she'd chosen. The document had gotten her over borders where the American passport would have caused problems. It was the name Jocco knew she travelled by.

In the back of the passport was a ten-dollar bill. Her worldly wealth. She'd stared at it for ages, hoping it might multiply. It wouldn't get her very far. And a *Hindenburg* ticket without cash was just paper. Ten dollars might get her to the coast of England if she was lucky, never mind the rest of the way. Besides, she couldn't board the cruise liner of the air in the only clothes she had—nurses' castoffs.

Through all the pain of her rehabilitation, every operation, every exercise, Roxy had rarely cried. But she thought she might cry now at the cruelty of the two choices Jocco had offered her, because she didn't have the means to act on either of them.

Her hand was on something. In all the excitement and tragedy, she'd forgotten about the other letter, from Herr Bochner.

She sniffed, then ran her finger under the flap. She needed cheering up and the old tailor had always succeeded in doing so in the three previous letters he'd sent her. Perhaps he felt that was his job, because he didn't dwell on what still had to be his terrible loss: the death of his wife. Instead he was enthusiastic all the time, with life a succession of miracles to him. They began when he'd walked away from the plane crash with nothing more than bruises. Continued with a cousin sponsoring him to come to the US, where another relative found him work straightaway in a high-end design house.

He had embraced everything American. He watched the Brooklyn Dodgers play every Saturday, munched his kosher hot dogs, cheered on "*die* Bums." In his last letter, he'd told Roxy that his daughters would be arriving very soon from Belgium.

She pulled out the pages, prepared to be cheered with that news.

But like Jocco's letter, this too had an enclosure. As she unfolded the sheets, something fell onto the coverlet. A separate envelope. She opened that and withdrew a single piece of paper.

It was a banker's draft, made out to her. And it was for three hundred dollars. More than what she'd given to Herr Bochner to bribe the guard to free his wife.

Roxy did start to cry then, careful not to get any liquid on the draft. Because now she had the money to go wherever she wanted. Though, she thought, as she wiped her nose, there really was only one choice, and one way to travel.

One step at a time. Brick by brick.

EIGHTEEN

ZEPPELIN

"FRÄULEIN LILLE? FRÄULEIN LILLE?"

Roxy was distracted by the mirrors in the Frankfurter Hof's ball-room. They were vast, gilt framed, opulent, as befitted one of Europe's finest hotels. They were also vintage, which meant that there was significant corroding and some distortion of her reflection. Either that, or she truly wasn't looking her best. Her mirror image seemed to accentuate the side of her face where she'd had the plastic surgery. Her hair, dyed midnight black now, had looked reasonable in the cut she'd gotten in London before catching the night train from Victoria Station. But tossing and turning all night on the narrow bunk had sculpted it into strange spikes. That, together with the dark glasses she wore for her new-found light sensitivity and her extremely pale skin, gave her a ghoulish quality. What was that German movie she'd seen, the last of the great silents? *Nosferatu*? That was it—she was one of the Undead.

She looked up. Aside from the customs officials in their uniforms, there were two other men standing by, scanning the passengers, appearing uncomfortable in their dark suits. Military or police, she guessed, posing as civilians. They returned her stare and she looked away.

The whisper came from right beside her. "Excuse me! Miss? Isn't that you?"

She turned to the whisperer. She couldn't remember his name, though he'd introduced himself just two minutes before. A fellow Yank, she knew that, though he had a German name. Hans? Wolfgang?

He was jerking his head, indicating the table about ten feet away before which they sat. She looked and saw the official in his tight black uniform beckoning her. "That's 'Frau Lille' to you," she said, rising, moving forward to sink again into the chair right before the customs table.

"'Frau'?" The officer lifted her passport and peered at it. "It is written here—"

"I know, I know! But 'Fräulein'? At my age? May as well call me 'spinster.'" She beamed at the official. "Know anyone round here who might care to change that status?" She glanced at the youngest of the two military men in mufti. "How about you? You married, sweetheart?"

The man just stared back before turning to whisper to his colleague. The customs man waved at her. "Please to take off your glasses."

She took off her glasses. She'd been smiling in the photographer's store near Victoria Station when the picture was taken, so she smiled now. She'd rather the guy focused on her face, not the photo. She wasn't sure she'd done her usual bang-up job replacing the old one.

He studied her for a long moment before closing the passport and handing it back. Then he nodded to a uniformed porter standing to the side, holding a small valise. "This is all you have?" the official asked.

There hadn't been a lot of time to shop in London—she'd arrived at noon and had had to be on the night train by eight. She'd hit Harrods and bought a few items, but they weren't up to Bochner standards. "And this," she replied, putting her satchel up. He frowned at the burned canvas, the dirt. Shaking his head, he opened it and tipped it upside down.

"Hey!" she snapped. "Go easy there."

The man just grunted.

Only a few essentials fell out of the bag. Lipstick, compact, her small penknife, cigarette case, a carton of Player's Navy Cut, change purse. A few essentials—and one weapon.

"What is this?" the official said, holding the derringer up by its pearl handle.

"Cigarette lighter."

"This?" He peered at it, turning it every way.

"It's a novelty, uh, a keepsake," she said, praying that he wouldn't attempt to bring forth flame. She'd removed the bullet as a precaution, had that stashed somewhere she felt sure no gentleman would ever look. But the lie could be pretty speedily exposed, nonetheless. "May I keep it?"

"Fräulein, you are going on an airship filled with hydrogen gas. There are no open flames allowed."

"You're telling me I can't smoke?"

"No. Yes, you can smoke. In the sealed smoking room. Using an electric lighter. Everything else—*verboten*." He dropped the gun into a separate cloth bag, with "Deutsche Zeppelin Reederei" printed on the front, before slipping the rest back into the satchel. This he then slid across the table. "Your suitcase will be searched and any other unsuitable items removed and also placed here." He tapped the cloth bag.

"But—" She wasn't happy with the idea of her only weapon being taken away. "If I promise not to use it?"

He shook his head. "Nein. This will be returned to you in America." He gestured to a woman standing at his right. "Now, you will please to go with Frau Gruber."

Watched by the two men she was now convinced were military, Roxy followed Frau Gruber. The woman led her into a curtained cubicle and ordered her to take off her dress, then searched it before running her hands up and down Roxy's slip. She was rough and thorough.

As they exited the cubicle, Frau Gruber nodded, and the male officer rose, clicked his heels together and handed her the passport. Even managed a smile. "Enjoy your flight, Fräulein Lille. Heil Hitler."

"Yes, indeed," Roxy replied, grabbing her satchel. The young American man she had spoken to earlier was waiting there. "Your turn," she said.

"Oh, I've already been. I was just waiting for you and wondering if you wanted to travel on the coach to the airship together."

He smiled bashfully and she looked at him a little more closely. Tall, about her age, floppy hair, a wide grin, blue eyes behind bifocal glasses, tweed suit. Willie, she remembered now. He was a little Ivy League for her tastes. But since her sole plan so far was to keep a low profile and surprise Munroe only once they were in flight, when neither would have anywhere to go, she realized she might stand out less in a couple.

"Let's," she said, linking arms.

Willie grinned and led her through the revolving doors—he was one of those who liked to go two per cubicle—and onto the second of the two coaches that waited beyond, just as the first one pulled away. They were seen aboard by another uniformed guard.

The coach was nearly full—she'd been one of the last examined. But keeping her head down as she made her way back, she could not see Munroe anywhere. The size of him, he'd be kinda hard to miss. First coach or . . .

Please, she thought, don't tell me he's changed his plans. She knew she didn't have a solid one, not yet. She just trusted that since God and Jocco had placed them on an airship together, something would come up. Odds had a way of evening out and she was owed some luck.

They found seats near the back. The coach was just starting to roll, when the two soldiers in poor disguise ran up. One hit the side, the driver opened the doors, they came aboard and then the vehicle moved off again.

"Those guys?" said Willie, pointing with his chin. "They must be security of some kind."

"Think so?"

"Yeah. I've been on Zeppelins twice and never been searched before. Bags, yeah, but everyone seems a little more on edge. Hope nothing's up."

"Like what?"

"I don't know." He pushed his glasses up his nose. "You gotta figure there are some pretty crazy types around in Germany right now."

"You mean someone might try to sabotage the airship?" When he only shrugged, she laughed and said, "Well, thanks a lot. I'm nervous enough about my first flight without that."

"Oh," he said quickly. "I wouldn't worry. Germans, right. Too efficient to allow that to happen." He smiled. "Where did you say you were from again, uh, Madeleine Lille? French name, right?"

"French father. French passport. US born and raised. You?"

"Philadelphia. German parents. Though I live in DC now."

The short journey to the airport passed in a swift exchange of information. Hers was all false, the story she'd made up to go with the passport. His sounded ordinary, a little dull—commerce degree, rich dad, in paper. Then again, she thought, he could be lying too.

She looked away as the bus stopped a short time later under a sign that read FLUGHAFEN: FRANKFURT AM MAIN. It always gave her a little lift, an airport. She sought out the window for a plane, any plane. She saw one landing in the distance, but once through the gates the coach was driven at speed past several buildings and finally into a hangar that was larger than any she'd ever seen. Which was necessary, she supposed, as gasps arose all around her from adults, kids, old and young, bound together in wonder. Because this hangar also housed the biggest bird she'd ever seen.

The *Hindenburg*.

Roxy couldn't help her own gasp. She knew her aerodynamics, the physics of flight. So how the hell anything as huge as this could ever get into the air was beyond her. And she'd seen it in the air, at the Olympics opening ceremony. On that occasion, though, it had just been up above; she didn't know how high; there had been no way to contrast it with anything. Here, people moving about below it looked like ants beneath a giant slug. A locomotive engine was opposite her, near the behemoth's tip—and it resembled a kid's toy. She was good at calculating distance—she needed to be for some of the landings she'd made in less than ideal circumstances. So now, as she stepped down from the coach steps, she didn't look up any more but along. Reckoned that the fuel truck to her left was one hundred yards away—a football field. The set of stairs even now being wheeled up to a gantry near the ship's aft was another gridiron away, perhaps a little more. "Two hundred twenty yards long," she murmured.

"You doing the stats?" Willie had followed her out, and stood beside her now. "They do metres here, of course, but you're close. Two hundred forty-five metres makes, uh, about 268 yards. Or eight hundred feet." He pointed. "The diameter is 41.2 metres. That's, uh, uh—"

"One hundred thirty-five feet." She looked up at the height, whistled, then smiled at his surprise. "Oh, I do metres. Have to when—" She broke off. She'd decided to keep her flying, and everything else personal, to herself. "When you're raised partly in France," she explained, then looked back up. "So that makes it about, what, ten storeys high?"

"Uh-huh. Quite something, ain't she?"

"Sure. Apart from one thing—there's no possibility that something that size could ever fly." She shuddered. "So I'm not going on board."

"On board it gets even better." He grinned. "You just wait till you see her on the inside."

Roxy didn't have to wait long. She and Willie joined the mob of passengers—mainly older, mostly men, a few women, and there was a family with younger boys. Munroe was still not among them.

Willie touched her arm, and they headed toward the set of stairs just being driven up to meet those lowered from the ship. Despite the encouragement of the attendant, she felt strange stepping onto them, leaving the ground—she, who would pilot anything, eagerly, without a qualm. Truth was, she never much liked being flown. And in something so unfeasible . . .

Then she forced herself to remember why she was there. Who she was there for. This wasn't a jaunt; it wasn't about pleasure in any way. She was there for her enemy. What she would do about him she hadn't figured out yet. She just assumed that the answer would be somewhere at the top of these metal stairs. Where Munroe was.

She was wrong. She realized it when she reached the platform and glanced back before entering the body of the ship. A Hispano-Suiza J12 roared into the hangar. Laughing at its wheel was Hermann Göring. Grinning back at him was Sydney Munroe.

The flight attendant urged her on. But Roxy didn't move, only stood and stared as the two big men levered themselves from the vehicle. The Reichsmarschall was dressed as if for hunting, in a cap with pheasant feathers in the band, a grey jacket with leather shoulder patches, and tweed trousers. A white linen suit swathed Munroe's bulk. The two men shook hands, slapped each other's backs, and the impression of Tweedledum and Tweedledee returned. But she couldn't find a smile now. Nor could she find that place inside where her courage usually lay. The sight of Munroe, the memory of all he'd done, all he'd meant to her and her family over the years, made her dizzy.

"Shall we?" said Willie, offering his arm.

"Gladly," she replied, taking it. Turning away from the two monsters, she entered the belly of the third.

Five stewards in white coats and black ties awaited them. A sixth man, in a dark suit, was speaking as she and Willie came onto the platform within the hull. His English was clear, lightly accented. "... accompany you to your cabins, where your luggage has already been placed. Once you are situated, we encourage you to unpack, and make yourself at home, as you say. Very shortly a steward will come by to explain about the cabin. Again, my name is Chief Steward Kubis." As someone spoke, he raised a white-gloved hand. "Please, Captain Lehmann has indicated that he wishes to make a speedy departure. Save all questions for later—perhaps over a nice glass of chilled Riesling in the salon, ja?" He smiled. "Tickets, please."

The passengers shuffled forward. All were asked again if they had any lighters, though none did, those having been taken away at the hotel. Cameras were also confiscated.

"Air regulations," murmured Willie, handing over a Leica. "They are given back once we pass the three-mile limit beyond Frankfurt. Germans don't want snaps of the air base being built."

Having no lighter and no camera, Roxy held out her ticket. It was studied and handed back. She took a step after the other passengers up the next flight of stairs, but Chief Steward Kubis halted her. "You are on this deck, mademoiselle. The B deck," he said, his French as flawless as his English. "We added these cabins only this year and they have several advantages. Larger, and they also have windows to look out from, as they are on the side of the vessel, not in the centre, as above." He glanced down at her yellow-stained fingers. "Also, the smoking room is on this deck, if mademoiselle and monsieur are smokers."

"Mademoiselle sure is," she replied. "Not sure about monsieur."

"Oh. I am sorry, I—" Kubis looked at Willie's ticket, adding in German, "Ah, apologies, sir. It is A deck for you."

"Come again?" Willie replied in English, putting a hand behind his ear. "German name, no German. Got 'A deck'—that's about it."

The family and she were the only ones who were bound for B deck. As Willie headed up the stairs, he called back, "Drink later?"

"Drink soon," she answered, and followed the white coat of a younger steward around a corner and down a corridor. Her cabin was the fifth down, opposite the WCs. The steward opened the door for her, and said, in heavily accented French, "I will return in a moment, mademoiselle." Then he took the family on to the end of the corridor.

She went in, closed the door behind her and leaned against it. If this was a larger cabin, what the hell size was on A deck? It was perhaps a hair bigger than the train compartment she'd taken from London. About seven feet deep, five and a half across. The walls were lined in pearl-coloured fabric. No bunk beds like on the train, but a single to her left, running along and flush to the outer wall; her suitcase was on it. She flung her singed satchel beside it. What gave the sense of more space was the window, which ran the width of the cabin, alongside the bed. She was startled to look out and see the sides of the hangar passing; she hadn't felt any movement at all. But the chief steward had said that the captain wanted a speedy departure. Within ten seconds, the hangar wall had given way to a different shade of grey—drizzle. They passed a marching band, the men's blue-and-yellow uniforms dulled by the wet. Beside them, in their brown shirts and shorts, was a troop of Hitler Youth. Both troops fell into their ranks and, at a shouted command, began to march beside the ship.

Roxy sank onto the end of the bed. She suddenly felt queasy, and she wasn't sure if it was motion, exhaustion, her ongoing balance problems or the sight of Sydney Munroe. Her course had seemed so clear when she'd read about his return to the States. She was certain that he'd be accompanied by the booty he'd stolen from them. She'd also read the omens to boost her certainty: a ticket for the *Hindenburg* had arrived in the same mail as money from Herr Bochner, for god's sake. But the journey had taxed her diminished strength to its limit. And her faith had waned with the simple sight of her nemesis saying farewell to the second most powerful man in Germany, the man who'd nearly caused her death. Who was she to oppose these guys? And, truly—what did she intend to do now that she was on board? Kill Munroe? He certainly deserved it, for her father's death alone, for all the pain he'd caused since. But she'd had that chance in a Madrid cellar and hadn't taken it. Roxy knew that she was not a killer. A thief, though? She'd helped steal the Bruegel once. Could she steal it again? It didn't seem likely. Seeing how she could barely lift herself, she wasn't sure how she would manage that hefty slab of wood. She could recruit—her new friend, Willie, appeared taken with her. But enough to be her accomplice in grand larceny while she kept him at arm's length?

A knock. "Come in," she called.

Her young guide—he couldn't have been more than nineteen—put his head around the door. She'd spoken English so he replied in the same, which was better than his French. "Is all clear with your cabin, miss?"

"Uh, not really."

He took her on a swift tour: the basin, with its hot and cold taps; the narrow closet, curtained off on the corridor side, with a rail from which she could hang her dresses. There was a fold-down writing table. "The shower is opposite in the corridor, but I should warn you it is not so strong and it is on a timer. The yellow light goes off and— *phft!*—the water stops, no matter how much soap you have still on your head. On this deck, at the very end of this corridor, you also find

the smoking room and the bar. Restaurant and lounges are upstairs."
A bell sounded and he smiled. "Excuse me, but I must get to my station for departure. Any other questions you will be kind enough to keep for later? Most passengers meet in the promenade on A deck—" he pointed to the ceiling "—to watch the 'up ship.'"

"'Up ship'?"

"It is the command. It is logical, no?" He laughed. "'Up, ship.'" He turned to go. "Wait," she said, standing and reaching for her purse.

"No, miss. All tips included in your fare. We are forbidden."

"Well, let it be our secret, eh?" she said, and crammed a five-dollar bill in his hands.

He stared at it a moment, then pocketed it. "Auf Wiedersehen," he called cheerfully as he left.

Outside, the band began to play and the Hitler Youth to sing. Some folk song—she didn't know it. She sat again. She could do without Munroe for a little longer. Hell, she thought, maybe I'll spend the entire trip in the cabin and get off quietly at the end. It's about all I have the strength for.

The song changed tempo and mood. This one she recognized: the "Horst Wessel." Jocco had told her that it was named for some thug killed in a street fight with the Commies. The first Nazi martyr. This one piece of patriotism led to the next. From below and, chorused within the structure, she heard the national anthem:

"'Deutschland, Deutschland, über alles' . . ."

It was reprised. It ended with drums and timpani. And then the cheering began. There was no other sound, no motor. There was barely any movement. Except there was, because she looked out the window and people began to recede.

"Up, ship," she murmured.

∾∾

She'd lain down and slept. When she woke, it was past ten, the voyage already three hours in. She still could hear only the faintest purr of an engine. Below, the lights of some city shimmered; the airship was flying low enough and she could see the bulk of buildings.

Waking brought its usual pangs. Once she'd smoothed down her dress—which did about as much for the wrinkles as her fingers did for her crazy hair—she slipped into her shoes, grabbed her purse and followed the corridor. Quite soon she came to a small room on her right. There was a counter, a man in a white jacket. He was wielding a cocktail shaker. "Madam needs a drink?" he inquired.

What she most needed was nicotine. But alcohol sounded good too. "Can you make me a Rusty Nail?"

"Of course. Which whisky would madam like?"

"Johnnie Walker, if you've got it. And shaken, straight up."

"Lemon twist?"

"Sure. Where can I smoke? Here?"

"No, madam." He pointed to another door. "This takes you to the airlock. Close it behind you before you open the next door. No leaking hydrogen to get through to fire, yes?"

"Does hydrogen leak?"

"Never. But we do not take this chance." He finished shaking and poured white frothy liquid into two stemmed glasses. "I will bring your drink," he said.

Roxy opened the door, stepped into the small space and closed the door behind her. There was noise from beyond the next one, a party heard through a thick wall. When she opened the door, that sound exploded, and though she was craving a smoke, she was almost overcome by what hit her.

She entered a head-height cloud. She didn't know how big the room was since she couldn't see the other walls. Big enough, she realized, as there were at least half a dozen pairs of trousered legs over stools. A few were unoccupied and she took a step toward one.

The door opened behind her. The action swirled the smoke as the bartender walked in, and he parted it, heading toward the vacant stool she'd spotted. On the other side of the stool was a table and banquette, currently occupied.

"Hello, Roxy," said Sydney Munroe. "I've been expecting you."

NINETEEN

NEMESIS

THOUGH SHE TRIED NOT TO SHOW IT, ROXY WAS STARTLED. Not by him—she knew Munroe would be on the *Hindenburg*; it was why she was there.

But how did he know she'd be aboard?

Yet the man she turned to now, sitting next to Munroe, did surprise her, and she couldn't help showing it. She had the sudden urge to grab the heavy ashtray and dash it into Ferency's face.

She didn't. Instead she picked up the frothy drink the bartender had just put down and threw it at him, glass and all.

The Hungarian jumped up, shrieking fury in his native tongue. Conversations at the other tables stopped.

"Lover's tiff," Munroe called, causing laughter, reaching a vast hand to pull Ferency down beside him again. "Drinks on me for the disturbance my young friends have caused." As the hubbub returned, he continued, softer, "Of course you know each other, don't you? And please, won't you sit?"

"I don't sit with murderers and betrayers."

"Oh, you mean the explosion in the plane?" Munroe *tsked*. "I was angry about that. My friend here acted . . . precipitously. I was so relieved when I heard you'd survived." He beamed. "Indeed, Roxy, I have only ever wanted you alive. Alive—and in America. Which now I will get."

"It was not personal," Ferency muttered, wiping his face with a huge polka-dotted handkerchief. "It was . . . business. We needed to destroy the evidence." He looked straight at Roxy. "Once you delivered the painting to Wilhelm Zomack he would discover it was a fake. He would make it an international scandal and all paintings would be closely considered. My swift work, which the Reichsmarschall now possesses, would not have stood up to intense scrutiny. He already knows it is fake. But he does not want anyone else to know it." He put the handkerchief away. "But the bomb was set by an idiot. It was meant to explode on the ground, before you took off. I meant to give you a chance. I would never want to hurt you." His eyes went moony. "You of all people, Roxy."

His lies were as thick as his pomade. But Roxy swallowed her anger. Anger would have its place, as would some form of revenge, that was for damn sure. But there was context here she didn't understand, which was of more importance than her feelings for this Hungarian weasel.

She turned to Munroe. "So you're saying I'm on this Zeppelin because of you? Not how I see it."

"No?" The big man smiled. "Did you never think to question why your lover suddenly wrote to you? And with such a strange offer?" He gave a little chuckle. "I must admit I thought you were smarter than that, and that it would not work. But my young friend here convinced me otherwise. Said he'd observed you with this Zomack. And do they not say that love is blind? " He chuckled again. "Sit, Roxy, please. You look like you need to."

She didn't want to give him the satisfaction, but she had to hear this, about Jocco. There was no question he'd written the letter she'd gotten. Now she needed to know why—and what had happened to him next. "So where is Mr. Zomack?" she asked, as she sat.

Munroe shrugged. "I don't know. Spain, perhaps. Once he agreed to do what we asked of him . . ."

"He agreed to betray me?" She snorted. "Sure. Even you don't have that kind of money."

"You are right. Money would never have done it. Your friend has ideals. But suffering?" He smiled. "Even for the toughest man, that can be harder to withstand."

Roxy's stomach did a flip. "Suffering?"

Instead of answering directly, Munroe laid a meaty hand on Ferency's shoulder. "Perhaps I should let my young friend explain the rest. Since he was so involved."

"Well, I'd certainly like to know why I'm being forced to share a table with this cockroach. Why's he even aboard?"

The hand stayed on the shoulder, rubbed a little. "He is my personal art expert and portrait painter. Áttila is most talented. I think he felt you did not appreciate that." He reached for his glass. "But tell Roxy about her lover now. Why he cooperated."

A smirk replaced the glare Ferency had been giving her. "It is simple. He did not know I had betrayed him. So when I was 'allowed' to visit him on Prinz-Albrecht-Strasse—"

"Where?"

"It is the street where the Gestapo headquarters and their jail cells are situated. Zomack was caught at the airfield, after you had flown." Munroe waved a hand. "Sorry to interrupt. Please continue."

Roxy felt bile rise in her throat as Ferency spoke again.

"Your lover had been there a long while when I visited. He was not well. It is not a pleasant place. After six months he was, uh, open to an offer. But they'd broken his right hand—he'd punched too many guards. And they'd done . . . other things to him as well. So it was required of me to forge the letter."

"Why didn't you just do that, and leave him be?"

"We felt that unless he drafted the letter, with all the personal things that only he would know, you would not come."

"I still can't believe he agreed. Or that he wouldn't try to warn me—"

"It comes back to suffering and hope." Munroe leaned forward. "I do not think you understand what the taking away and then the giving of hope can do, even to the strongest man. He dictated, signed—yes, he could do that much—and the Reichsmarschall had him released."

She thought back. The signature had seemed shaky. "That seems out of character for you. Why would you and Göring honour that bargain and let him go?"

"Hmm." Munroe licked his lips. "The Van Gogh landscape his father donated to Hermann's private collection may have helped."

So it comes back to art, she thought. Coupled with torture. And desperation.

The bartender returned, bearing her Rusty Nail and a refill for Ferency. There was an electric lighter on the table. She lit a cigarette. "And why do you think he went to Spain?"

"Is it not where the comrades are mustering?" Munroe replied.

She dragged smoke deep. She still couldn't believe that Jocco had broken, and lured her into this trap. And yet? Munroe was right—suffering and hope were mighty persuaders. And she suddenly remembered the story of his best friend, Reinhardt, and how Jocco had failed to put him out of his misery, left him to be tortured to death by the Italians. No one was there on Prinz-Albrecht-Strasse to do that kindness for her man. He'd broken. But what she didn't understand was why he'd gone to Spain, not come looking for her. How, in the end, he'd chosen Joe Stalin and a cause over her and their love.

She didn't let her hurt show, however. Because there was one other thing she needed to find out. "Okay, so you got me here. Bravo. But why? Why do you want me in the States so badly?" He started to speak, but she rolled on. "You bankrupted my father, and sure, you can probably do the same to me. But what I am wearing is about all I possess. So good luck. And I know you don't like to be crossed. But this, all this, getting me on board—" she waved her hand, circulating smoke "—it seems a little elaborate, even for a spiteful sonofabitch like you."

His piggy eyes narrowed in anger. His voice, though, was calm when he replied. "You would be right. If that was what 'all this' was for. But it is not. It is more of what my friend here just called it. Business." Munroe picked up his cocktail, sipped, then continued. "You are forgetting something, Roxy. Or rather, somewhere." He paused, then added, "Tahawus."

"Where?" Though it rang a bell, she couldn't place it.

"In the Adirondack Mountains. Up near Newcomb, New York. You own land there."

"I . . . do." The words were going to come out as a question. But then she remembered the place. Only just. "Blood Hill," she said.

"Correct."

Munroe was looking smugger than a toad. "For crissake, man, spill it before you explode."

"It's quite simple. I am still your father's principal debtee. His estate must pay off his debts before it dispenses any inheritance. Tahawus is its only asset." He sighed. "I couldn't come after you when you were outside America. Tiresomely, the law demands that such papers are served only on US soil. They will be when we arrive in New Jersey." He smiled. "The courts will rule in my favour, and I will get your land."

"What—a thousand acres of forest? In a depression? What's that going to net you? Two hundred bucks?"

The smug smile spread. "Ah, but you are wrong. You see, Tahawus was once a mining community. Iron. It was abandoned mid last century, because there was an impurity in the ore that made it hard to process. No one knew what it was, but the profit wasn't there because of it." He beamed. "The impurity was titanium dioxide. And it's now worth a goddamn fortune."

"Why?"

"Because it is stronger than steel but lighter than aluminum." He nodded. "It will particularly appeal to you, Roxy, knowing that so much will come from your former land. Because from now on it will be one of the major components in airplanes. To make them lighter, faster. And there will be many more airplanes needed soon, in the war that is coming."

There were so many questions to ask. One struck her—prompted by what she remembered from the newspaper article on Munroe that had accompanied the air ticket. "And would most of this titanium be going to Germany?"

"Well—" Munroe shrugged "—since my friend Reichsmarschall Göring is currently offering the best price . . ."

She remembered it now, Blood Hill. Her dad had taken her up to see it when she was about nine. There was an old miner's cabin they'd made habitable enough for a short summer stay. Loons had cried at night; bears had grunted nearby. A pine marten had snatched bread from her hand. And now Munroe was going to cut down all the trees and open a mine for a metal to be used in building German planes. Maybe like the ones that had bombed that town in northern Spain the week before. Guernica.

Watch out, she warned herself, you're beginning to think like Jocco. And thinking of him, she thought of all the other things that were missing from Munroe's tale, and why she was there.

She sucked in another lungful, then carefully stubbed the cigarette out. There was half still to smoke and habits died hard. Slipping the butt into her packet, she drained her cocktail and stood.

Munroe frowned. "Leaving us, Roxy? Can't I buy you another drink?"

She was sure there was a comeback she could find if she tried. But she knew that the less effort she spent on him, the better she'd feel. So she turned and walked out the airlock door, and closed it behind her on her nemesis's mocking laugh. Caught between rooms, she leaned her head against the exit door and shut her eyes—just too late to trap the tear that fell.

"Oh, baby," she said. "Jocco."

The door opened. The bartender, tray in hand, let out a curse. Keeping her head low, she pushed past him and entered the corridor. Her cabin was just ahead. She could go there and have the good weep she wanted. But she felt a pang of hunger. When had she last eaten? Ten hours ago at lunch. She'd slept through her first dinner aboard. But in the pamphlet she'd been given when she'd collected her ticket, she was sure she'd read something about sandwiches. Maybe they'd be available in the lounges above that she hadn't yet explored.

She went up the stairs. On the landing, there were entrances on either side. After tossing a mental coin, she went right—starboard, she corrected herself—and entered a lounge. It was about thirty-five feet long, about half that wide. On the far side was a promenade, with windows through which she could see the night sky. Several people, singles and in pairs, were there admiring the view. Others were occupying tables, playing chess or cards. To her left, the wall was filled with a mural. It was a map of the world, and showed voyages ancient and new. She saw the names Magellan, Cook, Columbus; designations LZ 126 and LZ 127—other airships, with their routes across the Atlantic.

A young woman in the white uniform of a stewardess approached her. "Good evening, Fräulein," she said, her accent light. "May I bring you anything?"

"Is it true you can get a sandwich this late?"

"It is true. Cheese, ham—"

"Both, please. With mustard. And maybe a, uh, a beer?"

She nodded. "Will you take it here?"

"Is there anywhere less crowded?"

The stewardess gestured to the room's end. "If you go on the promenade, up there you will find the writing room. There are magazines, books—"

"Thanks. I'll take it there."

The stewardess departed and Roxy crossed the promenade, glancing out into the dark, before walking the few paces on. The wall divided the two rooms; a railing continued to the next entrance, a gap a few paces along. She reached that before she noticed the hunched figure. She paused, and sighed inwardly. Only one person was in there, scribbling away so feverishly that he didn't notice her. Willie. Her admirer. She was about to back out, when he looked up and hastily threw an arm over what he was writing. "Madeleine!" he exclaimed.

She stepped in. "State secrets?" she inquired.

He laughed. "Poetry. I have a fiancée, in Washington. She likes stuff like that." He ran his hand through his thick hair. "But I am a terrible poet! No one else must ever see."

"It's the thought that counts."

"Perhaps." He ripped the page off the pad, folded the paper over, pocketed it. He gestured to a chair opposite him. "Will you join me?"

When she'd seen him, she'd thought of getting the sandwich to go. The last thing she felt like, after the recent shocks, was fending off advances. But the fiancée changed things a little. And all she'd have for company in her cabin were her thoughts, and she wasn't sure she wanted to be alone with them just yet.

She sat in the brown upholstered chair. The writing room was small, cozy. On its pale-yellow walls were little paintings, scenes from the world. In one, a Chinese farmer followed a woman toward a temple. In another, in America, tribesmen stood before a teepee, contemplating a sleigh pulled by a reindeer.

He pointed at it. "I went to my psychiatrist and said, 'Doctor, sometimes I think I'm a wigwam and sometimes I think I'm a teepee.' Know what he said?"

She looked at him. She couldn't remember the last time she'd heard a gag. "What?"

"He replied, 'You're two tents.' Get it? Get it?"

She groaned, then laughed, a little harder than the joke deserved. When had she last really laughed? With Jocco, she supposed, and stopped laughing.

Her expression must have changed. "You okay?" Willie's pleasant, open face had narrowed in concern.

"Fine," she replied. Just then the stewardess appeared with a tray. She set it down. On it was a beautiful plate, gold rimmed around a blue band. At the top, an airship floated in a blue globe, the words "Deutsche Zeppelin Reederei" circling it. Positioned beneath was a ham-and-cheese sandwich on rye. Beside it, a flute of pilsner, bubbles rising into foam. She lifted the folded linen napkin and laid it on her lap. "*Dankeschön*," she said to the stewardess, who answered, "*Bitte sehr.*"

As she turned to go, Willie pointed at the beer and said, "I'll take one of those, please, uh, *bitte sehr*?" He looked at Roxy. "Is that right?"

"Just *bitte* when you're asking for something. *Bitte sehr* is 'You're welcome.'" The stewardess nodded, left, and Roxy continued, "What, you're half German and you don't speak any?"

"Nope. None." He shook his head. "My parents left Germany in 1900. All they wanted was to be American, and that's all they wanted for their kids too. No German, not even to each other."

The sandwich was good, but she found her thoughts had taken away her appetite. After three bites she put the sandwich down and sipped her beer. "So, your poem? You going to recite it when you land?"

"No, I've got to spend a week in New York on business before I get home to DC. So I'm going to mail it. Right from here."

"What? How?"

"Didn't you know? They have a post office on board. You can send mail, stamped from the *Hindenburg*. They parachuted a bag down over Cologne, didn't you see?"

"I was sleeping."

"And you could send a telegram immediately."

Roxy arched an eyebrow. "Really? Quite the ship, ain't she?"

"She sure is."

She munched her sandwich again, only half listening while Willie prattled on about the airship and its wonders. Because as soon as he'd said "telegram," an idea had come. The faintest hope of a way out of this mess. Well, the first part of it, anyway: being served papers at Lakehurst Airfield. Because an airfield meant planes, and planes meant flyers—and some of those flyers would be women.

Amelia would be in California, getting ready for her big flight. But Louise Thaden? Pancho Barnes? Any member of the Ninety-Nines? Couldn't one of them fly in to fly a friend in need out?

Roxy took a last bite of sandwich, then drained off half her beer. "Gotta go," she said, standing.

Willie did too. "For a smoke? I saw your cigarettes in Frankfurt. I don't smoke, but I could keep you company."

"No, I'm hitting the hay. See you at breakfast."

He'd looked disappointed but perked up at that. "Sure. I'll save a seat." He stood too. "I think I'm going to see if I can send my fiancée a telegram." The stewardess appeared with his sandwich. "I'll take that to go," he said.

They left together but quickly parted ways. Halfway to her cabin, she realized she'd forgotten her purse in the writing room. She went back. No one was in the room now. But her plate with her half-eaten sandwich was still there. As was the writing pad Willie had been using. Sweet, she thought, poetry for his girl. When had anyone ever written her poetry? Never was the answer. Though there was a certain poetry in the way Jocco rolled cigarettes. And in the way he kissed her.

She sighed deeply and looked down. Willie pressed hard when he wrote; some words were etched on what was now the top sheet. She bent, suddenly craving a touch of love, even someone else's. She sought an endearment.

And found an umlaut.

She couldn't make out the word. But she'd been drawn to umlauts ever since she'd focused on that one on the eye chart in Göring's cellar, just before she put the scalpel to the doctor's throat. So from her purse, she now drew her cigarette case, took out the half-smoked butt, rubbed its ashy end across the page. A word appeared.

Rüstungen.

She understood what it meant. It had been stamped on half the boxes she'd flown in Abyssinia. Armaments. Guns, essentially. But she struggled to understand the word's use in a love poem—and from a guy who claimed he didn't speak any German and so wouldn't know an umlaut from two piss holes in the snow.

She was going to have to watch the jolly Mr. Willie.

She replaced the cigarette, and thought of their last conversation. There was a brochure on the side table, and in the back of it was a small plan of the ship. The post office and radio room were forward, and on B deck. She was pretty sure she wasn't meant to wander down there alone.

Hell with that, she thought. Jersey was three days away and the girls would need some warning if they were going to get her out of this bind.

She left, descended the stairs then walked along the corridor, past the entrance to the bar and smoking room. Opposite it, the clang of pans and plates could be heard, a burst of raucous laughter. Had to be the kitchen. Beyond that, a door half ajar gave her a glimpse of a room with banquettes and chairs. Men—officers, by their stripes— were sitting around, reading, talking. No one noticed her slip by.

Through a little cubicle of an office was a door. Voices came from behind her, down the corridor. She pulled the door open fast, stepped through and closed it behind her. Turning back, she inhaled sharply, and blinked.

She was staring into immensity—a universe of semi-darkness, punctured occasionally by bright lamps like stars. These threw light on a vast web of cables and wires stretching all around the cavernous space. It was almost completely silent. If she listened hard, she could catch the faintest hum of engines. She didn't feel like she was in the sky at all. Up there she was used to roar, wind, storm, a place where you had to shout to be heard. Here it was like a submarine. Or a cathedral. She felt that if she even whispered, it might be a form of sacrilege it was so vast, empty, almost holy.

Except it wasn't entirely empty. Farther along the gangway that stretched ahead of her she could see other enclosed, lit spaces like the one she'd just left. Her map had told her that beyond the water, gas tanks and storage areas to either side were crew sleeping quarters and then both the post office and the radio room. Her destination was maybe two hundred feet away.

She was about halfway there, when she heard the door open behind her. She stopped, anticipating the hail from an irate crew member. But none came. Instead she heard the door close again, then soft footsteps on the rubber-floored gangway. She turned to see Áttila Ferency walking toward her.

TWENTY

THE HUN

THOUGH SHE HAD NO DESIRE TO SPEND TIME ALONE WITH the creep, he had been the last person to see Jocco. There might be something else she could learn. So she waited.

The forger stopped a few feet away. "I saw you come here."

"Uh-huh."

"I wanted to be alone with you."

"Why's that?"

"I can help you."

"Oh yeah?" She raised one eyebrow. "You tried to kill me."

"I did not. I told you that was a mistake. Bad timing."

"Bad for me."

"I am sorry you were hurt, Roxy." He took a step nearer. "Hurting you is the last thing I wish to do." He smiled. "In fact, I want the opposite."

She stared at him for a long moment before speaking. "You have got to be kidding me."

"No." He took another step. "You are a strong woman, Roxy. Clever also. We would make a good team."

"Really? And what game would we be playing?"

"One we both understand." He stepped even closer. "I am excited about going to your country. It is the land of opportunities, yes? And I learned, from our time together in that cellar when I paint, that you do know something about art, and art dealing in America."

"Something, sure. So?"

"So. I paint, you deal." He nodded. "You are—what do they call it—the front? Your father collected, bought and sold, no? You will already have the credibility that, perhaps, a newcomer would not."

"It's, uh, an interesting idea. A gal could always use an income. But you may have forgotten—Munroe has plans for me that may make me kinda notorious."

"He does. But Herr Munroe is not as clever as he thinks. And he does not appreciate art, like you and me. He is only truly interested in the price." He nodded again. "So I help you, yes? When we land in America."

"How exactly?"

He shrugged. "He will be busy. He has something else to think about when we land."

"You mean *Icarus*? The painting is on board?"

"Of course."

"Then how about we smuggle both me and him off this bird?"

"It's possible. Anything is possible. If we are a team."

She took her lower lip between her teeth, studied him a moment. "Okay then. We're a team. Why not?"

She held out her hand. He covered it in both of his. "But how can I be sure, Roxy? How can I trust you? Only one way." He closed the last inches of gap, till his face was a hand's span away. She could smell his breath, spearmint on gin, and his floral aftershave. His voice dropped lower. "It was torture in that small hotel. The walls so thin. Hearing you and that . . . that Communist together. He was a brute. But you, ah." He sighed, squeezing her hand. "You were raised to be with gentlemen. Especially a gentleman who appreciates what a woman like you needs."

The stench of him. Those lidded eyes full of lies. He'd tried to kill her, whatever he claimed. She'd seen the expression of joy he'd painted on the face of Icarus's father. He'd hoped she'd see that as she crashed in flames. For one moment, she considered still stringing him along, in case she could use him on arrival. Just for a moment, though—that one before she took back her hand and slapped him.

He staggered, shock and fury warring. Then he hissed, "You stinking little bitch!" and came for her.

He snaked one long arm around and pulled her to him hard. She'd thought he was a tall reed, frail. But he was stronger than he looked and she was weaker than she'd been. She tried to swing her knee between his legs, but he pushed her back against the guardrail; and raised a hand to cover her mouth, palm concave so she couldn't bite. He pressed his body hard against her. She tried to slip free. But she could barely breathe; her head throbbed. She was still not fully recovered, and though she tried to reach, grasp, twist flesh, she couldn't free her hands. She thought she was about to faint. And she had a pretty good idea what Ferency would try if she did.

A door opened somewhere. Someone yelled and immediately Ferency stepped away, as a pounding came along the gangway that made it shake.

They both turned to the approaching men—two, Roxy could see through the film over her sight. There were others behind.

"What are you doing here? What is happening?"

It was the chief steward, Kubis. She focused on recovering her breath, while Ferency blustered, "This lady left the bar. I thought perhaps she had a little much to drink. Then I saw her come the wrong way. I followed to . . . to help her. I think she fainted."

Kubis turned to her. "Is this true, Fräulein Lille?"

Breath had returned; the mist had cleared from her eyes and from her mind. There was her, and all these guys. Had he actually been about to rape her? Well, one thing she knew—guys believed each other. If she claimed rape, there'd be denial, questioning, lies. Her word against his. Perhaps Ferency would reveal who she really was, and that she didn't need. Besides, she thought, taking a deeper breath, she owed this guy. Even more so now. And the way to pay him back was not to give him a chance to wiggle out of this. The way to pay him back was when she had him alone. With a weapon in her hand.

"Yeah. Came over a little blurry. Sorry." She stood away from the guardrail. "Phew. Better now."

She could see doubt in the chief steward's eyes. He looked between her and Ferency again. Then he shrugged and said, "No one is allowed here without a guide. Why are you here?"

"I wanted to send a telegram. Still do."

"For this you must make an appointment. In the morning. Tell the purser."

"Oh, please. It's urgent."

She lowered her head, opened her eyes deliberately wide. They had their effect. He sighed. "It is okay. Only this once, you understand. But you do not tell your fellow passengers."

"Our secret, Herr Kubis."

She was led on in the direction she'd been heading, crewmen staring then dispersing as she approached. Ferency was escorted the opposite way. She'd glanced at him before he turned. He looked smug again. She supposed that since she hadn't ratted him out this time, he might think that left him free to try again. Well, she'd be ready next time.

Kubis showed her into the radio room, bowed and left her to the operator. She saw that they had both a short- and a long-wave transmitter. For a moment she was tempted to try to track Louise Thaden down, speak to her direct on long wave. But the time it would take and the chances of finding her or any of the other girls were slim. Morse was the better system. It was guaranteed to get through.

In the end she wrote down a simple message and got it sent to the last address she'd had for the Ninety-Nines:

ROXY ON HINDENBURG STOP SAME DEAL AS CURTISS FIELD
TWENTY-NINE STOP FAST BIRD REQUESTED STOP

If Louise didn't get it, one of the other girls in the association might. She felt her name alone would set off alarm bells. Anyone who knew it would remember her precipitous departure eight years before, and read between the dots and the dashes. Then, she hoped, they'd be standing by for a speedy getaway.

The telegram went. She was escorted back to her cabin. Her heart had settled—and it had been a pretty busy day. She lay down and was asleep in moments.

And awake faster. Hard to sleep through the insistent knocking. She staggered up, threw on a gown and opened the door.

Three men were standing there: Kubis, and the soldiers in plain clothes who Willie had spotted earlier on at customs. The older one of the two, with greying temples and greyer eyes, spoke straightaway, English in a German accent.

"How long have you been in bed, Fräulein Lille?"

Roxy rubbed her eyes. "I don't know. What time is it?"

"Three thirty-five a.m."

"I went to bed at eleven."

"Can you prove it?"

"Well, there's no one in here to testify, if that's what you're asking." She opened the door wide. "See for yourself." The younger officer peered around the door, checked, shook his head. "What's going on?"

"We are looking for a passenger. A Hungarian by the name of Ferency."

At the end of the corridor, a door opened on the larger cabin there. Two dark-haired boys glanced sleepily from under their father's arm. The older officer saw them. "Please," he said, waving Roxy back.

She didn't budge. "Gentlemen," she said, "my reputation."

The officer turned to Kubis. "You will stay here. The door will remain open."

"Yes, Colonel."

Colonel, eh? Roxy thought, stepping aside. She went and sat on her bunk. The two men loomed over her. Quietly, the colonel spoke. "My name is Colonel Schreiber. Luftwaffe Intelligence. This is Lieutenant Kloff."

"How can I help?"

"This Hungarian passenger. Witnesses say that earlier this evening you two were found either in an embrace or a confrontation. Can you tell me which it was?"

"I could. If you can tell me why it matters?"

"Why?" The colonel glanced behind him. There was murmuring now in the corridor; Kubis's voice raised to reassure. The colonel continued softly.

"Because Áttila Ferency is not missing. We know where he is. He is in his cabin. He has been murdered."

TWENTY-ONE

SUSPECT

THOUGHTS TUMBLED THROUGH HER HEAD.

She had no love for Ferency. The bastard had attacked her. Before that he'd tried to kill her. He was—had been—traitorous scum, and good riddance to him.

But murdered? That meant there was someone else on board who also hated the Hungarian. Or who wanted him out of the way for some reason. Her mind leaped to Munroe—though the forger had been his new pet and ally. Also, Munroe wasn't the kind who would do his own killing. He could have an ally on board, though, a hench-man to do the dirty work. Though why get his victim on board the *Hindenburg* before killing him? It didn't make sense.

Not much did at 3:30 a.m., seven hundred feet up in the air, after she'd been jolted from sleep. She needed a moment. The two officers had crowded into her room, while the steward kept guard at the door. "Listen," she said, "I'd be happy to answer your questions." She drew her silk gown tighter around her. "But not in my lingerie."

The colonel swallowed. "And we do not wish to disturb the pas-sengers. So you will accompany us to a place where we can talk?"

"Then, I'll get dressed."

"Quickly, if you please. The lieutenant will wait with you while you change."

He stepped out, but his subordinate didn't budge. "Does he have to wait inside?"

"He does. And you will bring your passport."

He closed the door behind him. The lieutenant—he looked like he'd stepped off a Nazi recruiting poster, with his shaved head and a duelling scar on his cheek—regarded her till she arched an eyebrow at him and he turned away. She changed fast, into faun slacks and a blouse. A glimpse in her mirror revealed her night face as a blizzard of white cream. She grabbed a towel, wiped that off and went to work. The officer turned, *tsked*. She ignored him. If she was going to be interrogated in the middle of the night, she might as well look reasonable. She ran lipstick over her mouth; dabbed some rouge on her cheeks, and a hint of shadow behind her eyes. Applying the makeup also gave her time to look at herself in the mirror and think. How much did they know about her? Would they already have questioned Munroe? Would he have revealed who she really was? Unlikely. He wanted her on US soil so he could get her served, get her into court. She'd come aboard as Madeleine Lille. She'd better stick to that. Speaking of, she thought. After checking that the lieutenant was still looking the other way, she took out her American passport and tucked it into the elasticated top of her slacks. Chances were, they'd search her room, and she didn't want them to know who she really was. She could only hope they wouldn't frisk her as well.

There was little she could do with the mess that was her hair. She merely wrapped a scarf around it, picked up her purse and said, "Let's go."

He led her back down the corridor, past the now-silent bar and smoking room, the kitchen. There she was ushered into the room she'd noticed earlier, the nicely furnished one. Colonel Schreiber was sitting on a banquette behind a table. He beckoned her to the seat opposite him, before nodding at Kloff, who turned and left.

"Passport."

She reached into her purse. First thing she pulled out were her cigarettes. "May I smoke?" Roxy asked.

"No."

He held out his hand and she put the passport into it. She hoped he wasn't going to examine the photo any more closely than the official had in Frankfurt.

"French," he stated.

"Yes. But I was raised in America."

"You do not have an American passport?"

"Expired."

"Would you rather speak in French?"

"Up to you."

"Do you speak German?"

"I can say *bitte* and *danke*. That's it."

"We speak English, then." He rifled through the pages.

She hadn't travelled much as Maddie Lille. In and out of England, Belgium. The stamps in her US passport—all over Africa, Spain and the rest—would have been a lot harder to explain. She knew she didn't have to be on the defensive here. Perhaps there was a way of steering the conversation. "So, uh . . . who are you again?"

"I have told you. Colonel Schreiber."

"Not a policeman, then?"

He shook his head.

"So why are you the one asking me questions in the middle of the night?"

His grey eyes narrowed. "There are no policemen aboard. But I am in Luftwaffe Intelligence."

"A spy? How thrilling! I wish I'd worn my red dress."

"I am not a spy. But information came that there may be some threat to the airship. So I and my colleague are aboard."

"Threat, eh? Do tell."

"Fräulein, I am not here to tell you things. You are here to tell me things." He dropped the passport onto the table. "How well did you know Herr Ferency?"

She'd already prepared the answer to that. "I didn't know him at all."

"No? Do you always throw drinks over strangers in bars?"

She'd been prepared for that one too. "If they are rude to me, I do."

"How was he rude?"

"He was drunk. And he made an obscene suggestion." She leaned a little across, lowered her voice. "Would you like me to tell you what it was?"

"There is no need. And did he repeat this suggestion on the gantry?"

"No. He came up with a few others there. Before he lunged at me."

"And yet Chief Steward Kubis says you told him there was no problem. Why did you not report this assault?"

"Ferency would have denied it. Claimed I was the one giving him the eye. And, Colonel, I've found that you guys tend to believe each other, rather than a girl who dresses like me."

He absorbed this for a moment. "So perhaps you thought you would wait, and take your own revenge later?"

Roxy laughed. "Colonel, if I murdered every drunk who made a pass at me, you'd have to call me Jane the Ripper."

At that moment, Kloff returned. Schreiber, having informed his subordinate that she didn't speak German—in German—then received his report. Roxy learned that there were no traces of blood on her clothes or in the cabin. Nothing suspicious—apart from a lack of possessions. Kloff was sent off again.

"Give me your hands," Schreiber said, returning to English.

"Why, Colonel, you sweet thing."

He grunted, took her hands, examined them. Her polish was a deep scarlet, but she knew there was no trace of the real thing under her nails.

He released her. Time for offence, she thought. "Find any blood?"

"I thought you did not speak German," he said, releasing her.

"Come on. I heard your colleague say the word *Blut*. Can't be that different. And I don't believe you're considering a career as a manicurist if the Luftwaffe Intelligence thing doesn't pan out."

"I will remind you, Fräulein, that a man is dead. This joking is not appropriate."

"He was a shithead. However, I apologize."

He frowned. "Herr Ferency was quite brutally murdered with a knife. There were also—" he held up his hands "—how do you call these? Defend wounds? Here." He lowered his hands. "He fought to live. And I do not think that you would have had the strength to overcome him."

"Oh, I don't know. I've been told that I punch above my weight." She smiled. "Does that mean I can go?"

"In a moment. First, I am to tell you that though I do not think you killed him yourself, I also do not believe that you only just met." He raised a hand against her interruption. "I think there was anger between you. That maybe you have a colleague—"

"I don't—"

"So we will be keeping an eye on you, Fräulein Lille. There is no jail aboard, and we are not going to confine you to your cabin. Where would you go?" He nodded. "Also, we do not want the passengers disturbed with any fuss. But the authorities in both Germany and the US have been informed, and they may wish to question you on landing in America." He stood. "Now you may leave."

She stood, so he did too. "May I have that cigarette now?"

"The smoking room is closed."

"Come on! You wake a girl in the middle of the night and accuse her of murder—I think she deserves a break, don't you?"

He thought for a few seconds, then went to the door, called down the corridor. In a moment, the steward appeared. The colonel told him to open the smoking room. Though he looked less than pleased, Kubis nodded.

Roxy smiled at Schreiber and left. But as soon as she hit the corridor, she stopped, because coming toward her, escorted by Kloff, was Sydney Munroe. He glared at her, raising his meaty hands as if he sought to wrap them round her neck. But he didn't say anything, and she just gave him a look.

Theirs was a private war, she knew. Ferency may have been a casualty of it, in a way she had yet to figure out. But it would help neither of them to get caught up in all this more than they were.

Out of earshot of the colonel, the steward grumbled. But he unlocked the door to the bar, held it aside for her. "The other doors are open. May I remind the Fräulein not to bring a cigarette from the room. And the bar is closed. Drinking forbidden." He reached in, flicked on a light. "I will be in my office at the end of the corridor. Please let me know when you leave. I close the door. No more passengers to come in now. Good evening," he said, beckoned her in, shut the door behind her.

She eyed the bar. The only thing that would taste better than a Navy Cut was a Navy Cut with Scotch on the side. She spotted her old friend Johnnie Walker and stepped around to pour herself a large dram. Then she went to the airlock door, closed the bar side and opened the room side. The scent of stale tobacco assailed her nostrils. There was a small red night light, making the place dim, but she couldn't find a switch. She decided not to go back, though; she quite liked the idea of sitting in the semi-dark.

She found the electric lighter, fell into a banquette, lit up and inhaled deeply. "Ah!" she sighed, on a plume of smoke.

She took a swig of the whisky, smoked the cigarette to the butt and lit another from it. She held up her hand to watch the smoke curl up into the red light and wondered at how she shook. Jeez, she thought, it's been a night. Now that she didn't have to keep up a front, she allowed herself to sag a little. There was a murderer on the *Hindenburg*—that was clear. And whoever he was—has to be a he, she thought, given the type of murder the colonel had indicated—he hadn't struck randomly. Ferency was connected with her, with Munroe, with all that happened in Berlin. Which either made the killer an ally—or her one of his next victims.

She had drained the Scotch and was considering another, when she heard, very faintly, through two doors, a sound. For a moment, the lights went on. Someone had thrown the switch. Whoever it was changed their mind, because the light went off again, the sudden change making the room seem darker than it was before. At the same time, she heard the airlock door on the bar side open.

She looked around. There was no place to hide. No point either. Whoever was coming in knew she was there. Munroe? She'd been trapped with him in that cellar in Madrid and he'd tried to attack her. There, she'd had her derringer to fend him off. Here, she had nothing except for the heavy, cut-glass whisky tumbler. Not much, but she hefted it anyway, and stood.

The door opened. She took three steps back, pressed herself against the wall. She thought of shouting but found she couldn't get her mouth to work.

A man came through the door. Tall, but not wide enough for Munroe. His jacket was white, a steward's, but he was the wrong shape for Kubis. A stranger then—yet there was something about him that seemed familiar, even in dim red light.

She found her voice. "I'm warning you. I got a really loud scream."

The man paused, then turned to close the door behind him. "I know," he said, turning back. "It got us thrown out of that hotel in Tripoli."

She gasped as the tumbler slipped from her hand.

TWENTY-TWO

BROKEN LOVER

SHE STARED AT JOCCO, TOO STUNNED TO MOVE, TO SPEAK.

He took a step farther in. "Hello, Roxy," he said.

His voice broke the spell. She was moving, then she was in his arms. "How . . . How?"

"Shh," he replied, and kissed her.

It was strange. It was like kissing a wraith. He didn't feel real. Even as she wanted to dissolve into it, as she always had with him, to lose herself, her mind stayed separate. Questions overwhelmed her. Too much had happened, to both of them.

The embrace didn't feel the same and neither did he. The body she squeezed? Her Jocco was huge—big hands, barrel chest, shoulders that went forever. But the man she held now was thin, wire taut, not brick built. Also, and this was the strangest thing, he didn't smell like he had. There had been a scent to him, a good one, a musk all his own, a touch of aviation fuel and tobacco. Now he smelled of cooking oil, overlain with cheap cologne.

Jesus, Roxy, she thought, get out of your head. But she couldn't and they fumbled apart. "Here," she said, and pulled him down onto a banquette.

The red light was still dim, but she was able to study with her eyes what she'd felt on her lips, in her arms. His face, which she'd teased him was that of a Saxon farmer, so wide and ruddy, had thinned. His hair, the cowlick gone, was now the crop of a soldier's. Or prisoner's. But it was the eyes that had changed most. There was a look to them that she couldn't place; until she did. She'd seen it for months, staring back at her from hospital mirrors. Haunted. "Baby," she said, reaching a hand to cradle the side of his face, "what have they done to you?"

He turned, kissed her palm, then mirrored her, cupped her face. "And you, Roxy?" He touched the shiny skin on her cheek and jaw. "The crash?"

"Yes."

"Your hair?" He looked up at the strands that peeked from under her scarf. "You are black now?"

"It got burned. Grew back white. So . . . this."

His jaw tightened. "That bastard Ferency."

She took his hand, kissed it. "Did you kill him?"

"No." He shook his head vigorously. "I wish it had been me. But someone else got to him first."

"Who?" She shook the hand she held. "What the hell's going on? Why . . . *how* are you here?"

"I tell you everything. But first, can we smoke one of your cigarettes?"

"I'd rather you rolled me one of your specials."

"I would but—" He withdrew his right hand from her grip, lifted it into the light, and she saw one other of the things she'd known was wrong.

His hand was misshapen. All the joints looked swollen, and the thumb and forefinger were bent. The nails were ragged, with dirt under all of them that looked like blood in the red light.

"They broke it, Roxy," he said, his voice low. "And it was the least of what they did. They—"

"Wait." She went out to the bar, poured two large whiskies, came back and sat down again. Handing him one, she said, "Mud in your eye," and drank. She snatched up her Player's, put two into her mouth, lit them, then slipped one between his lips. "Now," she said, and drew deep. "Tell me everything. From Templehof."

He inhaled, blew a stream out over her head. "The forger betrayed us."

"I know."

"He gave us the fake and the real *Icarus* to Munroe. But Ferency didn't know or didn't care that Munroe wanted you alive. So, the bomb on the plane. He told me in the jail that he waited for you to take off before calling the police."

"I knew he was lying, the bastard."

"They arrested me and gave me to the Gestapo, who took me to their cells. There they . . ." He pulled in a deep breath. "They worked on me."

She took his shattered hand again. "Did they use that drug on you?"

"No. They stuck to old-fashioned methods." He swallowed. "I lasted maybe two days. But then I broke." She saw moisture come into his eyes. "Roxy," he continued, his voice choked, "I told them everything."

She kissed his hand. "Of course you did! You had to."

"There was not so much to tell, in the end. All about us, our conspiracy. Some comrades." He wiped his nose. "When they'd gotten all they could, they . . . just left me."

There were horrors in his eyes. She couldn't think of any way to even begin to take them away. He stared above her, then went on, his voice soft.

"Winter came. I had one blanket. I froze, was surprised when I woke up each morning. No one to talk to when I did, nothing to do but think. Remember. Never a bath, the stench was—" He paused, looked at her. "I am sorry. I know my cologne is not of the best. But I stank so much in there I still smell that place upon me, and the only way I can get rid of it is . . ." He sighed. "I despaired. I would have done anything to get away from there. And then I was given the chance. Offered freedom for one more betrayal." He looked at her. "Yours."

"The letter?" He nodded. "Your writing—"

"I did not write it. Could not." He held up his hand. "Only the signature, and that took me five times."

"I thought it looked different."

He nodded. "Ferency did the rest. I told him what to say, what might bring you. Then, when my father had given Göring the Van Gogh, they let me go." He shook his head. "I was surprised. They kept the bargain. I was driven to the border with Belgium. Told to go and die for my cause in Spain. I waited two days and then I crossed back in the middle of the night."

"Why?"

"I didn't know what they planned for you. Munroe had told me it was only to get you to America, to serve his papers on you. But I couldn't be certain he wouldn't harm you. And I couldn't live with myself if he did."

"Oh, my love." She kissed his hand again. "But how did you get on board the *Hindenburg*?"

"I have a friend. He works for the Zeppelin company, in hiring. He arranged it. A cook was suddenly sick. Well—" he shrugged "—we made him sick. I was his replacement."

"This friend? Is he on board too?"

"No. But another comrade is." He shook his head. "It is the second reason I had to be here."

"What do you mean?"

Jocco leaned forward and stubbed out the cigarette. She did the same. "This other comrade is cold, confident, efficient—"

"Like you."

"Like I was, perhaps." He held up his mangled hand. It shook. "He is also fanatical. I am a believer in the cause, but he believes that only by great actions will we bring down the Reich. Something spectacular. Roxy, he has a bomb. And he is going to blow up the *Hindenburg*." Over her gasp, he continued, "He arranged for me to be on board to help him. And I will. But I was determined that you would be safe first."

"How will you delay him?"

"There is one way." He reached into his trouser pocket, pulled out a small piece of metal, wires attached. "He cannot set his bomb without this timer. I took it . . . but I cannot keep it. He will know it is me."

"Why not just get rid of it?"

"Because I believe in the cause. I would like to see this symbol of the Nazis destroyed—only not with you on board."

"Does this guy know about us?"

"No."

"Then give it to me."

He hesitated.

"Listen, I'd like to see this big Nazi bird destroyed nearly as much as you would. So give it to me and I'll return it when we are docking. Blow the sucker up in its hangar, swastikas and all."

He studied her for a moment, then shook his head, tucked the switch away. "No. I will keep it. Who knows what will happen when we dock? You are already under suspicion. Perhaps we will not be able to meet before—"

He broke off. He was shaking. She just wanted to take him away somewhere hot, like that beach hut in Africa. Bathe in the ocean. Smoke. Make love. Heal them both. But the dream was too much, too far away. All she could say was "Did this guy kill Ferency?"

"Perhaps. He knew the forger was my enemy." He bit his lip. "My comrade is not completely well in the head."

Again, she thought, a little like you. But she said, "Who is he?"

"I cannot tell you." He squeezed her hand. "It is not that I do not trust you. But if you do not know, you cannot tell. No matter . . . what they do to you." He shuddered. "Do you remember Reinhardt?"

It took a moment. "Your wounded friend. The one you couldn't—"

He finished for her. "Couldn't kill. I left him to the Italians to be taken alive. Later that week, we recaptured the air base. His body was there, hanging . . ." He closed his eyes. "The things they did to him. He betrayed us all. Like I have now done. Many more died. All because I didn't have the courage to put him from his misery."

"Oh, baby," she said, wrapping her arms around him. "To kill a friend? How could anyone do that?"

He let her hold him for a few moments, then pulled away. "And now, with the Gestapo on board—"

"Gestapo?"

"Schreiber and Kloff."

"He told me they were Luftwaffe Intelligence."

"He lied. They are here because there have been rumours of an anarchist outrage. They will be watching everyone. They will be watching you. Which means—" He stood. "We must not be seen together again. I must go."

"Hey." She stood too. "What will you do now?"

"Watch. Wait. Restrain my comrade."

"And if you do? If we dock, disembark, and you blow up the *Hindenburg*? Then what?"

"Then . . . I do not know. I learned in the prison to think only of surviving today. Tomorrow, do the same."

"Then let me think for us." She put her arms around him again. "The fifth cavalry may be at Lakehurst Aerodrome to rescue me."

"Fifth cavalry?"

"An American expression. But if they can save one, they can save two."

"Perhaps." He let a little smile come. "Is it not a cowboy expression that we 'take to the hills'? Shall we do that, Roxy?"

"I'll take to the hills with you anytime, Jocco. In fact, I even own some hills to take you to."

He bent. They kissed again. It was better. Then, too soon, he pulled away. "Don't follow immediately," he said, and left.

She barely moved for the two minutes it took to light and finish another cigarette. She just stood staring through the cloud they'd created, swirling in the red light. There was something wrong, about everything. Everything Jocco had said, everything Ferency had told her and the Gestapo weren't saying. Something beyond the obvious.

What's going to happen? she thought, exhaling hard. What the hell is going to happen now?

TWENTY-THREE

THE TOUR

SURPRISINGLY, SHE SLEPT.

A dreamless sleep, mostly, until the end, when images assailed her. Her mouth was dry, and that brought memories like shards of a broken mirror from her time in Berlin. A polar bear talked to her. A rat confided. Icarus fell again and again, while his father wept. Her father wept. The painted sky darkened to the tolling of some far away bell that got closer, closer . . .

"Lunch! Please take your places for the second sitting! Last call! Lunch is served!" The voice from the corridor alternated with a bell being struck.

She sat up fast, swayed woozily. Lunch? Clearly, she'd slept through breakfast.

She checked her watch. Three p.m. Seemed late for lunch. Then she remembered: they put the clocks back every day by two hours, to account for the time difference. It was one of the boasts of the flight— no lag. You adjusted from European to US time as you crossed the Atlantic.

She ran her tongue around her mouth and tasted stale cigarettes and Scotch. They woke her fully. "Jocco," she murmured, half amazement, half joy. Then she remembered how he was. What he'd been through; what he was doing there; what was to come. Joy faded, replaced by fear. It held her for a moment. Then, "Well," she told herself aloud, "no point in facing all that on an empty stomach."

She thought of having a shower—the cubicle was right opposite her cabin. But when she stepped out into the corridor and pressed the door, she found that it was locked. Water ran within. Cursing, she stepped back inside and dressed swiftly, again in her faun slacks and blouse. Her hair was the same mess and she hid it the same way: under a scarf.

The dining room, on the port side of the craft, looked full. However, once she'd given the steward her name, he led her across to a vacant table in the far corner. Her route took her past the family who occupied the one larger cabin and one other cabin on B deck—a middle-aged father and wife, a daughter about sixteen years old, two boys about seven or eight. She smiled, said, "Hi!" but only the youngest of the boys said hi back—and the mother grabbed his arm when he did. They'd been woken by the ruckus in the night, of course. They probably thought she was some kind of trouble. She couldn't blame them.

There was a bowl of cold green soup before her, a swirl of cream making an apostrophe at its centre. She shuddered. Since she'd just woken, this was breakfast and she'd prefer her usual: black coffee, ham and eggs, cigarette. She knew she wouldn't get the last till she slipped down to the smoking room later. So she settled for ignoring the soup and reaching for a bread roll. It was fresh, still warm, obviously baked aboard. She wondered if Jocco the assistant chef had a hand in its creation, and decided to believe he did. She split it, and ladled on the churned butter.

She was halfway through a second, when she noticed the steward approaching again with Willie from Washington in tow.

"Excuse, Fräulein. This gentleman is known to you?"

The gentleman peered around the white coat. "I'm so sorry. I was busy. Missed the first sitting."

"Busy with poetry?"

"Yeah. It's hell!" He smiled. "Guy says if you take pity on me, I can join you."

"Pity taken," she said, and nodded to the steward.

He looked less than pleased at this disruption to his routine. "I bring soup," he said, then swivelled.

"No, that's okay, he can have mine. But can you bring me a coffee?"

The man nodded, walked away.

"You sure?" said Willie, sitting. On her nod he reached over and took her plate. "Man, I could eat a horse."

"But could you drink the pond that it swam in?"

He looked down, made a face. "Well, now that you mention it—"

"Go ahead, I'm sure it's great."

"If you insist."

While he attacked it, breaking up a roll to dip in, she studied him. So, Mr. Umlaut, she wondered, what's your story? A thought came: maybe he was Jocco's fanatical accomplice. Willie's looks were just so clean-cut—though she knew that meant nothing. His Wasp-y face was shiny with sweat. His hair was wet; recently washed, hastily dried.

"Oh, so you were the one hogging the only shower!"

He looked up, spoon halfway to mouth. "Sorry. I'd done some exercise and—"

"Twice around the deck?"

"Hardly, no. Just a few things in my cabin. Push-ups and the like."

He shovelled up the soup again—and she stiffened. Each knuckle of his right hand was red, raw and scraped. The skin had been recently broken.

He looked up, and noticed her stare. "Oh yeah," he said, putting down the spoon. "Stupid, huh? Jumping jacks—I banged it on the bunk." He flexed his hand. "Must have thought I was in the gym back home." He lowered it. "And by the way, it's impossible to hog that shower. It's on a timer. Two minutes and it cuts out. German efficiency, huh?" He put on the accent. "Vun minute for zee soap, one for zee rinsing. Any more: verboten!"

She breathed out slowly. Was she sitting with the guy who'd killed Ferency? Calmly, she said, "I thought you were half German?"

"Yeah, but my American half likes ten-minute showers."

The steward returned, put her coffee down and glared at Willie for not finishing the soup faster. He scraped a last bit of bread around the sides of the bowl before surrendering it.

"See what I mean? Efficient."

Back came the steward once more to set down plates. On them was filet of poached salmon, with parslied potatoes and a cucumber salad with dill. "May we have a bottle of Riesling, please?" Willie asked.

The steward nodded, went and returned immediately. Once Willie had sipped, and nodded his approval, the wine was poured and the man left. "To horses and ponds," said Willie.

Roxy raised her glass, began her usual rejoinder. "Mud—" she began. But the toast froze on her lips. She'd toasted with it only a few hours before. And the memory of who she'd saluted overcame her. This—the dining room, the food, the dark-haired family, floating above the Atlantic, the cold green soup—it was all suddenly as unreal as the images from her dream. While flirting with a man whose right hand looked like it had seen a fight? Handling a butter knife now, had he wielded a different knife earlier and killed Ferency with it?

She thought of a sentence. It had an umlaut in it. "*Übergeben Sie das Salz, bitte,*" she said.

Willie reached for the salt cellar, as requested. Then his hand halted halfway there. "Uh, sorry, what did you say?"

Gotcha, she thought. "Salt, please."

He passed it over, went back to his buttering. She used the salt, then focused back on his face. It had flushed again. He began to talk some more about the glories of the Zeppelin, but she didn't pay much attention. After a few mouthfuls, she put her fork down and stood. "Cigarette time," she said.

He stood too. "I don't smoke, but I could—"

"No, no. You finish your lunch."

"Okay. But I'll see you later. On the tour."

"Tour?"

"Sure. They do tours of the interior. You get to go up into the sack itself. Visit the captain in the gondola. See those engines."

"I'm not sure, I—"

"Oh, come on! You gotta see how this bird stays aloft. Didn't you say you were a pilot?"

"Did I?"

"Sure you did. On the bus to the aerodrome." He laughed. "Anyway, you gotta see the hydrogen bags. They—"

He was about to launch into more airship wonders. But she'd learned enough already about him. "I'll see you on the tour, Willie."

"Promenade deck, 4:00 p.m."

She moved off. At the entrance to the dining room she looked back. He'd sat again, but he was no longer eating. Just staring ahead. In his right, scraped, hand he was still holding the butter knife.

After ordering a second black coffee from the barman—she'd decided against the Scotch—she passed through the airlock. The smoking room was full because of the post-lunch rush, its fan labouring to disperse the fog. In one corner sat the Luftwaffe Intelli—no, the Gestapo officers, Jocco had told her that. Schreiber rose, and indicated the empty chair before him. She crossed.

"Is that an order?"

"No, Fräulein Lille. We would merely like your company."

"Then I'd prefer my own company, thanks."

She picked up the electric lighter from their table, went to another on the opposite side, lit up. The barman came with her coffee. She sipped, smoked and brooded.

She was just about to stub out when the smoke around her swirled. Someone had entered. She didn't look up until the someone loomed above her.

"May I join you?"

She stared at him for a moment. "I'm expecting someone, Munroe."

"Who?"

"Anyone who could pass for a human."

"Roxy!" Munroe lowered himself onto the chair. "Is there any reason for this unpleasantness? Wouldn't it be much easier for you to just sign the land over to me? Save all the fuss in court?"

She stubbed the butt out, stood, took a step.

He caught her hand. "Are you going on the tour?" he asked.

"Are you?"

"I am."

She jerked her hand free as she answered. "Then I wouldn't miss it for the world."

∽◦∾

"This on which we stand is called the middle, or axial, gangway. It is, if you will, the spine of the whale."

Though the ship's officer—Lieutenant Glaumann was his name— had obviously conducted the tour many times, Roxy could hear in his voice the same pride, the same enthusiasm that all the personnel aboard displayed. They loved their ship in a way she, a pilot, completely understood.

He had already ascertained that most of his guests worked in feet and inches, not metres, and continued, "Here, we are exactly in the middle. Seventy-five feet up—" all looked, to the roof above, criss- crossed with wires and struts "—and seventy-five feet down." All looked down.

They'd climbed up ladders from the lower gangway, which also ran the length of the ship along the keel. That's where all the passenger and crew areas were, the storage, the control rooms.

She glanced around at her fellow tourists. Theirs was a small party, the second of the daily tours. The first, conducted by Captain Lehmann himself, had drawn a much bigger crowd. The dark-haired family— Mexican, it turned out—were all there. The father and mother were rapt; the daughter looked like she had vertigo and clutched the thin guardrail; the elder of the two boys fidgeted, obviously bored; the younger grinned widely at everything. Willie had a similar expression on his face that went with all the whistles and folksy expressions he'd let out. "Gosh, darn!" he'd said. "Outstanding!" She wondered if he ever let slip a German expression. Break the act. Apart from that one mistake in the dining room, he'd maintained his front.

And there was Munroe. He'd arrived late, sweating, and he still didn't appear comfortable. His bulk made ladder climbing hard, and he'd tripped a couple of times because the sneakers he'd been given—everyone had to wear the soft rubber soles to protect the gangways—were too large. She studied her enemy now, as he listened to their guide. She noticed that the front of his white suit had dark spots on it, as if he'd slurped and spilled his tomato soup.

Roxy didn't hear the next stats about the engines, one of which was at the end of a side gantry they stood upon. Because she was suddenly thinking about lunch. How Willie had so enthusiastically eaten his soup at lunchtime. Which had been green as a pond.

The spots on Munroe's suit were scarlet.

She took a step toward him, to confirm, but he noticed her and pivoted away, back to the guide. "And these," Glaumann said, laying his hand on the very bottom of a giant balloon, "are what keep us in the air."

Was that Ferency's blood on Munroe's jacket? Had there been a falling-out of thieves?

Roxy turned, her mind reeling. She looked along the length of the ship, at the sixteen giant bags that filled the upper half of the interior all the way to the front. They seemed sinister to her now, alive, like chrysalides waiting to hatch. Their lower halves rippled as if a creature within was breathing.

"When fully inflated," Glaumann continued, "the sixteen bags contain seven million cubic feet of hydrogen. That is enough to lift 236 *tonnes*." He emphasized the word.

"Outstanding," Willie said. Then added, "But with the weight of the frame, the engines, all the fuel tanks, ballast, electrical generators, the cabins, the crew . . . how much more weight can you carry?"

"Twenty tonnes." Glaumann smiled at the whistles that came. "Yes. It is why we have the pleasure of your company and can make your voyage pleasant with all that good wine and food."

"And the gas?" It was a harsher, yet higher pitched voice that spoke now, and the officer turned to face the speaker, Munroe. "Isn't hydrogen highly flammable? You take our lighters, you don't allow flashbulbs for our cameras. That smoking room, with its airlock?" He grunted. "Aren't you nervous all the time?"

Glaumann smiled. "No. Because hydrogen is not flammable. Not at all." He nodded. "It is only when hydrogen mixes with air that it becomes dangerous. So, we have precautions. But hydrogen is also lighter than air. It is up there." He pointed to the top of the bulging cell. "It is almost impossible for it to escape this sack and mix with air. Now," he said quickly, interrupting Munroe's next query, "if you permit, I will tell more as we progress, and more later in the lounge, if you wish. We must move a little faster to see everything because I have to have you back for dinner. Schnitzel tonight, I hear. Yum-yum. The *Hindenburg*'s is even better than my wife's. But please do not tell her I say this."

Amid the laughter that followed, he set out down the gangway, Roxy and Willie bringing up the rear of the group. "Gosh, it's truly amazing, isn't it?"

"Outstanding," she replied blankly. Her mind wasn't on the ship, its lengths and volumes. It was on the man in the white suit ahead of her, what he might have done and if she could prove it. Because if she could, Munroe wasn't going to be suing anyone. And Göring would get no planes made with the metal from her mines.

The tour rolled on, with more amazing statistics and gasps of wonder. They reached the bow, where the lower gantry curved up to meet them. Descending that, Glaumann led them almost immediately down a ladder into the control gondola. This was stuck onto the belly of the airship, like a sucker fish attached to a blue whale. The plane suddenly became a ship, for beneath the tall front windows was a ship's wheel, a helmsman at it, steering by a gyroscopic compass set before him. Halfway back was another wheel, facing sideways, which Glaumann informed them was the inclinometer. Beyond that was a chart room for navigation, and at the back of that a smaller room with tables. Three officers smiled as the party entered and again when they left.

They climbed back up. The tour was nearly at an end and couldn't end soon enough for her. She had to get back to her cabin and think. She had two more nights aboard. Two nights and two days to make something happen. What chance did she have to catch a murderer, prevent an explosion, reclaim a lover? Not much.

Emerging from the gondola, they could see the gantry stretching ahead back to the passenger areas. Glaumann was making his concluding remarks. "Here you see, *Damen und Herren,* the tanks for fuel, hydrogen and water—the kind you drink and the kind we collect and vent as ballast. Also some quarters for officers and men and storage—" he waved "—as you can see." To the left side was a large oilcloth wrapped around the unmistakable contours of a big car. "Your vehicle, is it not, Herr Munroe?" the officer inquired.

"Mercedes 770," said the big American. "Like airships, you Germans are producing the best damn vehicles in the world."

"Thank you." Glaumann nodded toward the stairs ahead. "May I show the—" He bent, put a hand on the cloth's edge.

"No!" Munroe shouted. "Damn well leave it alone."

The officer narrowed his eyes and dropped the cloth. "Excuse me," he said, and led the way.

Roxy had lingered at the back. So she was the last to pass Munroe's car and the first to notice the smell.

It was cologne. It was cheap. And she'd smelled it last on Jochen Zomack.

She stopped, dropped to one knee. Willie, who'd also lingered, turned back. "Need a hand?"

"No. Laces on these damn sneakers. I'll follow."

"Okay."

He caught up with the others, took the stairs. When his legs had gone, she glanced back. No one was around. She lifted an edge of the car's covering cloth. The scent grew stronger. "Jocco," she whispered. "Are you there?"

No reply. But she smelled something else now, mingling with the cheap cologne and oilcloth. She'd smelled it before—in destroyed villages, and bombed-out towns. Iron. "Jocco," she said again, more urgently, and lifted the cloth.

Munroe's Mercedes was vast and red, but it was a different red from the blood that covered the body of her lover, which stank of metal. He was sprawled on the back seat. His eyes were half-open, glassy—like the eyes of a man lying under a streetcar. Like the eyes of a bishop dying in a cellar.

The cathedral wasn't just quiet now. There was no sound. None. No vibrating wires, no faint hum of engines. No people moving, speaking, laughing. There was death, again, and it took all the sound away.

Letting the cloth fall, she sank down.

And then pushed herself up. Because there was sound. A voice, calling. She saw him ahead, blurred, until her eyes focused. Lieutenant Glaumann was coming toward her. She stood, swayed, walked. He asked her something, but she didn't hear it. She didn't want to be questioned. She knew she wouldn't be able to explain the blood on her hands, the horror on her face.

The murder in her heart.

TWENTY-FOUR

KILLER, LOOSE

ROXY THREW UP TILL THERE WAS NOTHING LEFT, TILL ONLY bile filled her mouth. Staggering out of the toilet and across the corridor to her cabin, she made it to the sink there, yet only retching came now. Reeling, she fell face down onto the bed, but when she closed her eyes, the world spun even worse. She dragged herself into a corner of the narrow bunk and drew her knees up. Gradually, the spasms subsided, the world steadied, she could think.

Jocco.

She'd let him go. She'd thought she had no choice except to do so since she'd had no news of him after Berlin and the crash. Then to have him back? It had revived a fire she'd thought was extinguished. She'd let the thought of him—of them—back in. She knew they'd never be the "white picket fence and a parcel of kids" kind of pair. But if they'd got off the *Hindenburg,* if her friends had come to their rescue? Maybe they'd have made it. Found another war where life, if not simple, was at least a simpler kind of complicated.

Now all that was gone. Her guts twisted into knots, but she knew she couldn't give in to sickness or to grief. There was still a madman on board with a bomb, and no Jocco restraining him.

That thought had her swinging her legs off the bed. Of course! Jocco had the mechanism for the bomb. If he still had it and she got it, they were safe. If he didn't . . .

She had no choice. She had to go and check a dead man's pockets. The thought, the image of him, made her breaths come more quickly. But she stood up anyway.

The dead. They upset most people, of course. But the first doc she'd talked to, in that brief time she'd spent in Montreal with Aunt Estelle after her dad's death, had noted that it appeared more advanced in her; it froze her, took away her senses. He'd called it shell shock because he'd been in the war and had seen a lot of that. He referred her to a psychiatrist, who'd given it a fancier name: acute stress disorder. But it only occurred when she first saw the body. In New York under a tram car. In a Madrid cellar. In the back of a car on an airship—

The knocking, sudden and loud, made her cry out.

"Madeleine? You okay?"

"I'm . . . I'm sick, Willie."

"Shall I fetch the doctor?"

"No. It's not that bad. I'll be fine."

"Okay." There was a pause. "First seating for dinner is about to start."

"You go ahead. I don't think I can make it."

"I'll, uh, I'll check in on you later."

"Thanks."

She heard him moving away. Maybe she should join him. Willie Schmidt was a heap of questions she needed to answer. Had he killed Ferency? Did he have a bomb?

Other voices came from the corridor, speaking rapid Spanish. Kids laughing, parents hushing. The Mexican family were passing. Roxy thought of the boys, the one bored, the one enthused by the airship.

All doomed if the madman could arm the bomb. She should go to the authorities, tell them, let them deal . . .

She sat down. Wait, she ordered herself. If I lead them to Jocco's body, I'll be the first one they arrest. I'm a suspect in Ferency's murder. Schreiber, the Gestapo officer, already said that the police stateside would want to interview me. And what good can I do locked in a brig, or in my cabin? No. I need to try and figure this out myself.

Who was the killer? Or was there more than one? Munroe for Jocco, and the anarchist for Ferency?

The more she thought it the more likely it became. Munroe had shouted at Glaumann, the tour guide, not to lift the car cover because he'd known that Jocco's corpse was there. And he'd joined the tour late, with spots of blood on his suit front that hadn't been there when she'd seen him in the smoking room.

She went to the sink, ran the cold tap and splashed her face again and again. She had to take this step by step. Munroe could wait. First she had to find out if the anarchist had just acquired the means to blow up the ship.

She decided to allow the cabins to empty and the corridors to clear before making her move. After a while, all noise reduced to the faint rumble of engines, and she left her cabin. The corridor was empty. She walked quickly toward the chief steward's tiny office and opened the door onto the gantry. No one was on it.

It had been half an hour since the end of the tour. But night had already fallen, and the electrical lights were on, throwing the vast interior into shadows where the spill did not reach. The gantry was well lit, though, and she marched down it fast. She could smell the blood from ten feet away, but she didn't hesitate—she knew she couldn't. She bent, grabbed a tarpaulin edge and, taking another deep breath, jerked it up.

The corpse was gone.

She gasped, looked wildly around. But the front seat was as empty as the rear. She reached in and pulled a lever to spring open the trunk. It was huge. There was no body in it, but it wasn't empty. Wrapped in a grey cloth was a rectangular object. Pulling the cloth aside, the first thing she saw was Daedalus's screaming face.

Munroe had been back and cleared away the evidence.

Voices from the gantry. Roxy jerked down the tarp then ran around to crouch behind the passenger's-side wheel arch. Two crew members passed by. She turned to peer into the gloom behind the car, into the deeper storage areas. Jocco's body was not there either.

But her name might be. Because she was looking into storage nets, and in them were piled about twenty black belongings bags with the name of the airship line—Deutsche Zeppelin Reederei—embroidered on them. Each had a label tied around the neck. The mesh was wide enough to let her slip her hands in, move the contents about. In half a minute she found the one with Madeleine Lille written on it.

She pulled her penknife from her purse and used it to cut through the twined rope. Once she'd parted three strands she was able to slide her bag out. Reaching into it, she felt among the few objects, seeking the one she was looking for. "Hello, baby," she said, lifting her derringer into the light.

She had the bullet in her cabin. Singular. One wasn't much to use against two murderers. But it was one more than nothing.

More voices on the gantry. She stayed low as two crewmen passed back the other way. When their voices had faded, she reached again into the bag and drew out her lighter before shoving her bag back into the netting. Then she stepped out and hurried back to the passenger area of the ship. The chief steward's office was still empty and shouting could be heard from the kitchen. She still wasn't hungry—at least, not for food.

The bartender greeted her. "Same again, *chère mademoiselle*?"

"Make it a double."

"Of course."

There was no one else beyond the airlock; the smoking room was empty. They all had to be in their cabins, at supper or on the promenade deck awaiting their seating.

The bartender came in and set down her drink. As he left, she lit up, and raised her glass. "To Jocco, old comrade. Wherever the hell you are." She took a sip, raised the glass again, made a second toast.

"And to revenge."

∽o∾

She woke to screams.

At first she thought they were in her tortured dreams. Then they penetrated sleep and she was awake, shooting up, focusing . . . realizing that the screams did not come from the corridor. No one was fleeing a bomb blast. A seagull was flying parallel to the ship. But the *Hindenburg* was faster and soon left the bird, and its harsh cries, behind. Roxy looked down and saw icebergs. If these were below, that meant the airship couldn't be that far from North America. The first landfall would be Newfoundland. She'd recognize that. It was the route every flyer took, the shortest hop between the continents.

It was May 5. The last full day of the flight. Tomorrow morning, they would dock in New Jersey. If—she remembered with a lurch of her heart—a madman didn't blow them up first.

She checked her watch—8:33 a.m. She'd slept long and hard. Her mouth was like an ashtray that had been poorly washed in whisky. Only coffee and more nicotine could take that taste away.

The shower was free. Remembering Willie's warning, she turned it on, soaked herself fast—no easy feat in the ensuing dribble—applied soap, scrubbed and rinsed. Got the last of the suds out of her hair just as the shower clicked off.

Towelling, she stepped out into the corridor and straight into the back of the younger Gestapo officer, Kloff. He was standing with his hand raised in front of her door. "You will come with me, please, Fräulein."

She peered up at him. "Why?"

"The colonel wishes a conversation."

"Then give me a second, will ya?" She squeezed past him into her cabin, shut the door and leaned against it for a moment. So, she thought, it begins.

Schreiber was where she'd left him, behind a table in the officers' mess. He did not ask her to sit down. Nor did he beat around the bush.

"Who is this man?" he said, spinning a photograph around.

She looked at a recent shot of Jocco, with his short hair and his haunted eyes. "No idea. You want to tell me?"

The colonel didn't answer, just spun something else around to land beside the portrait. This was a news clipping, and she recognized it straightaway because it was special. From the *Philadelphia Inquirer*, March 17, 1929, when she'd won her first big race, the St. Patrick's Day Derby, bringing crates of Guinness from Boston to Philly. Her smile in the photo was ecstatic.

"So, Miss . . . Loewen. I am not going to ask you to explain why you are travelling on a false passport. We do not really have time for another one of your stories. We have evidence enough to arrest you now."

"Oh yeah? Since when did the Luftwaffe get the power to arrest folk?"

"We will hold you till we can hand you to authorities. Perhaps in America or—" his eyes glinted "—perhaps we keep you quiet on board and take you back to Germany with us. It is there your offences were committed, after all. And I think our punishments might be more severe. The Americans are a soft nation."

"So you got me." Roxy leaned down, placing her hands on the table. "But I think you'll find my soft country would take it pretty hard if they found out that you had kidnapped one of their citizens."

"We have Americans on board. Not one with the name Madeleine Lille. There will not even be a murmur." He nodded toward the table. "Now, do not waste my time. Tell me about this man."

She didn't even look at the photo. "Told ya. Never seen him before."

Schreiber nodded but not to her. Kloff grabbed her, twisting her arms behind her back. She yelped, swung her heel into his shin. The man grunted, but he didn't let her go, just pushed her face down till she was nose to nose with the man in the photo.

"I did not ask you if you know him. I asked you to tell me about him. On the *Hindenburg,* he is called Helmut Mandt, an assistant chef. You know him as the Communist agitator Jochen Zomack."

Roxy squirmed; she couldn't shift the iron grip. "You know so much, why do you need me?"

"Because he is missing. And we need you to tell us where he is."

"I don't know. Ow! Jesus, you bastard, my arm." She struggled but couldn't move. "How can he be missing? The *Hindenburg's* big but not that big. Search for him."

"We would if we did not feel we would alarm the passengers. This is a very special flight. Important men are on board who will, ah, help forge the unity between our two nations."

Sydney Munroe, she thought, as Schreiber continued, "So the orders have come from on high that there will be no disruption. This Communist is a disruption." He leaned till his face was a few inches from hers. "Tell me where he is."

She thought of telling him that Jocco was dead, but dismissed the idea when she remembered that she had no body to prove it. She thought of sharing Jocco's news about a fanatical comrade not right in the head who by now might, or might not, have the timer to a bomb. But the idea of telling this guy anything did not appeal. Besides, tell him any of that and she could be found guilty by association. She didn't know where this little chase was leading, but incriminating herself further wasn't going to help.

So she managed the best smile she could under the circumstances before saying, "Can't help you, buddy," and waited for the pain to double.

It didn't. Instead another nod saw her released—thrown forward so she only just stopped her face planting on the table. She stood straight, rubbed her wrists, glared at both men.

"If we were in Germany now, there would be more options for you," Schreiber said softly. "But here we have only one." He looked up at his subordinate and snarled, in German, "Take her to her cabin. Lock her in." He looked at her, smiled sourly. "Oh yes, we know you speak German, Miss Loewen."

Kloff reached for her again. She shrugged his hand off. "I've got rights, you know. And friends on board."

"Like Mr. Munroe? He has been most helpful in identifying you to us and explaining some of his feelings toward you. Or are you refer- ring to Herr Willie Schmidt? We know he desires you. Perhaps he will do so less when he is informed, along with the crew, that you have come down with a nasty touch of Spanish flu." He nodded. "You will be kept in your cabin till we dock. Maybe afterwards too. We will decide later whether to hand you over to American authorities or return you to Germany with us."

"Till we dock? But that's . . . that's not till tomorrow morning. You're going to keep me in my cabin for twenty-four hours?"

"No." He smiled, a sight without humour. "Headwinds over the ocean have delayed the flight. We do not dock now till the late afternoon of the sixth. So we keep you even longer." He looked at Kloff. "Take her."

Ignoring her outrage, Kloff grabbed an arm. A couple of the chefs were standing outside the kitchen and eyed her curiously as they passed. Kloff murmured something about her not being able to hold her drink and they laughed. She thought of making a fuss and complaining, but to whom? The captain? A few words from the Gestapo and she was cooked. Either way. She hadn't thought of an alternative by the time they reached her cabin door. And then it was too late.

"I'm hungry," she called, as the door slammed shut.

There was no reply. It was back to the gulls' screams. Except now she realized she wasn't entirely alone.

She delved into her pockets, then pulled out her cigarette case and the lighter she'd retrieved from her bag in the hold. She lit up and blew the smoke at the door. She wasn't worried. She was about as low in the Zeppelin as she could get, and hadn't the tour guide said that hydrogen rises? There wasn't going to be any down here. Almost no chance that a cigarette would set it off.

Her hand paused halfway to her mouth. A cigarette, maybe not. But a bomb?

TWENTY-FIVE

THE LAST DAY OF THE *HINDENBURG*

SHE HAD NOTHING ELSE TO DO, SO ROXY SLEPT WHEN SHE could. When she was awake, which was most of the time, she sat up in the bed, staring out, thinking, remembering. Coming up with all kinds of plans. Ditching every one.

In the early evening she saw the familiar coastline of Newfoundland below. She watched the sun sink, and was awake again to watch the light come up. All she could do was consume her cigarettes. The little half window she could open took most of the smoke but not all. Four times the steward, always accompanied by Kloff, came with sandwiches and water. He'd sniff the air and glare. She smiled. What was he going to do? Confine her to her cabin? But she smoked so hard that her stock was swiftly reduced. She began rationing, alternating smokes with a good chew of her nails. Neither helped much.

Each time they visited, they let her out for the toilet, the Gestapo man and the steward forming a man-made corridor between the cubicle and the room. Yet even if she could slip by them, run, outdistance the pursuit, where would she go? She'd be caught. There had to be a better way to do what she had to do.

Which is what, Roxy? she wondered, for the hundredth time, as she stared down at the coastline passing below, the one she knew so well from all her training flights. Her options had boiled down to a few, all bad. Over Boston, she'd thought that she should just tell the captain: "Look, there may be a bomb aboard—it may be armed, set by an anarchist buddy of my old lover, whose body is hidden somewhere on the ship." It sounded absurd, and anyway, what were they going to do? Set down at the nearest airport? It was one of the great drawbacks of the Zeppelin as opposed to a normal bird: problems with her plane, she could at least try to make a runway or at worst a field. But the *Hindenburg* needed a specialized place to land, mooring towers, winches. There was one in Frankfurt, one somewhere in Brazil and one at Lakehurst, New Jersey. Where they were headed. If she ran around screaming "A bomb! A bomb!" what were people going to do? Put on parachutes and jump? She doubted they had any. And you couldn't jump from seven hundred feet anyway—the chute wouldn't deploy.

She supposed they could search the ship. But she'd been in that cavernous interior. Plus, looking for a small bomb? How many days would that take? On his last visit, Kloff had curtly informed her that they were now due to dock at 6:00 p.m. But a storm had shadowed them all the way down from Boston. A few miles to the west, towering cumulonimbus clouds shot lightning bolts to the ground and quaked with thunder. The storm was creeping ever closer to the ship.

She hadn't reached a decision by 3:00 p.m. But the ship had reached New York, and for a few relieving moments she lost herself looking over the city she loved, the home she had not visited since she'd fled it eight years earlier.

She didn't think of herself as sentimental. So Roxy was surprised to find tears in her eyes as the *Hindenburg* came in over the Hudson and she got her first sight of the most spectacular cityscape in the world. They were so low she could see individual people on the packed sidewalks, almost all of them staring up and waving. She could hear, very faintly, the car horns in the gridlocked traffic, some drivers no doubt saluting, others, especially the cabbies, no doubt yelling "So it's a Zeppelin. Big deal. Move your ass already!"

It was easy to trace the avenue arteries down from Central Park, follow Fifth, count the blocks until she could see Fifty-Second Street. It was as choked as any of the roads. There was a streetcar outside what she figured had to be the 21 Club. It was stopped so all could observe the marvel overhead. Not stopped so all could look down and gawk at the horror under the front wheels.

"Dad," Roxy whispered, turning away, allowing the tears to fall now. What had begun there that day was somehow ending on this one eight years later. The man who'd caused Richard Loewen's death was on this airship, about to get the last remainder of the dead man's legacy. No doubt the sheriffs were standing by to take her into custody, while Munroe's servants waited to drive his new Mercedes from the airfield, with the *Fall of Icarus* in its trunk, destined for a secret room in his mansion.

Of course, an anarchist's bomb might get them all first. But if it didn't? She was damned if she'd see Sydney Munroe gloat over a painting that had caused death and a lot of hurt. Or gain the last inheritance she had, to turn one thousand acres of Adirondack forest into a titanium mine whose product would build German bombers that would destroy more lives.

She wiped her eyes. Fury focused her and cleared her head. With the clarity came certainty. Suddenly, she knew why Jocco had died where he did. Where he had hidden the bomb.

Right where Icarus fell.

She went and tried the door. It was still locked, of course, with no give to jerk it free even if she'd had the strength to do that. She bent, studied the lock and fetched her penknife from her clutch. She contemplated inserting it, jiggling it about—she might get lucky. More likely she'd snap the blade. And she had a feeling she'd need that. That and the one bullet in her derringer were the only weapons she possessed.

She looked away, to the sink, and thought of wrenching it off the wall to see what was behind. But the mounting looked solid and there was no shift when she tugged. Beside that was the small alcove that served as her closet. She pulled the curtain across, removed the single dress that hung there and laid that on the bed. The closet's back panel had the same fabric covering, creamy off-white, as the rest of the cabin. She reached in and tapped, expecting metal or wood.

She pressed. Her finger sank in. Another, thicker, layer of insulation? She took her penknife, ran it along the top edge of the alcove. Gripping with both hands, she pulled. It was difficult at first, until the whole fabric backing gave and she peeled it away to reveal . . . foam.

The entire wall was made of plastic foam.

Roxy smiled. Every fixture on the *Hindenburg* was light. The chairs in the dining room, on the promenade, in the writing room, were all aluminum. So were the tables. She'd heard that on previous flights they'd carried an aluminum piano. But even that had been removed to free up the weight for what the company really wanted: paying customers and their goods.

She heard faint cheering from below her, more concentrated than had come from the streets. She went to the window, looked down, and recognized the sight instantly. It was Ebbets Field, Brooklyn. Home of the Dodgers. A baseball game was in progress, the Loewens' favourite team playing one she couldn't identify. She saw the scoreboard though.

The home team was down 3–5. "Come on, Bums," she whispered, then added, "and come on, Roxy."

She put her ear to the door and heard voices, footsteps. During the last food visit, the steward had confirmed the landing time of 6:00 p.m. This last hour, the passengers would be packing still, getting their landing papers sorted. The airship was going to turn around, and be on its way back to Germany by midnight. The crew would be preparing for that, moving up and down the B-deck corridor and the gantry beyond it. She had no intention of cutting her way out of her cabin and falling into the arms of the Gestapo or anyone else. Closer to landing, all crew would be at their stations, all passengers up on the promenade to observe the docking. Kind of like her derringer, she knew she only had one shot. She settled back on her bunk and smoked her second-to-last cigarette as the airship made the turn south, heading for Jersey.

She recognized Lakehurst when they reached it. She'd flown in there a few times. Now she watched it come and she watched it go. They sailed on over, and began cruising down the Jersey shore, its beaches white in afternoon sun. But beyond them, to the west, the clouds had only gotten denser, drawn nearer. Lightning still flashed in their roiling depths. Thunder growled, and though the Zeppelin was still cruising smoothly, seemingly invulnerable to the weather, she knew that no captain would try to land a plane or moor an airship in such conditions. And yet, there was something about the Germans, their efficiency, their sense of timing. The *Hindenburg* was already some hours off schedule and had just missed another docking. Six o'clock had changed to seven. If Captain Lehmann needed to head back to the fatherland by midnight, he'd have to dock soon— even if conditions weren't perfect.

Roxy had her sense of timing too. When, at quarter to seven, the airship turned north, she suspected this would have to be it. So she slipped into her dress, tucked her loaded derringer into one stocking top and her passports into the other, flicked her last cigarette out into the New Jersey evening and picked up her knife.

The foam wall gave like butter under her blade. She cut parallel to the alcove wall, an inch from each edge though leaving the bottom, withdrawing the knife whenever she heard people in the corridor. The steward passed twice, each time calling, "Damen und Herren, time to vacate the cabins. Please, the checking for all personal items. Docking in fifteen minutes." She heard footsteps, some conversations in Spanish as the Mexican family passed and went up the stairs. When all was silent for five minutes, at 7:00 p.m. exactly, she slit the bottom of the alcove and pushed her carving out.

There was no point in lingering. After throwing her shoes out, grabbing the curtain rod, putting as little weight on it as possible—it was anchored in foam too—she swung her legs up and thrust them through. She teetered, the rod gave, and for one moment she was on her back, her head in the cabin, her legs in the corridor. She managed to dig her hands into the cut foam rim and propel herself forward. Her feet hit the corridor's far wall, and she arched and slid out, falling to the floor.

She sat there for a moment, then stood, smoothed her dress down, put on her shoes and set out along the corridor.

It was empty, all the crew at their landing stations, front and aft. She passed the bar and smoking room on one side, the kitchen on the other, and edged into the chief steward's tiny cabin. As she opened the far door, once more the cathedral of the airship's interior was before her. It was nearly as dark as night; she could hear that they'd entered the clouds, rain hammering on the canvas. All the auxiliary lights were on. Ahead, she could see the crew quarters, beyond them the area of the post office and radio room. She set out, wondering if she'd ever gotten an answer to the telegram she'd sent to the Ninety-Nines.

He moved quietly for a big guy.

"Hello, Roxy," Munroe said, as he rose from the shadows on the offside of his car.

"Hello, Sydney," she said, looking not at his face but at the .38 in his hand. "Didn't they tell you that you shouldn't play with guns on a Zeppelin? How did you get it aboard?"

"You can hide a lot of things in a vehicle."

"Like a painting?"

His eyes narrowed. "I wondered if you'd snooped around and found it. Can't help yourself, can you? That makes it . . . awkward for me. For you too. Because if you were to tell the authorities about it, after I hand you over to them—"

"I see your problem." She *tsked*. "Whatever are we going to do?"

"For now, this." He flicked the barrel. "Get in the car."

What was her choice? Start screaming, Munroe could plug her and disappear before anyone came. But even if she somehow got away, there were things here she needed to know. So when he opened the door, she slid onto the back seat.

Munroe leaned in the window, gun leading. "Of course, you're the second person I've found snooping around my car. Imagine my surprise when I saw who that first one was. That goddamn Commie Zomack." He chuckled. "Well, I fixed him good."

Roxy went cold. He'd just confirmed it. The man who had caused the death of her father had also killed the only man she'd loved since.

Munroe kept talking. "One punch was all it took."

Roxy shook her head hard, found words. "You killed Jocco with one punch?"

"Killed? Don't be ridiculous. I knocked him over the door and into the back seat. Busted his jaw, though, I bet." He laughed, waved his big hands. "Princeton, Golden Gloves, Class of '99."

"You killed him, Munroe. I found him—"

"I didn't. But I had to leave him here. Damn crew came along. When I returned, he was gone."

"I don't believe you. Because if he's not dead, then where the hell is he?"

Another voice came, accompanying the Luger barrel that slid in behind Munroe's ear. "I am here, Roxy," Jocco said.

"Jocco," she cried. "I thought you were . . . I was sure—"

"I know. It is always so with you, isn't it, my love? Whenever you see death. Or think you do."

The shock of it. The joy of it. She pushed herself up from the seat.

"Do not move!" he shouted. "And you—" he jerked Munroe by his collar "—into the car. Fast!"

He screamed the last word, stripping Munroe of his pistol, opening the back door, shoving him in. Munroe fell on her, crushing, forcing out her air. She gasped, and tried to push him off, with no chance of success. Then Jocco yanked Munroe to the side. He fell off her, into one corner.

Jocco opened the door and slid into the front seat, dropping Munroe's pistol onto the floor. "Baby," she said, and tried to move toward him again. But the Luger now swung to her.

"No, Roxy," he said, rubbing at a huge blue swelling on his jaw. "You have to stay there. Because I fear you may try to stop what I must do. You, who are always for the little people." His voice was slurred, as if he'd had too many whiskies.

"Stop you doing what?" she asked.

Except she knew. Jocco merely confirmed it with a smile. It wasn't his normal one, that rare gift she'd get from him sometimes. This one wasn't for her anyway. This smile was aimed up into the *Hindenburg*'s immense interior and she knew exactly what it meant.

She swallowed. She had to keep him talking while she figured a way out. She thought of one thing, one desperate thing, and began to execute it, shifting back against the seat. "Where's your friend?" she asked softly. "Has he got the bomb?"

"There is no friend. Or perhaps I am my friend also. That cold, efficient man you said I used to be?" A faint smile came. "Perhaps that is me still, inside."

"No comrade on board?"

He shook his head.

"Then who killed Ferency?"

"I did!" He jerked the barrel of his Luger at himself. "I did. For his betrayal of us. For what he tried to do to you. For what he helped them do to me in . . . in that cell." His eyes fluttered half closed and she shifted again. They opened, and he looked up. "Listen!" He tipped his head to the roof.

For a moment, all she heard was the rain on the airship's shell, and the faint hum of the engines. Then those all but vanished, leaving just the rain.

"They have dropped the engines to idling," he continued. "This means they are in position over the mooring mast. Soon the yaw lines will be dropped, fore and aft. The vessel will be winched down, drawn into the hangar. Unless—" He shook his head. "It is my time."

Roxy was staring at the Luger's mouth, aimed straight at her. She took a deep breath. "For what?"

"The destruction of the *Hindenburg*, while it is still in the air." His voice got stronger. "Think! All the newspapermen down there, the radio guys, the film cameras. What a great show it will make as the swastikas dissolve into flame! What a blow against Fascism everywhere!"

Roxy looked into Jocco's eyes as he spoke. They reflected the lamp hanging directly above the car, but that wasn't what caused the fierceness of the glow. It was his fervour. And she saw, just as she had in his smile, that he was not with her anymore. He was in a place she couldn't reach—where the martyrs lived. Still, she had to try, for all they'd been to each other, for all she still felt. Before she made her one move.

"Jocco," she said quietly, "you'll die as well."

He shrugged. "I do not matter. I think . . . I think that I am maybe half dead already. That only half of me came out of their prison."

"But all the others? The women and children?"

He swallowed. "It is unfortunate. Yet some may live. I will wait till we are as close as we can be to the ground. The ship will fall fast. Some may live," he said again. "Besides, innocents must suffer sometimes. For the greater cause. Those who died last week in Guernica were innocent, yet the Fascists claimed them as the enemy. I will claim all these rich pigs as mine." His eyes, which had hardened as he spoke, now softened again as they moved onto her. "But you may live, Roxy. Go low in the ship. Jump when you can."

"And where will you be?"

He smiled. "With my other baby. With my bomb." He raised another hand. Something was now in it. "This is the ignition cap. When this scum hit me—" he moved the barrel to Munroe, who was sweating heavily beside her "—it must have fallen out of my pocket. I searched everywhere, until I realized it could only be in the car."

Munroe was staring almost cross-eyed at the muzzle pointed at him. "Listen," he said, his voice hoarse. "Take the painting. Sell it for a fortune. If that's not enough I'll—" He coughed. "I'll give you anything. Just don't—"

"Always with the money, Herr Munroe." Jocco's mouth tightened. "Don't you understand that for some people, money is not enough? Roxy knows this. I do." He raised the Luger again, till it was in line with Munroe's eyes. "You will."

"Stop!" Roxy yelled. "What are you doing?"

He gave a grim smile. "This capitalist pig—my enemy, your enemy, Roxy. The man who killed your father."

His knuckles whitened. "No!" She shouted it again, then continued softly, "Don't do this. You're not well right now. Let's get off this bird together. Take Munroe's money. Buy two planes. Go to Spain. Fight more of your enemies. There'll be a beach, a hut. You can roll me your cigarettes." She leaned forward. "Baby, I'll get you help."

"Help?" That same half smile came. "There is no help for me now. There is only sacrifice. Mine. His." He turned again. His eyes, which had burned before, were ice now. "Herr Munroe? This is the workers' punishment for all your crimes."

"Please!" Munroe's voice broke as he squirmed. "Please don't. Don't!"

"Goodbye," Jocco said.

A blast. There was a moment when Jocco's brow crinkled, a puzzled look coming into his eyes as the Luger slipped from his hand. When they rose, they fixed on only one person. "Roxy?" he whispered, then fell backward onto the steering wheel.

The horn sounded, shockingly loud in the silence of that vast space. The stench of cordite rose around them. She lowered the derringer's smoking mouth to the floor. She stared at him, knowing he was dead. And yet, for the first time in her life, she didn't blank out when she realized it. "So long, my love," she whispered. "Don't fly too close to the sun."

Munroe was gasping next to her. "My God! My God! You shot him. We're safe. Safe!" he cried.

They were—for the five seconds before the *Hindenburg* exploded.

Roxy saw it begin. She'd looked away from Jocco, back and up to the roof. A flash there caught her eye—one of the huge gas bags near the fin simply dissolved. Flames dropped, rather than climbed. Then some kind of further combustion occurred; the fire doubled, quadrupled and burst out of the roof. Balloons on either side caught, ignited, exploded. The ship began to sink at its stern and a giant blowtorch of fire shot past the car, singeing them as it soared for the cone.

"Jesus!" Munroe cried, trying to stand. But the car lurched, the sudden gravity behind it snapping ties that were only meant to hold it level. Then they were shooting backward, held by the force against the seat. The car smashed into something—the stairwell, Roxy thought.

She tried to get up, but a heavy hand shoved her down as Munroe forced himself up and out the car door, and staggered off into the smoke. She stood to follow—as the Zeppelin hit the ground, rose, then fell to the ground again. She swayed, somehow kept her balance. When the ship settled the second time, she took a huge breath and plunged into the smoke where Munroe had vanished.

She couldn't see it, but she could feel the hard edge of the steward's door. The corridor beyond was filled with smoke, and she lurched down it and down the next one, fast, debris falling all around her. Beyond the cabins was a gangway. The door was locked, but as she reached it, all its surrounds dissolved in flames. She saw the ground about ten feet below, readied herself for the jump.

"Help me!"

The voice was right behind her. She turned.

Sydney Munroe was pinned under a twist of fallen girder. He had one hand free, stretched toward her. "Help me," he cried again.

She was almost out of air. Still she reached, and a huge hand clamped over her wrist.

"Save me!" he commanded.

His eyes were still piggy, still cold. She looked into them and saw nothing there. Nothing she cared about, anyway.

"Save yourself," she said.

Wrenching herself clear, she turned and fell from the airship.

There were so many screams now she couldn't tell if one of them was his.

She landed badly, an ankle twisting. But there was no staying where she was, not with hot metal and burning fabric showering down. She got up, hopped, cried out, hopped more. When she was clear of the worst of the flaming debris, she turned back, sobbing.

The *Hindenburg* was already a blackened shell. Flames still ravaged its length. All the skin was gone, and most of the skeleton. The cone was the only thing with any shape to it.

She couldn't understand how she'd survived. How anyone had. But there were people staggering or crawling away from it, men and women still emerging from the smoke, backlit by fire. Others, some in uniform, were rushing past her to help the passengers.

She looked down at her hands. They were pretty badly burned. At the hangar, she saw people gathering. There would be emergency aid there, doctors. There would also be the law. Once she was tended there would be questions. None of which she cared to answer.

She swivelled left and saw the aerodrome she knew, before it had been equipped to receive Zeppelins. She started to limp toward the hangars.

She'd gone twenty paces, when she had to step around something in her path. Something that smoked. It was a corpse, burned almost beyond recognition. Not quite, though. She saw the bones of a hand. Some charred clothing. A woman's shoe. She was two paces past when she stopped and turned back. She reached under her dress, filled with holes now, burned beyond use—and pulled out one of the items under her left stocking. Then, bending, she shoved Roxanne Loewen's singed but intact passport into the centre of the body.

She had to stop a few times before she got to the other hangars. People were about, pilots and crew all staring, horror on their faces. She studied them for a moment and recognized one. "Louise?" she asked.

The aviatrix turned, started, and ran to her—just in time to catch her.

"Roxy?" Louise Thaden said, laying her gently down. "You're alive!"

"Just."

"Kid, I'll get you to a doc." She began to rise, looking to the hangars.

Roxy grabbed her arm. "No, Lou, please. Get me out of here. Get me out of here fast."

They were the last words she spoke, before she surrendered to the smoky dark.

TWENTY-SIX

IN THE HILLS

Blood Hill, near Newcomb, New York. July 5, 1937.

IT WAS PLEASANT AMONG THE TREES, ESPECIALLY IN THE birch grove by the stream. The cabin had been built close to seventy years before by miners who wanted to get through tough winters. When the sun beat down, it got hot inside fast, and after her two experiences of extreme heat in the previous twelve months Roxy found that she preferred it cool. For the first two weeks, she'd spent a lot of time with her burned feet and her burned hands in the water, sometimes following the stream down a ways to the small pool it made deeper in the woods, to immerse herself. Lately, though, since her skin had healed and her ankle was mended, she'd noticed that, conversely, she liked to move even less. Just lie in the clearing, watch the leaves dance against the bluest of skies, listen for the voices in the water as it gurgled through the banks. Sometimes she brought a book; her dad had left a lot of old ones in the cabin—*Tom Sawyer*, some Dickens, some O. Henry. But her concentration wasn't great. She'd found that though her body had healed fast enough, her soul was not so swift.

Jocco. She thought about him a lot during the day, and dreamed of him each night. Sometimes the dreams were lovely: cool memories of hot nights, making love where they had and in places they'd never been. Mostly, though, it was the later Jocco who came, the one with the Gestapo prison and its memories in his eyes; the fanatic who only had his cause left, and his hatred. And then she'd wake and remember the story he'd told her in Africa. About his friend Reinhardt, who he couldn't shoot when he'd had to leave him behind. Who the Italians had then tortured before they killed him. It wasn't the same, her killing of Jocco. Yet, in a way it was. She couldn't leave him behind. She had to stop him, and he'd been tortured enough.

In other dreams, she blamed him; confused the disaster with his actions, what he'd wanted to do. For a while she'd believed it was his fault, that the bomb had gone off even without his ignition cap. Then she'd made her first trip into Newcomb for supplies and, in a diner, found a pair of week-old newspapers. One was the *Washington Post* and had the headline "Preliminary Investigation on Disaster Only Reveals Doubt."

Back at the cabin, she'd read the article obsessively. Sabotage was ruled completely out; the randomness of storms was in. Soon she knew the stats by heart, along with the names of all the living and the dead. Of the sixty-one crewmen, twenty-two had died. Of the thirty-six passengers, thirteen had perished. People thought it a miracle of sorts, considering the speed and intensity of the conflagration. She wondered if the dead thought it a miracle, in whatever afterlife they dwelled. The Gestapo officers, Schreiber and Kloff. The Mexican father and his daughter. Captain Lehmann, going down with his ship. Of the others, most she hadn't known. She was pretty certain of one thing, though: that Sydney Aloysius Munroe, in whichever Circle of Hell he resided, was not grateful for the miracle of the survivors.

There was one other name she recognized. It was on one of the lists—but it really leaped at her from the front page of the second paper she'd found, a sensationalist rag called the *New York Bugle*. Under the headline "How I Survived *Hindenburg* Hell!" was the byline "Willie Schmidt—Ace Undercover Reporter." Willie, with his fluent German, was on board to investigate Nazis and their American pals, especially the millionaire Sydney Munroe. "I saved half a dozen dames myself!" he wrote, and described in detail his heroic actions during the disaster.

But he lamented one he couldn't save:

I used to cover the flying races. So I spotted her in Frankfurt straight-away despite her disguise—Roxy Loewen, who'd fled America back in '29. I was making nice, getting close, and was going to find out what her story was. Until the bigger story took over. A shame she died, though. She was one good-looking broad.

There was a photo of her beside her plane *Asteria 1*, at some air-field. Smiling away. She didn't recognize herself.

So it's official, she thought, laying the paper down again after a third read. I'm dead. Has to be true if the *Bugle* says so. And how do I feel about that?

Confused, she had to admit. Pretty damn confused.

It was unusual being dead but not. She wasn't quite sure how she was going to handle it. And she was going to have to, sooner rather than later. Louise Thaden had taken a collection of the other Ninety-Nines. The gals had been generous. Forty bucks was a princely sum, but it wasn't going to last forever. Not with cigarettes now twenty cents a pack, and whisky nearing two bucks a quart. She supposed she could economize, and delay the inevitable. But after her year, and figuring all the ways she could have died during it, she'd concluded that life was way too tenuous to smoke cheap cigarettes and drink bad Scotch.

Which left her with two choices: the resurrection of Roxy Loewen . . . or her real demise. Neither appealed. Though she wasn't ruling either of them out just yet.

She stubbed out her smoke and put the butt into the pack. She had just one pack left. Sighing, she rose and headed up the deer trail toward the cabin to fetch it.

She was halfway there, when she heard the motor—a car coming up the rough dirt track from the road. She'd thought that eventually someone would spot her cooking-fire smoke, come to check on the "abandoned" cabin. Sheriff, probably. She didn't see any point in hiding. So she sat down on the front stoop to wait.

It was no police cruiser, though, that rounded the bend and pulled up but a friend in her sleek Packard Coupe. "Louise," said Roxy, standing. "I hope you brought some cigarettes."

Louise Thaden got out. "Good to see you too, Roxy. I did." She hefted a carton of Camels. "And this—" She shook a bottle of Johnnie Walker. Then her smile faded. "I also brought something else." She lifted a copy of the *New York Times* from the seat beside her. "Yesterday's," she said. "But I stopped in a hotel on the way up for some food and heard an update on the radio."

"Update on what?"

"You haven't heard?"

"Heard what? Jeez, Louise, tell me, will ya?"

Her friend didn't reply, just took a step nearer and held up the front page. Its headline read: "Amelia Earhart Still Missing: Rescue Planes and Boats Seek Shelter from Storm as Hopes Fade."

Roxy swallowed. "You better come in," she said.

∽o∾

Roxy had known some of it. Louise had filled her in on her one previous visit to the cabin. Roxy had thought of asking for another map,
pinning down some blue thread. But she found she could picture it
all pretty well in her head. The most recent news that Roxy had heard,
on Louise's last drop-in at the end of June, was that Amelia had made
it as far as Singapore.

"Where'd she head after that?" she asked, refilling her friend's glass.

"Bandung."

"Where?"

"Java. On from there to Darwin, then New Guinea." Louise sipped.
"Then came what was always going to be the trickiest part. She was
heading for Hawaii, but she needed one refuel on the way. She'd
picked this dot in the Pacific—"

"Howland Island. Yeah, I remember. Wait a second." Roxy rose,
went to the bookshelves. There was an atlas up there. After blowing
dust off it, she looked at the inscription in copperplate on the inside
cover: "Richard Loewen. Aged eleven. Happy Birthday from your
father and mother." Her dad had received it when he was a boy, which
meant it was fifty years old. Still. She flicked the atlas open to the
South Pacific.

Louise peered. "It's somewhere . . . here." She tapped open water,
near the drawing of a whale. "There're actually lots of islands here,
mostly uninhabited. We're claiming some, the Japanese are claiming
some—it's a mess. But we've built a runway on Howland. That's
where she was heading."

"Last contact?"

"There'd been some messages, but the communication systems
were poor. We haven't heard them all yet." She sighed. "Some say
there was a message when she was close. Garbled. Also, the weather
was terrible. And the radio announcer when I stopped at that hotel?
He announced the storm's gotten so bad no search flights have taken

off in twenty-four hours. Even the ships are making for port." Her voice broke. "I'm scared, Roxy. She . . . she—"

"Hush, now." Roxy got up, went to the window. A noise had drawn her, distant, small, but recognizable. She stared into the immensity of blue until she saw it, a black speck. Wings flashed in the sunlight. "Hey, Lou," she called, "think that's Amelia up there?"

"Kid—"

Roxy watched the speck until it had vanished, listened until all the sound was gone. The airplane seemed to take something from her with it, that numbness in her chest that had been there for months. Suddenly, the feeling lifted, dispersing in the high summer clouds. She turned back. "Two things I know, Louise," she said, crossing to sit again before her friend. "First, that there is no chance in God's blue heaven Amelia has crashed into the Pacific."

"Glad you're so sure. And the second?"

"The second is that I'm going to go find her. Which means you're going to find me a plane."

"Hey! That's three things."

"Ain't that the truth," said Roxy Loewen.

Author's Note

I remember the exact moment when the idea for this novel completely changed. Like many of life's great moments, this one involved beer.

A few months before the pint in question, I'd come up with the concept of a pilot in the 1930s and an art heist, set against the backdrop of the Berlin Olympics and ending on the *Hindenburg*'s disastrous final voyage. The main character was to be Jack Warren, gun-and-rum runner, a "tarnished knight" of the kind I like to write about, a man ruined by experience (and perhaps by a woman), seeking solace in whisky and money but really seeking redemption in a cause, along the lines of Rick in *Casablanca*.

Then, one day in the late winter of 2016, I was in London and met my former editor Jon Wood of Orion, at the Black Friar pub. Though I'd moved on, changed publishers and written two books for Penguin Random House, we were still good friends. I told him the rough story of the new idea. He swigged, looked at me and said, "Why not make the pilot a woman?"

And so Roxy Loewen was born.

(I should add that Jon has "form," as we say in England, in drinking and changing my writing life. In 2005, after two bottles of claret at Blacks Club in Soho, he mumbled the name Dracula to me, and my novel *Vlad, the Last Confession* began.)

The rabbit hole of research led me to the lives of those extraordinary women flyers of the 1930s. Defying prejudice, determined to get airborne, these gals did everything the men did, and more. Amelia Earhart is the best known, for her records and, perhaps, her mysterious demise. But there were many others as brilliant—Beryl Markham, Louise Thaden and the cigar-chewing, whisky-quaffing, sexual adventurer Pancho Barnes. These are just a few. Roxy is a mix of several, yet also very much her own gal.

Thus the plot changed for the better. (I find women often have this effect on my life!) I wanted a love affair at the heart of things, and Roxy was so independent that she would only fall for a certain kind of guy. Hence Jocco Zomack was born. He has the idealism she thinks she doesn't care about. As always, love changes everything.

I've always believed that research in historical fiction is not so much about the details, though it is important to get them right. What research does for me is act as a springboard for my imagination. It launches me in cool, unforeseen directions. Discovering that there may have been an original *Fall of Icarus* painted on wood was one of those launches. Reading that the tightly scripted, Teutonically efficient opening ceremony of the Berlin Olympics was hijacked by five thousand crapping pigeons was another. Not to mention the little detail of Spaniards in early civil war Madrid pouring chocolate sauce over everything, including sardines!

There's always *the* book too, the one that contains the most springboards. I found it amid the crazy piles and teetering shelves of one of the world's great second-hand bookstores, Macleod's, in Vancouver, British Columbia. Looking under "Aviation," among all the glossy spines of coffee table tomes, I noticed a squat book with a battered black spine that had no writing on it. Irresistible. I pulled it out to discover its title: *Aviation Manual*. Published in the 1930s by the Popular Science Publishing Co., Inc., New York, it had *everything*. From the specificity of a water-cooled Wright J-4 engine to how to land a biplane on a bumpy field in a crosswind. I swear that after reading it, I could take to the air in a Lockheed Vega and have a reasonable chance of not dying. If anyone cares to join me, I promise not to attempt the falling leaf first time up. Though I make no guarantee about barrel rolls.

The manual made the book in so many ways, but several others also aided greatly. *Amelia Earhart*, a biography by Tanya Lee Stone, and especially *Powder Puff Derby*, by Mike Walker, were great on the women flyers of the 1930s; though the best book about being a woman pilot, the passion and the power, was beautifully written by one of them: Beryl Markham, with her *West with the Night*. Michael Hart's memoirs were filled with good stories. Michael M. Mooney's *The Hindenburg* had great detail—even if I don't agree with his conclusion that the disaster was bomb related. Another fascinating book with a similarly conspiratorial premise was *The Search for Amelia Earhart*, by Fred Goerner.

I do like actual books for research, and my desk gradually becomes covered with them. But I'd be a fool to ignore the internet and its wonders. From being able to swiftly discover the price for a mickey of Scotch in 1936 to . . .

Well, one thing was a little film I watched on YouTube on the brilliant but defiantly Nazi flyer Hanna Reitsch. Look her up, she's worth it. As a test pilot for jets during the war, she'd had a terrible crash. Doctors told her she'd never fly again due to vestibular disorders, or balance issues. She regained that balance and took to the air once more by doing what Roxy does—walking along the apex of high buildings.

There are great websites on that amazing airship the *Hindenburg*. The most comprehensive I found was http://www.airships.net/hindenburg/. This had every detail, from photos of the dining service to the full specs of the engines. The routes, the schedules, the passenger and crew lists . . . the wallpaper. Wonderful.

But I also got an app. Hindenburg 3DA 5 by Michal Barta let me use my iPhone to actually walk through the whole vessel. Into the cabins and lounges, along the gantries. Be where the passengers and crew smoked and drank, ate and played cards. Allowed me to study the decor and experience that vast, cathedral-like interior. (Though I am quite inept at moving about. My thirteen-year old-son, Reith, had to rescue me more than once when I got stuck among the gas bags at the top of the ship and couldn't get down!)

My passion for flight is not merely random, I come by it naturally. My dad was Flight Lieutenant Peter Humphreys, Royal Air Force, Battle of Britain, Hurricane pilot, later shot down in North Africa. He survived; otherwise I wouldn't be writing this. But his tales of flights and dogfights and the joys and terrors of being aloft certainly inspired much within these pages. This book is dedicated to him, in great gratitude.

There are, as always, so many people to thank for what you are now holding in your hand. On the home front, my son, Reith, for all high-tech assistance. My wife, Aletha, for all the support, advice and yummy food. While on the business end . . .

As with a pilot, though writing may sometimes seem a solo flight, there are so many who allow me to soar, who get and keep the bird in the air. A novel is very much a team effort. The mechanics might be that great crew at Doubleday Canada in Toronto, who actually print the book, or set the file, that you are reading now, its "paint job" (or cover) designed by the wonderful Rachel Cooper. Then there is the man who gets the word out about the next "stunt," makes sure that I show up at events on time and relatively sober, and pulls the chocks away to get me airborne in public—my tireless, affable and ever-dapper publicist, Max Arambulo.

Yet no air force gets off the ground without the senior personnel back at base. My publishers at Doubleday are wonderfully supportive—from Air Commodore Brad Martin, the CEO of Penguin Random House Canada; through Air Marshal Kristin Cochrane, president and publisher at PRHC; onto my former flying partner (editor) now promoted to squadron leader (publisher) at Doubleday, Amy Black.

My final and deepest thanks, though, have to go to my new editor, Zoe Maslow. The perfect co-pilot, she got me back on course when I lost my way across country, and pulled me out of many a stall. Her hand on the stick was light but firm; she knew exactly when to push the throttle way forward, and when to ease back. Her taste is impeccable, not least in gin-based cocktails. Roxy would not be half the gal she is without Zoe. Brava!

It has been a privilege to spend time with the men and women of Doubleday—and with the aviatrixes (yes, it is so a word!) of the 1930s. What they achieved in that male-dominated world was extraordinary. I could go on with their praises for pages, if Roxy wasn't telling me to shuddup and roll us another cigarette.

So I will.

C. C. Humphreys
Salt Spring Island, British Columbia
May 1, 2018